MAUCH CHUNK

A Novel of 1968

Richard Benyo

SPecific
Publications
P.O. Box 161
Forestville, CA 95436
USA

Library of Congress Cataloging-in-Publication Data

Benyo, Richard
    Mauch Chunk: A Novel of 1968 / Richard Benyo
    Summary: It is June 1968 in the little town of Mauch Chunk, Pennsylvania. Once one of the most prosperous towns in America, after the decline of King Coal, the millionaires moved out and the town is struggling. A recent journalism graduate returns to Mauch Chunk to work on the local newspaper, only to find there is a lot more going on in little Mauch Chunk than he thought—including a former friend who lives his life as though out of a science-fiction novel, a state cop friend who lives in a caboose, the great Indian athlete Jim Thorpe who works as a gardener, and a missing girl who knew too much about the local drug trade.
    [1. Drugs—Fiction, 2. Eastern Pennsylvania—Fiction, 3. Mystery and detective—Fiction, 4. Journalism—Fiction, 5. Alternate worlds—Fiction, 1968--Fiction.] I. Title. II. Title: Mauch Chunk: A novel of 1968.

ISBN 978-0-9886980-2-4 (6X9 trade paperback)
ISBN 978-0-9886980-3-1 (digital edition)

Cover photo by Drew Benyo.
Joe Boyle photo by Ed Gildea.
Author photo by Rhonda Provost.
Design by Judy Henderson.

This is a work of fiction. Many of the characters depicted are pure fiction, although some are not. Those who are not are depicted as accurately as possible based upon their own actions and long-running observations of them during the period of 1968-72. The author appreciates the permissions by various family members and relatives to bring these folks back to life through the device of fictional narrative.

Contents

Dedication

This one is for Joe Boyle,
a newspaperman who
was the real article.

1

A Tramp Shining

Monday, 3 June 1968

"Well, you're quite the bloody mess, aren't you?" Richard Harris had declared earlier in the day.

Joe Boyle, editor of the *Times-News* in Mauch Chunk, Pennsylvania, had assigned me—probably as a way of easing me into my first day on the job at the newspaper—to interview Harris about his LP, *A Tramp Shining*. I'd done just that while Harris sat in a director's chair sporting his name while lounging on Broadway between takes on the location of *The Molly Maguires*, a film about the rebel Irish coal miners who'd infected the region in 1876, some of whom were hanged in the courtyard of the Carbon County Jail a half mile up Broadway.

The Hollywood types had come to town and spread truckloads of dirt up and down Broadway to cause it to revert to its appearance of nearly a century ago. Broadway in Mauch Chunk would serve as "the big city" to which Harris and his lady friend would travel for a day away from the mines. The parking meters had been removed and replaced with iron horse heads and rings to look like hitching posts.

The bloody mess to which Harris was referring was the left side of my mug, which a decade ago had received a remarkable vertical scar when I'd tripped down a flight of stairs and smashed my face into a cast-iron hot-water radiator at the bottom, knocking myself senseless for I don't know how long but long enough to imprint

1

a scar that looked worthy of being the loser in a duel fought with sabers.

"My friends call me Skar," I'd replied, my typical reply when someone offered the courtesy of addressing the disfigurement head-on.

"You can call me Dickie," Harris said. "All my friends do."

We shook hands and for the next half hour I peppered him with inane questions about his recording career, especially about "Mac-Arthur Park," which early in May had reached number 2 on the charts.

"What does it mean?" I'd asked him.

"I'm not allowed to give away the secret," he said. "Jimmy Webb wouldn't like that. Song explains itself, it loses all of its mystery." Webb had written the song and the rest of the album.

I didn't think much of Harris as a singer. Maybe he didn't, either. I felt uncomfortable asking him to evaluate his own musical talents. His acting chops were a mite more reputable.

Now he was sitting on a bar stool to my left in Weiksner's Bar, across the alleyway from the side entrance of the courthouse, where later this month they'd be filming the crucial trial scenes where the leaders of the Molly Maguires would be found guilty of mayhem and murder and sentenced to die by the rope. The Hollywood bosses had contracted with an air-conditioning place in Hazleton to come down and install a magnificent air-conditioning unit behind the courthouse so that the coming July heat and humidity combined with the heat from the klieg lights would not cause any of the actors or crew to pass out.

Mrs. Gertrude Apfelbaum, copublisher of the *Times-News* with her brother, Joe Boyle, and semianonymous "Strictly Speaking" columnist, occupying column one of the back page of every issue, had put it this way:

"When Paramount Pictures films courtroom scenes for *The Molly Maguires* later this month, the players will be working in comfortable conditions notwithstanding summer heat. Workmen from a Hazleton firm are now engaged in installation of an air-conditioning system. Through the unique system, cool air will be pumped in from outside the courthouse so as to eliminate noise within the building. Courthouse employees have commented that the air-conditioning system as a permanent feature would be appreciated."

I've always been a sucker for "notwithstanding" and "heretofore" and "inasmuch." Mrs. Apfelbaum would prove to be a keen guide to my keeping my sometimes-wayward grammar on course. The fronts of our desks butted up against each other, and she'd develop the habit of calling me "Kid." At twenty-two I'd just graduated from Espy State College a week before. She, on the other hand, was securely middle-aged.

Weiksner's Bar was one of those coal-region institutions but with a little more flare than most inasmuch as Mauch Chunk had gained its fame and fortune from being the shipping center for coal to Allentown, Easton, and Philadelphia; the coal came from up the road, meaning Summit Hill, Lansford, Coaldale, Nesquehoning, etc., and not from under Mauch Chunk. The closest Mauch Chunk came to the devastation of mining was three holes in the side of the mountain on the road leading to Nesquehoning where they'd discovered uranium and then decided to leave it for posterity.

Dickie Harris was still wearing his 1870s miner's garb from the filming earlier in the day. He sported a paste-on mustache, as did Sean Connery, who sat to his left, leaning against the wall at the end of the L-shaped bar. To my right sat Ron Von Renner, a classmate from the 1964 graduating class of East Mauch Chunk High School, on the far side of the Lehigh River. I'd gone to a state college in the middle of the state that specialized in turning out teachers while Ron had gone to Hershey, which specialized in turning out Pennsylvania State Police officers. He was currently out of uniform, wearing jeans and a flannel shirt and drinking from glasses filled from a quart bottle of Columbia cold-water aged beer, the pride of Shenandoah, Pennsylvania. His hands were rough and scarred. He lived in a caboose a few blocks away, on the former New Jersey Central railroad tracks. His hobby was rebuilding steam locomotives and their rolling stock with some of his high school buddies.

We'd both been on the intramural track team (him in the 220, me in the 880). He played basketball and sometimes trained with the wrestlers; I ran cross-country and wrestled on dark cold winter nights, the endurance from cross-country helping me make it through the third period. In a short sprint, no known miscreant would stand a chance of outrunning Ron, although he liked to claim, "They didn't give me a gun and teach me how to use it so I'd have to run somebody down." He was working on two pickled eggs fished out of the three-gallon jar on the bar, salting them liberally. It was he who'd given me my nickname of Skar. He said it sounded Roman, and thereby highfalutin.

The stools to Ron's right arm were empty. It was still too early for the courthouse workers to stop by on their way home for a quick beer and a shot. None of the four of us were smoking, but John the bartender was.

Everything about John was elongated, like a cigarette standing on end. His head looked as though someone had taken two dictionaries and smashed them together with John's head in between. His head was tall and thin like the rest of him. His arms were long and gnarly, the tips of his fingers able to scratch his kneecaps when he was standing at attention, which wasn't often. He wore—always, day and night, winter and summer—a long-sleeve white shirt topped by a red-in-front and black-in-back vest, making him look like a circus barker. His fingernails were polished and he had a pencil-point-thin mustache, but his clothes on a close inspection were frayed and threadbare. As long as he stayed inside Weiksner's, dark and smoky, his shabbiness didn't show. He smoked unfiltered Camels, which contributed to the overall smokiness of a place that was about as ventilated as a deserted coal mine.

"A mean-spirited cigar would go a long way in cleaning up the air in here," Dickie said, sipping clear liquor from a glass the size of a coffee cup.

Connery, also outfitted in a miner's garb and a fake mustache, simply leaned against the wall and nodded. He seemed immensely tired. An on-the-rocks glass with a shot of clear liquor sat untasted in front of him.

"Scotch?" I asked.

"Heh?"

"Scotch?"

"Scot."

"Huh?"

"Scot."

Dimwitted. I get it.

"Scot," I said.

"Yes, goddamn it. Scot."

I smiled stupidly. "I guess I'd piss you off if I said you did a good job of playing James Bond."

He rolled his eyes. "Yes, it would."

"Sorry," I said.

Dickie poked Connery in the ribs. He nodded toward me. "Go ahead," he said. "Do it for him. He's a friend of mine. Please?"

Connery rolled his eyes again, trying to sink back into the wall. "Bond. James Bond." He glared at Dickie. "You happy?"

"Yeah," we both said at the same time.

I waved at John. "Yuengling and two eggs."

He drew the six-ounce beer and fished around in the jar with tongs until he captured two beet-red elusive eggs. He slapped the glass of beer down in front of me on the wet bar and put the two eggs in a small paper plate and shoved it toward me along with a salt shaker and a fork. As the paper plate hit the damp spot on the bar, it stalled.

"May wanna wipe the bar once in a while," Ron said, pouring a generous amount of salt onto the half of an egg he had left in his left hand.

I hadn't had anything to drink all afternoon, and when that combined with looking at the mound of salt Ron poured on his egg, I suddenly had a serious case of the dries. I put my Yuengling down in one toss-back and banged the glass down on the bar for a refill.

Dickie pushed a buck forward on the bar. "Didn't know talking to me could make a fellow so dry," he said, smiling.

"Are those mustaches itchy?" Ron asked.

"What? These—?" Dickie said, and as one, he and Connery got hold of one end of the mustaches and ripped them off. They held them out in front of them like dead caterpillars. Dickie took Sean's, joined it with his, and gently lowered it into his shirt pocket. "Company property, you know." He smiled a wan smile, as though it went against the greater sorrow he was feeling behind his eyes. "Amusement park's closed."

"Hah?" I asked as John smacked down my new beer.

Dickie continued to half-smile. "Don't ya know, then?"

I shrugged.

"When the 50-cent mustache ride closes up, so does the amusement park," he said.

"Known fact," Connery said before taking a generous gulp of his drink.

"So when was your graduation and who came by to see it?" Ron asked.

"Sunday afternoon, 26th," I said, cutting a red-dyed egg in half with my front teeth. Tasted good; the eggs might have actually been made less than a week ago. "Nobody came. Didn't expect them to come."

"Family still as weird as ever, huh?"

"Weird? Yeah. My mother hasn't been out of the house in years, still wears her widow rags. Ellie can't drive, doesn't want to learn. One brother in the Air Force in Alaska, another in jail. And my grandmother sure isn't gonna drive or be driven fifty miles to sit around with a bunch of strangers all day."

"So where you been stayin'?" He drained the six-ounce beer glass in front of him and refilled it from the quart bottle, then moved the second six-ounce glass of beer toward him. Ron never liked to drink cold beer. He always had to have it warm. Even when it was his ironic favorite, Columbia cold-water aged beer.

"Dragged my feet coming home, helped clean up the apartments for Professor Evans. Six guys can really make a serious mess of things in nine months of habituating. Then I moved into Granny's dungeon room."

Ron smiled. "She know you call her Granny?"

"Sure. I've always been her favorite. She doesn't care what I call her."

"The old castle still as dark and dank as always?"

6

My grandmother's "house" had undergone strange renovations over the years following my grandfather's death. She must have thought she was related to the Winchester widow who built the Winchester House in San Jose. Over the years it had sprouted turrets, balconies, secret passages, extensions, and additions, as though she lived in the Middle Ages instead of a block off Center Street on the east side of Fisher's Hill in the 20th century.

"It's tolerable, barely," I said.

"Watch this," Ron said, tossing the half-egg in his hand to within an inch of the tin ceiling and then moving under it to allow it to drop into his mouth. Dickie applauded.

"Can you do that with a watermelon?" Dickie asked, poking Connery in the ribs. Connery didn't seem to be paying attention.

I plopped the second half of my first egg into my mouth in a less-daring fashion.

"Reason I asked about your living arrangements," Ron said, moving around the sweating quart bottle until he had made three intersecting rings on the wet bar, like the Ballantine logo, "is you have an appointment tomorrow with old Miss Delaney." He nodded his head toward the Asa Packer Mansion just up behind the courthouse.

I looked at him with a completely blank expression. I'm a past master of blank.

Ron shrugged. "You don't wanna live with Granny the rest of your life, do ya?"

Dickie grabbed my left sleeve. I turned to him and he had screwed up his face into a sourpuss, shaking his head "No." He turned toward Connery, as though to solicit his opinion. Connery wearily shook his head "No."

"That's three to zero," Dickie said. "He'll be there. What time?"

"Noon," Ron said, biting into his second egg.

"She'll probably serve watercress sandwiches," Dickie said. "Is she pretty?"

"She's old," Ron said.

"That's not what I asked," Dickie said.

"She used to be," Ron said.

Dickie poked me in the ribs. "That so?"

"Yeah, I guess so. She's old enough to be my mother. In fact, she went to grade school with my mother."

"I'd go for it," Dickie said, taking a slow, deliberate drain of his glass before sitting it down with a nod for another. "John, me man," he said, pointing at the lonely ice cubes.

"Just knock on the front door," Ron said. "She's expecting you. She can give you a tour of what they've done so far to fix the old place up toward turning it into a tourist attraction that will save Mauch Chunk's sorry ass."

"You mean she's renting rooms in the Asa Packer Mansion?" I asked, astonishment apparent on my face.

Ron hit his forehead with the palm of his right hand. "No, mo-ron. She's apparently got some rental somewhere that she's trying to fill."

I took a long sip of beer. And shrugged. "Maybe," I said.

"Maybe nothing," Ron said. "You go for it. Get out from under Granny's claw."

"Yeah, fine," I muttered weakly. "I'll do it if Dickie tells me what 'MacArthur Park' is all about."

Dickie raised his eyebrows. "Don't rightly know," he said. "Maybe that's why everybody's buying it. To look for clues be-tween the lines."

There was a pause. John the bartender made a courtesy pass with his damp bar rag. All of us, like guys doing the wave at a ballpark, lifted our drinks and eggs as his rag slid in front of us.

I drained my Yuengling and motioned for another. John had al-ready refilled Dickie's glass.

"What ya doin' this weekend?" Ron wanted to know.

I shrugged. "Maybe moving. Maybe nothing. Why?"

"Got some guys coming around Sunday to help me move some wheels. We could use some help."

"Move wheels? That sounds pretty boring," I offered.

Ron snorted. "These hain't wheels from a '64 VW bug." He snorted again. "These are wheels, big steel wheels, from a ten Class T-2B 4-8-4 locomotive used to run for the Lehigh Valley, ole Wyoming No. 5212. Take six guys maybe three hours to move 'em to where I need 'em."

Dickie poked Connery in the ribs. "We're not doing anything Sunday. We should get ourselves into this. Sounds like fun."

"Fun?" Connery said. "Not fun by a long shot." He continued leaning against the wall.

"Guess we're out," Dickie said. "We only come as a couple."

"Maybe next time," Ron said. "So what da'ya say?" he asked, turning back to me now that Harris and Connery were out. "You'll be the sixth guy."

"What're we gonna do, pick them up and walk around the rail yard with 'em?"

"Ya remember Prof. Myers teaching us about fulcrums?" Ron said. Prof. Myers was the grizzled old fuddy-duddy science teacher we'd had in high school. He broke the ice in his classes by telling thirty-year-old jokes he had written in the margins of his teaching plan back when dirt was young.

I nodded my head, took the head off the new brew.

"Lots of fulcrum stuff goes on," Ron said. "But you *do* get a pretty good workout. Some of the guys from the old South Street Gang are gonna help. Maybe afterwards we can take a run along the railroad tracks down to Bowmanstown and back and then put some mats down and go a couple of rounds, see how rusty we are."

"Wrestle? In June?"

Dickie raised his right eyebrow. "Wrestlin's bloody good any time of the year, dependin' on who you're wrestlin' with or against."

"This won't be coed," Ron said.

"Well then, what's the sense of it?" Dickie said.

"Greco-Roman or pro?" I asked.

"Pro? What's pro? Like Haystacks Calhoun and Professor Toru Tanaka and Chief Jay Strongbow? Like rubbing foreign objects in your eyes?"

I smiled. "Yeah," I said. "Like rubbin' foreign objects in your eyes."

"That sounds like fun," Dickie said. He looked at Connery, who seemed uninterested in anything at the moment. "This town is

9

bloody boring. Wrestlin'—pro wrestlin'—that sounds like fun. Me 'en Connery here'll take you fellows on. We'll be Haystacks Calhoun. I kin sit on his shoulders"—Connery shook his head "No."— "or he kin sit on my shoulders, 'en you come at us one at a time, tag team like, 'en we'll go at it good." He swung his arm in the air with a theatrical flourish.

As he did the door opened, letting in a mess of fresh air.

"So you won't help us move locomotive wheels or run to Bowmanstown and back, but you'll come by later to wrestle," Ron said.

"Gotta pace ourselves—" Dickie began to say.

Someone from behind me grabbed my left arm above the elbow and turned me on my stool.

"You're given' up that stool so my woma— What the fuck? Lookit this ugly fucker." The guy was a dozen years older than me, his long hair going gray, his beard following suit, and he smelled of weed. He was also a good thirty pounds bigger than me. Behind him, looking over his shoulder, was his "woman"—a redhead wearing a black T-shirt and braids, freckles across her nose, and big loop earrings with skulls the size of quarters hanging from the ends of them. She had once been pretty but now was just pretty hard.

Three other guys and another woman were clustered behind them like a head of broccoli.

"I said get off that stool, you ugly fuck, so's my woman kin sit down here with Mr. Richard Harris so he can see why she oughta be in his movie."

I smiled at the dude and swung myself around on the stool so I was once again facing the bar and my beer and the second beetred pickled egg. I nodded off toward the right. "There's plenty of empty stools over there, from which Mr. Richard Harris can gainfully view your . . . woman."

"You ain't listenin' good," Mr. Hairy said to me from behind my back.

I could see that Mr. Harris and Mr. Connery were sprung for trouble. Maybe this was old hat to them. I'm sure this wasn't the first time they'd sat through an audition in a dark on-location bar.

"Plenty of stools over there," I said, reaching for my beer.

My hand never reached it.

The bastard tried to cold-cock me on the left—the ugly—side of my head. Maybe not wanting to touch the scar slowed down his punch or maybe he wasn't as fast and strong as he used to be. Who is?

His blow ricocheted off the left side of my head, just above the ear, and before he could recover from his forward motion, pure instinct kicked in, instinct from wrestling in high school and college, and I swung my left arm back, caught his neck in my armpit, and simultaneously pushed myself away from the bar with my right hand, spinning off the stool, dropping his back onto the now-vacant stool, my armpit trapping his neck and my weight readily available to snap his neck.

The guy's leg thrashed as though he was suffering a seizure and he tried in vain to get a grip on me, which was made difficult by the fact that I effectively had him in the position of an inverted turtle.

"Stop it or I'll snap your neck like a fuckin' wishbone," I hissed.

At that moment his woman let me have a fist in the left ear. The blow wasn't solidly placed and she was a bit off balance but I saw stars. The stars extinguished themselves in a moment, just in time for me to see her toppling backwards. Ron had administered a fist to her forehead. She landed against one of the other toughs and threw him off balance, which Ron took advantage of, stepping over her to get to him, where he threw a hard right to the guy's nose. Even in the bad, cigarette-smoke-tinged light, the color of blood spurting from his nose was very vivid.

The door opened and light rushed in from the afternoon sun. Several bodies hurled themselves out the door, and it slowly closed itself.

"I'm not gonna tell you again," I said to my left armpit. "Stop struggling or I'll stop you permanently." He stopped for a second, tried to shift himself to a more advantageous leverage, couldn't pull it off, and began struggling again. Ron walked over and punched *him* in the nose. He settled down.

Ron stood there shaking the soreness out of his fist, then slapped his fist up into his left armpit and shook his head. "She's got a hard forehead," he said.

John had come around the bar and was standing over the punk by the door, threatening him with Black Beauty, the Ted Williams Louisville Slugger that he kept behind the bar. The guy saw the wisdom in John's argument that he just sit there quietly and bleed. Not so much the woman. Still a bit unstable from Ron's blow to her forehead, she wobbled to her feet and began spewing a septic tank of curses at us, ending with "I'm gonna call the fuckin' cops to put you fuckin' assholes away forever!"

Ron reached into his back pocket and pulled out his Pennsylvania Statie shield. "Yes, ma'am," he drawled. "Your wish is our command."

She spit on the floor, a good-sized lunger.

John moved the baseball bat in her direction. "I hain't cleaning up your mess, bitch. Clean it up now, or I'll split your skull," he said quietly. She looked around as though somebody was supposed to come to a damsel's rescue. No luck. She reached over to one of the little tables near the door, pulled a paper napkin from the caddy, and got down on her knees and wiped it up, making sure to exhibit a snarl all the while.

Ron signaled John to give him the bat. "Go call Drizler to have some of the boys come down and take these bozos away," Ron said, spinning the big bat like a nightstick.

The guy I was holding down—the leader of the pack—began coming to and began making feeble struggling efforts. "Wanna let him have another one?" I asked Ron.

He shook his head. "Let him drop." I unwrapped my armpit from around his neck, and he rolled off the stool onto the floor.

During the height of the action, the two blows to the left side of my head had smarted, but now that things had quieted down, I could feel a huge headache beginning to flower inside my battered skull.

I shook my head in an effort to clear it but immediately stopped, because all that did was make the inside of my head hurt even worse.

I took a deep breath as John put a call in to the Mauch Chunk Police Department to come by and pick up the litter. They were reluctant at first. "Ron says to hurry it up," John added. He hung up. "They'll be here in less than a minute." Their office was a mere block away.

I realized, suddenly, that the stools where Dickie Harris and Sean Connery had been sitting were empty. Ron noticed, too. "They were the only smart ones in the place," he said, still twirling the baseball bat.

The guy who'd started it all lay on the bare wooden floor, a floor soiled by generations of drunk, semidrunk, and on-the-way-to-drunk patrons, and moaned.

"Hope you enjoyed your Welcome Home party," Ron said.

*   *   *

Ron's caboose, a mere two blocks away from the bar, was cozy if Spartan. We sat across from each other, drinking beers straight from the bottles. Ron's right hand was in a bucket of ice water, where he was hoping the hurt would be leached out of it and it wouldn't swell. I was sitting with a hot-water bottle filled with ice pressed up against the left side of my head.

"You gonna be able to go to work tomorrow with that hand?" I asked him.

"You betch'ya," he said, draining the last four ounces of Miller High Life from its clear bottle. "You're the one I'm worried about. All these years wrestling and you've managed to avoid getting a cauliflower ear, and now you might get a beaut—over what? Some numbnuts hippie biker."

Still being faithful to Yuengling, I gulped down a few ounces and tried to shake my head in the negative. "Not gonna happen," I said. "I'm gonna have a helluva bruise, but my ear'll be fine. And there's not much inside the head to rattle, so eventually that'll be okay, too."

"Maybe we ought to take you by Doc Dougherty's to have him take a look at it."

"I'm fine," I declared with all the confidence of an invalid. I set the empty green bottle on the table next to me. I tried to get up but the room began to spin. I sat back down. "I oughta get outta here and start working on my story on Dickie Harris, pop singer, so it can be shared with the panting public tomorrow afternoon."

Ron pulled his fist from the bucked and wrapped it in a towel. "Cold hurts worse than the bruised bones," he said, getting up to get himself another beer. I waved him away when he offered me another one. "You have two stories to write up," he said. "You were right there when there was a knock-down, drag-out bar fight at Weiksner's, an eyewitness to history. Joe Boyle's gonna insist that the paper carry a story on it. I kin give ya a couple of quotes if it'll help. Let's see." He stroked his chin. "A gang of out-of-town rowdies descended on Weiksner's Bar last night, looking to get an audition for a rising female star. Insert name here. Local theater critics were not enthused, causing her manager to abruptly cut off negotiations . . ."

I gave him the finger and left, a mile and a half walk in front of me, where I could write in peace in the damp, dank dungeon below my grandmother's castle.

"Don't forget to spell my name right," Ron called after me. If he had any sense he wouldn't want to see his name anywhere near that story.

2
Meeting Mr. Thorpe

The lame little feature story on Richard Harris's *A Tramp Shining* was into type and laid out by midmorning Tuesday, as was the unbylined news report on the little fracas at Weiksner's. Turns out the starlet and her manager and groupies were part of an Allentown motorcycle gang that had come to Mauch Chunk in a VW microbus held together by antiestablishment bumper stickers. The several who'd escaped before the police arrived were easily gathered up, their costumes giving them away in a town where almost everyone was years behind the hippie revolution in clothing. In fact, most of us were apparently well out of the sartorial swing, unaware that some motorcycle gangs had decided to jettison their traditional black leather jackets for soft brown leather with fringes and tie-dye shirts.

Did we prefer to press charges, Chief of Police Harvey Drizler wanted to know. Ron and I did prefer to press charges, figuring that a couple of days in jail being forced to eat Mrs. Harvey Drizler's home cooking would in large part punish them for their crime spree.

Now it was 11:50 as I left the *Times-News* offices on Race Street, walked down to Susquehanna, over to the courthouse, and up the steps next to the war memorial on my way to the Asa Packer Mansion to see Miss Delaney about a place to rest my weary head.

I'd driven to work in my low-end 1964 Rambler 440 four-door and parked it next to Ron's caboose. He wasn't awake at that hour; nobody but the milkman, the guys at the Mauch Chunk Baking Company, the Allentown *Morning Call* paperboys, the folks in the

Times-News, the waitress and short-order cook at Steve's Diner, and a few hung-over cats were awake at 5:00 a.m. On the way to work, my second day on the job, I advanced my daily habit of stopping in at Steve's for a cup of milked-down coffee and an apple turnover. It was conveniently on my route to work: an aluminum diner out of a bygone era, wedged in beside Weiksner's.

Turned in my stories, pulled stuff from the wires and marked up which wire stories we wanted typeset, said "Hello" to Cy Apfelbaum (the ad sales director), Mrs. Gertrude Apfelbaum (my deskmate and the lady who would teach me more about journalism in six months than I'd learned in four years of college), and Joe Boyle, who had already been in the office for an hour, knocking out a half-dozen stories in his hunt-and-peck two-finger typing style, all of them gleaned from a long thin notebook scribbled in the night before in a handwriting only he could interpret.

I'd learned the first day that I didn't want to be in the office just after the noon chimes when the presses started running down in the bowels of the building. The whole building shook, pencils rattled in their beer-can holders, and the place filled with dust motes that had to be as dangerous to a person's lungs as cigar smoke. I was convinced the dust motes were saturated with printer's ink, just looking for a healthy pink lung to settle into.

Better to listen to Dickie Harris not tell me what "MacArthur Park" meant.

Better to be climbing the steps behind the courthouse where the air-conditioning crew from Hazleton was making a racket banging on the monstrosity they were installing for what would turn out in the final edit to be thirty seconds of theater time in the 1970 release of *The Molly Maguires*. Just beyond them on this Sunny-Warm day (upper right "The Weather" report on the front page of the June 4, 1968, *Times-News*) stretched the manicured emerald-green lawn (Oops! Sorry Gertrude: redundant: emerald *is* green.) of the Asa Packer Mansion, three stories, eighteen rooms, and eleven thousand square feet of Victorian opulence being revivified after being closed up since 1912 when it was deeded over to the Borough of Mauch Chunk by Mary Packer Cummings, Asa's daughter.

I was to see about taking up residence on the ground behind the very haunted Harry Packer (Asa's son, who died young) Mansion that loomed above Asa's home. As kids we were certain the deserted Harry Packer Mansion was haunted; as teens we were absolutely certain of it; as a young adult, I still entertained the possibility. The place had such a brooding presence in those days that eventually, when the Walt Disney Company wanted to add a haunted mansion to its Disney World park in Orlando, it would use the Harry Packer Mansion as a model.

Oh, yeah, before I walk the rest of the way up to the Asa Packer Mansion and share watercress sandwiches with Miss Grace Delaney, I should report that nobody in the *Times-News* offices said a damned thing about the left side of my face looking like a ripening eggplant. Mrs. Apfelbaum held a sheet of copy paper in front of her face when I said "Hello," probably to hide a knowing smile; it's difficult to repress a smile when it comes to the eyes, though, and Gertrude's were twinkling. I was sure Joe would make some crack like, "How's it going, Slugger?" but he didn't even look up from his notes as he continued to poke the keys of his Underwood, the roll of copy paper merrily unspooling through the platen of his typewriter.

As I trudged up the pathway to the front porch of the Asa Packer Mansion, I plotted to approach Miss Delaney with my good (right) side always toward her. I hoped there were many dark shadows in the mansion where I could hide my messy side.

But as I reached the bottom of the steps leading up to the porch, I saw that a table had been set up in the side lawn, complete with a dewy crystal pitcher of iced tea, what looked like an angel food cake, and real china and silverware. Ugh. There were no dark shadows anywhere to be seen, except under the steps.

As though it was carefully rehearsed, as I reached the bottom step and began to climb toward the porch, Miss Grace Delaney appeared at the edge of the porch and began to carefully lower herself down the steps. She wore a light-blue dress that came to the ankles and had frill around the hem, at the wrists, and at the collar. The neckline dropped a foot and there was a brooch of the silhouette of a young woman tied around her neck with a black ribbon. Her shoes looked as though they were made out of fancy, very busy wallpaper—all in all, a stunning outfit, and perfectly unsuitable for Mauch Chunk 1968. But probably the effect the mansion folks were shooting for when it came to capturing the height of the era when Mauch Chunk was home to a dozen millionaires back in the 1870s.

I stood there waiting for her to descend into a world symbolically below her, keeping the good side of my face toward her.

She moved slowly, as I supposed ladies did nearly a century before, when things around them moved slower and where one's sartorial presentation was all-important. She introduced herself in a low voice and led me toward the little table. As we reached it, the bells of St. Mark's struck noon and the hammering and banging of the air-conditioning crew at the courthouse stopped.

I pulled a chair out for her and she sat, rather properly or in a fashion that good old improper me would have thought was proper. I put a little pressure on the chair to push it in and she smiled and motioned me to take my own seat.

I saw several workingmen leave the mansion on the far side, apparently off to take their lunch, maybe down at Steve's Diner. An elderly man who was pushing a lawn mower on the huge lawn between us and the looming Harry Packer Mansion didn't stop mowing just because it was noon.

Miss Delaney broke the ice.

"What brings you back to Mauch Chunk?" she asked.

I thought that was an odd question because this is where I was born and raised and had a job, but I decided to answer it anyway. She poured iced tea into our glasses and then passed the silver sugar bowl.

"My plans are not to stay in Mauch Chunk," I said, "although with the draft and all, I may be required to leave sooner than I plan."

"Ah, yes," she said. "The war." As though she'd just learned about Vietnam earlier this morning.

"Since I know a lot of people my age who say they aren't going to come back to Mauch Chunk but then do, I thought I'd do it just the opposite: come back after college, get my fill, then leave for good."

She sipped her tea, just enough to determine whether she needed more sugar. She apparently didn't.

"You're not especially fond of Mauch Chunk," she said.

I'd sipped an ounce of tea out of my glass, and although it tasted a bit different from iced tea I was used to, it didn't need any more sugar.

"Not especially," I said.

"But your family has lived here for quite a long time."

"And some of them still do."

"But not you."

"I haven't much to hold me here."

"But your mother—"

I must have made that uncontrolled twitch of my nose that I always seemed to make anytime someone mentioned my mother.

Miss Delaney cocked her head an inch. "You're not fond of your mother."

I shrugged.

"She's had a difficult life, what with your father dying and then being left alone," Miss Delaney said.

My father had died in a mine collapse when I was ten. My mother had " married down" and always held it against my father, who'd given her three boys and then a girl, Ellie, who still lived at home and took care of mother.

"She wasn't left alone," I said. "She had four of us for quite a few years, and my grandmother—"

"How is your grandmother?" Miss Delaney asked.

"Not well," I said. "She's always been strong but not well; lately she's not strong and not well."

Miss Delaney raised her eyebrows over the rim of her glass. "And you're living there at the moment—"

I nodded. "Yes. In what we refer to as the dungeon . . . the basement. It's quite nice but a little on the damp side and a lot too big for my tastes. I'd prefer something smaller and a little drier."

"Do you know that I used to go to school with your mother? We used to play house in the basement."

"I assume she was . . . happier back in those days." I sipped more tea. A butterfly, as though programmed to add to the wistfulness of the mansion grounds, flitted around a hanging plant up on the porch, and the elderly man went slowly back and forth up on the lawn with his lawn mower humming.

"She certainly seemed to be," Miss Delaney said. "Perhaps she wasn't properly suited to raising a family."

"You make that sound as though we gave her a run for her money," I supplied.

"Well, you know how boys are—" she said, not meaning to. "Well, what I mean is that boys can be a handful." She straightened the front of her very straightened dress.

"We were energetic but not necessarily a strain," I said. "I don't think my mother was built to have children. Motherhood seemed to confuse her. It's not like playing house."

Miss Delaney sipped her tea, very little at a time. "I suppose that's something that I'll never know," she said. "But I do have my nephews and nieces. I'm sure you know them."

I did. The two boys, Michael and Jack, were one and two years older than me, and the girls, Elizabeth and Bertha, one and two years younger. "I went to St. Joe's around the same time they did," I said. I knew of Michael and Elizabeth, but not very well. At one point, when I was around nine years old, Michael and Elizabeth asked me to come by after school to play. But when I showed up and knocked on the door, Mr. Delaney, a lawyer, took me into his office and explained to me, in very nice language, why he didn't want kids like me playing with his children and how he would appreciate it if I would stay away from them. This was before I got my scar; I can't imagine what he'd have said when he saw me sporting that monstrosity.

I followed his instructions and stayed away from them, which they didn't seem to appreciate, thinking I was being standoffish—which, of course, I was. When they graduated from eighth grade, they went off to Marian High School and I trotted off to public high school, and that was that.

"How are they?" I asked, not really caring to know. I wondered when we'd get around to the apartment—or to the swell bruises on the left side of my face. Somewhere other than her family.

"Well, Michael is studying to be a doctor, and Jack is following in his father's footsteps and is nearly a lawyer in Philadelphia, and Bertha is still in college."

"And Elizabeth?"

The flush that washed over Miss Delaney went from her forehead all the way down her chest. "Well—" she said, and then stopped, lowering her head and depositing her hands in her lap. "Ah—this is awkward, but Elizabeth is one of the reasons I wanted to talk with you . . ." She fluttered her hands above her lap like a big white moth.

"Okay," I said, not knowing what else I should say. I hadn't seen Elizabeth Delaney in, like, eight years, and probably wouldn't recognize her if she walked up the lawn and sat on my lap. I wondered if there really was an apartment for rent. I wondered if dear buddy Ron Von Renner had set me up for this meeting, knowing well in advance what weird directions it would take. "Okay," I repeated.

Miss Delaney seemed eager to start but unsure where, exactly, to begin.

"Elizabeth has vanished," she said.

"Is that unusual?" I asked, probably too quickly. Something was telling me that Elizabeth Delaney's disappearance was nothing new.

Miss Delaney looked taken aback. "You know about Elizabeth?" she asked.

I shrugged. "Lots of kids these days vanish; then they turn up looking for money and place to stay for a while, before vanishing again when they don't like the house rules," I supplied.

Miss Delaney sat quietly for a moment, as though contemplating that concept, as though the whole possibility was new to her. "They do, don't they?" she mused, looking toward the courthouse where the air-conditioning guys weren't making noise. The butterfly—orange and black and probably a monarch—fluttered past us, headed toward the side porch.

"Not uncommon," I said, hoping to lure her back into the world of consciousness and conversation. "So Elizabeth has vanished before," I added.

Miss Delaney nodded her head. "But never for this long—"

"What do the police say?"

She looked startled by the word "police."

"Oh, no," she fluttered like the butterfly. "Oh, no. We don't want to get the police involved."

Weird. Vanished. But the police aren't to know.

"They can't help you find her if they don't know she's missing," I said, realizing how incredibly obvious—and stupid—what I said was.

She shook her head, vigorously. "No, no."

"And who's 'we'?" I asked.

"Why her father . . . and her mother . . . and me."

"What? You're afraid the police won't be sympathetic because she's 'vanished' before? Or that it might make the family look bad--?"

Her expression seemed to give a vote to both of those possibilities.

I was becoming very uncomfortable about this whole line of conversation. Does electricity come with the apartment, or do I have to pay that myself? Help.

In a stalling maneuver and to give her a moment to formulate an answer, I glanced up the hillside at the elderly gentleman in bluejeans and blue work shirt mowing the lawn. I wished I were up there with him, dealing only with a gnarly blade of grass or two.

When she didn't answer after thirty seconds, I felt obliged to fill the vacuum with something. "Is *anybody* looking into her disappearance? Has there been a ransom note or call?"

She shook her head vehemently. "No, no. No ransom. Nothing like that. My brother, her father—he's a lawyer, you know—he hired a private investigator, but he hasn't accomplished much. Says she'll probably come home when she's good and ready. Sleazy man. From Lansford."

"And you want me to look into this because--?" I knew I should just excuse myself and look for an apartment another day—an apartment without a dramatic story attached to it like a barnacle.

"Well—" she said, raised her hands, palm up. "You're a reporter. You know things. You get to ask questions. You go places where most other people don't. You have resources . . ."

"But this is only my second day on the job—"

"But the newspaper in Danville. When you were in college. Early this spring. The stories you wrote. About the . . . you know . . . drug trade . . . among young people." That seemed to sum up her argument as far as she was concerned.

I'd written a series of features for the Danville paper about the fledgling drug trade on campus at Espy State, where I was matriculating and spending too much time learning journalism and too little earning good grades in arts and sciences subjects that I needed to graduate. I'd managed to escape with two credits beyond the required 128, with an average of 2.46, most of which came in my senior year; before that I'd skimmed along at 2.0 looking over my shoulder for the Selective Service hounds who were prepared to pounce if a guy's GPA slipped below 2.0. Several of my buddies had let 'er slip and were now faithfully if not enthusiastically serving our county in foreign climes. They'd be coming after me any day now that I was free and clear of college deferment. I could go get married to avoid the draft or become my mother's sole means of support, neither of which was all that appealing at the moment.

It was no big news that young people in college were using drugs at a far higher rate than their parents ever had, not that many of the parents of my friends in the Mauch Chunks had ever stepped onto the grounds of a college. The series I'd written dealt directly with the drug trade at my particular college, but its tentacles stretched out into the surrounding community, spider-webbed-together colleges in the area, and my suspicions were that there was a sophisticated corridor up through which the drugs were pumped toward the colleges throughout the middle of Pennsylvania and into upper New York State.

I'd managed to get a modest advance from Atheneum to do a book on the subject, which I would start researching once I got up to speed on my newspaper job and once I found an apartment and if the Selective Service didn't decide to latch onto my sorry ass day after next.

"Your theory is that Elizabeth's disappearance has something to do with drugs," I said, voicing the obvious.

Miss Delaney nodded her head.

"Elizabeth has been involved in drugs," I supplied.

Miss Delaney nodded her head.

"What kind of drugs?"

"Weed."

"Marijuana," I supplied.

"Yes." She played with her hands, "Personally, I don't think it should be illegal to smoke marijuana. It's relaxing." She looked again toward the courthouse and the absence of burly guys banging hammers on aluminum air-conditioning units.

I didn't know what to say. I didn't want to get into a philosophical discussion of drug laws, and I didn't want to send her off on a reverie about the time she spent a memorable week in Greenwich Village smoking pot while listening to a cool jazz combo.

Thing is, I could easily imagine that: the smoky club, the tinkling of glasses, the Scotch on the rocks, the after-hours jazz club, Miss Delaney right in the thick of it, sucking down a reefer. Reefer madness. We'd had a music teacher in high school who spent every available weekend she could in Manhattan taking in what she referred to as "light operas" and which we put down as "musicals." She took us on a bus trip one weekend to see some light operas, and she knew everybody along the way, from the Trailways bus driver who drove us the ninety minutes into Manhattan to the folks checking us in at the Royalton Hotel on Forty-Fourth Street, to the ushers in the theaters.

Yet during the school week she kept her class well under control and disciplined and never caused an eyebrow to be raised in East Mauch Chunk, although some of the men and quite a few of the women did comment on her sometimes colorful outfits—snappy and cosmopolitan against the usually gray costumes of the citizens of a down-and-out coal-region burg.

Yeah, Miss Delaney would have fit right in down there in Greenwich Village.

"But there may be other drugs involved," she was saying, while I was still daydreaming of Miss Delaney tapping her foot to the jazz greats.

"Do you know what these other drugs might be?" I asked.

"Maybe heroin, LSD, cocaine," she said, as though her daily talk was peppered with references to a pharmacology of street drugs. "I hear they're even experimenting with horse tranquilizers," she added.

I hoped my head wouldn't spin around and give away the fact that I was being shocked here. "Can you describe Elizabeth?" I asked, hoping to regain a more benign track. "And tell me about previous . . . vanishings."

"I have pictures," she said, rising from her chair. I rose, too, being polite and all, and watched her go up the stairs to the mansion. I sipped some iced tea, ran my tongue around the inside of my mouth trying to identify the sort of not-iced-tea patina, and thought about all the excuses I could logically come up with to refuse to get involved in what was all the time sounding more sinister and difficult. I already knew that if I were to get involved, I'd have to visit Elizabeth's father, the one who warned me off playing with her when we were kids. I doubted he would remember our brief encounter, but I was sure he hadn't changed his stripes over the past decade. "Elizabeth! Elizabeth! What did I tell you about staying away from that dirty, filthy coal-miner's kid—"

But he hadn't said that to her. He'd let it up to me to be a prick by seeming to brush off Elizabeth and her brother, as though it was my decision and he was totally innocent of being involved in the least way. I ran my left index finger down the ridge of my scar. I should make a point of visiting him after dark so that when he turned on the porch light, I could really freak him out. "Boo! Here early for Halloween. Got something for me?"

As I waited for the return of Miss Delaney with the photos of Elizabeth, I drummed my fingers on the little table, being patient and impatient at the same time—patient for her return, impatient with my being suckered into this.

When she came back, she handed me a studio portrait that was obviously Elizabeth's Marian High School yearbook photo; I knew that because she was wearing a school uniform like the girls at Marian. There was also a set of snapshots from what looked like a picnic, some kind of a picnic at a park, where she was dressed in a white summer blouse and pink Bermuda shorts, and barefooted and sitting on a blanket holding an A-Treat black cherry soda. Her left front tooth was chipped.

I pointed at the photo.

"Chipped it sidewalk surfing," Miss Delaney supplied.

Sitting with her on the blanket were two other girls. In one of the photos, one of the girls, a blonde, was thumbing her nose at whoever was taking the picture. In the background several group-ings of adults and young people were standing around as though waiting for whomsoever was roasting the weenies and burning the burgers to get the job done so they could all eat. They were all a bit out of focus.

In the graduation portrait, Elizabeth looked like a normal, sweet brunette chick dressed in a plaid school uniform in what was likely one of the last years that a Catholic high school managed to require its girls to wear uniforms—to the dismay of perverts who like to see pictures of attractive girls dressed in school uniforms.

"Very lovely," I said, making to hand the photos back to Miss Delaney.

"You may keep those," she said. "I had them made for you."

"You—?" I started but stopped myself. How the hell would she have known far enough in advance to have those done up so she could give them to me today? That I'd be sitting here today to get lured into this? Because in the shallow recesses of my slow-twitch mind, I already knew I was going to do what she wanted, if for no other reason than it was a perfect place to start research on my book. Elizabeth might even come to constitute the first chapter, a spring-board into the whole damned, ugly topic by putting a face to it.

I placed the pictures on the edge of the table, compulsively straightening them so all the edges facing the courthouse were lined up perfectly. "So tell me about Elizabeth's . . . increasing bad habits."

Her hands again began to graze in her lap. She began to speak, then stopped, then tried to restart from a different direction. "She was fine in high school, a near-perfect student. A little moody once in a while, but what teenage girl isn't? She spent summers as a camp counselor out at Lake Harmony. In September of '65 she started at St. Elizabeth's School for Girls in Bethlehem." Miss Delaney gazed at the top of the courthouse for a moment, lost in thought. "She seemed to thrive there the first year. When she came home for Thanksgiving that first year, she was excited. 'Look, Aunt Grace, the school printed my name on everything I bought there.' She showed me her sweatshirt, her gym outfit, a half-dozen pieces of clothing she'd bought, all of them with 'St. Elizabeth' embroidered or stenciled on them. It was a wonderful Thanksgiving. Everybody in the family was home, and we had some early snow, and we celebrated at the house up at the lake. It was wonderful." She paused, as though getting things set up chronologically. "Christmas was nice, too. We stayed close to home for Christmas. She brought one of her school chums home with her, Barbara Kottke. The one you see thumbing her nose in that snapshot from the following spring."

She sipped her iced tea. "Then, a little at a time, too little to notice if you weren't looking for it, things began to change. She didn't write or call as often—"

"Often happens when somebody gets caught up in college life," I supplied.

"But that should have happened in her freshman year," Miss Delaney said.

I shrugged. "Not necessarily. She may have been in touch more in her freshman year because she was a bit homesick, then when sophomore year came around, she was more in the groove, and more of her life revolved around school than home."

Miss Delaney seemed to think about that for a while. She shook her head slowly. "That may be," she said, "but really, the changes, they increased and she . . . withdrew. And started going to the homes of her friends for vacations instead of coming home."

"But the Kottke girl came here for Christmas, you said," I said. "Seems natural that Elizabeth would then go to her house the next year."

Miss Delaney seemed to be getting frustrated with me. Her hands, like white spiders, chased each other across the blue of her lap. "It's difficult to explain," she said. "You—"

"—had to be there," I finished for her.

She nodded. "Yes. I don't think any of us noticed too much at the time. But later, it all made sense."

"Then what happened?" I asked, noting by the tower clock that the workmen would be back soon banging on the air-conditioning unit and that I'd be expected back at the *Times-News* office.

"Well, she started vanishing."

"Not like a magic trick," I said, unable at this point to stifle being a wise ass.

Miss Delaney cocked her head. "What *do* you mean?" she asked.

"Nothing, nothing," I said. "She began to vanish."

"Yes. From school. From home, on the rare occasions when she was home."

"How many times did that happen?"

"Half a dozen times a year."

"But she always came back."

"Yes. Eventually."

"Her father didn't send anyone out looking for her?"

"The first few times."

"And did they find her?"

"No. She'd eventually come home on her own."

"And what makes you think she won't turn up on your front step this time?"

Miss Delaney pursed her lips. "Funny. It sounds funny. Women's intuition."

I nearly reached across to stroke her fluttering spider hands. "Women's intuition is often underrated," I said.

She smiled a half-hearted smile.

"So what, exactly, do you want me to do?"

"Find her. Bring her back, so we can get her into a hospital where they can help her through this."

"Does your brother have any idea what you're doing?"

She shook her head. "He thinks he's doing all he can by hiring that worthless private dick." She spit the word "dick" out as though she knew him better than she should have.

"You must know that today is only my second day on the job at the newspaper," I said. "You seem to know things like that—"

28

"Sometimes I think a newspaper in these towns is superfluous," she said. "By the time it finds its way to peoples' doorsteps, they already know everything that's happened."

"So everyone will know that we had this little chat," I said.

"They will not learn it from me."

"Well, my point is that with getting up to speed with the news-paper and getting research rolling for this book—"

"But," she interrupted, "Elizabeth is like research for your book. It's all part of the same subject . . . but now with a face put to it."

My first instinct was this: hey, lady, maybe you ought to write the damned book. "That's kind of true," I said instead.

"And some of your research might find its way into the *Times-News* also."

I was starting to feel a little overwhelmed. I'd always been good at doing research papers in high school and college, in fact that talent brought in a bunch of extra cash and some fashionable sweaters in college by doing term papers for some of the guys in my dorm who were term paper averse, but the research I was now facing, especially that with the face of Elizabeth Delaney on it, wasn't going to be confined to library shelves.

"I'll need some information and a letter from your brother to St. Elizabeth's authorizing me to see her records there."

Miss Delaney nodded, as though she expected no less.

"I'll need the address and phone number of the Kottke girl and any other friends—from here in town and from college—she hung with the last few years. And I'll need $500."

She looked startled, as though she thought all of this was going to happen for free. "Ah—" she started. "I'll need a couple of days."

"If her father can afford a private investigator, he can afford $500," I said, trying not to appear like a mercenary, but then that was what she was recruiting me to be. "What--?"

She looked blankly.

"For expenses . . . and for bribes," I supplied. "I suspect if I start digging into this, I'll encounter some people who aren't prone to give away information for free. Make the 500 in ones, fives, and tens."

She nodded, as though it was all beginning to make sense.

"And I'll need a quiet place to work," I added. "The newspaper office is no place where a guy can think straight, which is why I suspect Joe Boyle is always out and about on assignments. And I can't work in my grandmother's cellar, and I won't work at my mother's." She nodded, just as the clock tolled one o'clock. "You'll want to see the room I advertised. I think it is just what you are looking for."

I nodded, took another sip of iced tea.

She got up slowly, as though she'd aged a decade in the past hour. I'd have thought that getting some of that off her chest would have lightened her mood, but it apparently did just the opposite.

"Come," she said. "I'll introduce you to Mr. Thorpe, your new roommate."

I got up from my chair just as the air-conditioning guys began beating their hammers against the aluminum. And sat right back down. I felt lightheaded and woozy.

Miss Delaney turned around and came back to the table, gently taking my right upper arm. "Oh dear," she said. "I may have put too much gin in the iced tea." She put her free hand to her mouth, whether a learned reaction to something embarrassing or to hide a smile, I wasn't sure.

"Gimme a moment," I said, and pushed myself off the seat very slowly and gently. I felt a little unsteady, but by concentrating on each deliberate step, I was able to get myself going in the right direction. Gin for lunch! Just what I needed in the middle of the workday.

We walked like an old coot and his nurse up the wide lawn toward Mr. Thorpe, who calmly and steadily continued to push the lawn mower across the perfect lawn. Apparently he'd skipped the ginned-up iced tea.

He saw Miss Delaney approaching and stopped in his tracks, ran a forearm across his forehead to wipe off perspiration, and let loose with a wide smile. He didn't reach six feet but he was well muscled although sporting a bit of the thickness some men get when their muscles begin to turn soft. His face was rough, the skin the texture of cottage cheese. His hair was combed straight back and his handshake was as firm as a twenty-five-year-old wrestler.

I kept it together as I realized this was *the* Jim Thorpe, Olympian superstar. "Howdy," he said when Miss Delaney introduced us. "Miss Delaney told me I wouldn't be living alone forever up there next to the haunted castle," he said, waving a thumb up the hill at the Harry Packer Mansion.

"I was going to tell Miss Delaney that when we were kids we all thought the place was haunted," I said.

Mr. Thorpe's eyebrows rose and he smiled. "It still is," he said. "I hear noises coming out of it all the time."

"Probably squirrels running about," Miss Delaney said, as though a next-door house being haunted was going to make me change my mind about wanting to live in the neighborhood.

"Heard you're a wrestler," Mr. Thorpe said.

"Wrestled in high school and college—and last night," I said.

Mr. Thorpe patted me on the shoulder. "Heard about that," he said and laughed. "I'm sure you fellas gave them as good as you got, and got to still be standing at the end."

"Mr. Thorpe used to wrestle a bit," Miss Delaney said.

He nodded his head. "Yes, indeed. I did some wrestling, but not a lot."

"It's an honor to meet you," I said, again extending my hand, shaking hands a second time, feeling like an idiot.

For a moment Mr. Thorpe looked confused, and then he grasped my hand and gave it a good clamp.

"What brings you here, to Mauch Chunk?"

"A nice clean quiet job in a nice quiet—usually quiet—place, at least for a bit, before I head back to California."

"But aren't you way past retirement age?"

"I have no plans to retire," he said. "When you retire, all you do is sit around doin' nothing. 'Cept wait for the Grim Reaper." He smiled a warm smile. "I figure if I keep movin', he won't know where to find me. Besides, I can use the money workin' brings in."

"We should do a story on you," I suggested.

He held up his hand. "Too late. Mr. Boyle did a nice story on me last month when I turned eighty years of age." He nodded, obviously pleased with the story Joe Boyle had done on him. "He even went so far as to publish an editorial arguing, persuasively mind you, for the return of those medals I won in the Olympics of '12."

"Well, you should have 'em," I said. "You certainly earned 'em."

"Well, perhaps," he said. "There were rules, rules I didn't know about as well as I should have, and we need to have rules about things or everything'll fall apart."

"Would you care to take your potential new roommate up and show him around while I get back to work, Mr. Thorpe?"

"Glad to," Mr. Thorpe said, putting his arm around my shoulders and steering me up the hill, while Miss Delaney turned to go back to the Asa Packer Mansion.

"Come and see me when you're done and we'll finalize everything," she said.

"You don't have to worry about ghosts or goblins getting you," Mr. Thorpe said, as we walked around the side of the brooding mansion. "Our rooms are out the back in the carriage house. The ghosts don't come back there. Besides, if they did, I do believe you'd scare them more than they'd scare you."

He laughed and put his arm around me.

"Did you have the iced tea?"

"Did I—"

He laughed. "I make sure to keep working over lunch so she doesn't invite me to have iced tea and cake with her or I never get anything done in the afternoon. Then at the end of the day she complains that I didn't do my work, that I'm a drunken red man."

My eyebrows went up.

"So to not insult her and to save my job, I bring my own birch beer—"

"—you know birch beer?"

"Not where I come from, but I learned it here. Not much different from root beer."

"But there's a difference."

"If you learn to listen—with your tongue."

"Like a snake."

He laughed; I laughed.

"So what brand gin does she use?" I asked.

3

Beaking News

The day's *Times-News*, in the upper-right corner of the front page, under the silhouette of a rooster and the words "The Weather," would declare that Wednesday, June 5, 1968, was to be CLEAR-COOL. And it was. Or it would be.

But at 4:35, sitting above Fisher's Hill on the east side of town in the ole '64 Rambler Classic 440 while the in-line six bathed its innards in squishy motor oil, it was dark and cool. The streetlights were still on.

I'd gotten to the Dungeon early enough that I'd had time to box up a bunch of my stuff—most of it had never made it out of the boxes I'd used to bring it back from college—and move it to the trunk of the car. Sometime during the coming day I'd force the poor Rambler to crawl up Packer Hill, make it turn left into the driveway behind the still-haunted Harry Packer Mansion, and pull up in front of the carriage house, where Mr. James Thorpe and I would commence being roommates, occupying nearly identical apartments on either side of a common area that included a kitchen and a living room. The whole place, small but comfortable, was furnished entirely with antiques. The newest item in the place was a plastic shower curtain sporting big yellow daisies, wrapping itself around a claw-footed metal tub. All this for $50/mo.

But I hadn't spent most of the evening contemplating the bliss of sort of having my own place, unattached in any way to my previous life, other than it was on the property of a mansion that we kids knew was haunted. I'd spent half of the evening writing up yet another story about the Paramount Pictures effort to enshrine *The Molly Maguires* as a symbol of the unrest and antiestablishment bent that increasingly marked the 1960s. Like ninety years after the Mollies, the spirit of rebellion was pocking the land. The story for this afternoon's paper was a profile of my old drinking buddy, Dickie Harris, concentrating most on his role in *Camelot*, a . . . er . . . light opera.

The rest of the evening I'd spent going back and forth between the two photos of Elizabeth Delaney, first the high school graduation portrait and then the picnic with her friend thumbing her nose. The rest of them I just let lie there. Those two, I thought, were the important ones. I also thought a lot about how the whole damned thing must be a carbon copy of what's going on all over the country, maybe all over much of the world: a young person discovers drugs as a key to unlock deep and profound recesses of self, expanding the worldview, giving access to all known and unknown human knowledge, and putting that young person in conflict with the whole complex structured world that took thousands of years to get that way, a wrong way, a way obviously not sympathetic to deep thinkers and mystics, one that must be scratched off like a scab.

Then I had another beer and of course the whole picture got even clearer. Just how cookie cutter was Elizabeth Delaney's case? Well-off parents, dominant father, submissive mother, perfect symbol of the 1950s family, ripped down the middle by a couple of semesters of college and supercharged by fellow wanderers, all fueled by an increasing availability and assortment of drugs.

It wouldn't surprise me if I took an afternoon off, drove down to Allentown, knocked at the door of the parents of the nose thumber, and Elizabeth looked over the shoulder of whomsoever answered. If it were that easy, the private dick lawyer Delaney hired would have already found her, and Elizabeth would be home safely cooking up new ways to escape her overprotective dysfunctional family. Private dicks know how to do such mundane things, don't they? He had seen the photos, hadn't he? He knew about her college buddies, didn't he?

I popped the top off yet another Yuengling longneck there in the deep, dank, dark dungeon and wondered when I'd have time to follow up on all this. Joe Boyle had already assigned me to my first East Mauch Chunk borough council meeting tomorrow night. "They'll spend ninety minutes arguing over whether to put in another parking meter but pass the annual budget in five minutes," he warned. "Drink a lot of coffee before you go into the meeting."

I dropped the three-on-the-column into first, turned on the lights, and eased the Rambler onto Eighth, heading over to North. The streets were pretty much bare. Headed down North toward the river, wondering what it would be like living with Jim Thorpe, famed Indian athlete. Not very stereotypical, that's for sure. He spoke well, in complete sentences, not like Tonto, and seemed to be born with a smile on his face. Don't take yourself too seriously. Maybe I could learn that from him.

On the other side of the bridge I turned left and eased the car off the road to park it next to Ron's caboose. He had one of the state police cruisers home overnight: must be going out on patrol earlier than usual. "Anything but riding the desk," he'd said. Problem was that's probably where he'd end up. He was way too organized, couldn't help himself, and they'd be blind to miss that trait.

I locked the car, zipped up my light jacket, and walked toward Steve's Diner to get my morning joe and apple turnover. This was my third day on the job and the joe and turnover had already established themselves as bad habits.

I pushed open the glass door and it was like entering the lobby of the Tower of Babel. A radio up on the shelf above the Bun coffee maker was on, with a stressed, frantic announcer going on about "updating" this and "updates" yet to come, and Joe Jeske, the owner of Steve's (don't ask), was waving his hands and muttering to himself, while Barney, the short-order cook, was waving his hands back at him, and the two customers at the counter were sitting with their heads together as though trading bomber gun-sight secrets at a Paris café during World War II.

I made a sign that I hoped over the weeks would take on a life of its own and metastasize into my "usual" order, meaning coffee and apple turnover, but nobody was paying me any attention.

The radio cut to a remote in Philadelphia, where Mayor James Tate was saying something was "very, very terrible."

"What's terrible?" I asked Joe.

He slapped himself on the forehead. "You haven't heard?" he asked. "You, a newspaperman, haven't heard?"

"What?" I said again.

"They shot another Kennedy," he said. "Like that's what the Kennedys are there for, to be shot at."

"What Kennedy?" I asked.

"The younger brother, Bobby."

"In Los Angeles, early this morning," Barney said from behind his spatula. He waved it in front of his face like a sword.

The normal first-thing-in-the-morning humidity got even steamier.

"At a hotel in L.A.," Joe said. "After a victory speech."

"Yeah," Barney said, "while he was leaving through the kitchen."

He said it as though he was personally offended that such a thing should happen in a kingdom over which he and his brethren reigned.

"How is he?" I asked. And got three different answers:

Joe: "Near death."

Barney: "Badly wounded."

One of the two elderly gentlemen customers: "He'll make it. He's tough, took on the city bosses."

Before it got any more crazy, I decided to put myself through the black-ink coffee at the *Times-News* office. Besides which, it was hooked up to the wire services, to AP, and would be getting more current reports than a bunch of guys in an aluminum early-morning diner.

I turned around and went back out through the glass door, Joe calling after me, "Hey! Where ya goin'? Don't you want your regular?"

It took a minute to jog between Weiksner's and the courthouse, across Broadway, along Susquehanna, and up Race Street, where the *Times-News* office was lighted up brighter than Christmas. When I pushed open the door, everyone was in a scrum around the wire machine except for Mrs. Apfelbaum, who sat at her desk with her head in her hands. A Roman Catholic, Irish, she'd always been a grass-roots supporter of the Kennedys.

36

I dropped into my seat across the desk from her. She looked out from between the forest of her long fingers. "They've done it again," she said. "Why can't they leave the Kennedys alone?"

"What's the latest?" I asked.

Mrs. Gertrude Apfelbaum, raised most of her life on gathering and disseminating news, clicked into her newswoman gear. She put her hands on the desk in front of her and suddenly looked like a mature, female version of Edward R. Murrow, giving the news to an anxious world.

"Shot in the back of the head, with a .22, around 12:15 Pacific time, leaving a rally at a hotel after he won the California Democratic primary," she dictated. "Not much yet on the assassin . . . ah, assailant."

Her eyes began to well up and she put her face back into her hands. I got up and put my arm around her shoulders. She patted my hand with one of hers.

She shook with sobs for a minute and then stopped, unraveled herself, and reached for her purse, from which she extracted a handkerchief and wiped her nose. She made a dismissive gesture with her right hand, signaling that I should go join the guys at the wire machines, where the bells signaling a major story moving over the wires clanged hollowly for the rest of the morning. Like Pavlov's dogs, every time the bells rang, we rushed to the machines to read the latest. Ironically, it was usually Cy Apfelbaum, Gertrude's Jewish very-mixed-marriage husband and head of the ad department, who read the news to us.

We walked back and forth between the snug little newsroom and the composition room where the day's issue was being put together like a jigsaw puzzle, to the press room, where the mighty-armed trolls of that subterranean kingdom drank rank ink-black coffee, sported eternally black fingers from the indelible ink, and walked around like miners trapped underground. Our pressmen were all Slovaks from up the road, in Summit Hill and Lansford, knotted arms from wrestling Volkswagen-sized rolls of newsprint and tightening down screws on the finicky old letterpress. They sat on stools, morose, waiting for us to come down and update them, coming up shyly to invade the newsroom when we didn't come down often enough to keep them informed. All of them Roman Catholics, they had a spiritual stake in Bobby Kennedy.

At one point I slid the pages of my story on Richard Harris into the top drawer of my scarred navy desk. Mrs. Apfelbaum occasionally made attempts at small talk. She sort of apologized for my first week on the job being so crazy, as though she had something to do with Kennedy's shooting. I told her about lining up the apartment in the carriage house of the Harry Packer Mansion, and about Mr. Jim Thorpe. She seemed to approve of my moves to date. "He's a very nice man, but very troubled," she said simply.

In an attempt to make her smile, I told her the Harry Packer Mansion is haunted. "The place is haunted, you know," I said.

She frowned and then smiled. I was sure she was going to assure me that it wasn't but instead, playing along with it, she simply said, "But of course it is."

My expression, my confusion, made her smile.

"Mr. Thorpe says that the carriage house is all right, though," I added.

She periodically dabbed at items for her "Strictly Personal" column, which would not be as long today as it usually was and which would make no mention of Robert F. Kennedy since that was front-page straight news and there was no legitimate reason yet for it to crop up on the "society" column, as I thought of the column. Better than "rumor" column.

The guys laying out the pages locked in all of the interior pages but kept the front page fluid, ready to replace any information with still-fresher information. They laid out a few local pieces on the bottom of the front page (things like "Lehighton High Athletes Cited," "Woman's Scrap Book Gets Honorable Mention," and "Vo-Tech Graduates First Class of Practical Nurses").

News about the assailant came across, not terribly well edited, rushed. Bob Thomas of the Associated Press filed the piece that we used on the far-right column under the 48-point headline KENNEDY STILL CRITICAL:

LOS ANGELES (AP)—Sen. Robert F. Kennedy was shot in the head by a mysteriously silent gunman today after winning the California Democratic presidential primary. He emerged from more than three hours of surgery in "extremely critical condition."

An aide said all but a fragment of a bullet was removed from Kennedy's brain and a second bullet, less serious, remains in the back of his neck.

The sixth graph held some information about the would-be assassin:

"With stunning rapidity at 12:25 a.m., a man police described as a Caucasian, about 25, 5 feet 5 and 120 pounds, with dark hair and complexion, emptied the chamber of an eight-shot .22 pistol."

Caucasian, dark complexion . . . confused us.

We kept part of column one open for news that dribbled in moments before we began to run the presses at noon, and news of the assailant began to jell:

"The man arrested in the shooting of Sen. Robert F. Kennedy was identified as Sirhan Sirhan, 23, who has a brother who lives in nearby Pasadena."

Several graphs later it was revealed that Sirhan Sirhan once lived in Jerusalem and that he had four one hundred dollar bills in his pocket, "with which he was planning on leaving if he could get away," L. A. Mayor Samuel Yorty reported.

"The AP burped on the name," Joe Boyle said. "That can't be his real name. That'd be like Apfelbaum Apfelbaum."

"We don't have time to wait for clarification," Nate Dermott, the managing editor, always a nervous wreck, said. "We gotta run with it."

People had been calling the newspaper all morning to get updated information, and Mrs. Apfelbaum and our receptionist were constantly on the phone. Now, with the presses about to run, they could tell the callers that the paper would be on their doorstep real soon now.

Under the top headline on the top of the front page were three additional pieces: World Reacts to News, The Irony, and Violence Stalks Kennedy Family.

Ten minutes later, the AP bell began to ring again, as it had been all morning. We could feel the rumbling through the floor as the presses began to run, building up speed like a locomotive, starting slowly in a deep rumble and spiraling up to a drumbeat and on to a jet-plane engine at full throttle.

Pencils and pens on our desks began to vibrate, the Better Business Bureau plaque on the wall began to shake, and Mrs. Apfelbaum put her hands over her ears. She mouthed the words: "Some day this whole building is going to come down and kill all of us."

I moved around in my swivel chair as though riding a car with bad springs over a bumpy road.

She shook her head sadly, the tragedy of today mixing with the tragedies of life in general. Even hardened news folks get the blues.

Once we had regained our equilibrium, like sailors aboard a tossing ship, Joe Boyle decided it was time to get the hell out of the office and take the pulse of the community. "Who's going with me?" he asked the newsroom. Nate Dermott demurred.

"I'm going home," he said, "and get drunk."

Cy Apfelbaum and I decided to go with Joe to get some critical quotes about RFK's shooting from the citizens of Mauch Chunk. We started at Weiksner's Bar.

There were a half-dozen denizens of the dark bar. Two of them were sitting at a table. The other four were at the bar, two of them drinking boilermakers, one of those digging into a pickled sausage half. John was behind the bar. "Hey, slugger," he said when he saw me. He made a motion with his hand, indicating that he wanted me to turn my head a bit so he could survey the damage. "Yuck," he said. "It's gonna look even worse once it begins to turn green and yellow. Lots worse."

"Thanks," I said as we took our stools at the small arm of the L-shaped bar. John drew drafts of Yuengling. Cy drained his in one chug, motioned for a refill.

"Helluva day," Cy sighed. "Helluva mess."

John, always the agreeable bartender, nodded in agreement.

The guy wrestling with the sausage nodded. "Kill a Kennedy," he said. "Is that the new national sport?"

Joe drained off half of his beer, shook his head, pulled his notebook out of his back pocket and sat it on the bar, and made a note to himself.

"Any news on who did it?" the sausage guy asked. I sort of recognized him but couldn't quite place him.

Joe shook his head. "Too early to tell for sure. Information keeps coming in, but it'll be a few more hours until everything's sorted out. Name's Sirhan Sirhan, we do know that." He finished his beer and tapped the rim for a refill. John was particularly energetic today and got right to it.

"Doesn't sound like an American, that's for sure," one of the guys at the table said. "Sirhan Sirhan," he said slowly, trying to get more familiar with the alien sound of the name. "What kind of a parent names their kid the same thing twice. Like Tommie Thomas or Bill Williams, for god's sake."

"Sounds Arab," sausage guy said. "Some cultures over there use repeated names. Or string together names that are a block long."

Joe nodded. "Seems this Sirhan Sirhan didn't care for Bobby Kennedy. Some paper in Pasadena wrote something negative about Bobby, and this Sirhan guy was carrying a clipping in his pocket when they searched him."

"Pretty bad when somebody goes to kill somebody just because some newspaper jerk—sorry Joe—wrote something bad about a guy," John said, again refilling Cy's six-ounce beer glass.

"Maybe he got put up to it, like Lee Harvey Oswald," the guy at the table said. "Oswald worked for the Russians, you know. Maybe this guy's working for the Arabs."

"Lotta hate over in that part of the world," Cy said. "They hate everybody over there, even each other." He raised his beer. "To Bobby."

Everybody in the bar raised glasses, with murmurs of "To Bobby."

There was a long moment of silence. The sound of the Hazleton air-conditioning guys banging away filtered through the bar's windows. A car horn somewhere out on Broadway sounded once, twice.

"You know, they let those assholes out of jail this morning," John reported, looking at me.

"I hope you're pressing charges," Joe said.

I nodded that I was.

"They'll be going to trial," John said, "as soon as the Molly Maguires get done using the courthouse."

"Maybe we can get a group hanging rate," the sausage guy said, around a two-pinch wad of preserved meat. He pointed his fork at me. "That thing hurt? Heard it was a real good fight."

"Just when I try to use my jaw," I said, moving my jaw back and forth. It made a popping sound.

"Any of you ever pop a woman?" John asked.

Nobody answered.

"Didn't seem to bother ole Ronnie," John said.

"Nothing bothers Ronnie," I said. "But everything bothers Ronnie."

There was silence again, guys looking at their drinks as though they weren't sure just what they were and what they were good for. The two guys at the table lit cigarettes and blew the smoke up toward the ceiling, where dollar bills had been tacked over the years, many of them turning a dull gray in response to all the smoke blown their way.

"I don't know what the world's coming to," Cy said to nobody in particular. "Killing Kennedys, punching women in the face."

Nods of agreement, sips of beer. It was the first time in modern history a bar full of guys didn't have an answer that would correct all the ills of the world.

"Sure hope there's no Jack Ruby out there in L.A.," Joe said. "That'd make things worse still."

More nods of agreement.

"L.A. ain't Dallas," one of the guys at the table said, as though that summed things up perfectly.

"You ain't been to L.A. *or* Dallas, Macky," John said. "How d'ya know they hain't the same?"

Macky blew some smoke in John's direction.

Joe scribbled something in his notebook.

I suddenly felt low, empty. I had been way too young to vote for Jack Kennedy in 1960 and wasn't sure I'd have voted for Bobby Kennedy this year after what he'd had the FBI do to Martin Luther King, the wiretapping and all. But you had to admire his guts in going after crime figures in cities where those same crime figures may have figured in his brother getting elected in 1960. I liked to see the world as black and white, and it was proving to be about the color of the left side of my face. But killing somebody because of his politics or because somebody had written something bad about a guy in the newspaper: Jesus.

Joe dropped a bill on the bar and motioned for us to head out. I finished up my beer, Cy finished up his, Joe collected his notebook from the bar, and we headed back out into the sunshine, waving goodbye as we went.

"Not in the mood for another bar," Joe said. "Let's swing by Queenie's"—the local beer and soft drink distributor—"and get a cold case and go up to the Flagstaff so can contemplate the world from a perch better and higher than a bar stool."

That seemed like a good idea to Cy, who picked up his pace over to the railroad station where his car was parked. He waved his hand up Broadway, which was still covered in dirt for the movie. "Need a long-handled shovel to scoop up all the shit," he said.

I had no idea what that meant.

We piled into Cy's car, went by Queen Beverage, had them bring a case of Ballantine out of the cooler, put in into the trunk, and Cy drove us up to Flagstaff Park, the pavilion complex that hangs over the mountain's ledge overlooking the Lehigh River, Bear Mountain, and both Chunks. The place had been a beehive of activity during the 1930s and '40s, with big bands like Jimmy Dorsey playing there on a regular basis. Now it was open sporadically for proms and the occasional special occasion. It was currently in one of its dormant phases.

Cy parked outside the cyclone fence. I pulled the case of beer from the trunk, and Joe walked down the fence to where vandals had opened a slit. We bent down and went through, over to the rocks on the edge, where we each took a rock seat and began passing around beers.

It was a brilliant day, cool and blue. The town below looked like it was assembled on a tabletop as a Christmas display, compete with railroad station and parallel rail lines. On the other side of the river, Bear Mountain squatted in front of us, Pleasant Hill (known to one and all as Nigger Hill for the coal-smeared miners who lived there; it was where I'd grown up; my mother and kid sister still lived there) clung precariously to the other side of the mountain, and across the little valley where the lumberyard sprawled, East Mauch Chunk spread out along an ancient alluvial fan, the streets laid out straight and logical, breaks coming only when the topography refused to cooperate, a hillock making it impossible for a proper street to continue along its grid, only to continue a few blocks farther along.

Cy took a log drag of his beer. He swept his hand out in front of him, his overcoat too much for such a nice day but something he seldom left the indoors without. "Out there," he said. "They wanna kill all the Jews, the Catholics, and the Negroes. They got King this year and now they nearly got Bobby." He spat. "Bastards!"

I was more saddened than irate, something that beers at noon only exaggerate. I looked over toward the Asa Packer Mansion. It looked as though Mr. Thorpe was working at the flower garden, down on his knees. I remembered that I still needed to drive my stuff up Packer Hill and deposit it in our apartment.

Joe stared at the left side of my face. "Out in the sun here it looks a lot worse than it does in the darkness of a bar—"

"—or in our offices," Cy added.

I ran a finger down along the scar and then up along the bruise. With everything going on I didn't much have time to think about it. I could feel the bruise when I worked my jaw, but so what? At least I hadn't been shot in the head with a .22.

"What if he dies?" Cy said.

"Who?" Joe said.

"Bobby."

"Probably will," Joe said. "And if he lives he won't be Bobby anymore."

"Jesus," Cy said. "Gimme another beer."

4

By Rail to Packerton

"You know he's gonna die, right?" Ronnie said as I pulled the T-shirt over my head. "Either that or he'll be a veg the rest of his life."

He was talking about Bobby Kennedy. I groggily understood what he was saying but didn't particularly like the way he was saying it.

"That's pretty cold," I said.

He snickered. "And it's pretty damned righteous."

As a state trooper who'd seen his fair share of head-shot and crash-mashed head injuries, I had no way of arguing with him, although I wanted to.

We were suiting up to take a little jog down the gravel road that paralleled the Jersey Central Railroad tracks to the rail yards at Packerton. I was groggy because I was here with Ronnie at the end of his workday after having spent the afternoon perched on the edge of the Flagstaff boulders contemplating the world and drinking copious amounts of beer. When Joe and Cy and I came down off the mountain, I'd seen that Ronnie's cruiser was parked in front of his caboose, so I'd knocked to see if he'd like to help me unload my shit up at the Harry Packer Mansion carriage house. "Sure," he said, "as soon as we get in a few miles."

So here we were throwing on our running stuff and talking about head injuries.

I laced up my well-worn Converse running flats, stood up, and bounced a little to loosen up my ankles. Ronnie was contorting himself into a pretzel on the carpet in front of the coal stove. I'm not a big proponent of stretching before you run. I can picture cold, stiff muscle fibers being snapped like icicles.

Besides, with so much beer onboard I'd probably pass out if I stressed my body too much too early.

When he was sufficiently loosened up, we went out the door, down the steps, and began immediately skipping over railroad tracks in order to get off the side of the road. We jogged past the Jersey Central Railroad Station, now an empty husk. There was word the Carbon County Tourist Bureau had plans to move in and fix it up and use some of the square footage as a museum celebrating coal and railroads.

The tracks were seldom used these days, so rust had built up on them. Ronnie was muttering under his breath about how the rust would be gone once he and his buddies got their steam locomotive up and running. "And we'll run tourists out to Glen Onoco during the high foliage season and maybe stop out there and have a picnic," he said.

We weren't more than a hundred yards past the station when an old coot wearing a red plaid Woolrich jacket came out running after us, yelling for us to get off railroad property. "Yo, Mr. Fogel!" Ronnie yelled. "It's only us joggers!"

Mr. Fogel stopped in his tracks. "Oh, okay. Didn't recognize you, Ronnie. Okay." He seemed disappointed he didn't get to ream out some trespasser's ass.

"His one remaining joy in life is hassling trespassers," Ronnie said.

"Shouldn't he be retired by now?"

"Yeah, sure. But what would he do with himself? He has no family and this gives him a chance to interact with other human beings—"

"By hassling them," I said. "Nice."

"Well, we *are* technically trespassing."

An A&P grocery store trailer truck downshifted as it began to lumber up the Mansion House Hill to our right. The hill paralleled the road we were on, which paralleled the railroad tracks, which, coming out of the Mauch Chunk yard, were narrowing down to a mere two tracks. High above the struggling tractor-trailer squatted Flagstaff Park. It seemed like days since I'd been up there drinking beer and commiserating with Joe and Cy.

"How many trains come along here these days?" I asked.

"None on this side. Maybe two a week over on the Lehigh Valley side."

Ron raised his hands over his head, stretching the battered East Mauch Chunk High School T-shirt he was wearing. He windmilled his arms. "Pretty tight today," he said. "Don't know why." He windmilled some more, this time spinning his arms in the opposite direction.

We skirted a few puddles that lay in the middle of the road. The surface of the road was black from years of spilled coal. When we were kids, on the Lehigh Valley Railroad side of the river, we used to take our Radio Flyer wagons down to the road over there and shovel the spilled coal into buckets and try to sell it on the east side of town. Twenty-five cents a bucket. Then we'd blow our profits on Topps baseball cards, which our mothers would proceed to throw out as soon as we left for college.

A souped-up car of some type came rumbling down Mansion House Hill in a low gear, letting the engine hold it back.

"So how'd the meeting with Grace Delaney go?" Ron asked.

I shrugged my shoulders. "Okay, I guess. But she spent most of the time talking about her niece, Elizabeth. How she's vanished."

"She vanishes on a regular basis. But she always comes back," Ron said. "What about it does she think is different this time?"

"I dunno. Something she feels, some female intuition or something. She wants me to go look for her."

Ron snorted, then laughed. "You? Why you?"

"Because I'm used to asking questions and digging into things."

"And of course you said you'd do it—"

"I don't know that I had much choice. She got me drunk first and then had her way with me."

"You didn't drink the iced tea."

"'Fraid so."

He snorted again. "Well, good luck on your quest to locate the damsel in distress."

"Good luck hain't got nothin' to do with it."

"What are you counting on, raw talent?"

"Hell, we'll have no trouble finding a little girl like that."

"What's this 'we,' Kemo Sabe?"

"You're gonna help me."

Ron shook his head. "No way. I got important things to do with my spare time."

"More important than finding a fair maiden?"

"Don't kid yourself. She hain't all that fair."

"How would you know?"

"I took her out a couple of times."

My stride skipped a beat. "You dated her?"

"Hell, man," Ron said over his shoulder, "I'll bet that I've dated every eligible female on both sides of the river. Hell, I might even get around to dating the fair Miss Delaney, and I don't mean Elizabeth."

I caught up to him. "You know, you're more of a hopeless case than I thought."

"Why? What's wrong with dating women? You got something against dating women?" He snorted again. "Who you want me to date?" He held up his hand. "Don't even answer that." He windmilled his arms again. "Tense. Real tense today."

"So what was dating Elizabeth Delaney like?"

"Why don't you find out for yourself?"

"What da'ya mean?"

"When you find her, you can date her."

I shook my head.

"She's okay," Ron said. "Nothing special. Not especially bright, even though she's in college and all. But then, considering that you just graduated from college, the standards can't be all that high these days."

"When did you last date her?"

"Couple-a months ago."

"Did she seem like she was into drugs?"

"She wasn't using anything while we were out on our date, if that's what you mean. But if she was using on her own time, she wouldn't be the only chick from around here who was."

"Would you have arrested her if she was using?"

"While we were out on a date?"

"Yeah. No. Anytime."

"If I did it on a date, that'd be entrapment."

"But you would, under other circumstances."

"Depend on the circumstances."

"Would you arrest me if I was smoking marijuana?"

He was quiet for a dozen strides. "Yeah, yeah. I probably would. Because that'd give you a record and then the Selective Service couldn't latch onto your sorry ass and send you to 'Nam."

I reached over and gently slapped him on the back. "My pal. What a guy."

We were approaching the place where the Lehigh Valley tracks came across the river on a steel bridge and ran parallel with the Jersey Central tracks down to the Packerton yard.

"So what're you gonna do about the draft?" he asked.

I shrugged. "What can I do?"

"Get married. Tell them you already have a brother serving. Tell them you're your mother's sole means of support. Shoot yourself in the foot. Act like you wanna go to 'Nam. That's always a dead giveaway that you're nuts. Tell them your butt-ugly mug is a form of handicap. Did I say shoot yourself in the foot?"

"I might actually like the military service," I said, not meaning it.

Now it was his turn to slap me on the back. "See, yeah. That's a good start toward acting like you're a nut case. Keep practicing that. Memorize the annual rice production in Vietnam, stuff like that, that makes it seem like you really wanna tour exotic Viet-fuckin'-nam."

I smiled to myself, wondering how I'd put up with such a putz since first grade. "But back to Elizabeth," I said, as the tracks in front of us began to increase, growing out of each other like branches out of a trunk. The brickwork sheds were partially visible around the

49

corner. The roadway above us was dropping toward our level, and the sound of traffic increased. They were rushing downhill into what was known locally as the Packerton Dip—a bottoming out of the road at railroad and stream level before immediately shooting up the other side headed toward Lehighton. The dip was famous during snowstorms for creating a giant parking lot as cars came down from either side and then couldn't get up the opposite side without a forty mph running start and a speed limit that was thirty-five.

Ronnie again windmilled his arms. The motion was creating a pattern that seemed to be saying to me "When-I-wind-mill-my-arms-it-means-I-wanna-change-the-topic."

Our turnaround point, level with the bottom of the dip, was coming up, and Ronnie was still windmilling like crazy.

"Look," he said, as he made an elaborate turn, his arms still whirling. "She's been gone this time like a week, maybe not quite. For all I know, she heard you were coming back to Chunk to live and work and that drove her away from the hearth and home of her ever-loving family. All I know is that she's done it before, nobody in her family has bothered to formally file a missing-persons report, very much *un*like the first two times, and no police personnel that I know of have to date started an investigation because (a) there has been no formal request for them to do that, and (b) if habits are to work like habits, she's in the habit of eventually getting bored or running out of money, whereupon she returns home . . . before she again decides to cut out." He blew some snot from his right nostril; it plopped in front of my left shoe.

"So officially, you are not at this time concerned," I supplied.

"Jesus," he said, shaking his head. "Didn't you listen to a thing I just said?" His right hand snapped out as though to slap me upside the head, but he would have connected with my already-bruised left cheek and jaw. He pulled the punch at the last moment and hit me on the left shoulder. "There's no official anything here. No official missing-persons report filled out. No official investigation. No official nothing."

I turned my palms up in front of me. "But her old man has a private dick out looking for her."

Ron's right eyebrow went up and he again snorted. "Good point," he said. "Why's he bothering if he didn't bother filing a missing persons?" He shrugged. "I'll cogitate on that for a while." He smacked his forehead. "Shit!" he said.

"What?"

"I almost forgot to warn you away from Chief Drizler and his brood."

"What da'ya mean?"

"Somehow your comment about the biker assholes being punished by having to eat old lady Drizler's cooking got back to her and she's on the warpath."

"What's she gonna do if she catches me? Force me to eat some of her deer venison stew? All I have to do to get off scot-free is pass a sample of that shit around the courtroom 'en I could have her dead to rights on attempted murder."

Ronnie laughed. "Just steer clear of the Drizlers until this blows over. And don't park your car at a meter downtown or he'll have his goons ticket your butt."

I did my own snort, but it didn't come off as well as Ronnie's well-practiced versions. "Hey," I said, "why don't we sneak up on old man Fogel on our way back and spook him?"

Ronnie turned to look at me as though I was a mass murderer. "What the hell's wrong with you? Sometimes you act like you're eight years old."

"Come on," I said. "It'd be a hoot—"

He shook his head. "Old Mr. Fogel has done me a lot of favors by keeping an eye on my rolling stock. Some of the little bastards in town like to cause trouble by breaking into the cars and partying there. Just like we'd do if we were eight-year-olds. Mr. F keeps an eye on my stuff so to repay him, on the first of each month I issue him a Traffic Ticket Nullifier card."

"A what?"

"Like a Get Out Of Jail card."

"But he doesn't drive."

"That hain't the point."

The downtown began to grow larger as we loped along, both of us now loose and limber. We'd both broken a reasonable sweat. Ronnie pointed toward Race Street, like a vertical slash off to the left of Broadway. St. Mark's Church towered off the corner, and across the little street loomed the red-brick Lehigh Coal & Navigation Company building. Just above St. Mark's was the red, three-story *Times-News* building and beyond that the European-like stone row homes that made Race Street famous. "Why don't you buy one of the row homes instead of paying rent? Some of 'em're dirt cheap. One of 'em's like down to $800."

"The one that looks like it's a model home from postwar East Germany?"

"It's gutted, but the walls and roof are solid."

"I hain't buying nothing 'til I see if I get drafted."

"Hmmmmm," Ronnie said. "Good point."

"Why don't you buy on Race Street? You hain't gonna get drafted and you make a lot more money than I do."

"I like living in a caboose. And once I get the locomotive up and running, if I ever get tired of ole Mauch Chunk, I can hook my cars and the caboose behind the loco and head off to anywhere the rails go."

"Like a hobo."

"But a prosperous one."

We were approaching the railroad station.

"I ever tell you the story about the Easter bunny?" Ronnie asked.

"No. And there's probably a good reason for that. Every story you tell ends up in disaster."

"Naw," he said. "This one's uplifting."

"I know I'm gonna be sorry, but what about your Easter bunny story?"

We had slowed to a walk, cooling down on our way back to his elegant caboose-house.

"This was like April of 1965. I came home from the academy for Easter and I no sooner walk in the house than the old man pulls me aside and tells me my kid sister's bunny rabbit has to be put down because it's been puking pus from both ears for the past week and the old man's too damned cheap to take it to a vet and too chicken-shit, big brave World War II never-heard-a-shot-fired-in-anger guy that he is, to off the bunny himself. So I go out the back to the rabbit hutch and sure enough, Spunky the rabbit is producing pus like you'd squeeze cream out of a chocolate éclair. It was a big bunny, big and white, and it was twitching its nose like they do, and I picked it up and it felt hot like it had a fever."

We climbed the steps to Ron's caboose-house and filed inside. I sat down with a sigh while Ron kept his story going real fast like he'd had too much caffeine or something.

While he talked, he went over to the fridge and pulled out two green bottles of Rolling Rock and popped off the caps with his teeth, handed me one, which I began to gulp greedily, both because I was thirsty and because I wasn't too cool with the direction this stupid story was going.

"Hell. I didn't want my kid sister to hate me for the rest of her life. So I got a cardboard box, stuffed Spunky into it. He didn't seem to care or nothing. Just settled down in there. I took him down the back where there were some big flat stones, sat the box down on one of them, wrestled up another one, said 'Goodbye, Spunky,' and squished that harmless big ole white rabbit. Squish, just like that. So fast there was no blood, nothing. Then I dug a shallow grave and without opening the flattened box, slid it in and covered it up."

I must have looked like I expected more, which I did.

"No, that's it. The end. At dinner that night, the old man told us that Spunky had escaped and was probably halfway to Allentown by now. The kid sister cried and we put together a search party and spent about an hour knocking on doors, asking if anybody's seen a big ole white Easter bunny. Half the people thought this was some kinda joke. Easter weekend, looking for the Easter bunny."

I swallowed the mouthful of beer I'd been entertaining and shook my head. "I thought this was gonna be one of your gross-out stories."

"Like what?"

"Like we ate roasted rabbit for Easter that year, and it was really good because it had been tenderized."

Ron smiled. "Hey, that's good. Can I borrow it?"

"Yeah, sure. I'll send a transcript to the SPCA to clear it with them."

"Cool," he said. "Now let's have one more beer and move your crap up to your new digs."

He was wrong about that. It turned out to be three more beers before we drove all my crap—mostly paperback books—up to unload in my digs in the nearly haunted Harry Packer Mansion carriage house.

He was right about something, though. Bobby Kennedy didn't survive his headshot.

5
Rudy's Room

Thursday was no better, on the whole. All of us in the newspaper office spent much of the day checking the wires every five minutes for the latest on Bobby Kennedy. He'd died, just as Ronnie said he would. His assassin, Sirhan Sirhan, hadn't been a hiccup on the AP wire; he turned out to be a Palestinian. That fact struck fear into the hearts of many in the Arab world for fear the U.S. would take severe measures against them the way they would have done against somebody else if the positions had been reversed. We began hearing that RFK's body would be transported by train from New York to Washington, DC, and it would pass through far southeastern Pennsylvania.

Other work got done, but there was little enthusiasm for it. Everybody was pretty well worn down emotionally.

I was now Jim Thorpe's roommate. Ron and I had managed to unload the Rambler's trunk in less than ten minutes. Most of the boxes of books were piled against a wall in the central living room. Mr. Thorpe, who had been reading a Zane Gray novel when we arrived, had offered to help us, but there wasn't much to help with. The three of us sat around for a few minutes and shot the bull the way three guys tend to do. Ron had on several occasions met Mr. Thorpe, so there was no need for introductions. Mr. Thorpe admonished me for my dreadful taste in friends and Ronnie enthusiastically endorsed his take on that.

We spoke briefly of Bobby Kennedy and agreed that it was a terrible thing and the assassination of Martin Luther King and Robert

F. Kennedy in the same year made us look like a Third-World country. Mr. Thorpe said he didn't exactly know what a Third-World country was, but it didn't sound good.

Because I had to get up early, I went to bed at 10:15 when Ron left. Mr. Thorpe stayed up an additional half hour or so before the light in the living room went out. When I got up at 4:30 to get cleaned up for work, his door was closed and I could hear him snoring.

I walked down the steep Packer Hill to Steve's Diner, had my usual, agreeing with everyone there that this Kennedy thing was a horror, then walked the two blocks to the *Times-News*, where everyone there felt pretty much the same way.

When the floor began to vibrate at noon when the presses in the basement began to pick up speed, I left the office and headed up Broadway, where the *Molly Maguire* film crew wasn't filming today but where the street was still covered with dirt and the parking meters were still disguised as hitching posts.

I'd decided to pay a visit to my incarcerated young brother Rudy, up at the county prison, which just happened to be where they'd imprisoned the captured Molly Maguires and where, in the courtyard, they'd constructed a scaffold so they could hang the renegades.

When I got to the prison, a stone monument to the last century, I was greeted by lanky, angular Sheriff Neast, who warned me to avoid the Drizlers.

"Why's she so hyped about this?" I asked Mr. Neast. I'd gone to high school with his son "T. C." and we'd played around in the jail cells when we were kids.

"Well," he said, "she went out and bought a real genuine Betty Crocker cookbook and she's trying to improve her cooking, so she's somewhat sensitive about it. Their attitude is, like she's trying, doggone it, so give her a break—or else you'll incur the wrath of the Drizlers." He laughed.

"I thought the only thing she knew and the only thing she wanted to know is what her mother taught her."

"Seems she's trying to evolve, get past her mother, so she's especially sensitive while she molts from caterpillar to butterfly." The

56

sheriff was a heavyweight reader of poetry and practiced rhyming once in a while himself

"Maybe I ought to go apologize," I said, "before they up and kill me."

He shook his head. "That'd only cause her to think she's on the right path and it would harden her resolve and"—he paused, looked to the ceiling for the right way to put it—"I was over there for dinner two nights ago and . . . well . . . the transition isn't going well. The chicken was undercooked, the frozen peas were still half-frozen. I can't imagine what Thanksgiving is like at that house."

I shrugged. "Whatever you say." I changed the subject. "How's T. C.?"

"Managed to flunk two courses so he couldn't graduate on time so he's taking the two courses over now so he can get his diploma in August, hoping the draft forgets all about him. After that, I don't know."

"Tell him I said hello. I'm living in the Harry Packer carriage house. Tell him to drop by when he's in town. We can catch up."

Sheriff Neast ushered me inside. In the courtyard the movie people had constructed a scaffold where they planned to film the hangings of the Mollies. He pointed toward the row of cells. "He's in number six," he said, extending his hand so I could shake it. "I'm leaving for a lunch meeting. Take as long as you like." He turned and walked away, probably one of the mellowest sheriffs in all of Christendom.

Brother Rudy was sprawled on his bunk reading *The Panther Valley Pugilist*, a tabloid shopper out of Summit Hill, owned and operated by Buddy Sward, who fancied himself a crusading journalist in the mold of Edward R. Murrow. He was also one of the two Republicans on the three-man county commissioners.

Rudy looked up when he heard me approaching. The door to his cell was wide open. "Yo," he said. "Come on in." He set down the paper and sat up on his cot. I took the bare wooden chair near the commode. I reached out to shake his hand; he awkwardly did the same.

"So how's prison life?" I asked.

He extended his arms to encompass the cell. "Home, sweet home," he said.

"When ya getting out?"

"When my sentence is up."

I shrugged.

"Two weeks, two days, and three hours."

"And you're sure you don't want me to take up a collection to bail you out?"

"Nope," he said.

"How about a hacksaw inside a triple-layer chocolate cake?"

"Cake would be nice, but you can get me something down at the bakery. A half-dozen wedding bells maybe." Wedding bells are what the Mauch Chunk Bakery called a devilish delight of an upside-down German chocolate cupcake minus the paper but entirely covered with chocolate icing. Each one contained enough sugar to rival Cuba in sugar production.

"You need anything from home to make you more comfortable?" I asked, thinking of a change of clothes. The stuff he was wearing was giving off a noticeable aroma. He'd always been a bit of a slob, the youngest of three boys and indulged by our mother, who felt she'd never have any more children—until Ellie came along.

"I'm fine with what I got. Unless you could manage to smuggle in some m.j."

I raised an eyebrow. "You're joking, right?"

He smiled that ingratiating smile that won him the okay to go a little further than most of us. "Only partially."

"If I bring it, will you share it with Sheriff Neast?"

He smiled again. "I will with T. C., but I'll be gone by the time he gets back from college."

"So T. C. smokes weed . . . Here, in the jail?" I asked.

"Sure. Up on the wall, out in the yard."

"You're lying. He's never even around. He's away at school. Why don't you just stop lying? And I suppose you sell it to him—"

"Yeah, sure. Okay, maybe not, but I would if he was here."

"You sell it to anyone else?"

"Sometimes."

"How about Elizabeth Delaney?"

"Sometimes I *buy* it from her, when I'm low."

"When's the last time you did?"

He shrugged. "I dunno. Four, five weeks. Why?"

"Just curious. Her aunt says she's vanished and she wants me to poke around and help find her."

"She vanishes every once in a while—but she always comes back."

"Her aunt has a feeling it's more serious this time."

"The aunt that likes to dress up in fancy costumes?"

"The one at the Asa Packer—"

"That's the one. Did she offer you iced tea to make you more pliable?"

I couldn't help smiling. "Am I the only one who didn't know about that?"

"Appears so."

There was quiet for a few moments, kind of awkward, like searching in the dark for a light switch that would allow you to continue into the strange room without knocking over stuff. Somewhere at the other end of the jail somebody dropped a metal pail and said "Shit."

"So what else am I naïve about?"

"Probably everything."

"No hints?"

Rudy shook his head. "I wouldn't want to disillusion you all at one time."

I wasn't sure where to go after that. So I asked: "Is this bust going to keep you out of the army?"

"I don't think so. It's not a felony. I got caught for using, not selling. I may stay out by declaring that I'm the sole support of the old lady."

"I was gonna use that one," I joked.

"Maybe both of us can." He smiled and I could see him changing gears. "Maybe you could crack a big drug ring, be a muckraking newspaper hero like Buddy Sward here." He held up his copy of *The Pugilist*. "Were I you, the first person I'd talk to would be Nully Schwartz. He's in the mix, in real deep."

"What makes you think he'd talk to me if he's in that deep?"

"You two sci-fi nut bags go back a long way, and that urge to leave here and live on another planet runs deep."

"Null-A" Schwartz had received his nickname—his real name was and is Albert—in sophomore year when he got hung up real bad on the science-fiction author A. E. van Vogt, especially his novel *The World of A* . . . with a horizontal line atop the lowercase, which we pronounced "Null-a." Which, with Albert, became Null-A or Nully.

We'd spent an inordinately large amount of time in high school trading sf novels back and forth—especially Ace double novels (two for the price—35 cents—of one)—and reading them right in class behind the camouflage of our textbooks. But in our senior year, Nully's father got killed in a car crash coming down off the Broad Mountain, and Albert withdrew into their house on Broadway and took his kid brother with him, and we all just stopped seeing them. They'd already lost their mother to breast cancer, which nobody talked about back then because it involved the breast, and people in our town always tried to keep a medical diagnosis from patients so as to spare them the anguish, so Mrs. Schwartz might have died not knowing what she was dying from. Albert was eight at the time, his brother six. Albert sneaked a look at the death certificate and told me about it. We treated it like it was an international Cold War secret revealed. He developed a fixation with breasts and started a nice collection of cheap men's magazines, one or two tiers down from *Playboy*.

Then the death of his father, and the death of his interactions with the world outside his front door.

"He still live in the old house?" I asked.

"Yeah. Just a block up the street from here."

"Maybe I'll go see him."

"When you knock at the door, be sure to stand off to one side in case he's in one of his weird moods, thinking you're the fuzz, and he fires a round through the door."

"That weird, huh?"

"Oh, yeah. But weird like he's not always like that. But if you know him, it's easy to tell which mood he's in. You may wanna talk to him through the door before you go in—if he invites you in."

I reached over and picked up Rudy's copy of *The Pugilist*. On the front page there was a muddied photo of a valley with a creek running through it. An old swayback barn stood in the foreground. NO DAM DAM shouted the 48-point headline.

"No dam dam?" I said, holding up the paper, pointing at the headline. "Does this guy speak English?"

"What da'ya mean?"

"If he's sending a dam to perdition, it's d-a-m-n, not d-a-m."

Rudy screwed up his nose. "So what? People know what he means! He doesn't want the dam dam put up."

"Sounds like you're with him."

"Damn right, with an *n*."

"You wouldn't be saying that if you lived on Broadway when the next downpour comes and the water backs up."

"You dumb bastard. Where the hell you think I'm currently residing?"

He had me on that one. The county prison was on Broadway but built well above the street level. "Got me," I said, feeling stung for being dumber than my dumb-enough-to-go-to-jail brother.

"So how's this"—I indicated the jail cell—"going over at home? Has mother rendered an opinion?"

"I'm not sure she even knows."

"You serious? If you've been here for weeks, you haven't been home. Wouldn't she be suspicious? Think something's up?"

"Not necessarily. I'm gone a lot, like lots. Who wants to live in that nuthouse? I notice you didn't stay long."

"She sleeps all day and walks the floors all night. Creeps me out."

"There ya go."

"Creeps me out even more than Granny's dungeon and bat-cave."

"So where you livin' now?"

"With Olympian Jim Thorpe at the Harry Packer Mansion's carriage house."

"You two must make a terrific couple. Anybody speculating yet about whether you two are getting it on?"

"What the hell you talking about?"

"You know how eternally bored people like to speculate and gossip."

"Yeah, but—"

"They're already spreading the word that I'm getting butt-fucked twice a day since I've been in here."

"Well? Are you?"

"Not even if I wanted to. They've currently got a shortage of clients."

"The sheriff's deputies on strike or something?"

"Most of them take vacation this time of year."

This was getting nowhere. I looked for a way to graciously exit. I slowly stood up. "I'd better get going if I wanna see Null-A before my lunch hour is over." I tossed *The Pugilist* back onto his cot. "You need anything? Really. Like a change of clothes?" I pointed at him. "Those you've got on are starting to stink up the place."

Rudy laughed. "I like 'em like that." He laughed again. "No, really. Mrs. Neast is laundering a new set of clothes for me. I think they were left over from the last guy they hanged. By tonight I'll be smelling like roses."

Rudy didn't make an attempt to get off his bunk. I awkwardly reached down to shake his hand, but he didn't bother to take up his half of the deal. "Get outta here," he said, "so I can start missing you already. And remember to stay to one side of Null-A's front door."

I smiled and the effort put pressure on my jaw. "Aren't you going to ask about my bruises?" I said, running my left index finger down the left side of my face.

"Naw. I know all about it. You 'en Ronnie made them look even worse than you do, right?"

I nodded.

"You'll look worse than that if Mrs. Drizler ever runs into you."

I snorted. "Everybody in town *does* know everybody else's business, don't they?"

"I can't imagine why the Boyles continue to publish the ole *Times-News*. By the time it plops down on doorsteps, it's old news."

"How 'bout poor Bobby Kennedy, huh?"

"The Kennedy curse continues. Guess Teddy's next to make the news."

"Let's hope not," I said, turned and walked out to the street, wondering if and when Rudy was ever going to get himself together. Like I'd know when and if that happened to either him or me. I suddenly envied Donald, up there in Alaska in the USAF, fixing jet engines, keeping the world safe for democracy, and fighting polar bears single-handedly while riding on the back of a whale.

Null-A, Null-A, is your gun loaded, are you in the mood today to kill?

6

The World of Null-A

Null-A Schwartz's front stoop looked as though nobody had stepped on it in a decade, which I knew wasn't true because I'd stepped on it numerous times six or seven years ago, before Mr. Schwartz took himself out and got himself killed. Mr. Schwartz had graduated from East Mauch Chunk High School and insisted that Null-A and his brother go to school on the other side of the river from where they lived, so every day they took the bus to high school.

There was a covey of dead leaves blown up against the threshold, the front door looked as though it had been sandblasted, and the front of the house was wearing itself down to bare, gray wood. There was a peephole in the upper middle of the gray door, and today's edition of *The Times-News* lay forlornly in the middle of a welcome mat that was frayed at the edges and nearly unreadable.

I picked up the newspaper and tentatively stepped onto the stoop, remembering Rudy's admonition to stand to the side of the door in case Albert sent a .30-06 slug through to discourage Fuller Brush salesmen.

There was an electric doorbell to the left of the door but it, too, looked weathered and tired out. I was certain it was dead and that I'd have to knock, but just for the hell of it, I pressed the button and immediately heard from inside a bounding version of Wagner's "Ride of the Valkyries."

Ah-ha, I thought.

The tune was by far our favorite classical gas.

In our sophomore year we had written a screenplay having to do with epic battles between diverse and incompatible cultures, much of it stolen from both Wagner's *Ring of the Nibelung* and Tolkien's *Lord of the Rings*, which, of course, Tolkien had stolen from Wagner, who had stolen it from Scandinavian legends. We had a climactic scene, even though we never finished the screenplay (we jumped around a lot throwing together the most exciting scenes) where the good guys came charging in from the air on sentient dragons (Andre Norton had taught us early on that animals are sentient to a certain extent and perhaps could be worked with to become a member of a human/animal team) to destroy the evil and grotesque enemy. Get this: all the time, my own grotesque scars from my own disfigurement were still pink and fresh.

We later that year worked on yet another screenplay, this one involving motorcycle gangs where the Good Motorcycle Gang came tsunamiing over the hill while "Ride of the Valkyries" boomed in the background. We suspected it would be a musical, but neither of us had the first idea how to play a musical instrument and the two of us yodeling to Everly Brothers' tunes sounded like a cat being skinned alive.

I actually jumped back a step and simultaneously jumped off to the left side to best avoid a bullet in the gut. I heard footsteps inside the house, and footsteps loud enough to be heard over Wagner, them's heavy footsteps. I recalled that Albert was a big lad, built like a tackle or fullback, with sandy crewcut hair, light-blue eyes, and a crooked smile. I mentally tried to add five years' worth of age and abuse of recreational drugs to the last imagine I had of him, the day before his father died, in Mr. Allenworth's algebra class.

When the door opened, what stood before me came as a shock.

Albert—my old sci-fi buddy, notorious Mauch Chunk pothead—looked as though he hadn't aged a day. His hair was a little longer, but his crooked smile was in place, and he looked fit and clean—cleaner than in high school, when he tended toward tattered jeans and polo shirts. He was wearing a blue golf shirt with an alligator on one breast, khaki sand-colored slacks (with a sharp crease), and penny loafers complete with pennies, but no socks—what we used to call a "lut" look back in high school.

He looked surprised, as though he had just come to the door without bothering to peek out the peephole to see who was bothering him in the middle of the day. I could have been anybody, a Mormon or a Jehovah's Witness or an insurance salesman.

"Yo, Skar," he said, smiling his big old happy smile. He looked closer at me. "Yo, Skar, you really did get pounded. Looks like you been kicked in the head by a Clydesdale." He reached out to shake my hand, and confused, I put the copy of *The Times-News* in his hand. He quickly switched the paper to his other hand and reoffered his hand to shake. I took it. It was warm and dry and strong. "Shit, man, come on in. I saw you were back"—he tapped the newspaper—"and was wondering how long it would take for you to drop by."

I gulped and followed him inside.

There was no musky smell, no rat droppings on the long rug that ran the length of the hallway. In fact, the place looked about as well kept as a museum with funds to burn. The walls were off-white and looked as though the paint wasn't more than a year old.

We passed the doorway to the front room off to the right and another off to the left. The one on the left was a comfortable-looking parlor, complete with stuffed chairs, an upright piano, and a long sofa; an entertainment center covered one wall; on both sides of the entertainment center were shelves filled with LPs.

The front room to the right was, quite simply, laid out like a rich man's library: floor-to-ceiling bookshelves filled with hardbound books in various shapes and sizes and colors and a long table in the middle with six chairs around it. A half-dozen volumes were open on the table, as though someone was doing research.

Null-A kept walking, and I kept following. Toward the back of the hall there was a room off to the left that looked like an office, with a desk, a banker's lamp on the desk, a blackboard filled with numbers and symbols, and a corkboard with the business sections of the *Wall Street Journal* tacked up. The banker's light was turned on and under it a huge ledger-like book lay open.

To the right was the kitchen, exactly as I remembered it. Null-A hadn't bothered upgrading a thing. It was just as his mother had left it before she died. Everything was clean and in its place. He opened the refrigerator door. "You want some iced tea or lemonade?" he asked.

I shook my head . . . yeah, the head that was spinning. So far I hadn't seen one gun, and I didn't smell the aroma of marijuana. What gives? How could a whole town be so 180 degrees off?

Null-A poured himself some iced tea. I wondered if it was "fortified."

The house had a set of stairs just off the kitchen and a set inside the front door that went up to the second floor. Null-A motioned for me to follow him as he walked up the stairs. When we reached the hallway on the second floor, he led me into one of the bedrooms, which had been turned into a sort of sf museum. The walls were filled with books and tables and stands sporting models of robots and rocket ships. The single closet door was locked with three locks. He undid the locks, opened the door, and turned on a set of lights. "What d'ya think?" he asked. "My shrine to A. E."

The closet wasn't a closet at all. It looked as though a bank vault had been stuffed into the closet. Everything was metal. Half of the shelves were crowded with books and magazines, all neatly placed as though by someone who was terminally neurotic— someone like Null-A.

"Everything he's ever written, every damned edition, even the trashy ones," Null-A said. On the right side were a half-dozen bound manuscripts. "Originals," he said. "Including *Slan*." He slowly and lovingly stroked the *Slan* manuscript the way a romantic would caress a madonna. His eyes sparkled and his grin widened. I expected to see little twinkly stars explode from the tips of his teeth. He was a drug head all right—drugged by A. E. van Vogt, science-fiction author of the second tier.

He stood there, iced tea glass frosty in his one hand, his other hand resting on the cover of the manuscript as though transported to another plane of existence, as though in the middle of a religious experience—which it probably was. I could picture him locking himself in the vault/closet, breathing in all of van Vogt. It was more than a little spooky. Okay, it was a *lot* spooky. I have no idea how long he would have stood there gazing raptly around his reinforced closet filled with the works of A. E. van Vogt if I hadn't coughed. The cough sort of broke his spell. "Somethin', huh?" he said, waving his manuscript-stroking hand around.

"It's something, all right," I said, waving my right arm around. "Just van Vogt?" I asked.

"Isn't he enough?" Null-A asked.

I shrugged.

"Come on," he said. "You used to like him, too.

"Too much, huh? Over the top?" Null-A said, a mite crestfallen that I had not been nearly as mesmerized my whole life by an sf writer. "Well, it's not like I'm hurting anybody, right?"

Spoken like a true addict.

He closed and locked the door to his shrine and indicated with his head tilt that we were going back into the hallway. We went toward the back of the house, in the direction from which we'd come, and he walked past the stairs and to the window in the very back of the hall. He raised the window; it went up without any fuss or bother, as though it was on ball bearings. He stepped over the sill and onto a metal fire escape. I followed.

He went up the steps and walked onto the flat part of the roof, where he had three chaise longues, a telescope, and an elaborate Arab-looking ashtray on a metal stand that looked as though it could hold a dozen cartons of cigarette butts. Instead, I could tell by the smell, it held a fist-sized clot of Parodi cigar butts, the same kind we'd pilfered from Dugan's Store next to the library when we were kids, then hiked to the top of Mount Pisgah where the old Switchback Railroad used to be, where we sat on a boulder and smoked the things.

He sat down on one of the chaise longues and pulled out one of the distinctive red, black, and green Parodi boxes that contained five individually wrapped smokes. He held the box out to me. I took it and extracted one of the root-like cigars, peeled away the transparent cover, and slid it out of its little cardboard bed. Why not? I smoked them occasionally in college, just for the passing comfort they provided.

Null-A pulled one out, ran it through his mouth to moisten it, and fired it up with a silver Zippo lighter. He passed the lighter to me, and I moistened my cigar and fired it up. The smoke I pulled into my mouth was tart but mild. It brought back lots of memories, all of them good. We sat for some moments just sucking in smoke and blowing it out, trying—with varying success—to make smoke rings. Then, like we'd done in high school, with the burning tip hot enough to produce plenty of smoke, we tried blowing smoke rings at each other, hoping two of them would hook themselves together like links in a chain. Two of them did just that, and for that moment I was happier than I'd been in years.

One success seemed to be enough, and we leaned back and simply puffed away, effectively polluting the air above Broadway. The slight breeze nudged the smoke toward downtown.

It seemed as though we would be sitting there silently until our smokes burned themselves out, so I broke the silence. "So how come you aren't the drugged-out whack job everybody thinks you are?"

He smiled, pursed his lips, and executed a perfect smoke ring about eight inches across. "Because I choose not to be—anymore."

I couldn't help crunching my forehead into a frown.

"I was, right after Dad died. So was Ricky. We spent about six months feeling sorry for ourselves, hating everybody and everything—especially God—and going through about every kind of drug we could find short of Ajax." He blew another ring, one that slowly expanded. "But eventually we got bored and tired of it, Ricky before me. He just looked at me one day after we'd tooted a cigar-sized doobie and said, 'What the fuck are we doing to ourselves?' I didn't have an easy answer, so I wiseassed it. 'Gettin' stoned,' I said. 'What's the point?' Ricky said. 'All we're doin' is making the pizza delivery kid rich.' I couldn't help laughing at that. And of course we'd just sucked down so much m. j. that we were already looking at the phone, ready to order a large pepperoni. The thought of it made me laugh even more, and then I started coughing and came close to throwing my back out. Ricky slapped me on the back some, and it eventually stopped, and we eventually ordered a pepperoni and a combo, and we stopped the drug stuff that day."

"And the drug stuff was started over your dad getting killed?"

He shrugged. "We'd both tried pot before, but only every once in a while. But after Dad's accident, we went full time, overtime. I can't speak for Ricky, but for me it worked to dull the whole damned thing. I became a dirtbag rat." He pointed his finger at me. "You know about that. I just turned on my friends, closed the door behind me, and got high as much as I could. And I could a lot, because addictions must run in the family. The way I'm nutty about collecting sf books—I have every damned Ace sf book ever published—Dad was into collecting life insurance policies. After he died and we buried him, we found more than a dozen life insurance policies. Beaucoup money. Could have bought most of Mauch Chunk and still had some left."

"So where's Ricky?"

"California. He was a big Beach Boys and Jan and Dean fan so once we came out from under our pot fog, he up and headed west. 'The west is the best' is his slogan. He calls once a week or so trying to get me to move out there, but I'm anchored here. And besides collecting sf stuff, I've got another hobby that makes being inside tolerable."

"What's that?"

"Making money make money. Playing the market. Get rid of your Bethlehem Steel stock and buy big into tech."

"I don't have any stock."

"I'll give you some to play with. Remind me when you leave. I'll sign some stuff over to you, send it down to your office. IBM's good, H-P, stuff like that."

"But it can't be good for you buttoning yourself up in the house like this. Don't you get rammy?"

"I've got a gym in the basement, and sometimes after dark I sneak out and roam the neighborhoods."

"Sneak out and do what? Skulk around like the Phantom?"

He shook his head, executed another perfect smoke ring. "Put in some miles. Run a little, walk a lot, get the stink blown off me.

71

Clears my head. But I wouldn't do it in the daylight because I'd have to go to a costume shop to rent a stoner outfit so I'd fit everybody's idea of who I am."

"Does anybody know you're straighter than a Boy Scout?"

"Couple-a people. Just a handful. It's really nobody's business but my own."

"So you're not into the drug cult at all?"

"No."

"So you wouldn't know any of the players."

"I didn't say that. I do keep up on what's happening around town."

"You know Elizabeth Delaney?"

He nodded. "Sure. Her father's the ambulance chaser over the east side. Came by and wanted me to sue a bunch of people when my dad died. Still bills himself as working at Delaney & Markowski, even though Bill Markowski's been dead for three years. The guy's too cheap to pay for a new sign. I go by there a lot on my walks. His place could use a new coat of paint."

"But you know her."

"Used to. Not lately."

"But she was a regular when you knew her?"

"Yeah. She started in high school. Her and a couple of her Catholic virgins. Mary Jane Fitch, Gloria Jarko, Rita Wright."

"She's missing again."

"Not so unusual."

"Her aunt thinks it's more serious this time. Women's intuition."

Null-A raised an eyebrow. "Never underestimate it."

"She wants me to find her."

"Why not go to the cops?"

"Ya got me. First thing I'd do."

"So you're gonna drop everything and go find her."

My Parodi had exhausted itself and I tossed it into the elaborate butt bucket. "Not drop everything. Just inquire here and there as I have time."

"Like now."

"Like now."

"So you didn't come to see me as an old buddy, just as a potential source."

"Both," I said. "And you never returned my copy of *Dangerous Visions*. You used your dad's death as an excuse to keep the book, right?"

He frowned. "When I locate it I'll get it back to you. I'll bundle it up with the stocks I'm gonna sign over to you so you can plan toward retirement. But in the meantime, on this Elizabeth Delaney things, I'd go see Alice Finkel."

I must have looked perplexed. "Why's that?"

"She knows a lot of . . . unusual people."

"Like you."

"And you. You're the one took her to the senior prom."

"I think it was the other way around."

"How so?"

"I think she took me."

7
What Joe Knows

Null-A gave me a quick tour of his science-fiction collections and then sent me on my way with the promise of my first edition of *Dangerous Visions* and a handful of tech stocks to follow. We'll see.

The contrast between the interior of his house and the exterior was startling. I stood on the front stoop, semistunned, noting all the signs of wear and tear and wondering how everybody could be so wrong about Null-A's life. In a small town like this, secrets aren't secrets for very long, but Null-A had managed to keep his secret a secret for years. Maybe he was using a form of mass hypnosis he'd learned about in one of his thousands of sf novels. Well, for what it was worth, his secret was safe with me.

I walked down Broadway, headed for Race Street. Null-A said it would be easy to find Alice Finkel's house. It was one of the stone row homes on the south side of Race Street, the one with the purple door. That side of Race Street was a long block of stone row homes where the back wall was actually built into the mountainside. Most of the houses were in ill repair and some were empty, like the one Ronnie felt I should buy for $800.

What a contrast to their heyday in the second half of the 19th century when the sixteen shoulder-to-shoulder three-story homes were known as "Millionaires' Row." But one at a time, Asa Packer and his friends moved "down the road" to Bethlehem, and most of the row homes went slumming.

Race Street angled off from Broadway at the intersection where Doc Dougherty's huge house squatted on one corner, the movie theater (formerly the opera house) on another, and Cy and Gertrude Apfelbaum's home on a third. At that point, Race Street stayed level while Broadway dipped, so halfway down Race Street, you were parallel to Broadway, but Broadway at that point was two stories below you.

At the intersection of Race Street and Broadway there is a public spring: a pipe coming out of the mountainside where fresh water eternally runs into a stone box that is hip high. Just as I made the turn onto Race Street, I saw Joe Boyle approaching under a good head of steam. He was wearing his sports jacket and had a Polaroid camera slung around his neck, as though he was off to cover a hot story.

But it was me he was looking for. "There you are," he said, as he came even with me. He put his arm around my shoulders and steered me to the bench that sat next to the spring pipe. "We gotta talk," he said.

"I know I'm a little late coming back from lunch," I said.

"Oh, you'll make up that time tonight when you cover the borough council meeting on the East Side. No, no, it's not that." He looked both ways, up and down Race Street, as though we were spies about to exchange secrets in the middle of Budapest. "Grace Delaney came by the office. Left an envelope for you, big fat one. I put it in your desk drawer, the top drawer. She said you'd know what it was for. But being the nosy reporter that I am, I asked her what it was for, thinking it might be newsworthy and all," he said, slinging his arm across the back of the bench and patting me on the back. "News is news, ya know? So she told me. Said it wasn't any secret you were helping her find Elizabeth. But what I want to know"—he leaned in close—"is why you didn't come to me first to get the goods. I could tell you a lot about the Delaneys."

Joe smiled one of those Cheshire cat grins that indicates he's hiding a whole bushel basket of secret shit that he's dying to spew forth in a vomit of good, bad, and really bad data, all mixed together, maybe to be separated later—or maybe not.

"I'd like to know a lot more about the Delaneys," I said, feeling low as a spit-out piece of chewing gum for not going to Joe first.

But I had my reasons. "I already know some. I grew up on the same side of town and went to the same grade school as his kids." I held up my hand to stop myself because I was getting off course if I wanted to elevate my discarded chewing gum status to at least have it end up in a garbage can.

"The reason I didn't come to you yet was that I hadn't talked to enough people and I wouldn't have had time to formulate the right questions to ask you, and you're a busy guy, and I don't want to waste your time with half-assed questions day after day."

He looked up and down the street again. "That's a good answer," he said. "Of course, I don't believe it." He laughed. "We journalists are supposed to be filled with doubt through which we can assuage our poor feelings about ourselves by filling the rest of the space with cynicism. So really, why didn't you ask me for the scoop?"

"You're the expert, and I didn't want to waste the expert's time until I had something decent worth asking. Honest." I made the sign of the cross.

"Okay, okay," he said. "Just keep all the information you get sieved through the cheesecloth of Elizabeth Delaney's father being a sleazy lawyer and his father before him being an even sleazier lawyer, and I hope if one of his sons succeeds in following him in the family business, he can swim through the lye bath to get some of the sleaziness washed off."

I rifled through my memory of the Delaney boys and couldn't find anything especially horrid about them, at least not for the limited exposure I'd had to them. "The boys always seemed fine by me," I said, expecting Joe to correct me in no uncertain terms with details so sordid that I'd be embarrassed to hear them. He didn't.

Instead, he shrugged. "I guess I'm gonna have to agree with you on that one. But they still have lots of time—and the bad genes—to get corrupted." He laughed. "The same way I have a lot of time to corrupt you to the ways of big-time, small-town journalism, kid."

He got up from the bench and his Polaroid camera banged against his belly. "Where to?" I asked.

He laughed again. "Big-time journalism. The Mauch Chunk Bakery is putting the finishing touches on the tallest wedding cake they've ever made."

"Stop the presses. Who's it for? Anybody we know?"

"That's one of the reasons I'm going by. To find out. Good investigative journalism. Nobody I can think of would order a six-foot-tall wedding cake with alternating layers of chocolate and vanilla. Must be for somebody from out of town."

I dug into my pocket and pulled out two bucks. "Can you bring me some apple turnovers for a late lunch?"

"Sure," Joe said. "So who's next on your list of suspects?"

"Not suspects, informants." I pointed a thumb down Race Street. "Alice Finkel."

"Ah," Joe said, "the town gypsy."

8
Go Ask Alice

The stone row homes had bohemian potential but currently were "enjoying" a continued existence as the down-and-out slice of town. Three of the sixteen houses were abandoned, most of the rest occupied but deteriorating at glacial speed. Across the narrow street stood a narrow row of aluminum garbage cans, in bad shape themselves, half of them spilling their contents. As far as the houses went, you could place a safe bet not one of them had seen a tightened screw, pounded nail, or dab of paint in the last decade.

The Times-News building, painted red, marked the end of the row homes but was not one of them. The purple door I was looking for was halfway down the row. The purple was closer to lavender and looked like it went against the grain of the neighborhood and might have received a coat of paint four or five years ago. In the windows on both sides of the door, a handful of flowers sprouted from the necks of wine bottles, the one on the left a Chianti and on the right Annie Green Springs, a college favorite.

A multicolored (looked like crayon) sheet of paper was hung in the right-hand window just above the flowers, advertising Alice's services:

ALICE FINKEL
Séances
Psychic Readings
Palm Readings
Limited Psychoanalysis
Plumbing Services

No phone number, no hours listed.

I raised my fist to knock on the door, but then hesitated.

In too many ways, I lead a life of uptightness. Alice, on the other hand, led one of untightness. She'd always lived a bit—actually, a lot—on the edge. She and her mother had moved to town when she was about twelve. Nobody knew where her father was and nobody ever asked. Alice's mother, Ruby, only went out after dark and pretty much let Alice do whatever came into her mind.

She *did* go to school, public school, and was a decent student, apparently, running a straight line of Bs which, come to think of it, was very strange: no As, no Cs, no Ds, no Fs. How'd she manage to do that? When you stopped and thought about it, getting all Bs would be more difficult than getting all As.

The public grade school on the east side was just across Sixth Street from St. Joe's Catholic School, so kids from one school occasionally saw kids from the other school. Especially the boys, who got together evenings and weekends to play basketball on the asphalt courts of the Bevan School. With baskets with steel-chain nets.

Alice, though, kind of floated around at the edges, a small blonde sprite, remarkable only in her elusiveness. She seemed to have no friends and didn't seem deprived or concerned about that.

My first face-to-face encounter with her came at the start of our freshman school year at East Mauch Chunk High School, when public and Catholic kids mixed. I'd been scarred by then, and on the first day of school she came up to me, stood in front of me, stared at me for a good fifteen seconds, nodded, and walked away.

She'd once sat down next to me at lunch back when we used to bring our own lunches in brown bags and talked for a half hour straight about the Peloponnesian Wars, never even opening her brown lunch bag. When lunch ended, she got up, walked away, and didn't say another word to me for two months.

I used to think of her as Tinker Bell, on whom, as a kid, I'd had a crush. She was small, blonde, filled with a sort of inner light that was on a wavelength not everyone could see, and a bit flighty . . . in a charming sort of way.

Halfway through our senior year, she stopped me between classes and told me that I should stop kidding myself, that I didn't trip and fall down the stairs and crash into the iron radiator, causing my scar, that I'd been pushed. "Take that for what it's worth," she said. And once again, she didn't speak to me for a month or two after that. What it did do, though, was implant doubt and suspicion in my mind. Could I have been pushed—but by whom?—and then rewritten history in order to avoid dealing with it?

Alice didn't seem to have any friends, so on occasion when she was in study hall in the library, salted away by herself over near the magazine stacks, I'd sit across from her, sometimes dragging Null-A with me. We never said anything or passed notes or kicked each other under the tables. I was in what was referred to as the "academic" class, which meant I had vague intentions of some-day going to college; she was in the "commercial" section, which meant she could type and would probably go into some area of work where that would be a plus, like being a secretary. So we had no classes together.

Then, with the senior prom two weeks away and my figuring to do exactly what I'd done for the night of the junior prom, which was stay at home reading science-fiction novels while wishing I was battling a monster on Barsoom, she confronted me in the hall between classes and asked if I was going to the prom. When I said "No," she informed me that I was and that I should pick her up at 6:00, which I did, in a borrowed car, and we went to the prom and danced the slow ones and talked about inconsequential stuff and sat with some other couples we knew, and afterward a bunch of us went out to the Sportsman's Lodge and had lobster tail (for her) and prime rib (for me), with draft beers on the side. (On prom night they lifted the ban against serving minors.)

I got her home around 1:00, walked her to her stoop, and she stood on her toes and kissed me on my ugly cheek and went inside, where there was a light on but nobody home.

And that was that.

I didn't see her during the few weeks that were left in high school, and then I began working awful shifts at the Bethlehem

Steel iron foundry over the summer to make money to go to that bastion of academia, Espy State College, and we completely lost touch.

Maybe when she found me standing at her front door she'd think I came to ask for a date. That made me laugh. A date with Alice wasn't exactly a date.

I was about to go through with a rap on the door when a white VW microbus sporting a peace symbol on the front came puttering up the street. It pulled over on the side of the street opposite where I stood, bumped gently into one of the metal garbage cans overflowing with crud, and came to a stop.

The door opened and Alice floated out and pointed at the door. "Go ahead in. It's not locked. I've been expecting you," she said. She wore a pair of tight jeans, a tie-dye T-shirt and no bra, a necklace of what looked like bright red Ping-Pong balls tightly drawn around her neck, and a blue ribbon tied and swirled throughout her hair, which was still very blonde and very long and looked as though she hadn't bothered to comb it in a week. Her lipstick was as red as the Ping-Pong balls. She wore dark leather sandals and seemed to levitate across the narrow street. She came up to my chin and went up on tiptoe to kiss me on the ugly cheek the way she'd done four years and a month ago. She reached past me and opened the door, then pushed me inside.

"I knew you'd come," she said, "because I'm psychic." She went up on her toes again and kissed me on the lips. She tasted like peppermint.

I tried to slow things down. "If you knew I was coming, how come you weren't waiting for me?"

"I was off by all of thirty seconds," she said, and kissed me again, her arms wrapped around my neck like a pet monkey.

I hadn't yet gotten it together enough to kiss her back and wasn't sure if I wanted to. This whole encounter was obviously confusing. What did all this mean? She mashed her lips up against mine again as though she was trying to administer artificial resuscitation, and maybe she was. Her breasts pressed against my chest and her peppermint lips were starting to bring me around.

I wanted to slow things down, to get all of this onto a logical track, but increasingly I was losing focus.

When she flicked her tongue inside my mouth, my will to resist withered while everything else blossomed.

I gently sucked on her tongue and she began thrusting it in and out. I started to get lightheaded and ran my hands down her back and cupped her ass, gently pulling her closer to me, as though she wasn't as close as it was possible for her to get short of being glued together. Her pelvis rubbed against my leg and my dick swelled and rubbed against her. She moaned and rubbed her belly against it. I caught my breath and used my tongue to push hers back inside her mouth, where I played my tongue along her teeth, like a finger across piano ivory.

I began to move my hips against hers and she thrust back, our hips meshing and mashing. Gently at first, and then more insistently, she herded me toward the long, black crushed-velvet sofa that squatted against the sidewall. She sucked at my tongue, the peppermint flavor exploding.

I peeled her off me and carried her to the sofa—she seemed to weigh nothing—and gently laid her down on it, her arms still locked around my neck. For being so small, she was strong enough to pull me down, still sucking my tongue deeper into her mouth. My left leg went down between her legs, and she began to rub her pelvis against it. My expanding dick became tangled in my shorts, and for a second I thought about repositioning it to relieve the pressure and discomfort, but instead I gently ran my left hand across her right breast, rubbing my palm against her stiffened nipple. She moaned. "Pinch it, pinch it," she moaned.

I did and it got harder still. "More, more, harder," she cried. "More. Pinch it good." I tightened my thumb and index finger on it, feeling it swell through her T-shirt, let go of it. "No, no, pinch it," she cried. I pulled her shirt out of her jeans and reached up under it and rubbed my hand over the nipple, then grasped it again. It was firm and slightly slick, as though it was polished or perspiring. "More, more, harder," she moaned. But each time I tried to squeeze it harder, my fingers slipped off. The challenge of doing exactly what she insisted became the focus of my whole world as I pinched and squeezed it and she kept insisting I do it harder.

Frustrated, I pulled my mouth away from hers and moved it to her nipple. I kissed it, sucked it, and put it between my teeth, which allowed me to get a good grip. Her moaning increased and her hips moved more insistently against my left leg, and in a blind rush, I came.

Like a kid outside in the middle of winter who urinates in his pants rather than go inside, it felt good for the first few seconds but terrible afterward. A moan escaped my lips, but it was very much a different kind of moan from Alice's.

"Don't . . . don't stop," she moaned, and in a smooth, swift motion she unzipped her jeans and pulled them ten or twelve inches down her hips. She spread her legs, exposing blonde, curly public hair. She moved my left hand to where it would do some good. "Do it, stroke it," she pleaded, so I did. Not very experienced in doing what she wanted me to do, the basics came naturally. She pulled her tie-dye shirt up over her head and threw it on the floor. She cupped her left breast. "Now do this one," she commanded. "Hard."

Now kneeling on the floor in front of the sofa, I stroked her between her legs and sucked on and nibbled on her left nipple. Her moan began to rise in pitch and she moved her hips against my hand and thrashed her head from side to side.

I increased the speed of my left hand and she increased her thrusting until she tensed and then shuddered with a squeak escaping her mouth. Then she relaxed, her eyes closed, her body covered with a sweat sheen.

I kissed her on the forehead and she pulled my head toward her and locked her arms around my neck. "Nice," she whispered.

All I could say was "Mmmmmmmmm."

She released my head and took my face in her hands and smiled at me. "You can go in the back and throw your shorts away, then come back. You'll feel better. And you'll be just like Ernest Hemingway—he never wore underwear."

I was reluctant to leave, afraid that when I came back she'd be gone. But I rose and walked to the back of the house, where there was a half-bathroom. I dropped my jeans and took off my shorts and wiped myself and dropped them in the wastebasket, then pulled my jeans back on.

My shirt was soaked with sweat and clung to me.

When I returned to the front room, the curtains were pulled and Alice lay spread out on the sofa like a three-quarter-size "Naked Maja," but blonde on blonde. She'd removed the red necklace but left the blue ribbon in her hair.

She motioned for me to come over. When I did, she ran her left hand against my crotch, very lightly. "You don't have to keep your clothes on, unless you're planning to leave within the next minute."

I threw off my shirt, one of the buttons spinning off across the floor, and dropped my jeans and stepped out of them.

She stroked me and I came alive again. Her hands were rough, unlike everything else about her. She was lithe and compact and the contrast of her white skin and blonde hair against the black of the sofa was startling, even in the partial gloom.

I knelt down in front of her and kissed her. She stroked me as she spread her legs and then guided me on top of her and into her. For a minute that seemed to last forever, we didn't move at all, just lay there, warm and growing. Then a little at a time, then more insistently, she moved her hips. I tried to match her rhythm and pretty much did.

And that's the story of how I lost my virginity.

* * *

We sat across from each other at her kitchen table drinking a mint tea that tasted similar to her kiss. Add forty years and we could have been an old married retired couple whiling away a late-spring afternoon.

She said she had a plumbing job at 5:30 after an old guy near retirement got home from work over on the East Side. "Good work," she said, "but hard on the hands." She explained how she'd taken shop classes in high school and learned plumbing easily enough. I remembered taking plastic shop and metal shop: my plastic-shop projects never came out round like I wanted them, and I'd sand them mercilessly looking for that perfect roundness until there wasn't much left of the project other than what I made pass as a lopsided keychain; in metal shop I'd tried to make a crossbow by using a leaf spring off a '40 DeSoto, but I could never get the triggering mechanism down safely so for the sake of all sentient beings in East Mauch Chunk—including myself—I gave it up.

She told me how she had worked a deal with Butch Kirk, who'd graduated two years before we did, where he'd come and replace the roof on her row home and she'd do the plumbing work on a spec house he was building out in Hacklebarnie, a sort of scabbed-on village to the west of town.

Apparently she didn't make a whole lot from her readings but did have a half-dozen regular clients. One of her séance clients was one of the most prominent women in either town, who demanded séances in her own home, away from prying eyes, where she wanted to hear from her dead husband to find out where he'd hidden the German bonds he'd been so proud of. I hoped to hell it wasn't my grandmother but couldn't be sure it wasn't.

Around 2:30, when I'd finished my tea and was explaining that I had to get back to work at the paper just down the street, her two cats decided to come downstairs. The bigger one, Pandora, a purple-point Siamese, jumped onto my lap against Alice's apologies but was unfazed when I didn't complain. The cat rolled over in my lap and wanted to play patty-cake. I rubbed her belly and she purred and announced to me she had bad breath. The smaller one, a Burmese, was named Mahogany, and the name fit her coloring; she kind of sailed up onto the windowsill in the front room where the light was and stared outside.

"You've got something on your mind, something you wanna ask," she said. "Something you're asking everyone else around town."

I smiled and nodded.

"I don't know much about her. We didn't move in the same circles—"

"Does anybody here move in your circles?" I interjected.

She smiled back. "You'd be surprised." She sipped the last of her tea, set the cup down gently, and reached across the table to take my right hand in hers. She spread my hand open, palm up, and ran her left index finger across the lines. She seemed absorbed for a minute or two and then said "Hmmmmm" and turned my hand loose.

"You're a troubled young fella," she whispered across the table. "You may need quite a few sessions before you can be cured." She licked the palm of my hand. "Long lifeline but other aspects very troubling."

I reluctantly pulled my hand away. "I really gotta get going. This is probably the longest lunch break in the history of the newspaper."

"All I can tell you about Elizabeth Delaney is that she likes to get high, doesn't much care where or how . . . or with whom. And I think if I were you, I'd talk to her old man before he comes looking to talk to you. He's gotta know you're snooping around. And everybody knows how he loves people sticking their noses into his affairs. Better still, though, if you can somehow manage to get past him and talk to the Mrs."

"I noticed that you didn't refer to Elizabeth in the past tense."

Alice smiled faintly. "I don't get the vibes that she's dead—yet. But I *could* be wrong."

"But if she keeps going the way she's been going, that's a real possibility—"

"If *any* of us keep going the way we're going we're gonna end up dead," Alice said. Who could argue with that?

"So it's not gonna mean anything to old man Delaney that his own sister asked me to do this?"

Pandora rolled over onto her stomach and sprawled out on my right leg, looking over her shoulder as though giving a command that I apply my hand to the top of her head and scratch. At least from this angle I didn't have to endure her bad breath.

"They're close enough, but they each think the other is kinda nuts. Him with his sleazy legal deals and her with her Victorian playacting. Most of the town is surprised the Packer Mansion lets her work as their front, but I can see it myself. She's good PR . . . and it doesn't cost the mansion anything but the occasional bottle of gin."

"Maybe I can collar the old man tonight after the East Side's borough council meeting. Joe Boyle tells me he comes to every meeting, always with something new to complain about."

Alice laughed a good laugh. "His latest thing is he wants to fence off the lot behind his house and raise pigs." She laughed again. "Some people would say he already did."

I didn't get it at first. "Oh," I said. "Oh. Like you mean Elizabeth." The look on my face must have said I was appalled that Alice would be so crass. "You never seemed to me to be the gossipy, slashing type."

"I never had anybody to gossip with before," she said.

I stood up and set Pandora on the floor. She looked up at me disapprovingly, turned, and walked off to the front of the house, where Mahogany continued to sit in the window sunning herself. "On that note I'd better get back to the office so I can bone up on who's who on the borough council before I go over there and try to interpret what they're doing to the town."

Alice shot from her chair as I made my way to the front of the house. She grabbed my right arm and stopped me, way stronger than she should have been for her size. "Not yet," she hissed. "Wait."

Outside her front windows, a Mauch Chunk Police cruiser slowly drove down Race Street. "How'd you do that?" I asked her.

She went up on her toes and kissed me. "Comes naturally," she said.

All of this nonsense of the Drizlers being after me for badmouthing the old lady's cooking seemed absurd.

"Since you can see such things, just what will the Drizlers do to me if they catch me?" I smiled, trying to make little of it.

Alice wasn't smiling. "They'll tie you down to a chair, force open your mouth, and force-feed you her famous—and infamous—squatter's stew."

I made a face. "That bad, huh?"

"You been away from here way too long."

9

Lizzie's Old Man

It was less than a block from Alice's house to the *Times-News* building, the garish red-fronted building and the first in the row to not be part of the row homes.

As I walked in, I received a quizzical glance from Gertrude Apfelbaum, as though inquiring where I'd been. I smiled at her. "There's something different about you," she said. "Did you have lunch at a bar?"

I laughed nervously, not certain that a sign hadn't been painted on me indicating that I was no longer a virgin. I certainly wasn't going to discuss my recent sexual activity with Mrs. Apfelbaum.

"Anything more on RFK?" I asked.

Mrs. Apfelbaum pulled together a pile of wire stories on the top of her desk, shuffled them expertly, and passed them across. She also passed across our desks a big brown envelope. "This came for you."

I sat the wire news on RFK in the center of my desk, swung my chair halfway around, and opened the envelope. My copy of *Dangerous Visions* slid out and dropped into my lap. I opened the front cover and there was a twenty-dollar bill and a note. "Hope the 20 covers overdue penalties. Null-A." I slid the rest of the contents out. There were two sets of official-looking documents that indicated that I was now a member of the Wall Street set: one hundred shares of Hewlett-Packard and an equal number of IBM. Old Null-A didn't waste much time following up on his promises.

I carefully slid both certificates and the book back into the envelope, pulled open the bottom drawer of my desk, and dropped the envelope in. I pulled open the top drawer and, as promised, there was a chubby brown envelope filled with ones, fives, and tens. Totaling $500, I assumed, just like I'd asked for. I guess that sealed the deal: I was now on the payroll of Grace Delaney.

I reopened the bottom drawer and dropped the money-filled envelope in on top of the other envelope. In a matter of days, I'd become richer than I'd ever been in my entire life. I could get used to this.

I swung back to my desk and shuffled through the wire stories. The basic story was not advancing much. Just elaborations on what went before, filling in the blank spots. RFK would be buried next to his brother in Arlington Cemetery. Not much more on this Sirhan Sirhan fellow.

I slid open the middle desk drawer and pulled out a notebook and three pens. Mrs. Apfelbaum looked up at me and smiled. "You're going to thoroughly enjoy your first East Mauch Chunk Borough Council meeting tonight," she said, smiling as Madame Defarge did while looking up from her knitting to see yet another royal head lopped off.

"Joe already briefed me," I said, not smiling.

I put the cover over my typewriter and left the office, headed home. Mr. Thorpe was pushing a wheelbarrow filled with mulch across the lawn between the Asa Packer and Harry Packer mansions. He paused a moment to wave. I waved back, chugging steadily up the hill to our shared domicile.

Once inside, I pulled three Sultana 25-cent chicken potpies from the freezer and slid them into the oven so they could bake while I showered. I ran the water until it was hot, sniffed my arm to check if there was any evidence of Alice left on my skin, and then thoroughly scrubbed down. After drying off, I changed into a pair of khaki pants, a button-down shirt, and a tie. Wanted to look professional when appearing before the borough council.

The potpies were not quite done, so I popped a brew and turned on the TV, hoping to get some local news, but I was too early, but not too early to catch the end of *General Hospital* on one channel and *American Bandstand* on another. I went through a dozen channels (one of the benefits of living in the cradle of CATV) but didn't see anything I liked, so I pulled out the morning's edition of the *Morning Call* and checked out what was going on in the Allentown-Bethlehem-Easton area. Nothing very exciting.

I put on an oven mitt and pulled out the three potpies, lined them up on the table, and paged through the *Saturday Evening Post*. Mr. Thorpe apparently liked to keep up with events 'cause he sure had a bunch of magazine subscriptions. They were scattered, in neat piles, all over the place. I should probably contribute to the cost of the subscriptions if I was going to read them.

I poked a fork through the top of the first potpie and then used the fork to fold the edges of the crust into the interior of the pie, thereby absorbing some of the thick juices into the crust. It didn't take long before I was working on number two. I opened another beer between number two and number three, paid some attention to a story about the Peace Corps in Africa, then decided I'd had a pretty exciting day and the council meeting wasn't until 7:00, so I went to my bedroom and set the alarm for 6:15 and took a long nap.

I don't remember dreaming anything, and I never heard Mr. Thorpe come in and make his own supper. He was a real quiet Indian. I started when the alarm went off, straightened my tie, gathered up my notebook and pens, and found Mr. Thorpe sitting in the living room watching the television with the sound turned down.

"Yo," I said, which is what I always say when I don't know what else to say. "You could have turned up the sound."

"Watching a baseball game. Don't need sound to know what's happening."

I thought for a moment about sitting down to join him. I was sure even a dull baseball game would be more interesting than sitting through a borough council meeting.

"I have to go cover the monthly council meeting over the east side," I said, as though it was important that Mr. Thorpe knew where I was going, as though he was my father or something. "Not sure when I'll be back. I'll try to be quiet when I come in."

"Okay," he said and went back to watching the silent ballgame.

The ole Rambler started right up. I gave it thirty seconds or so for the cold oil to get itself pumped into the upper regions of the motor and then backed out onto Packer Hill. The drive across the bridge and up North Street to Ninth took all of four minutes.

The East Mauch Chunk Borough Council held its monthly meetings in a back room of the firehouse at Ninth and School Streets. "Then, when they're finished, most of them retire to the bar and rehash what they just spent two hours hashing," Joe Boyle had warned me. "If you have the energy left, you might make some points by joining them. They won't mind. In fact, it'll make you seem like one of the boys." He pulled a fiver out of his wallet and handed it to me. "Break the ice by buying a round."

"How many of them are there?" I asked, wondering how far five bucks would go to buying drinks for serious drinkers.

"Five council members, their lawyer, and a secretary. If it goes beyond five bucks, pay for it and turn in a chit tomorrow." Something else dawned on him. "And this is going to seem really weird, especially for a firehouse meeting room: nobody smokes in the meeting room; they all go outside; it's in tribute to Mike O'Reilly; he died of lung cancer last year after smoking like a chimney since he was seven. He was a member of council, and I have no idea of how many other council members *he* gave lung cancer to during two-hour-long meetings in a closed room, but I know I used to come out of there feeling I'd sucked down two packs. They replaced ole Mike with Billy Stikk, another heavy smoker."

I parked on the School Street side of the building. There were a half-dozen cars already parked there. Several guys were standing and leaning in front of the side door sucking in cigarette smoke. Among them was an elderly woman dressed in a black-and-white floral-print dress; her hair was tied in the back in a tight bun. She looked familiar, and after a few seconds I recognized her: Mrs. Rudy, formerly the secretary at the high school, since retired, and by the looks of the notepad that stuck out of her big black-vinyl purse, she must be serving in the same secretarial capacity here at borough council. She was smoking an unfiltered Camel, which she dropped on the ground and ground out with her sensible brown shoes. Didn't she have any black shoes to go with her dress and purse?

She saw me as I crawled out of the car, where I turned and put the key in the driver's door to lock it. "No need to do that," she said. "All the thieves and bungling burglars and ne'er-do-wells'll be in the meeting with us."

I walked across the narrow street, and she reached out a nicotine-stained hand to shake mine. She asked about my grandmother and I told her she wasn't feeling well, and then she asked me about my mother and I told her she wasn't feeling well, and Mrs. Rudy said she'd have to visit both of them. *Good luck on that,* I thought. She introduced me to three of the smokers, each apparently a proponent of a specific brand.

"Martin Schiller," she said, he nodded, a Marlboro man, tall, reedy, and wan looking. "Alexander Sarkosky," our local displaced Russian from Lansford, a Chesterfield man, stocky and plain faced. "Billy Stikk," with a pack of Pall Malls in his pocket but a Chesterfield (apparently borrowed) on his lower lip, a youngish-looking guy with dirty-blond crewcut and the faint beginnings of a brush mustache above his upper lip. A stupid bumper sticker from college popped into my mind: Mustache Rides 50 cents.

At five minutes of seven, Stikk opened the side door for Mrs. Rudy to enter. The side door was the "family entrance," which simply meant in this case that it bypassed the bar, where the boys hung out, and where ladies and kids were not allowed. In a bar/restaurant, the family entrance would have led directly to the restaurant and the front entrance to the bar, with a discreet closed door between the two, just like at Rock's Steak House in Espy, where we college dudes used to hang out once we turned twenty-one—and sometimes before—after we'd finished up our homework for the day.

"Billy," Mrs. Rudy said, "can you detour through the bar to let the rest of them know we're about it sit down?"

Billy did just that as we filed into a room about forty-by-thirty-five with a table and chairs on one side and a riot of folding chairs sitting about carelessly on the other side.

There were already people occupying half the chairs, including a man of the cloth who had a thick file folder resting in his lap that he kept petting as though it was an overweight cat, and next to him Lawrence Delaney, with a thick file folder resting in his lap . . . like a file folder resting in his lap. No anthropomorphism for him. He looked as though he had aged ten years in the last five and not an aging that looked like aging—more like dissipation, like he got himself a good case of cancer. He wore horn-rimmed glasses and brown wingtips, and between those two extremes came a pair of worn bluejeans, a plain white long-sleeved shirt with the sleeves rolled up, and a plain red tie, carelessly knotted.

Mrs. Rudy directed me to the front row seat closest to the door. A red scarf was draped over both my seat and the one next to me. The seat next to me would be occupied by Stace Dornbeckkoffer, the local reporter for the *Morning Call* out of Allentown. Joe Boyle had already given me the scoop on how these things worked. If Stace was unable to make the meeting, I was to get my notes to him as soon as I was finished writing my story so he could use them to write his own; if I was absent from the meeting for some reason, he would extend the same courtesy.

The barflies marched in slowly, more like shuffled in, and took their assigned chairs at the wide table. Martin Schiller, the mayor, sat in the middle, flanked on one side by smokers Sarkosky and Stikk and on the other side by drinkers Bakker and Tighe, according to the nameplates on the table in front of them. For a borough council meeting, there was a curious lack of paperwork in front of them. That was made up for by Mrs. Rudy at one end of the table and the borough attorney, Russell Craigo. Craigo's pile was three inches thick and needed straightening; Mrs. Rudy's was half that thick but was neatly shuffled, like a deck of cards.

A moment before Mayor Schiller's gavel fell, Stace Dornbeckkoffer huffed and puffed in, sat down on his chair, or rather filled out his chair, and reached over and shook hands with me. He was middle-aged, heavy-set, sweated a lot, breathed heavily but had no scent of tobacco on him, and wore a twenty-year-old brown suit with appropriately scuffed pant cuffs and leather patches on his elbows. I hoped he had run here from Lehighton and that his breathing would settle in soon; if not, I was afraid they'd have to call an ambulance for me, a victim of being throw off my natural rhythms. Stace pulled a reporter's notebook from his back pocket and pulled a half-dozen bank-issued pens from his jacket pocket, selected one that looked brand new, and returned the rest to his pocket. He breathed a sigh that would have filled a hot-air balloon.

As far as the meeting went, I'll spare you the details, except to say that Joe Boyle had schooled me well on what to expect.

"The annual budget will get passed in ninety seconds and they'll spend the next hour on something inconsequential," Joe said.

That's exactly what happened.

The annual budget, taking effect on July 1, was put out for public comment, nobody commented, Bakker made a motion to accept, Stikk seconded, and that, as they say, was that.

For the next hour things got lively as the borough council members went back and forth about a proposal to install parking meters on both sides of North Street between Fifth and Sixth. Which is where the priest—Father Slavinsky—came in. He represented St. Joseph's Catholic Church, where I'd been baptized, which took up the upper half of the block on the eastern side of North Street. He didn't want meters to tax his flock. Joe Brown, who owned the newsstand across the street where I used to buy my Ace sf novels, was perched back in the shadows, and he, too, was vehemently against meters, which would greatly affect his customers.

"But they wouldn't be enforced on Sundays and after six o'clock on weekdays," Mayor Schiller argued.

An elderly woman in the back row got up and squeaked that she lives just a few doors below St. Joe's, and she has lived there all her life, and she has always parked her car in front of her house, and she'll be damned if she is going to pay for that privilege. Most of the members of the studio audience clapped their approval of her disapproval.

Father Slavinsky went off on a tangent about old ladies attending the 5:15 Mass on weekdays, and Mr. Sarkosky said that the meters wouldn't be active at 5:15, and besides, none of the old ladies who came to 5:15 Mass drove.

Mercifully, Mayor Schiller entertained a motion to table the subject for the time being. Tighe made the motion, perhaps eager to get back to the bar. Bakker seconded, and none of the council members raised any opposition.

The mayor looked around at the restive audience and at his own restless council and seemed about to entertain a motion to adjourn when Lawrence Delaney jumped to his feet, his file folder falling out of his lap on the floor, his papers shuffling themselves toward the council table. He ignored the papers. "What about me?" he said in a voice almost as squeaky as the little old lady from North Street. He cleared his throat and lowered his voice to a more male level. "What about my topic?"

The mayor banged his gavel once to retake control. Most of the audience, having exhausted the subject of the parking meters, seemed inclined to get up and leave but were reluctant to because they had not yet been dismissed.

"I told you earlier today, Larry, that we were not going to hear from you because you did not get your topic onto the agenda a week in advance of the meeting, as required by law," the mayor said.

"You should know that, Mr. Delaney," Russell Craigo said. "You're a lawyer. The law requires that we post the agenda a week before our meeting so that the public can acquaint itself with the topics we will address." He seemed pleased with himself that he made that quite clear.

"But you don't understand," Lawrence Delaney said, shaking his right index finger in the direction of the council. "They're coming next week, they'll be delivered on Wednesday, and I want this settled now!" His whole body quivered as though he'd stepped on a live wire.

Attorney Craigo turned to Mayor Schiller. "What's this all about, Martin?"

Mayor Schiller blew out a mouthful of air as though to force himself to relax. "Delaney here," he said, waving his hand in Delaney's direction, "wants to raise pigs—pigs!—behind his house, his office. Pigs."

The word was taken up by half the folks in the audience as though it was a word new to them. "Pigs. Pigs?"

Attorney Craigo mouthed the word but didn't say it aloud.

Delaney continued to vibrate, about to explode. "Yes, pigs," he said. "And why not?"

"Well, because it's illegal," Attorney Craigo said. "This isn't a farm community."

"But people all over town raise chickens," Delaney said.

That fact seemed to come as a revelation to Mayor Schiller.

But not to Attorney Craigo. "Chickens are allowed," he said. "No problem with chickens."

"Even if they're nasty beasts," Stace Dornbeckkoffer whispered to me.

The topic of pigs, with chickens thrown in, seemed to energize the room. Everybody failed to raise the subject of adjournment.

"Chickens are a personal food choice for people who may not be able to afford to go to Bernie Leinhard's store and buy a chicken," Bill Stikk said.

"And so are pigs!" Delaney shouted above the growing din.

"Ya gonna slaughter 'em on your front porch?" Billy Stikk shot back.

"None of your damned business," Delaney said.

Mrs. Rudy gave Delaney the hairy eyeball. "Language," she said simply, making a notation on her pad.

"Language yourself," Delaney said, his face now crimson. "I want this approved now, tonight, or—"

"Or what?" Mayor Schiller said.

"Or I'll sue," Delaney said.

"On what grounds?" Attorney Craigo asked.

"Restraint of trade," Delaney shot back.

"I thought you said these pigs were for personal use," Craigo said.

"What they're for is my business," Delaney said.

"What they're for is our business," said Mayor Schiller. He banged the gavel hard on the table. "This meeting is adjourned!"

"But you need a motion," Attorney Craigo began.

"Adjourned!" the mayor repeated.

Stace Dornbeckkoffer gave me an elbow in the ribs as he lumbered to his feet. "Can't wait to read your lead," he said as he waddled out the door.

I followed, wanting to position myself to be able to catch Lawrence Delaney when he exited the hall.

The squabbling continued, with nobody much inclined to leave the fun behind.

The night had turned cool, or else the superheated air inside the council meeting had turned overly muggy after two and a half hours of fermenting. I leaned against the side wall of the fire station, three feet away from the door through which anybody who was leaving would have to pass. I remembered the five-spot Joe Boyle had given me to buy drinks for the folks after the meeting but decided it was more important to confront Delaney than it was to make points with the barflies.

Two and three at a time, people began to leave the hall, giving their own takes and reviews on the subject of raising pigs in East Mauch Chunk. The consensus seemed to be that it wasn't such a good idea. A corollary consensus was that Attorney Lawrence Delaney was progressively getting stranger all the time, and add to that a fomenting of his well-known anger, and it might be worthwhile to plan on coming back to next month's borough council meeting. More lively than Thursday-night television.

Mrs. Rudy left, smiled at me under the bare bulb above the doorway, and immediately lit up a cigarette, pulling in the smoke as though it was oxygen to a deep-sea diver. "Welcome back to East Mauch Chunk," she said before walking away, her sizable file of folders tucked neatly under her arm.

Almost everyone who came out immediately lit up. They wandered off in twos and threes, still discussing chickens and pigs.

The place should have been pretty much emptied by now if I factored in the number of council members and spectators who would opt for the bar rather than the exit.

Finally, I heard a high-decibel "No!" coming from the mouth of Mayor Schiller. "Come on, Russ, let's have one for the road and let old Delaney here find his own way home."

"You'll be sorry," I heard Delaney say through the closed door. Then the door opened as though somebody was trying to get out of a burning building, and I placed myself directly in front of the door, square under the bare light bulb so he could see me, and blocked his way.

He stopped in his tracks, the spring-loaded door being held back by his right hand, his left hand filled with file folders. He glared at me. "Whadda *you* want?" he hissed.

I smiled my most ingratiating smile, but it didn't melt his frozen heart one iota. "A terrific quote about chickens and pigs would be a big help with my article," I said, my notebook and pen poised.

That seemed to throw him off a bit. He looked confused.

"Aren't you gonna ask about my daughter?"

"Of course I am. But first things first."

He looked down at the concrete stoop and let the door pull itself closed. We were alone in the night, everyone else either gone home or cozied up to the bar inside. From across the street it would look like a little one-act play, lit noir style by the bare light bulb above our heads.

He ran his tongue over his lips the way a smoker does when he's searching for that stray bit of tobacco that didn't stay in the business end of the cigarette.

"Pigs are smart. They make good pets. They're easy to raise. They'll eat anything."

My eyebrows raised up all by themselves and I quickly jotted down that quote. "Pigs smart. Good pets."

"But don't they make a mess, take up a lot of space, get ornery?"

"They're smart and they're good eating," he said.

I jotted that down. "But if they're pets, why would you eat them? You don't eat cats or dogs or horses—unless you're French."

"They're not the same kind of pets as cats and dogs and horses. And you know that. Why're you baiting me?"

"I'm just a little confused. Your daughter has gone missing and instead of concentrating your energies on finding her, you're obsessed with raising and eating pigs."

His look confirmed that by bringing up his daughter I had crossed the line, and this interview was over. "I've hired a PI to find her," he said through gritted teeth. "She's done this before, and it's none of your fucking business."

I made like I was writing that down.

He didn't much like me doing that.

He tried to move past me, but I was no longer a ten-year-old snot-nosed kid who could be scared at will. "Get the fuck out of my way, you little prick!"

Since I was two inches taller than him and twenty pounds heavier and in nearly the best condition I was ever going to get into in my life, I let that go as the ranting of a nasty little old man. "I'll get the fuck out of your way when you answer some questions," I said.

He tried to fake me out by moving right and then reversing field, but his eyes gave him away, and I continued to block him. He was a lawyer, so I was almost certain he was going to claim kidnapping and call the police, but he didn't.

"We can do this all night," I said, actually moving in on him a few inches, causing him to back up. It was like herding . . . pigs?

"When did Elizabeth disappear?" I asked.

He looked like he was going to spit in my face but then thought better of it and answered, "I dunno."

"Was she involved with anyone?"

"I dunno." He shuffled back and forth as though he was going to again try the fake-out move to the left.

"She into drugs?"

"I dunno. Yeah, maybe. Every kid is."

"I hain't," I said.

"You drink booze. That's a drug."

"Perfectly legal," I said. "As a lawyer, I'm sure you've heard of the repeal of Prohibition." He either didn't let that sink in or wasn't listening. He kept eyeing somewhere past me—anywhere past me. "You don't seem to know much. Mind if I talk to your wife?"

"You stay the fuck away from my family!" he sputtered.

"I was invited to connect with your wonderful family," I said. "By your sister."

"You mind your own goddamned business. I have a good PI on this case. You keep your nose out of it."

"I don't take orders from you," I said, which I guess was fairly obvious. "I don't work for you."

"You don't work for anybody. You're supposed to be Clark Fuckin' Kent, boy journalist."

"What makes you think I'm not?"

"You're nosing around for a cheap, sick tabloid story, and you're milking my slightly delusional sister to extort money from her . . . for your beer. I suppose if you *do* find anything, you'll come slithering to me, wanting to be paid to keep it quiet, you ignorant little shit." He took a deep breath, and an idea lit up behind his squinting eyes. "I'll call your mother. See how you like that—"

"You wanna mess with my family, why not go all the way and call my grandmother. I'm sure she'd like to drill you a new one. She's always said she doesn't like you."

I could see by the way his eyes dropped that the last thing in the world he wanted to do was deal with Dear Granny. Even I had to dial it up a notch at times to enter her chambers.

Lawyer Delaney's eyes came up again, another bright idea festering behind them. "I told you years ago to stay away from my kids."

"I did," I said. "Shit, I was ten years old at the time, you moron."

"So you haven't learned anything in the meantime. You fuckin' stay away from my kids, you ugly little prick!"

"Do I have to stay away from your sister, too?"

His eyes glared.

"I was thinking about dating your sister. Hell, if we got married, you'd be my brother-in-law, and we could do Thanksgiving dinner," I threw in, knowing the instant it came out of my mouth it was as moronic as this whole sordid charade.

But at that point I didn't much care. I needed some answers and wasn't above lowering myself to Lawyer Delaney's level to get them. Hell, most people loved to talk to a journalist. "You can be my best man," I said, continuing to lower the bar.

I tried another tack. "So you're not going to be cooperative in helping people take positive steps to find your daughter."

A frown crossed his brow. "You just got that, mastermind?" he said.

The whole frustrating effort was beginning to drain me, and I could feel I was going to either slug him or step aside and let him go. For some reason I glanced over my right shoulder. There were only two cars left on School Street: mine and a '68 four-door Chevy, and framed by the streetlight over the Chevy, I could make out someone in the passenger's seat.

"You made Mrs. Delaney sit in your car for two and a half hours while you talked pigs in that meeting?" I said, and then, before he could react, I pivoted on my right foot and jogged over to his car and rapped on the passenger's window. In a very natural reaction, Mrs. Delaney rolled down her window before Mr. Delaney could recover sufficiently to run toward the car, yelling, "No! No!"

I leaned down and put my forearm on the open window. "Mrs. Delaney," I said. "I'm looking to find your daughter, and I seem to be running into a lot of dead ends."

Lawyer Delaney wrenched open the driver's door and slid in, fumbling for his keys, tossing his pig files onto his wife's lap.

"I'd like to talk to you about Elizabeth," I said. When she heard the name Elizabeth, Mrs. Delaney's eyes brightened, which was the only thing bright about her. She looked twenty years older than she was, a poor woman beaten down for decades by her husband and buffeted by a daughter who was not living up to the dreams a mother had for her.

Lawyer Delaney fumbled the keys into the ignition and fired up the engine, dropped it into Drive, and stepped on the gas, but not before Mrs. Delaney mouthed the words "Call. Noon."

I didn't even notice the gravel that got thrown up onto my legs from the rear tires as Mr. Delaney roared up School Street, halfway up the street remembering to turn on his lights.

I slid into my own driver's seat, fired up the car, and sat there as it idled—and decided I'd made more progress than I'd expected to. I had three phone calls to make tomorrow as soon as things quieted down at work: one to Hazleton, one to Allentown, and one to Mrs. Delaney.

I eased the car into first gear, wrestling with the shift on the column, and eased out the clutch. I drove to the carriage house, apologized to Mr. Thorpe, who was reading a book, because I'd be making some noise for an hour or so typing up my borough council article for tomorrow's paper (Council Cuts Pork from Budget and from Backyards) while sipping some suds.

I finished up at 11:00, sat with Mr. Thorpe for a few minutes of aimless conversation, and then went to bed. The light in the common living room was still on at 2:30 when I got up to take a piss. Mr. Thorpe loved to read. Must be a good book. I'd have to sneak a look at the title in the morning.

10

Road Trip

"You should keep an eye on Delaney," Joe Boyle said, handing back the galley proof of the borough council story with the pig lead.

"I'm scheduled to talk to Mrs. Delaney today at noon," I said.

Joe looked perplexed. "Doris Delaney doesn't talk to anybody. She's like a hermit."

I explained how she sat in their car for two and a half hours last night while the borough council meeting went on and how after I had confronted the Lawyer Delaney, as they were scratching out, she mouthed the words "Call. Noon."

Joe shook his head. "You must have a mysterious way with women."

I shrugged.

"Is it all right with you if I make that call and a couple of others from home?" I asked. "There's awful background noise here, and I don't want to freak her out."

"Wouldn't want to do that," Joe said, "certainly wouldn't want to do that." He patted me on the knee then pointed to the galley proof in my hand. "I'm nominating you to be our regular foreign correspondent to the East Mauch Chunk Borough Council."

I almost said, "Shit, thanks," but managed to keep the shit out of it.

I let Mrs. Apfelbaum and Nate Dermott, the managing editor, know that I was going to conduct interviews from the quiet of my own digs. "Don't blame you," Nate said. "Once those presses start, I can't even hear myself think."

I turned in the marked-up galley to one of the typesetters for correction, then headed out the door. I'd walked to work, so I walked home, up Packer Hill but out in the street, not through the Asa Packer Mansion lawn. I didn't want to run into Grace Delaney until I had something solid I could give her for her $500 investment.

Mr. Thorpe was out somewhere on the Packer grounds, and he didn't tend to take his lunch until midafternoon so I had the little place all to myself. I set a notebook on the dining room table, sharpened a couple of number 2 pencils, and spun the dial on the rotary phone.

After three rings, there was a faint "Yes?" that sounded as though it was coming from Mars, passing through a solar storm on the way.

"Mrs. Delaney?" I whispered, not wanting to startle her.

"Yes?" she said again, as though not certain she was Mrs. Delaney. "Yes. This is she. To whom am I speaking?"

I told her.

"Oh, yes," she said. "Last night." Pause. "I may have changed my mind."

"About what?"

"About talking to you, of course."

"Well, that's certainly your prerogative," I said. "But I am trying to help find Elizabeth."

The mention of Elizabeth's name caused Mrs. Delaney to sigh.

"She's done this before, but I . . . have a feeling . . . a different feeling this time."

"So does your sister-in-law."

Instead of Lawyer Delaney's derisive reaction to mention of his sister Grace, Mrs. Delaney's response was the opposite. "Grace, dear Grace," she said. "She is so supportive."

"She asked me to help . . . if I can," I said.

"Yes. Yes, I know. How kind of you." There was a pause marked by a sort of static from Mrs. Delaney that sounded as though she was about to say something. Then she did. "Mr. Delaney doesn't like you . . . doesn't want you anywhere around my Elizabeth."

"He told me that when I was ten years old and Elizabeth asked me to come to your house to play. He didn't want me anywhere near his . . . your kids. Like I had the plague or something."

She actually laughed. "He's just always hated your entire family," she said. "He never said why, but it had something to do with your grandmother. Some business thing, I think."

"But what can that possibly have to do with my trying to find Elizabeth?"

"He doesn't want anyone from outside to be involved with our family. He needs to say what we do . . . "

"But he's not doing anything constructive to find her."

"Oh, no. That's wrong. He did hire Mr. Calahan . . . "

"The private investigator."

"Yes. So you see, he is concerned . . . about all of us, but especially Elizabeth."

"But he doesn't agree that it's different this time, that she maybe didn't run away again."

She sighed again. I assumed that she was doing a lot of that lately. "No. No. Of course not. Mr. Delaney does not put much faith in the intuition of women." She sighed again.

I was going to tell her that I had heard on good authority that neither of them should put much faith in the abilities of Mr. Calahan but thought better of it.

"So am I to believe that you are not opposed to my looking into Elizabeth's disappearance?"

"Well. Oh," she said, as though that question presented a particularly daunting quandary. "Oh, no, I do not. But Mr. Delaney must not know that." Pause. "He would be very upset if he knew that. Very upset, at both of us . . . all of us. He *does* get upset sometimes."

"I'm sure he doesn't get upset with you," I said, eager to hear her answer to that one.

"Oh, you don't know Mr. Delaney. He gets upset with everyone."

"But not with himself."

"Of course not. Why would you say that?"

"Just wondering."

"And is this a good time of day to call you if I have questions or news about Elizabeth?"

At first she didn't answer, implying that she was reluctant to possibly get caught talking to the "enemy." Finally, she spoke. "Yes. Yes it is. Mr. Delaney is away from the house and the office every day at this time."

Now I paused, not sure where to go next. "So I have your support in looking for Elizabeth."

Another pause. "Yes. Certainly. But you can't tell anyone. It would just make a mess . . . more of a mess."

"Do you have a phone number for Barbara Kottke?"

Again a pause. "Oh, Barbara. Yes, yes I do. Please hold while I find it."

She was gone a good three minutes. When she came back, she told me what it was. It was a prefix in the Allentown area.

"But you won't tell her or her mother you got the number from me, will you?" she asked.

"Not if you don't want me to."

"Oh, no. I most certainly don't want my name brought up." Another pause. "You tell her you got the number from one of her friends—if she asks."

"But I don't know any of her friends."

"Then tell her Grace gave it to you. Grace knows Barbara . . . a little."

"Yes. She showed me a picture of Barbara and Elizabeth. In fact, I have it right here." I slid the photo from the folder I'd started on Elizabeth Delaney.

"You do? What picture? Oh, wait, yes, the one at the picnic. I've seen it. I'd like to have it back at some point."

"Grace had a copy made for me. Along with a copy of her high school graduation portrait."

"Oh, yes. I have that one right here. Framed."

"I appreciate you talking to me. I'm going to call Barbara now and see if I can go down and interview her, to see what she knows about Elizabeth."

"Yes, yes. That's a good idea. Two of the times Elizabeth ran off she ended up at Barbara's. They were close at school, you know."

I agreed that I did know that. "And Barbara is Elizabeth's closest friend?"

"From school, yes. None of her close friends from high school went to college at St. Elizabeth's."

"I'll see what Barbara has to say, and if I turn up anything I'll let you know. At this time of day, to avoid any trouble from your end."

"Yes," she said, and the phone line went dead.

I dialed Barbara Kottke's number. It rang three times and then a woman answered. I explained who I was and asked if I could talk to Barbara. I heard a girl's voice in the background say, "Who is it, mother?" but Mother Kottke told me that Barbara was not home at the moment and she didn't expect her home until later tonight.

I asked Mother Kottke if she had seen Elizabeth recently, and she said she hadn't. "When was the last time you saw her, ma'am, do you recall?"

The pause was long enough that it sounded like one of those where the wheels are turning rapidly in order to decide which lie to use. "Why it must have been a week or two before school let out . . . back in mid-May. She came over to visit for a few hours while she waited for Lawrence . . . her father to come pick her up."

"Then you live close to St. Elizabeth's."

"Oh yes, five . . . six blocks away."

"And Barbara lives at home."

Pause. "Yes. Why do you ask?"

"Elizabeth stays at a dorm and Barbara lives at home."

"Yes. They have some classes together and they became friends, and then we got to know Elizabeth's family, most of them."

"Have you been contacted by a Mr. Calahan?"

"Who? No. Should I have?"

"I'd have thought so."

"Who is he?"

"A private investigator Mr. Delaney hired to help find Elizabeth," I said, wondering what kind of a PI wouldn't start an investigation by looking at Barbara's house, which is where Elizabeth ended up on several other occasions when she'd vanished.

"Are you a private investigator, too?" she asked.

"No, no. I'm just a journalist helping look into this, at the request of Elizabeth's aunt."

"Grace? She's a character," Mrs. Kottke said. "Very unique."

"I would say," I said. Pause. "Would you mind if I called back later tonight to see if Barbara is in?"

"Well, you can try, but I genuinely don't know what her schedule is at this point."

Genuinely? Where's that come from? "But she *is* living at home for the summer . . . "

"Of course she is. Where else would she be?"

"Well, some college students spend the summer abroad, traveling or taking courses at some exotic locale."

"Oh, I see. Yes, I suppose they do."

"Or they go off to a dude ranch in Arizona to work for the summer. That's something I always wished I could have done, instead of working at the Steel."

"Well I'm sure there is nothing wrong with working at the Steel for the summer," she said, trying hard to not be condescending.

"Very educational," I said. "Taught me what I *don't* want to do for the rest of my life."

"Then it was all worth the experience," she said, as though talking to a little kid.

"Please let me give you my number," I said. "Do you have a pen handy?"

"Right here," she said.

I repeated my name and gave her my home number and the number at the newspaper. I didn't hear any scratching of pen on paper. I was sure she wasn't copying either number down.

"I very much appreciate your talking to me," I said. "And please let me know if you hear from Elizabeth. Of course, that's after you call her parents to give them the good news."

"Yes, of course," she said, and vanished from the line.

I flipped open my address book and looked up Marie Martinelli.

Ah, Marie. My closest friend at Espy State. A unique gal. Barely five feet tall, olive-skinned, dark-haired, straight As, Coke-bottle glasses, chain-smoker, skinny but always worried about her weight. "You oughta see my mamma," she always said. "'Nuff said." To help keep her skinny, she and her roommate, Gayle Cleaver, tall and blonde and a nonsmoker (and straight Bs), had cajoled permission from our cross-country coach to train with the boys because the college didn't have a girls' team.

If we'd had a mixed team, Marie would have been our sixth and Gayle our seventh best. In our senior year, I was number three man and always aware that Marie was back there somewhere nipping at my butt—in spite of or perhaps because of her chain-smoking. I don't know if she actually inhaled, but she was as accomplished at blowing smoke rings as any of us were armed with our Parodi cigars. On our 18-milers along under-construction I-80, she could hawk a lunger like a retired coal miner. She had dearly wanted to go to college in Manhattan, so she frequently dressed all in black and sometimes sported a beret. And she could curse like an iron-foundry laborer.

Which I assume she learned from her father, an Italian immigrant who changed the family name from Martinelli and opened a bakery in Hazleton called Martin's Baked Goods. In quick succession he opened Martin's Baked Good shops in Berwick, Blooms-burg, Danville, Avoca, and half the towns in the hard-coal region: Pottsville, Nanticoke, Gerardville, Shenandoah, etc.

It was no secret that Mr. Martinelli had "connections" in New York and New Jersey, and people suspected that the truck from his Hazleton bakery that ran special orders to restaurants in Manhattan and Brooklyn early every morning might have numbers salted into the cannolis. I'd met Mr. Martinelli on many an occasion, especially when we had a home Saturday-morning cross-country meet. We'd top the hill with a half mile to go to the finish line beside the gym, and there at the top of the hill cheering us on would be Marie and her father with his arm around her as she applauded our efforts, both of them framed with the step-through Chevy van Mr. Martinelli was driving between bakery locations. On several occasions he stopped in at the gym on his way back through to catch us wrestling, always an unlit cigar the size of a rattlesnake stuck in the right side of his mouth.

He was one of the most jovial human beings I'd ever met. "Ah, my baby's best friend," he'd call when he saw me after a meet. "If you were a nice Italian boy I'd force you to marry her." Hahaha. He'd force us into the bakery van and drive us downtown and treat us to a nice meal. "Both of youse"—coal region for the plural of you—"could put some meat on your bones." Hahaha.

He also loved one of our rival schools, Slippery Rock State College, and after one meet where we barely beat them, he shanghaied both teams and took them downtown for lunch at the tony Hotel Harrison. At the end of the meal, when presented with the bill, his eyebrows rose into pyramids. Football players might have big appetites, but long-distance runners are tapeworms with legs.

Everyone in the coal region feared . . . respected Mr. Martinelli. He was a generous man but firm in his opinions. Whenever there were rumors of trouble in the underworld and yet another hoodlum body was found sprawled along the Northeast Extension of the Pennsylvania Turnpike, credit was always given to Mr. Martinelli.

Then, just before Christmas in our junior year, Mr. Martinelli dropped dead. Just like that. While overseeing the loading of his van behind the Hazleton bakery. I went to the funeral and stayed in the back, out of the way, pushed against the wall by the throng of mourners. And as though there had been absolutely, positively no whitecaps on the sea, Mrs. Martinelli—Mother Sophia—stepped in and took over. Not from the driver's seat of the van but from a little office in the back of the Hazleton bakery.

Marie had been kind enough during my researching the drug-trade route through Espy to steer me in directions that kept me on track, without in any way betraying any information about her involvement or that of her family in supplying information. The Martinellis were, to put it mildly, very much antidrugs. Both on general principles and because they felt that anyone bringing drugs into the mix was going to throw a law-enforcement spotlight on their activities. And it was personal as well. Marie has two older brothers, Carlo and Christopher. Christopher *had* gone to school in Manhattan and had come back home with a heroin habit, which they'd dealt with quickly. Carlo had gone into the Marines but was still stateside in some intelligence capacity in northern Virginia. Mrs. Martinelli, and now Marie, stayed home and took care of business, Marie fluent in legit business matters after majoring in business administration at Espy, where biz ed and special ed were the school's two acclaimed majors.

I dialed Marie's mom's house in Hazleton, where I would not be surprised to find that Marie, two weeks past graduation, had taken over the whole store.

"Hello," she said.

"Yo, I need a ciggie," I said, which for years had been Marie's greeting to anyone she ran into.

"Yo yourself, shithead Skar, what the fuck's happenin'?"

"Nice to speak to you, too," I said. "I can't believe your mother allows you to bring that filthy mouth into the family home."

"She loves the rest of me so much she lets me bring the mouth along." A pause where I could hear her sucking cigarette smoke. "So whaddya want, a job? They already got a good bakery in Mauch Chunk, those Nazis over on Broadway." She was referring to the Schantzes, who ran the local bakery and made swell apple turnovers.

"Nazis and fascist Italians got along real well during the war. Why not go into partnership with them? I'd be glad to march out front with a sign reading DOWN WITH AXIS BAKED GOODS!"

She snorted, which was a substitute for a laugh, dictated, in part, by her excessive smoking.

"So really, what's up? I know you don't like telephones all that much, so this isn't a social call."

"It's a Christopher thing," I said, which had always been our code for "it has to do with drugs."

"More research on your book?"

I winced. "The only research I'm getting done on that is what I'm finding out looking into a disappearance."

"Is she cute?"

"Yeah, sorta, but it's not that. Her aunt wants me to help find her, her mother wants me to help find her, and her father wishes I was dead and out of the way."

"And this disappearing thing is new behavior for this chick—?"

"Nope."

"And she's into the drug scene."

"Yup."

"And somebody thinks this time it's different."

"Aunt and mother."

"But not father."

"He's probably the one who's right. At least looking back at Christopher's trajectory."

"So she's on the ole downhill escalator—?"

"I haven't seen her, but that's the impression I'm getting."

"They usually develop fairly predictable habits. Including thinking they're way smarter than anyone around them."

"I checked in with the chick she usually ends up with, and she's not there this time."

"She have a lot of friends?"

"Doesn't seem to."

"Probably made new friends, 'specially if she has any money. Her folks have any money?"

"Her father's a lawyer."

"It's a fallacy to think all lawyers are rich—especially small-town lawyers."

"So what're you saying, that her father might be dealing drugs to supplement his lawyering fees? Using his daughter as an 'in'?"

"No, that's *not* what I was saying, but now that *you* said it, I'd add it to your list of theories to check out."

"I don't currently have a very big list of theories—other than that she's using and losing."

"Well, add the old man, just in case."

"Hmmmm," I said.

"Hmmmm what?"

"Nothing. Maybe. Maybe something, but something really weird."

"Whazz'dat?"

"Her father went to a borough council meeting last night demanding that they allow him to raise hogs on his property."

"What—?"

"Hogs. Says he wants to raise them as pets and then wants to slaughter and sell 'em."

A pause. "Maybe that's what happened to his daughter—he raised her and sold her for slaughter."

Now I paused before asking. "Ya know," I finally said, "you're really one sick bitch."

"Ya think?"

"Well, yeah."

"We had a hog problem up here," she said. "The outskirts of town ended up circling a guy's farm—Bixby I think the guy's name was—and he raised horses and pigs and a bunch of his neighbors got together and went to council and tried to have the law changed to consider him to be inside the city's suburbs and therefore unable to continue raising horses and hogs. 'Specially hogs. Some of the neighbors liked having horses around. At the same time he got up in arms because a lot of the neighbors owned dogs that they didn't properly train or control and they used to go over to his farm and harass the horses and the hogs, mostly the horses, 'cause the hogs wouldn't put up with it. Really got a lot of lawyers happy and rich when the queen-bee bitch going on about his hogs lost one of her prized dogs when it got loose, ran over to Bixby's, started harassing a sow, and got blindsided by a boar that broke the dog's back legs, then started eating it from the back, while the dog was still alive. But anyway, I digress."

I felt like somebody had just hit me between the eyes with a sledgehammer. "Man, I really gotta get you together with my buddy Ronnie Von Renner, two animal lovers, you guys'd be great together."

"Von Renner doesn't sound Italian. Mama Sophia would never have it."

I looked at the clock on the wall and decided that I'd spent enough time socializing with my buddy Marie. "I'd like to come up there this afternoon and talk to your mother—about this drug thing."

Marie produced one of her patented snorts, but this one hurt my ear. "You're putting me on, right? You wanna come up and spend some quality time with Mama Sophia asking her questions—direct questions—about a subject she would rather see confined to the fires of Hell? Are you mad? Are *you* on drugs?"

"Let's see here. From your first question to your last: no, yes, no, no."

She snorted again. "She'd sic Teddy on you and then have Teddy take what was left of you out to Bixby's to feed his hogs." Although I'd never met either Marie's mother or Teddy, I knew that Teddy was Mrs. Martinelli's body . . . er . . . assistant, and I don't mean assistant baker. He was reputedly big and bad.

"Besides," I said, "isn't it about time I met your mother? After all, your father liked me and I'd guess your mother—"

"My father liked everybody—almost. And he often confided in me that he didn't see what I saw in you. 'If he'd put on an extra hundred pounds and we could put some makeup on him so his scar would stand out even more, we could hire him as a debt collector' is what he told me."

Naw, I thought to myself. *She's making that up*. Mr. Martinelli and I got along capitally. Really. Although he made it clear that Marie and I would never be more than friends. "I could convert to Italian," I had said, joking. He turned the color of an eggplant. "That's nothing, that Italian stuff, to be joking about."

I said I was sorry, only joking around, and he reverted to his normal color and said 'Okay, that's fine, but . . .' He left it hanging.

Me as a bill collector in a loan-shark world. In a dumb way it held some appeal: I could put my malady to good use. Knock, knock. Door creaks open, woman of the house sees me, screams with back of hand thrown over mouth, "I'm here to collect hubby's debt," I'd say, and she'd pay up right away. "Here, take it all, take more than he owes you, but please don't hurt me." Easy money. Scars work good that way.

"Don't even think about it," Marie was saying, wheeling me back in from my romantic reverie of being a well-shod gangster.

"You go ask her, see if it's okay with her. I'll wait."

She actually put down the phone, and I could hear her walking away from wherever the phone was located. Sounded like high heels on linoleum.

While I waited I whistled and watched the second hand of the wall clock spin around. At last I heard, as though through an echo chamber, "No, Mama, no!" Then clicking heels again and the phone being picked up.

"What's with the heels? You got a big lunch date?"

That threw her off for a second. "Just back from a funeral Mass." Pause. "And the next one I'll be going to is yours."

I laughed. "She said yes," I said, not certain that she had but led in that direction by Marie's reaction.

I heard a match strike and a long inhalation of breath, a slight cough, and an exhale. "I tried to keep your sorry ass safe, and this is what I get in return."

"Is your address still—?" I said, reading it out of my address book. "I'll be there in a half hour." She hung up, and I hung up and went out to the ole Rambler, whistling along the way. Whistling through the graveyard, maybe, but whistling.

* * *

The drive to Hazleton from Mauch Chunk skirted the eastern edge of Nesquehoning, then took a 90-degree right turn and headed up and over the Broad Mountain, a real bear in the winter and steep enough that I had to drop from third gear to second, then downhill and through the village of Beaver Meadows, where Jack Palance was born and raised, and in no time at all into the outskirts of Hazleton, a city as stuck on the shank end of the shit shovel as Mauch Chunk, and maybe moreso. I kept my eyes open for the Bixby farm.

Hazleton looked gray even though the sky was blue. The streets were cracked and broken, rusted railroad tracks going through town here and there and heading off to pretty much nowhere.

I cut off the main street and headed north and within four blocks was on a stretch with houses that were a mix of well-kept-up, needs work, and downright decrepit. The houses on the left side of the street were on the upside of a hill, so each house had a set of steps— always concrete—leading up to a front porch. They were all 2 1/2 stories. The houses on the right side were on the downside of the hill, and you had to walk *down* a set of concrete steps to get to the front porch. I wondered if the basements of the houses on the right side regularly flooded in the spring when the snows melted.

The postage-stamp lawns in the front of the houses ran the gamut of filled with flowers, well-tended flowers, to a sanctuary for weeds. One house halfway down the block on the right was a half-dozen shades of gray, the roofline like a tired nag, and a gray-haired woman out front pushing around gray leaves while wearing a gray dress that looked like she'd picked it up from an Amish thrift shop. Her sad house featured a star in one window, indicating a son had died in World War II (which was now twenty-three years gone) and in the other window a sign that proudly proclaimed WE BURN COAL.

Marie's mother's house was at the end of the block, on the corner, on the "up" side of the street, and actually had a lawn that started small in front, next to the steps, and continued around the side of the house until it encountered an actual backyard that had been covered with paving stones. A swing swung from a huge maple tree at the back of the yard.

I parked on the side street, on the side of the house, for no very good reason other than I felt like it.

The house was vying to be in the top three on the block as far as being kept up went. It was painted dark green with light-green trim, actual wood sides, no aluminum siding. A green awning extended out from under the roof of the porch both in front and on the side. It looked like a porch where you could sit on a June night sipping beer while waiting for the lightning bugs to come up out of the grass.

There was lawn furniture on the porch and each of the cushions was upholstered in clear plastic. *Ah, jeez*, I thought, *they aren't going to have all the furniture in the house covered in clear plastic, are they?* I tried to remember if Marie had ever mentioned it, or if I was already spinning out the stereotypes of the traditional Italian family in America. As I would learn in a few minutes, you should be careful to not denigrate stereotypes. They come from somewhere, and often enough to make a groove as deep as those in the vinyl of the latest Frank Sinatra smash.

I was confronted by a screen door. The house's door was open so fresh air could circulate inside. I was about to depress the doorbell when I heard the pitter-patter of little feet, a pitter-patter I recognized as Marie Martinelli's. And even if I had had a cold, I would have been able to smell the stale cigarette smoke trying to escape onto the front porch.

Marie came around an archway, an archway on the other side of the front room, which, like many front rooms in the Coal Region, was reserved for very special events like Christmas and wakes and which was never desecrated by normal use the remainder of the year. And yes, the furniture was protected from the real world by clear plastic covers. Somehow, they had managed to get doilies to stay put on the sleek plastic sofa backs and armrests.

Marie was wearing an Espy Field Hockey T-shirt and bluejeans and desert boots. As far as I knew, she'd never played field hockey. She kind of flounced across the room and pushed open the screen door, kind of scowling at me from behind her heavy black glasses. She tiptoed up to kiss me with her ashtray lips and whispered, "You stupid bastard. I'll get you for this bonehead move." She undid the tiptoe and stood in front of me and in a normal voice that I was sure carried to the back of the house said, "It's so nice to see you. Come on back and met Mama Sophia and Teddy."

"What happened to the heels?" I whispered to her as she turned to lead me to the back of the house.

"Pervert," she hissed.

I followed her through the condomed front room, around the archway, down a hall, and into a big kitchen. Standing in front of the refrigerator, and roughly the same size, was a crewcut guy wearing a dark suit and a white shirt with a thin black tie. That, I assumed, was Teddy.

Mama Sophia sat at the kitchen table, a cup of coffee in front of her, muddied by cream with a saucer under it. I stood across from her, waiting for Marie to introduce us, which she did with a flourish that was riddled with ridicule. She referred to me as "that dirt-digging journalist."

Mama Sophia was pretty much what I anticipated and pretty much what I'd glimpsed at her husband's funeral: short, stocky, dressed completely in black, ample salt-and-pepper hair tied up into a crown, the beginning of a mustache on her upper lip. She didn't wear glasses at the moment, but she usually did; she had the indentations on both sides of her nose from where they usually rested. Her eyes were rheumy and blue rimmed, although they were dark brown. She could have been any age from forty to sixty. She had no wrinkles in her olive skin, except around the corners of her mouth and the sides of her eyes.

It was easy to see she was staring at my scar, while Teddy stared at me as though I might attempt to steal the silverware. He held hands with himself in front of his belt buckle.

Mrs. Martinelli continued to stare at me, nodding slowly, as though she was contemplating falling asleep. For a moment, nobody spoke. Then Mrs. Martinelli waved her right hand in front of herself, as if waving away a lazy fly. "Is not so bad," she said, "your scar. My brother, Anthony, god bless him, a propane tank exploded near him and he was scarred for life, all over his body, a beautiful face ruined for all eternity. And Father Lewis, the cancer eating his face away, his jaw nearly falling off, afraid to go outside, now that was horrible. You, you're a handsome devil." She made a sound that fell between a laugh and a cackle. "You come to visit, my daughter's friend."

"Skar wants to ask you some questions about the drug trade in this part of the state," Marie said, taking a seat at the table, a seat in front of an overflowing ashtray where a half-smoked cigarette sat smoldering.

Mrs. Martinelli looked at Marie with what can only be described as a stinky eye. "What would I, an old widow, know about that?" she asked, innocent as all hell.

Afraid of the direction things were going, I jumped right in. "Marie says you know many things, that you are an astute observer."

Her left eyebrow rose. "Astute?" she asked, and I wasn't sure if she truly didn't know the word or if she was teasing me. "What's astute?"

"Critical, perceptive, focused," I supplied.

Mama Sophia scowled. "Well she's wrong. I go to the bakery, I go to church, I sit here. I know little." She sported a thick Italian accent, but I'd grown up around so many accents, from my German grandmother's to my grandfather on my father's side's broken Slovak, that I had no trouble following her.

"But you're a member of a close-knit Italian community—"

"And what? Italians are all Cosa Nostra and they know all the inside poop about all the crime that goes on because they're in the middle of all of it?"

So far this was going very well.

"My daughter, for all of her fine education, doesn't know half as much as she thinks she does." She nodded at Marie, who, standing next to Teddy, looked the size of a doll.

"That's probably true of most of us," I said, trying desperately to lighten up the kitchen. I glanced around nervously. The kitchen still had a coal stove. A door with glass in the upper half was off to the left and it led to a small mudroom and from there to the backyard. I wished at the moment I was sitting on the tree swing, swinging the day away.

Mrs. Martinelli hadn't found my leavening comment amusing. "What is it you want here?" she asked. "That I should give you the names of some people to go to talk to about drugs, about crime?"

I nodded.

"All you need to do is go downtown and talk to the chief of police, a captain"—she nodded at Marie to get the captain's name— "Captain McMurdock. He'll tell you all you need to know. I'm just an old woman with a too-smart-for-her-own-britches daughter."

I shot a glance at Marie, and she merely shrugged her shoulders, an I-told-you-so smirk on her face. Mrs. Martinelli glanced at Marie and caught the look. "And you," she said. "You and I will talk later."

"If you want me to leave, Mrs. Martinelli, I'll be more than willing to oblige."

That seemed to catch her off guard. She took a toothpick from her saucer and poked it around her teeth, as though stalling. "You wrote those stories in the Danville paper?" she asked.

I nodded.

"They carried them in our paper," she said, nodding toward the door to the cellar, where a pile of newspapers sat atop a stool. "Did they stop the drugs from going to those colleges, that Bucknell and Penn State, and the one youse two went to?"

I shook my head. "Can't say that they did, but maybe they slowed down the flow a little, and maybe got the police taking a longer look."

She nodded. Then turned to Teddy. "You and Marie go out back, out in the yard, and wait until I call you. I want to talk to this young man—alone."

"But, Mama," Marie protested, rushing over to Mama Sophia's side as though to save her from a mugging.

Mama Sophia shrugged Marie off in such an offhanded way that it should have shattered her self-esteem. "Out," Mama Sophia said. Teddy was already headed for the backdoor, and he nodded his head in the direction of the backyard, indicating that Marie should follow him. "I'm not going to tell you twice," Mama Sophia said. And that was that.

Marie, the headstrong pushy broad I'd known for nearly four years, meekly shuffled to the backdoor, which Teddy was holding open for her, and walked into the backyard.

"Sit," Mama Sophia said, indicating the chair across from her. I did as I was told. Mama Sophia pushed the ashtray away from her, a look of contempt on her face. "You've tried to get her to stop this disgusting habit. She told me. You nag at her."

I nodded.

"That's good. I hate it, this cigarette smoking. It's no good for you, nothing but trouble and misery . . . and the world has enough of that already."

I nodded.

"She coughs at night, in the middle of the night, in the middle of her sleep, I hear her."

"It's a hard habit to break," I said. "Better to never start. Tobacco is a drug—a bad drug."

"The Surgeon General says it will kill you, we all know it will, it's as bad as black lung disease, the disease of the coal miners, the same thing." She folded her hands and shook her head slowly. "You keep after her; she listens to you, even if you think she doesn't. You keep after her to stop this terrible habit." She made a sour face, which I suspected she did often, and again shook her head. "This drug. These drugs. They'll be the downfall of all of us. One of my sons, Christopher, he goes off to New York City and he comes back hooked on heroin. Heroin. We had to send him away. To get him off it. And now we have to watch him, constantly, to make sure he doesn't go back to it, become a drug addict again." She let out a sigh and bowed her head. "You don't have kids. Don't have them," she said from under her bowed head.

I thought, not for the first time, of becoming either a priest or a psychologist. Given a bit of time around me, people tended to open themselves up and dump their stuff on me, maybe because I look damaged, that because of that I'll understand their problems. Maybe I should get paid for it. Maybe if I'd had enough time alone with Lawyer Delaney, I could have gotten him to bare his soul—if he has one.

"But you must hear this all the time," Mama Sophia whispered. "You, a reporter, you must hear terrible things all the time."

I wanted to tell her that I'd only been a real professional getting-paid reporter for less than a week, but I didn't want to add more disillusionment to her already disillusioned life.

She didn't say anything more for a full two minutes, and I decided I wasn't going to egg her on, I'd just wait until she was ready to say something. Finally, she did. "This drug business, I don't know how to stop it, even slow it down. It's just growing, fast, feeding the colleges mostly, making the kids addicts. Comes out of Philadelphia and through Mauch Chunk on its way to Bucknell, Susquehanna, Penn State—Espy. And in from New York along that 80 interstate. Even if some gets stopped, enough gets through to keep the business going. Most people, they know nothing about it. Nothing."

I nodded. "Most of my father's generation got their kicks from hard liquor."

Mama Sophia nodded.

This wasn't progressing as I originally thought it would. Instead of a fiercely contested battle of wills, it was more like a dialogue dance on some uppity PBS talkfest.

"No good will come of this," Mama Sophia said spreading out her arms, palms up as though waiting for someone to hammer nails into the palms of her hands. "But what can we do?"

"Expose as much of it as we can," I ventured.

"Like taking away the Dutch boy's thumb in the dike," she said.

I nodded again. We were sounding very profound.

"We have discussed this problem, my . . . associates and me, and in what little ways we can slow it, we have. Rumors to police, flat tires, a car run off a road, but still it comes, this marijuana. Young people, they just nod and smile, as though it's nothing."

"They see no harm in it, and it's a way to rebel against their parents," I said, knowing that it sounded exactly like a nerd's words would sound, like I was my father's father or something. I didn't want to tell her, but I had tried marijuana a couple of times, and both times it made me fall asleep. I wasn't awake when the pizza arrived.

"All we can do is put sand in the gears," she said, as though she'd been matriculating at Berkeley.

I couldn't help smiling.

"What?" she said.

"You sound like a campus radical."

Now she smiled. "I read the newspapers. I have a lot of time to read the newspapers."

I pulled my notebook from my back pocket and pulled out a sheet of paper and wrote my two phone numbers down and slid the paper across the table. Mama Sophia took it and folded it and slid it into her apron pocket.

"I'll be in touch," I said, standing, wishing I'd parked the car out front so I could escape without Marie seeing me go. From past experience, I knew she was capable of holding a grudge for a helluva long time.

Reading my dilemma, Mama Sophia said simply, "Sometimes it's best to go right at a problem." She didn't make any move to get up, and I felt I should shake her hand or give her a hug or something, but maybe not. "Go straight out through the backdoor and say goodbye to her, and if she has a cigarette in her mouth, which she probably does, take it out and stomp on it. Maybe she'll get the message."

So I did just that.

11
Wrasslin' U.

Although I knew from long-running experience that Marie carried a grudge for a very long time, I also knew that eventually it would wear itself out and she'd come around. I did take the half-burned cigarette out of her mouth and stomped it into the grass. Ole Teddy hid a smile as Marie went off like a Roman candle, all cursing and sputtering, but I think it was half-hearted because she was glad to see that her mother had not turned me into a pile of cheap gelato.

I left Hazleton, and when I hit the top of the Broad Mountain, I pulled off the right side and parked near where our father had taken us boys before deer season every year to sight in our long rifles. I could see through the trees that the bench was still there and that the firing range was being kept reasonably free of random vegetation.

I had some running shorts and running shoes in the trunk, changed into them, and crossed the road and began running down one of the dirt roads that led over toward the Oxbow. Our father used to take us out hiking along these roads after deer season ended; we went with him and a couple of his miner buddies, and we'd take wax-paper-wrapped summer sausage and cheese sandwiches and a TastyKake pie, mine always cherry. We'd get a few miles in, and they'd have us bushwhack a few hundred yards, and we'd end up at a clearing under a big tree, where somebody years ago had built a fire ring out of conglomerate rocks and where there were some flat rocks to sit on while we listened to the birds and the stories of storied hunts in the past, and while we were doing that, one of the men would pull a couple of crumpled pages of yesterday's newspaper out of the game pouch in the back of his coat, put them in the middle of the fire ring, gather some twigs, stack them into a tepee formation, then lean in a few half-inch-thick dried branches, then give one of us a match from a waterproof container, and we got to strike it on a flat rock and ignite the paper and wood. When the fire was going nicely and some of the thicker branches had caught, one of them would wander off into the woods and come back with a coffeepot and a can of coffee they hid in a cache under a rock, and they'd put together a pot of coffee, and when it was ready we'd all hold out our tin cups to get some. Then we'd chip some powdered milk out of a jar and stir it into the coffee, watching the milky clouds form to match the milky clouds in the sky, and we'd sit back and the men would still be telling tales, and we'd be blowing the hot off the top of the cup and sipping a little coffee off, warming our hands on the cheap cup, feeling all grown up and ready to shoot a deer or wrestle a bear to the ground or camp out for a week, no matter what the weather held, until we'd built up a sack of our own stories of living in the woods.

The late afternoon became warm, warm enough to soften the memory banks, to let them spew. Warm enough, sweating a little sheen, the shoes sending up little puffs of light-brown dirt, the sun coming down through the trees like a blessing. A pair of squirrels sent up an annoyed chatter, their domain disturbed, taunting, like somebody was actually going to spring up into their tree, like Tarzan, and grab them in his fist—where the squirrel would proceed to bite open a good-sized wound on the thumb.

I smiled at the foolishness of it all, the absolute lack of necessity for taking a jog in the woods, against the real need to do so.

I went in about two and a half miles and then turned around and came back. As I got closer to the highway, I could hear the occasional car laboring past. I tried to remember how many chicken potpies I had left in the freezer. Decided to not stop off at the A&P on the way home, certain I could find something to eat.

Back at the car, changed shoes, pulled my pants on over my shorts, left on the sweaty T-shirt and headed home, keeping the ole Rambler around forty-five coming down off the mountain, not wanting it to get away from me.

I was looking forward to a hot shower when I turned into the Harry Packer Mansion driveway but slowed suddenly when I was confronted by a black Chevy Suburban that had a lot of hard miles on it. It had a New Jersey license plate. Over the Rambler's idling motor, I could hear a wave of rough laughter, like a bunch of guys at a fraternity party. It was coming from the carriage house.

I shut down the car, got out, and approached the front door cautiously. The wave of sound increased, occasionally cut through by an even louder bark of laughter.

I opened the door and was faced with a small army of massive men sitting, lounging, knocking back long-neck beers, hooting and hollering, sitting around listening to Mr. Thorpe, who sat in his easy chair like King Tut. Mr. Thorpe pointed at me and a half-dozen boulder heads turned in my direction. "Ah, here he is now," Mr. Thorpe said, as though he'd been previewing my appearance with his massive audience. The living room was generous in its proportions, but with the six of them and Mr. Thorpe, real estate was wanting.

The guy closest to me, filling out a chair, was well tanned and weather beaten. He handed me a Budweiser from a cardboard case that was open at his feet. "Ya want two, white eyes, and you kin have 'em. Plenty fer everybody."

"Give 'im a whole case," a pasty-faced guy as big as half a sofa said.

Thirsty from my run, I took a long drag of the Bud in my hand, and before I could lower it, there was another cold one in my other hand.

"Looks like he's been doin' roadwork," a big Oriental guy sitting like the Buddha in the middle of the floor said. He was playing with a deck of cards. And even though he was in jeans and a cowboy hat, I recognized him: Charles Kalani Jr., aka Professor Toru Tanaka, one of the most famous/infamous pro wrestlers in the world, always ready to pull a "foreign object" (usually salt) from his shorts so he could use it to gouge out the eyes of an opponent. The big fella who'd given me beers was none other than my all-time favorite pro wrestler, Chief Jay Strongbow, out of uniform, but still the Man.

"Hope you don't mind the boys dropping by on their way to matches in Hamburg tomorrow," Mr. Thorpe said.

All I could manage to do was stand there stunned and open mouthed. It was like an all-star wrestling convention. Killer Kowalski, Pedro Morales, Victor Rivera, and Waldo Von Erich, the pasty-faced guy, who in the ring assumed the role of a Nazi thug. In a pair of Bermuda shorts and a tank top as though he'd just blown in from Southern California, he didn't much look like a Nazi. Maybe like a big-boned accountant who didn't get out in the sun often enough.

"Pull up a seat and have something to eat," the Chief said, pushing a folding chair toward me with an open pizza box sitting on it: pepperoni, with half the slices still there. It wasn't the only pizza box in the room. "We travel with folding chairs that we steal from the arenas," Chief said, "because nowhere we go has enough chairs handy for all of us." He tapped the mouth of my Bud with his Bud. "The Professor is trying to learn some card tricks." The Chief leaned close to me and whispered, "He's not very good, but we can't say that out loud 'cause he's got a quick temper." Chief laughed. "Only kidding. He's a teddy bear."

The Professor was spreading cards out on the floor and only Killer Kowalski was paying any attention to him. Pedro and Victor were talking to each other in what sounded like Spanish.

Mr. Thorpe was telling a story about wrestling in the 1940s in Ohio. It involved a match that went extra rounds, and there was a lot of betting involved, and the guys who were supposed to throw it decided not to, and there were bloody noses and fistycuffs in the audience.

I felt like jumping in and telling the story of Ronnie Von Renner and me last year at the Little Palestra in Allentown when Pedro Morales was fighting Waldo and the balcony was so close overhead that when Waldo began fighting dirty and was getting the better of Pedro, a half-dozen Puerto Rican fans jumped off the balcony into the ring to come to his aid, a dozen of them surrounded me and Ronnie and threatened us because we were white guys, and a bunch of other white guys—none of us pretending to be Nazis, by the way—sitting nearby had to come to our aid to save our sorry asses from getting stomped.

The referee had one helluva time clearing the ring so the match could go on.

Thinking about that episode, I waved at Mr. Thorpe to get his attention and asked if I could interrupt his story long enough to ask if it was okay by him if I invited Ronnie up to join the fun. He waved me to do that, so I went across the room and dialed Ronnie's number, and he picked it up on the second ring and wanted to know right away if I was in the middle of a bar brawl, because of all the background noise and all, and to lead him along, told him there was a brawl going on in the carriage house and he needed to get himself up her right away before it was over, and that I'd save at least a couple of guys for him to trounce.

He hung up and two minutes later he was standing in the doorway, his fists ready at his sides, trying to shift gears to take in what was actually going on. I pointed to my new best friend, Chief Jay Strongbow, who was extending his fist with a Bud inside it, and I said, "Ronnie, meet Chief Jay Strongbow."

For the first time in my life, I actually witnessed Ronnie's jaw drop.

"Holy shit," was how he put it.

He accepted the Bud from Chief, pulled up his own folding chair, clinked bottles with the Chief, and shrugged, soaking up what was happening like a happy sponge.

I explained, over the din, that the best I could gather so far is that the six of them travel together in the big Suburban and they knew Mr. Thorpe from when he used to be involved in just about every sport you could imagine, including professional wrestling, and when they had a card of bouts nearby, they dropped off to visit. They had a card at the area in Hamburg on Saturday night, so they swung by to visit and—I was assuming—sleep over. I didn't know of a hotel for miles that would be able to accommodate this circus.

"Hey, Chief," I said, "you guys staying over tonight?"

"We usually do," he answered, turning his attention back to the Professor, who was making absolutely no progress in the matter of becoming a cardsharp.

Mr. Thorpe's story ended and another one began, and it was easy to see he was in his glory. Waldo and Pedro and Victor were all paying rapt attention, about what appeared to be protogroupies and a hotel detective who was also a wrestling fan who lost his job over the ruckus they caused and who traveled with them as a "bodyguard" for the next two years. As though a group of 250-pound bruisers needed bodyguarding.

The tales spun out, the empty beer bottles piled up, the pizza boxes were emptied and more called for, and before we knew it, the clock had wound itself to 11:00 and Ronnie and I had early calls, him with a Saturday morning patrol and me with the Saturday paper to get out. (Thank god there was no Sunday edition; the *Morning Call*'s Sunday edition would have been way to difficult to challenge.)

Ronnie agreed that I could move to the caboose with him so we could get some sleep and the boys could take over the carriage house, including my bed. We bid adieu to the boys, who Mr. Thorpe assured us would be hitting the sack within the next hour or so, and walked—a little wobbly—down the hill to the caboose, where Ronnie pulled out an old army blanket I could crawl under while sleeping on his sofa. In less than five minutes we were out.

*   *   *

The phone rang at 3:32.

It took the third ring to allow me time to figure our just where in the hell I was. Ronnie bounded out of bed and picked up the receiver. "Yeah. Yeah," Ronnie said. "Mr. Thorpe needs us."

I looked down at myself. I was still in my clothes.

I put on my shoes and we marched up the hill.

The lights were on in the carriage house and the door was open. There were low-slung conversations going on. We walked into what looked like a prayer circle—of a very pagan variety, where there were human sacrifices involved.

The seven men had formed a circle, and in the middle of the circle, among the empty beer bottles and ravaged pizza boxes, knelt two guys I didn't recognize who I wouldn't have recognized even if I did know them, because they were bloodied and broken and bruised and bandaged.

Chief held up a left sneaker and what looked like a black rag. "The third one got away," he said. "But we got part of his shirt."

"When they broke in and tripped over his leg, the Chief went on the warpath," Waldo Von Erich said.

"They broke in—?" I said dumbly, still half asleep.

"Yeah," the Chief said, "as in entered a property not their own. Broke in."

"They were looking for you," Mr. Thorpe said.

"Looking for me—?" I said dumbly.

Ronnie slapped me a good, hard one in the middle of the back. "Wake the fuck up," he said. "Mr. Thorpe said these mugs"—he pointed his left thumb at the mugged mugs in the center of the room—"were looking for you . . . and I doubt it was to sell you a magazine subscription or to convert you to Mormonism."

One of the two mugs groaned, as though he was just coming to after spending a week in a coma.

"The three of them had lead pipes and one of them had a sap," Chief said. Waldo held up a sap and a lead pipe as a way of making it easier for me to get the picture

"You shoulda heard the Chief," Pedro said. "Best warpath I've ever heard from him." The Chief's signature act in the ring was to get the shit beat out of him by the bad guy until he'd had enough, whereupon he'd "go on the warpath," and god help anyone in his way. He'd start to vibrate and he'd get agitated and he'd start to do a war dance and the crowd would get into it, on the side of the good guy finally coming around to put it to the bad guy, and the Chief would go crazy and in thirty seconds turn the bout completely around, pummeling the bad guy into a gibbering mess of Jell-O. His ire during the warpath was ecumenical; if a referee got in his way, the referee was fair game as was, during tag-team matches, his own partner. When he started on the warpath, the Chief took no prisoners.

"Wish we'd had a tape recorder," Pedro said. "He took on all three of 'em, the greedy bastard. We had to rouse ourselves enough and break through the warpath daze to let him know he should leave some of them for the rest of us." Pedro snorted. "Rat bastards!" He made like to spit at the two mugs. Both of them winced.

I took a long look at the two of them. Both wore dark clothing, most of which was ripped. From what I could tell under the blood and the burgeoning bruises, both were about mid-twenties, one of them apparently a bodybuilder, the other broad in the shoulders but going a little soft in the middle. Both were dark haired, and the softer one sported a goatee.

"You know either of these sucks?" Ronnie asked.

I shook my head. "Never seen 'em before, that I can tell. Maybe if we cleaned them up a bit, I'd recognize them."

"Not gonna happen," Professor Tanaka said. "If anything, they're gonna get more bloody and messed up." He made a huge fist at them and they again winced.

Not very elegantly, Killer Kowalski drew himself up from the floor. There wasn't enough space for him to roll into a crouch like he was capable of doing in the middle of a match. "I asked them questions," Killer said. "They talk too easy but they don't know much."

"They said they're from Slatington, wherever that is," Pedro said.

"Down the road a few towns, out past Palmerton," Ronnie said.

"They said they were hired to come up and work your sorry ass over," Waldo said. "To discourage you from looking for some gal."

"Elizabeth Delaney," I supplied.

"Yeah, that's her," Waldo said.

"She your girlfriend?" Killer asked. "Her old man wants you to stay away from her 'cause you're so damned ugly?" He smiled and winked at me.

"She's a college gal, disappeared," I said.

"And you're looking for her and somebody doesn't want you to find her," The Chief said.

"That's what they said," Killer said. "Said they got paid $250 each."

"Fuck!" Waldo said. "That's more then I get paid for throwing a match."

"They say they don't know the guy hired 'em," Killer supplied. "Got a phone call, then money in the mail, with a Mauch Chunk postmark."

"What d'ya wanna do with 'em?" the Professor asked.

"We should turn 'em over to the police," Mr. Thorpe said.

"Hell no," Ronnie said, thank god. "Our boy here doesn't want to get involved with the Mauch Chunk cops. They got it in for him ever since he became a food critic."

"What--?" Killer said.

"Never mind," Ronnie said. "Long story."

"But he doesn't have to be involved," the Chief said. "He wasn't even here. We were. *We* could file the complaint."

"I don't like getting mixed up with cops," Victor said.

"But I'm a cop," Ronnie said.

"Hell," Pedro said. "You made the mistake of hanging out with us. You're now tainted blue."

"The local cops won't get anything out of 'em, and if they go to trial, we'll have to come back here and maybe miss a match or two," the Chief said.

"Leave 'em to me," Killer said, as he kicked the bodybuilder a good one to the butt. "Go ahead, cry, ya little sissy. Three guys against one, in the middle of the night, ya sneaky bastards." He went into a fierce pose, pumping up his arms. "Leave 'em to me. If they don't cooperate, there's a lot of abandoned mines around here where we can deposit the bodies." A moan escaped Mister Bodybuilder.

"Go ahead, get a little more out of 'em," the Professor said. "Find out how badly they were supposed to beat him and find out what they were supposed to do with Jim, here. He's an old man and coulda got a heart attack or something."

Mr. Thorpe growled. "I'll 'old man' you, ya puffed-up Hawaiian," Mr. Thorpe said, shaking a fist at the Professor.

"You fellas better go back to sleep," the Chief said. "Leave these mugs to us. The less you know about this, the better off you'll be."

Ronnie looked at his watch. "We'd only get ten minutes before the alarm goes off. We might as well stay awake."

"They'll need the bodies to be able to prosecute me, right?" Killer said.

"We told ya what we know," Mr. Goatee whined. "Please . . ."

"You boys might wanna leave to get ready for work, and just leave this to us," Mr. Thorpe said, herding Ronnie and me out the door and into the chilly morning. "Steve's'll be open soon. We'll get some coffee and doughnuts and have a heart-to-heart talk with these fellas while we have our breakfast." He pushed us the last few inches out the door. We turned to go down to the caboose and looked back briefly to see the tribe of wrestlers closing in on the two mugs.

"They won't really kill 'em, will they?" I asked Ronnie.

"How the hell do I know?"

12

Glow in the Dark

We didn't bother to try to go back to bed, instead put on a pot of coffee and took showers, then grabbed a couple apple turnovers from Steve's. We left around the same time, Ronnie off to patrol the highways and byways of Carbon County, me to help get out the Saturday paper.

Joe was already in the office when I arrived at 5:00. He was banging on his typewriter keys with both of his index fingers while ignoring a cracked cup of 10W40- strength black coffee.

Without looking up: "You wanna write up a piece about the ruckus at your place early this morning?"

Jeez. Nothing in these flyspeck towns escapes the all-seeing eye of Boy Journalist, Joe "Scoop" Boyle.

"No," I said simply. "Nothing happened. At least nothing worth bothering the public with. Just a party."

"Hmmmmmm," Joe said, stopping his fingers in midstrike. "Not what I heard."

I shrugged.

"My spies tell me the party ended around midnight, but the real action got going around three in the a.m."

"Nothing worth reporting," I said. "Ronnie Von Renner and I took care of it."

"Hmmmmmm," Joe said and went back to banging out his story. "Little later you need to go out to the uranium mines and talk to a"—he stopped typing again, rummaged through the messy pile of notes next to his typewriter, and pulled out a frayed piece

135

of notepaper—"Mr. William Schute, the engineer who's going to oversee the sealing up of those old eyesores. He'll be expecting you around 9:00."

"Sure," I said, accepting Joe's slip of paper written in Joe's scrawl—a scrawl that in no way could be interpreted to read "Mr. William Schute."

The uranium mines were three holes cut into the lower shoulder of Mount Pisgah along Route 209. Years ago uranium had been discovered there, but the feds decided it should be preserved as a backup source for the atom/hydrogen bomb program. The three entrances had been "sealed up" by the application of a bunch of boards that looked like a set for a low-budget cowboy movie. Most kids in town had long ago breached the high-security boards, some of us going so far as to attach hinges to one of the boards so we could swing it out of the way when we wanted to enter instead of having to pull nails and then renail it when we left.

Nobody in town knew much about uranium and nobody seemed to care, beyond learning the duck-and-cover routine in case of a nuclear attack. Us kids were fascinated at that time by radium watch hands that glowed in the dark, so we spent a bunch of time in the uranium mines with the (unfulfilled) promise of the ability to glow in the dark. We even thought that when it took hold, we could be second-tier superheroes, maybe get our own comic book. Nobody said kids were smart.

Apparently the newer kids were even more stupid than we were, because the authorities found out that their security had been breached, so now they were going to cinder-block the entrance closed so no goofy kids could break in and get themselves hurt or killed. Sealing up abandoned mines. Very newsworthy. Bet it would make it onto the front page of Monday's paper. That's what passes for news in the Mauch Chunks.

I went to work sorting through wire copy, marking up what we wanted the gals to typeset for this afternoon's paper, then did a bit of editing on some of the stuff we'd produced in-house, then checked the updates on the ad pages so we could let the pressmen know how many pages to expect, and then checked in with Sally

Slotvok to make sure she was nearly finished with the tabloid insert that carried the television listings.

At 8:50 I wished everyone a pleasant weekend and drove up the road to find Mr. William Schute. The mine entrances were on the inside of a curve in the highway, and on the outside of the curve was a two hundred foot drop down to the Jersey Central Railroad tracks, and it was way too tight to pull the car off the side so I parked it at the gas station at the bottom of the Liberties, the tight switchback that came down from the Heights to join Highway 209. I walked the seventy-five yards along the inside of the road to the first mine entrance.

Sitting on a table-sized rock that had fallen off the side of the mountain and ended up next to the mine entrance was a skinny guy with disheveled dirty-blond hair wearing a sand-colored shirt with the sleeves rolled up and a pair of shorts the same color. He kinda looked like he was going on safari, like Marlin Perkins on TV. He wore glasses and had one of those goofy pocket protectors in his shirt pocket—a pocket that was chock-full of pencils and pens.

He stood up when he saw me. I'd already pulled my notebook from my back pocket, so he obviously knew I was the guy he was expecting. We shook hands, both dry, and made introductions. He wore a Lehigh University ring. "I wanted to go to Lehigh, but it was a little too expensive," I said. He seemed confused. "Your ring," I explained. "I worked over the summer with a Lehigh grad student at the Bethlehem Steel's quarry. He had a ring just like that."

"Good school," he said. "Started by Mauch Chunk's own Asa Packer."

I nodded toward the haphazardly boarded-up mine entrance. "We used to play in there when we were kids," I said. "Hoped we'd come out able to glow in the dark . . . like a superhero. Firefly. Something like that."

"Lots of footprints just inside," he said. "Like why bother to waste the boards when they aren't keeping anybody out."

"We never did get that glow-in-the-dark thing down."

"We spent our time in an abandoned, condemned house that we swore was haunted, but all we got out of it was dirty," he said.

"Although one time I did come home with about fifty spiders hanging on my back. I didn't even know they were there. Really freaked out my mom something fierce."

"Firefly meets Spiderman," I said.

He chuckled.

He proceeded to give me a step-by-step outline of how they were going to go about sealing up the mines: make a last sweep to make sure there were no hobos living inside, leave the air vents alone (too small for somebody to crawl through), then use cinder blocks to build a wall within the entrance, and then use concrete over the cinder-block wall to make it look like the side of the mountain. "It won't be perfect," William said, "but we've got some coloration we're going to mix in with the concrete to get as close to the color of the nearby rock as to make it nearly indistinguishable."

I had been taking all of that down in my own version of shorthand. "When is all of this gonna happen?" I asked.

"Wednesday morning. We'll close the road down to one lane so we have space for the flatbed trucks and the cement mixers. Probably have it done in one day. We have three separate crews, so it should get finished up pretty fast."

"SPCA hain't gonna come after you to make sure there's no rats or mice trapped in there," I said, smiling.

"They're welcome to take the walk-through first thing Wednesday morning," he said, "although the air shafts are big enough to allow rats and mice access, both in and out."

I nodded.

"Let's take a last look inside, just for old times' sake," I said.

He nodded and walked to the boarded-up entrance, where he pulled one of the boards out toward us. It was hinged on the inside and swung out easily, allowing us enough space to squirm through. "You involved in this engineering spectacular?" he asked.

"Yeah. We stole the hinges from shop class."

Naturally, as soon as we got inside, the temperature dropped. The inside of mines say pretty constant in the fifties, which is why so many wineries dig their cellars into the sides of mountains. Perfect natural air conditioning. Of course, if you dig down far enough, the temperatures start to increase.

There had never been bats in these mines, and there weren't any flying out at us in waves now. There was a cool breeze coming from inside, where the air let in from the vents farther back into the mine kept the air fresh.

William had been correct. There were numerous footprints in the soft dirt and some in the mud formed where the mine seeped water. Many of the prints appeared to be recent.

He played his flashlight along the walls. The tunnel was as wide as a lane-and-a-half road and the ceiling was eight feet high. There were no rails. If the mine were going to be run, it would probably have been serviced by trucks. On the right wall water seeped down, tinkling a drop at a time into a little puddle. At some points there was still shoring holding up the ceiling, while at other segments the shoring—along with some of the ceiling—had fallen. Not good to be in a mine when that happened.

The tunnel continued back another fifty yards, but where we stood, about seventy-five yards in from the entrance, another tunnel went off to the left at a ninety-degree angle.

"Whew," William said, as we turned toward the left. "What's that?" He sniffed the air. It took me a few seconds longer to catch the scent being blown toward us by the airshaft. It was the sweet, nauseating smell of something rotting.

"Smells like something crawled in here to die," I said. "We had a dog that did that. Knew he was going to die and crawled under a pile of rocks up the mountainside where we played so he'd die in a familiar place."

We advanced on the smell coming from the side tunnel, and each step the odor became more pronounced. William played his flashlight well ahead of us, running it back and forth. It passed over something on the floor ahead, and William brought it back to center on whatever it was.

Even from this distance, it was obvious that it was a body—a body lying on its back, its feet pointed in our direction. I involuntarily wrapped the crook of my left arm over my nose in an attempt to hold off the smell.

William went down to his knees beside me, retching. He extended the flashlight to me and I took it, moving forward slowly.

Between the smells from the body mixed with the smell of William's vomit, I fought to control my own guts.

I held my breath and moved forward, walking the flashlight's beam over what was obviously a woman's body, a body bloated from internal fermentation, the skin darkened and expanded like a gas-filled balloon, like a fat woman attempting to make a too-small granny dress fit. The fat feet threatened to tear apart the cheap sandals she wore.

Her head was bent at a radical angle as though she was attempting to rest the side of her head in her armpit. Just beyond her head was a Ball canning jar with the remains of a white candle standing inside. A filigree of nearly phosphorescent mold covered the lower half of her body.

I fought to hold onto the breath, as though I was diving far underwater, afraid to open my mouth and nose to take a new, vile breath of death air. I fought down a belch and tasted sour apples in the back of my mouth.

I played the light over the woman's balloon face and was virtually certain it was Elizabeth Delaney. Still jealously clutching the lungful of air, I knelt down next to her, and put my fingers between her lips and parted them. They offered no resistance and felt like two small water balloons. Her left front tooth was chipped, exactly like Elizabeth Delaney's in the picnic photograph.

I felt a bubble rising inside me, something that was desperately trying to overwhelm the reporter's objectivity that I'd been able to marshal, something that was making me as sick in the stomach as in the soul.

I'd seen dead people before; it was part of the job. I'd seen some utterly grotesque bodies mangled and broken in traffic accidents, several—like this—left to decompose, but they'd never been anyone I personally knew. My mouth had gone dry and the queasiness began spreading.

I turned back to William and helped him to his feet. "We don't want to disturb any evidence," I hissed to him as I let the tired air leak from my mouth. I led him away; he didn't offer any resistance.

Once we turned the corner into the main shaft, we both stopped and took deep lungfuls of air. William ran his forearm across his mouth, trying to clean it. "Oh, god," he said. "Horrible."

"Never quite get used to it," I said lamely, putting my arm around his shoulders and leading him toward the light.

* * *

The rest of the day ran together and went on forever.

I asked William to stay at the entrance of the mine, out in the fresh air, to keep people away from the mine, and then ran down and got into my car and drove directly to the Mauch Chunk Police Department, where I was met by an officer I didn't recognize. I told him we'd found a dead body, likely Elizabeth Delaney, in the #1 shaft of the old uranium mines.

He looked, at first, like he didn't believe me. "Get the chief up there as soon as possible and get some of your men to guard the scene," I said as I jogged out and across the street and from there to the newspaper office.

Joe was still there. I took him aside and told him what we'd found, and he pulled me out the door and toward his car. "Call the State Police and have them get to the uranium mines," he called to Gertrude Apfelbaum as we left. "Tell 'em to make it quick!"

He put his arm across my chest, as though to hold me back. "You're too close to this. I'll take it over from here." I expected that I'd put up some resistance to that idea, but I knew he was right. Besides, there was something I had to do.

I nodded. "I'll come up a little later," I said.

"I'll need to interview you at some point," he said, and was off.

I went back into the office and sat down on my swivel chair, pulled open the bottom drawer of the desk, removed the fat envelope filled with one-, five-, and ten-dollar bills, and set it on the blotter. Mrs. Apfelbaum was finishing up with the State Police dispatcher. "The uranium mines, up on 209, by the Liberties," she said, nodding at me to get my confirmation. I nodded back.

She hung up and took a long look at me. "You look terrible, like you've been frightened to death."

I took a deep swallow but couldn't get it down. My throat was still dry as broken glass. "We found Elizabeth," I mumbled, my hand waving in front of my face as though it was weightless. "She's dead . . . dead for a while, in the mine." I felt tears start to form and ran my forearm over them.

Mrs. Apfelbaum made as though to reach out her hand to me, but her arm wasn't long enough. "How terrible," she said. "How terribly tragic." She shook her head and her jowls quivered. She pulled back the arm she'd tried to reach over the desks and put her face in her hands. "Her poor mother's going to be devastated," she said through her cupped hands.

I got up, picked up the fat envelope, and on the way out patted Mrs. Apfelbaum on the back. "What's this world coming to?" she asked.

"I'm sure I don't know," I said. "I've got to do something, but I'll be around later in case Joe has any questions I can answer."

"I'm sure he will," Mrs. Apfelbaum said. "After all, you're a key witness."

"Or something—" I said as I walked out the door and down Race Street to Susquehanna, where I took a left turn toward the courthouse and the steps beyond it leading up to the Asa Packer Mansion. There was still some sun shining down on ole Mauch Chunk, but there were also some high, dark clouds moving in quickly from the west like a squadron of enemy dirigibles. *Looks like rain*, I said to myself. Ya think so?

I ignored the traffic light and walked across Broadway, lost in my thoughts, and nearly lost it all to the temporal world as a beat-up '49 Buick slammed on the brakes and got on the horn. "Moron!" he yelled.

"You got that right," I said.

He didn't know what to say to that so he just sat there idling as I made it across the street.

Each of the steep steps leading up to Packer Hill seemed like an obstacle course taken on by leaden legs.

I made my way to the side lawn where Grace Delaney made a habit of enjoying lunch with some lovely baked goods and spiked iced tea, where she lived a lively life in a world that no longer existed.

Indeed, the cakes and the sweating pitcher of iced tea sat there, waiting. I sat down, placed the envelope at the edge of the table, and poured myself a generous glass of iced tea.

There was no banging of hammer on metal from the air-conditioning guys from Hazleton perched on scaffolding against the courthouse. Word was that *The Molly Maguires* people would begin shooting the climactic courthouse scenes Tuesday or Wednesday of next week. I was scheduled to report on all of it for the paper.

I sipped the iced tea, put a packet of fake sugar into it, sipped it again, eyed one of the cakes, some *fou-fou* fancy things designed primarily for women—sensitive women who need not watch their weight.

In a few minutes Grace Delaney came out onto the porch and began her descent of the steps that fronted the mansion, and from there down to the little patch of garden.

I stood up to greet her.

"Why, how nice," she said. "I didn't have a date for lunch and now I do." She sat in the same chair she'd used the other time I did this. I turned my chair to face her.

"You have some news?" she asked. "Or is this flagrantly social?"

I gently pushed the envelope across the table. Her right eyebrow went up. "I won't need this," I said.

Her right eyebrow stayed up. She looked rather fetching for a woman my mother's age. Today she wore a white, long-sleeve frilly blouse with a silver cross at the end of a shiny necklace. Her skirt was black and went to her ankles and at the ankles featured a spider web of lace. And again she wore low boots that looked as though they'd been made from expensive wallpaper. She had begun to reach for a glass into which she could pour herself some iced tea. She stopped. "You've found her," she said, and smiled. "I knew I could count on you. I just knew it." She slapped her palms together and then held her hands together as though in prayer or delight.

I couldn't help bowing my head and that was a dead giveaway.

Her right palm went to her mouth. "Oh no—" she said.

I nodded, feeling sweaty and dirty.

"She's . . . a . . . in the first uranium mine, up past the Liberties. The police are there." I wanted to move closer to her, to try to comfort her, but I didn't know how, had never been shown how, so I couldn't. I wanted to turn the chair back under the table and begin banging my head against the tabletop.

"And she's—"

"—dead," I filled in.

"And you're certain . . ."

I thought back to the bloated off-purple thing that was festering inside the tunnel, looking like a giant blood-filled tick, no relation to a young girl smiling her cute chipped-tooth smile in the middle of a picnic. I once knew Elizabeth Delaney, when we were kids, and that wasn't her.

I nodded that I was certain.

Miss Delaney put both hands into her lap and raised her chin. Trying to be brave and tough, I figured. "And how did she die? An overdose?"

I shook my head. "It's not important how she died," I said.

"Oh, but it is. It certainly is," Miss Delaney said, firmly. "It most certainly is."

I didn't want to talk about it anymore. I just wanted to take a huge swig of ginned iced tea . . . and maybe take a long nap.

"How?" she insisted.

"Broken neck," I supplied. "Ten days, two weeks ago—"

Miss Delaney shook her head. Closed her eyes for several long moments. A dollop of mucus slid out of her right nostril and paused on her upper lip. She didn't bother to wipe it away. An eighteen-wheeler lumbered through the dogleg between the railroad station and the courthouse.

She opened her eyes and stared at me. She blinked away tears. Above us, on the upper end of the lawn, I could hear the mechanical snipping of blades of grass under Mr. Thorpe's push-mower.

Miss Delaney pushed the envelope of cash across the table. "Find out who did that to her," she said simply, got up, and laboriously, as though she was carrying a great weight, made her way up the stairs.

I patted the envelope and then took another long swallow of the iced tea. I sat for a long moment, then got up and jogged up to the carriage house, tossed the envelope on my bed, ignored the mess from the night before, splashed some water on my face, then jogged up Packer Hill, into the Heights, then down the Liberties and toward the uranium mine.

When I arrived, the State Police had the highway down to one lane. Ronnie was directing traffic going west, another statie doing the same thing at the far edge of the curve. Joe Boyle's car was pulled up against the side of the mountain, just in front of the black coroner's van. Beyond it, an unmarked State Police cruiser sat with its red-and-blues flashing.

I walked up to Ronnie, who was good enough at what he was doing that he could talk into his walkie-talkie to the other statie, direct traffic, and talk to me at the same time. I stood next to him so as not to block oncoming traffic's view of his hand signals.

"For an amateur, you're pretty fuckin' good," he said.

"Whaddya mean?"

"You went lookin' for her, and in no time at all you found her."

"It was all coincidence."

He snorted. "Being good at anything involves some degree of luck. Your luck at the moment is like syrup on hotcakes." I assumed immediately that he hadn't yet had breakfast.

Now I snorted. "Where are Mauch Chunk's boys in blue?"

"They—wisely, I think—don't want nothin' to do with this."

A little wind squall came down 209 and blew a thin wall of grit in front of it. I blinked; Ronnie didn't.

"You been in there?" I asked.

Ronnie shook his head, directed the next line of waiting cars through. "Nope. Not sure I wanna see her."

I nodded, although being beside him and not in front of him, there was no way he could see it. "Not very pretty. Doesn't even look like a human being. Definitely doesn't look like Elizabeth."

"This is gonna kill her mother," Ronnie said. "Her father, I don't know. I don't know what he cares much about these days."

"Except pigs," I added.

"Yeah. You'll have to explain that to me at some point." He looked over his shoulder. "You're about to be questioned about your part in all this." He gave the next car the signal to wait. "Want you to meet Inspector T. James Farrell," he said, indicating the crewcut guy wearing a Brooks Brothers suit who walked up to us from behind.

Inspector Farrell did a double take at my face—a reaction I'd absorbed a million times—and introduced himself, formally, coldly, like he'd just eaten a garlic dill pickle, pushing a business card into my free hand. Behind his back, Ronnie turned and winked at me.

"You found the body," Inspector Farrell said.

"William Schute was with me."

"We already spoke," he said, motioning me to follow him away from the traffic and toward the side of the mountain.

"He was pretty shook up," I said, thereby ignoring the first commandment of a police interview: answer only what is asked and as briefly as possible; add nothing.

"But you weren't."

"Of course I was," I said.

"But he was more shook up." Although Inspector Farrell had a notebook in his hand, he didn't bother to write anything in it.

"Yes." I decided to come to my senses and just answer the damned question.

"And you were looking for her."

"Yes."

"On whose behalf?"

"Her aunt's, her mother's."

"But not her father's?"

I shook my head.

"You know her father?"

"Slightly."

"And you have an opinion about him?"

"Yes, I guess I do."

"And what is that opinion?"

"He doesn't like me. I don't like to be not liked."

"And how do you know that?"

146

"When I was ten, he told me to stay away from his kids."

Inspector Farrell's right eyebrow went up. "Because—?"

"Because I wasn't the proper caste to be interacting with his children."

"Because you were poor and he wasn't."

"Something like that," I said, then couldn't help adding, "but my grandmother's probably the richest person in either town," figuring he probably already knew about that and if I didn't clarify it, he would be suspicious about why I hadn't. This finding a dead body was getting way too complicated.

"But to Mr. Delaney, your grandmother didn't count."

"If you mean she didn't shower money on us, so we weren't well off, and I think he had some dealings—legal stuff—with her that did not end well for him."

"So he didn't care for you—"

"That's my distinct impression, although the other distinct impression I had is that he didn't much care for most people." There I went again, shooting off my mouth. Stop.

"But you wouldn't have held a grudge against his family after all that time—"

"A grudge?"

"A grudge. That you'd want to get back at him by hurting members of his family."

"What?"

"That you might in any way be involved in this . . . this death."

"It was a murder," I said.

"You don't know that."

"She didn't break her own neck."

"There is no official cause of death at this time."

"There is to me. And from the looks of Elizabeth's body, this happened ten days to two weeks ago, and in case it's important to the case you're trying to build, I have an alibi for that time period. I was taking final exams and graduating from college."

"And people will swear to that—"

"Yeah. Even Vincent Price. I got to interview him after he spoke at our commencement."

"No one has accused you of anything."

"It sounds like you're trying very hard to do just that."

"Quite the contrary. I am merely trying to explore all leads."

"Well, here's a headline for you: I DID NOT KILL ELIZABETH."

"You knew her well, then," he said.

"I what?"

"You just referred to her, for the second time, by her first name only."

"I knew her—slightly—when I was a kid." I found myself shaking my head. "Hell, in a town this size, almost every kid knows every other kid, unless a kid's mother locks her in the closet."

"So you contend that Mrs. Delaney locked her daughter in a closet."

I felt like running my hand down the front of my face in frustration, the way the Three Stooges used to do. "I contend nothing of the sort." Another wind squall came down the road and stirred up more dust, but this time a wall of huge raindrops followed it. My back was to the oncoming storm. Inspector Farrell was facing it. He took a handful of meaty raindrops directly in the face and a basket more made his suit jacket look like it was sporting polka dots. His interest in questioning me further suddenly seemed to vanish.

"I expect you to be available for additional questioning, and you are to mention to no one the fact that there was a candle at the head of the victim. We keep certain information under our hats," he said as he hurried off.

"I hain't going anywhere, unless the draft gets me, and I hain't sayin' nothin' to nobody about no candle," I shouted after him. He did not look back. I wondered if he was related to the Wicked Witch of the North—that he might melt right in front of us if he got hit with enough water.

I sidled over to Ronnie, who was doing his duties almost unconsciously. "You enjoy talking to Farrell?" he asked.

"He think everybody's guilty?" I asked.

"That's the premise he uses to start every investigation—that everybody is guilty, if not for the crime of the day, then for something."

"Maybe somebody should begin questioning him."

Ronnie smiled. "Could be interesting—"

"Would I go to jail if the next time he questions me I begin to question him right back? Can you pull a file on him that I can borrow so I can get together some lines of questioning that will make him very, very uneasy?"

Ronnie smiled again. Then shrugged. "I know a couple a lovely ladies in personnel."

I was about to say something else, some wiseass thing, but at that moment the coroner and his assistant wheeled the gurney out of the mine with Elizabeth's body encased in a dark-green plastic zip bag. The cars passing by on the outside lane slowed their speed so they could gawk. They didn't even know what they were gawking at because news of Elizabeth's body being found had not yet hit the news. They just gawked to gawk. Behind me I heard Ronnie raising his voice. "Move it! Let's keep it moving! Move along!"

I walked over to the coroner's van, not to gawk but because that was where Joe Boyle was standing, taking notes furiously. The raindrops were now smaller, and there were a lot more of them, and they were being pushed in front of a rising wind. Joe's sports jacket flapped around him, and the edges of his notebook flapped like a white bird. Without looking up, he said, "Let's go back to the office. I have a couple of questions for you."

I followed him back to his car, and we drove off. As usual, it was filled with trash: used coffee cups, deli sandwich wrappers, rifled-through notebooks with his distinct antipenmanship.

He parked in his usual spot on Susquehanna Street, the one the cops kept open for him, and turned off the motor, but he didn't make a move to exit. He suddenly had his notebook back in his hand, ready to take notes. "We can do it here," he said, a gray expression mottling his face.

"What's wrong?" I asked.

"This'll sound heartless," he said, "but we're gonna get beaten to the punch on one of the biggest stories around here in years."

I saw what he meant. The *Times-News* for Saturday was already plopping on customers' front porches. We wouldn't have another edition until Monday afternoon— which meant that the *Morning*

Call, which had a Sunday edition, would have Elizabeth Delaney's murder all over the front page tomorrow morning.

"It's not exactly heartless," I said. "I understand the frustration. We were first on the scene, but we'll be the last to make hay with it."

"We even have an inside line to it," he said. "You."

"Well, maybe we won't be the first with the news, but we can make up for it by doing a more thorough job."

"We should have you write up your experience as a sidebar," he said. "Yeah, we should do that." He made a note to himself.

"How long?" I asked.

"As long as it takes to tell what you know. But just the facts. Just re-create this morning."

"I can do that," I said, realizing it would be no major-league chore. "I'll try to get it out later today."

"Okay," Joe said. "Now tell me all you know, but just the facts. Keep the cheesy descriptions for your own story. But don't get into how you were looking for her. That's not part of the story of how you found her."

So I told him what I knew, which wasn't much. William Schute and I walked into the mine, smelled something awful, and went to find out what it was and we found a body—a body that I thought had a good chance of being Elizabeth Delaney. I did not tell him about forcing open her lips to check for the chipped tooth.

When I was finished, I asked him what I should do when somebody from the *Morning Call* got in touch with me, as they certainly would. "Just give them the facts, just like you did for me. We've gotta cooperate." Then he paged backward in his notebook. "Did you get the first name of the inspector who questioned you?"

"James," I said.

"Great. That's all." He began to open his door. "You'll be home all weekend?" The rain had caught up to us and was peppering the back window of Joe's car. "In case I have any more questions."

"Sure," I said.

He closed his door and fired up the car. "You shouldn't walk home in this rain. I'll drop you off," he said, did a U-turn, and drove me to my driveway in front of the carriage house. He reached across the seat and shook my hand. "Quite a week," he said. "You had quite a week for your first week on the job."

I realized that I'd completely forgotten that Robert Kennedy had been killed just a few days ago.

I sprinted for the front door as Joe backed his car out onto Packer Hill. The rain was coming down with a vengeance, the wind whipping it along, the mountainside that was the Heights the only thing protecting the carriage house and the mansions from the full force of the storm as it roared in from the west.

Inside, Mr. Thorpe was at work trying to straighten the place up. He had shopping bags filled with empty beer bottles and a three-foot stack of empty pizza boxes just inside and to the right of the front door. If we had a fireplace, we would have been able to feed it on pizza boxes for several hours.

I fell into his slow, unstoppable pace, as the rain and wind roared around outside. The carriage house was built like a fort and didn't even notice the storm.

"Did the boys get away safely?" I asked.

He laughed. "They left in a big rush, like air out of a tire."

"Did they take the two assassins with them?"

"Oh, yes."

"Will they really drop them down a mine shaft?" Of course I knew they wouldn't, but what the hell . . . He laughed again, waving a pair of white boxer shorts before depositing them in the garbage can. "They'll have some fun with them, scare them a bit, but I'm sure they wont be coming back this way for a long time. Put a bad taste in their mouths for visiting Mauch Chunk."

He hummed to himself as he worked, but I couldn't make out what the tune was. We fell into a rhythm as the rain beat its own rhythm on the roof.

Within an hour we were finished. Mr. Thorpe plopped down into his big chair with a copy of *Moby Dick* sitting next to him. I'd snuck a peek at it the day before, curious as to what he'd been reading so intently. "You like that?" I asked, nodding toward the book.

"I've always been passionate about hunting and fishing," he said.

I sat at the table quietly for a few minutes, shuffling papers around, until the picnic photo of Elizabeth Delaney worked its way to the top. I ran my fingers down the right side of the photo, my eyes frozen on the chipped tooth. Wondering how the swollen bundle in the mine could have at one point in time been this girl. To make the connection between the two was something that my mind—was it my mind?—was reluctant to do, as though to meld the two would be to confirm that, Yes, it was her, and yes, she was very much, very horribly dead . . . and expanded and diminished at the same time.

Tears welled up and rolled down my cheeks, but I didn't make a sound. Mr. Thorpe sat in his chair looking out the window, trying to not embarrass me by seeing the tears.

Outside, it continued to rain . . . and rain . . . and rain.

13

The Profound Effects of Rain

I brought the Royal portable typewriter out to the kitchen table after asking Mr. Thorpe if the banging of the keys would bother him. He waved the question away, his face still stuck in the challenge of pursuing the white whale.

I'd never been one to be struck down by writer's block, but for the longest time I sat looking at the blank white page in front of me, then looking out the window at the slashing rain, now coming down in sheets as though sliding across the landscape on a giant clothesline or yardarm. It was so thick I couldn't see the clock tower on the courthouse.

Look at the paper, look at the rain, glance at the photo of Elizabeth Delaney at the summer picnic, smiling, her chipped front tooth making her look way more innocent than she turned out to be. I couldn't stop looking at the chipped tooth. A victim of sidewalk surfing. Eventually a victim of her own self-indulgences. What pain could have driven her to want to escape life? Her pigheaded and pig-loving old man? Her wimpy mother? Losing her religion? Never having it to start with? Helped along by her privileged girl-friends at St. Elizabeth's? Lured to the weed and beyond by some-one in town? A boyfriend? A pusher looking for more customers?

I needed a headline for my sidebar about how I'd found Elizabeth. "You just referred to her by her first name only." Again. Yes. As though I did know her. But that was only slightly.

"The Subterranean."

No. Too Greenwich Village.

"The Smell of Death."

No. Too Edgar Allan Poe.

"Dead in the Dark."

No. Too Arkham House, too H. P. Lovecraft."

"Found in a Mine."

Too Tom Sawyer.

"Found, by Chance."

Too cute.

"Found."

Found. Period. Simple.

Since this was to be a sidebar and not straight news, I had a great deal of latitude and I could be a little more creative on it, but not to any extent that would have Joe Boyle reining me in.

My visit to the abandoned Uranium Mine #1 along Route 209 west of town was scheduled as a last chance to examine the mine before its scheduled Wednesday sealing up. Engineer William Schute, after explaining how the mine entrance would be sealed in two stages—cinder block, then concrete—led us into the bowels of the long-abandoned mine that has traditionally been an off-limits but much-explored playground for generations of young Chunkers.

Now with a head of steam, I rolled along, and in fifteen minutes more it was finished. I had no sooner banged in the last period than the phone rang. As Joe and I had anticipated, it was a reporter from the *Morning Call*, a Harold Monk from the Allentown office, not someone from the satellite office in Lehighton.

We spoke for a few minutes, and what I ended up telling him was pretty much what I'd just written for the sidebar. Without getting into my search for her, there wasn't much to relate. Went to the mine, smelled something horrible, found her body. The reporter had already spoken with William Schute, so what I told him ran pretty much parallel with what William told him. "Anything else you'd like to add?" the reporter asked.

"Nothing but the obvious," I said. "It's a real tragedy, and we all hope that the killer is found quickly."

"The State Police have not yet classified it as a homicide," Harold Monk said.

"Perhaps they have a way of ignoring the obvious," I said.

Harold Monk briefly laughed the laugh of the hardened journalist. "Sometimes takes a while for the obvious to become obvious," he said and signed off.

The gray day was going to put me in a gray mood—grayer than it already was—if I sat around like this. I felt like taking a nap but instead pulled on a jacket and hauled out my umbrella, said goodbye to Mr. Thorpe, and walked up Broadway to the jail to see my kid brother, well-known criminal mastermind. The walk up Broadway was an experience. I should have worn boots. Water was running down the middle of the street, and at several sewer drains, water was coming up out of them instead of going down them like it should. Very expensive Hollywood dirt—now mud—was being swept into the river.

Broadway in Mauch Chunk was like the neck of a funnel, the wide part of it miles above town in the area marked by farms and framed by mountains on both sides so that rain water flowed down off both mountainsides and came down the middle of the valley along Mauch Chunk Creek, picking up speed and force as the creek reached town.

Halfway up Broadway the creek went underground, running under the street, on its now-rapid way to the Lehigh River.

In some sections of Broadway and also on the lower side of Race Street, folks who lived there had trapdoors to the creek. In a fit of incredible stupidity and laziness, some of those people used the trapdoor as a garbage basket, dropping any waste they had down into the creek where, when it rose, it carried the effluvia down to the river. Unfortunately, some of the morons went so far as to drop mattresses and box springs through the trapdoor, which had the potential to make a mess, because something big was liable to get stuck, hung up, forming a dam, backing up the flow of the creek until it came back up above ground.

The current storm, only a few hours old, was already hitting some obstacles against its efficient rush to the river. I should have worn boots. But I had already chastised myself for that.

I stood outside the jail, watching the water run down the street. Inside, the rain was making a racket as it poured down on the courtyard, where the *Molly Maguire* crew had erected a gallows for the upcoming filming of the Mollies being hanged in the very same courtyard where it had really happened in 1878.

The rain hissed down out of the gray sky into the gray courtyard. The gallows were wooden and designed to dispatch more than one Molly at a time. The nooses had already been laced their thirteen turns and strung. All that was needed now were the convicted, the executioner, and the witnesses. The current weather would set the right tone for the hangings.

It was like the setting of a hanging in a cowboy book kids would love.

I couldn't help smiling to myself about how dopey kids are. Joe Boyle and Nate Dermott were spending their spare time putting together a special souvenir edition of the newspaper celebrating the Molly Maguires. They were doing it in conjunction with the Mauch Chunk Tourist Promotion Agency. Most of it consisted of a photocopy of the editions of the *Mauch Chunk Democrat* from June of 1878 that pertained to the trial and execution of the Mollies. But before the formal hanging of the Mollies, there was nearly another hanging:

CHARLEY BOOTH AND PETE McGEADY PLAYING MOLLY MAGUIRE HANGING.

While everyone around here was talking about executions, Molly Maguires, Courts of Justice, etc., is it not to be wondered at that two such bright little fellows as Charley Booth and Pete McGeady should conclude to engage in a game of Molly Maguires? With this determination they last Saturday betook themselves to "Prospect Rock" where Pete was to play Molly and Charley act the part of Judge, hangman, etc. Whether they went through a regular course or not has not transpired, but that Pete had been sentenced by his bosom friend to "suffer the extreme penalty of the law" is certain. A piece of wash-line was procured, tied around Pete's neck, and Charley led him off the stone he was standing on. His critical position was attested to by the terrible cries uttered by the juvenile judge and hangman when he found Pete struggling for life and himself unable to relieve him. Happily another youngster, somewhat taller than either, was near at hand and it was only to his resolution and exertions that Pete's life was spared. A few minutes longer and Pete McGeady would have been a dead Molly indeed, and Mauch Chunk have lost what promises, in the course of time, to be one of its brightest luminaries.

Sounds exactly like some stupid stunt my kid brother Rudy would have gotten himself involved in.

I waved at Mrs. Neast and walked across the courtyard to the cells. The door to Rudy's cell was once again open, and Rudy was once again sprawled on his bunk reading the *Panther Valley Pugilist*.

"Is that the only thing you read these days?" I asked as I walked in and sat down on the wooden chair. Rudy looked over the top of the tabloid, surprised to see a visitor on such a lousy day.

"I'm rereading it," he said. "Be nice if you worked at a real newspaper instead of the *Times-News*. This paper's got punch, it takes a stand, it puts up with nothing." He dropped the paper onto his bunk, and I noticed it was not the same one he had been reading during my last visit. I thought about extending my hand to shake his, but it had been awkward last time, so I didn't bother.

Rudy was smiling as though everything was swell with the world. Kind of inappropriate to the current situation—spending a damp, rainy day in a damp jail cell that was a century old. "Somebody smuggling you drugs?" I asked him.

"I wish," he said.

"Null-A lives just up the street. You could probably get him to drop some good stuff by for you."

He smiled, one of those smiles that say that I know a whole lot more than you think I know. "So you saw him," Rudy said.

"Yeah," I said. "He wasn't anything like I expected."

"He's a real chameleon. One day this, another day that."

"He was in his stockbroker mode when I saw him."

"So'd he help you out with some leads on Elizabeth?"

I shook my head. "Not much. Not that it matters much anymore."

Rudy was obviously confused. "What da'ya mean?"

"Elizabeth Delaney is dead, murdered."

Rudy looked stunned. "How do you know that?"

"Because I found her. In the Uranium Mine #1, complete with a broken neck. She'd been there a while."

Rudy looked around, like the cell was suddenly way too big for his liking, that he wanted a little corner into which he could crawl.

"Dead," he said. "Killed."

At least he was buying the killed more readily than the State Police were.

"And you found her," he said, as though shuffling a handful of simple ideas around in his head, attempting to put them into some logical order. "That was fast. You were fast . . ."

"It was a coincidence."

He shook his head. "There are no such things as coincidences. If there were, there are too many things that would be coincidental to be coincidental."

"You sure somebody isn't slipping you drugs?" I said before I could stop myself.

Rudy merely smiled. "Don't always need drugs." Then his smile faded. "Elizabeth dead." His gaze wandered again. "We did it—a couple of times. She liked to talk dirty while she was doing it. She liked to talk—a lot." Something, an idea, crossed behind his eyes. "Maybe that's why somebody killed her. She liked to talk a lot, always needed something to talk about."

Rudy's reasoning on that made sense. Loose lips sink ships. That's what the posters in World War II read. We had one of them nailed to the wall in our cellar, next to the furnace. "Loose lips sink ships."

Rudy pointed his finger at me. "There you go."

Something else began moving around behind his eyes. "It's probably nothing, but the couple of times we did it in the daytime, she had bruises—on her sides, under her arms, on her ass."

"And she said she fell down a lot."

Rudy shook his head. "No. From playing sports. Softball, stuff like that."

"I didn't know she played sports."

"I didn't either, but at the time it didn't much matter to me 'cause I was getting screwed." He shrugged. "I can only do one thing at a time, you know."

Neither of us said another word for a good two minutes. Without our voices bouncing around the close walls of the cell, I could hear the pounding of the rain on the roof and against the dirt in the courtyard. Every few seconds a *whooshing* sound ran through the old building, like banshees playing tag.

"Storm's getting worse," I said.

"It'll be okay," Rudy said.

"What will?"

"Everything. Mauch Chunk, the people who live here."

"You haven't seen what it's like out on Broadway," I said.

"It'll be fine."

"You're full of shit. I just walked up here, and Broadway is filling with water, like a walled-in river. Water's coming up out of the sewer drains instead of going down them."

"Buster says it'll be fine."

"Buster? Who's Buster?"

"Buster Sward," Rudy said, reaching over and picking up his copy of the *Panther Valley Pugilist*, rifling through it, finding what he was looking for, and folding the paper upon itself, pushing the preferred page toward me. It was page 4, the editorial and opinion page. The lead editorial was pretty simple—and pretty absurd: Mauch Chunk Does NOT Need the Mauch Chunk Creek Watershed. I scanned the lead. Buster Sward, editor-in-chief, one-third of the Carbon County Commissioners, was responding to a speech the previous week by Mrs. Agnes McCartney, executive director of the Carbon County Tourist Agency, who continued to push the building of the dam above Mauch Chunk.

"This fallacy-spouting harridan, this McCartney woman, obviously has an agenda—an agenda that does not have the needs of the residents and taxpayers of Carbon County at its center. The Mauch Chunk Creek Watershed or Dam or Lake or whatever she wants to name it—maybe even McCartney Dam—is not needed, is not worth the enormous amount of taxpayer funds it will require. In a sentence, Mauch Chunk Does NOT Need the Mauch Chunk Creek Watershed."

I raised my eyebrows. "What?" said Rudy.

"Lots of hyperbole, no facts," I said.

"What da'ya mean?"

"He's off on a rant but doesn't present any facts to bolster his argument. Not one fact. Not one citation of how the center of Mauch Chunk, Broadway, has not flooded in the last century. Because, of course, that'd be bullshit. It floods on a regular basis."

"Not enough to make it worth building a dam that'll cost millions and millions of our dollars—"

"Your dollars? You're sitting here letting those same taxpayers foot the bill to pay to feed and house you."

For a moment he was at a loss.

"I work when I can," he said, lamely. "Nobody gets hurt when Broadway floods, just a few damp basements."

"That's easy for you to say, sitting up here some feet above the coming flood."

"Ninety-nine percent of the people in Mauch Chunk don't get affected when Broadway floods," he said. "And those that do can move."

That didn't leave much room for maneuvering. Our obvious impasse seemed like a good place to make my exit. "Anything I can bring you next time I come by—other than drugs?"

"Naw," he said. "They take pretty good care of me."

A thought occurred to me. "Mind if I take that with me?" I said, pointing at his copy of the *Pugilist*.

"Naw. Maybe if you read it thoroughly and with an open mind some of what Buster Sward says will get through to you and you'll see the light." He gave me a condescending smile.

I gave him one back. "Yeah, I'm almost certain of that."

I got up and didn't bother to offer to shake his hand. I shoved the folded-up newspaper down the front of my pants and closed my jacket over it. I walked through the courtyard where, if it was possible, the rain was coming down even harder than before, waved again to Mrs. Neast, retrieved my umbrella, which I'd parked just inside the huge front door, and headed out into the maelstrom.

The wind still blew, but harder. The rain came down, but thicker. The level of the water running down the middle of Broadway had risen at least an inch and was working its way to the top of the curbs. In fact, looking down the street, I saw that at places where the street curved, the water was already rushing over the curb onto the sidewalk, bringing with it a wave of dirt and small gravel.

I briskly made my way down the street, and the farther I went, the worse it got. A few cars slowly picked their way down the street. Usually, Broadway was a bumper-to-bumper parking lot on both sides of the street. Now there were numerous holes; apparently some car owners who'd been through this before were taking their cars to higher ground.

I should have worn boots. My shoes were thoroughly soaked. When I reached the carriage house, I took them off before going inside and then set them on the small pile of newspapers just inside the door. Mr. Thorpe was still sitting in his chair, still reading *Moby Dick*. He waved and told me that Joe Boyle had called, wanted me to call him back, at home.

Joe lived on Fifth Street on the East Side. Probably wanted to get his news team set up to cover the coming flood. Or maybe he had a few more questions about my finding Elizabeth Delaney's body. "Miss Delaney also called. Says Mrs. Delaney is distraught. No need to call back. She'll be hard to reach for the rest of the day," Mr. Thorpe said. "She seemed real calm," he added.

I sat down at the table and dialed Joe Boyle. He must have been sitting next to his phone because he picked it up immediately.

"Nice storm," he said. "How's Broadway?"

"Going underwater rapidly."

"We'll have to execute our usual coverage," he said. That reminded me. I pulled the folded copy of the *Pugilist* out of my waistband and put it on the table. "But that's not why I called." Pause. "I talked to a friend of mine who works at the courthouse. He says Lawyer Delaney is very, very deeply in debt. Very deeply. Deep like a mine shaft." He was quiet for a moment. "Just thought you ought to know."

"I didn't realize the courthouse was open over the weekend," I said.

Joe laughed. "It's not. You just have to know the right people—especially the people who can literally memorize every file in their office."

"So Lawyer Delaney's fiscal distress could motivate him to do all sorts of things to get his head above water," I said, sounding very professional. At that moment the wind blew a sheet of rain against the window. Talk about Hollywood timing.

"Yeah, sure," Joe said. "He'd do just about anything to save his ass. Even going so far as to raise pigs in his backyard. Which, by the way, he is."

About that I wasn't completely surprised. My little phone conversation with Mrs. Delaney sort of hinted that the pigs he wanted to raise were already there or were on the way. "How's that going to go over with the borough council? That'll really piss 'em off."

"I suspect that some of them already know, but they aren't going to chance being the object of Delaney's ire until a regular citizen files a complaint, which I assume will be whenever the wind changes and the stink heads in their direction."

"But now they're not likely to raise the subject until after he buries his daughter."

"And nobody's quite sure when that'll be. The staties still have the body." I could hear him say something to someone else in the room, but I couldn't make out what he said. "The staties will be in touch with you and the engineer on Monday so they can get shoe prints from the both of you in hopes of narrowing down who the other prints belong to."

"Any time," I said. Then thought of something to ask Joe while he was on the line. "What's your take on Buddy Sward?"

"Why do you ask? Going to apply for a job on his rag?"

I laughed at the concept. "How pissed off is he likely to get if we were to take a picture under the streetlight tonight of the Mauch Chunk Creek running down the middle of Broadway and publish it on the editorial page Monday under the headline of his quote . . . wait a second till I find it here . . . yeah: Mauch Chunk Does NOT Need the Mauch Chunk Creek Watershed?"

Joe let out a slow whistle. "You make a career out of looking for trouble?"

"It just seems appropriate. And we are a newspaper. With a perfectly good editorial page, same as him. It's not like we're calling him names—"

"Not like I usually do under my breath every time I come across his rag," Joe added.

"It would be short, simple, and in this case a picture will be worth a thousand words."

"You have a decent camera?"

"I still have the one I used on the college paper."

There was a pause, and when Joe came back he was using his seriously funny big-city editor mode: "Listen here, son. The *Times-News* has an extremely important assignment for you. Tonight, after night falls, when it's dark, you are to proceed to Broadway, the center of Mauch Chunk proper, where you are to take long-exposure pictures of just why Mauch Chunk doesn't need a watershed. Let nothing, most of all common sense, stand in your way."

"We'll make Buddy Sward squeal like a pig," I said.

"Ouch," Joe said, and hung up.

But before I did anything else, I had to force myself to sit down at the typewriter to knock out the second draft of the sidebar on finding Elizabeth Delaney's body. Not easy. How to keep it objective. Just the facts, but keeping myself out of it. I changed it around to be told in the third person. One slow line at a time while Mr. Thorpe sat under the flickering reading lamp following the progress of the Great White Whale.

When I finally finished it—all five hundred words—I pulled it out of the typewriter and sat it on the table. It would do well to enjoy some rest before I came back at it tomorrow to tighten it up . . . or to add something that suddenly felt pertinent that I'd forgotten. I was being spoiled on this piece and was becoming worried that having the luxury of time that seldom applies to journalism, I'd overthink it and therefore overwrite it, losing the immediacy in the process.

The wind pushed the rain against the window like the sea pushed waves to shore, which was impressive, especially since the rain wasn't even coming directly at us. It was coming down the river valley and we were sheltered from the worst of it by the hills that formed the Heights. For a moment, I had the urge to strip naked and run out into the storm, around the sheltering hillside, and straight into the worst of it, the wind-driven needles of hard rain stripping the skin from my body and sucking the smell of death from my nose and lungs.

It all suddenly felt overwhelming. Shit. I'd graduated college on May 26 and here it was June 8, just short of two weeks later, and I'd already lived a lifetime. I had a vague insight into why some of my classmates were going on to graduate school in subjects that wouldn't possibly land them a decent job when they graduated. They just plain wanted to stay away from the real world, the real world of sweat and dirt and death and rot. I thought of Sartre. I thought of Nietzsche. I thought of a photograph taken at a family picnic where a young girl smiles for the camera, revealing a chipped tooth and a death's skull just under the skin. I thought of the profoundly natural process that had been working for weeks to reclaim Elizabeth's now-useless body, decaying slowly from the inside out in a naturally regulated meat locker.

There was a pause in the wind, a startling vacuum. Was the storm over? I peered out the window at the still-thick rain, through it to the orange streetlights out there along Susquehanna Avenue. Then the wind came on again, like a misshapen thug that had been battering at the door, and decided to back up a little to get a running start to take a really good try at destroying it.

The windows rattled—enough to make Mr. Thorpe look up from his book. He smiled. "At least there's no tornado out there moving up on us through the wall of rain." He smiled again, went back to his book. I fingered the sheet of paper I'd just used to sum up what we knew about the finding of a young girl's body in a deserted mine. I thought about Stephen Crane, about the two versions of the sinking of the *Commodore* he'd written, one for newspaper consumption, the other as the short story "The Open Boat." I thought for a moment of writing an alternate version of the sidebar I'd just done, this one as a short story, complete with more gruesome description of the body and loaded with speculation.

But in the end, I pulled on a pair of knee-high rubber boots and got my camera and put on my hooded jacket and went to see about shooting some flood pictures.

The wind was so profound that walking down Packer Hill to the steps leading down to the courthouse was like trying to walk the deck of a ship being lashed and tossed by fifty-foot waves. Fortunately, most of the onslaught was coming from the west, so on the way down it was hitting me in the back. The streetlights glowed a Halloween orange, the rain blowing in front of them highlighted like grains of salt.

With my left hand I pushed the camera to my chest under the hooded coat; I used my right hand to hold onto the rail going down the steps.

When I turned the corner at Susquehanna and Broadway, there was a moment of near quiet as the edge of the courthouse held back the worst of the storm. In front of me the streetlights marched up Broadway, illuminating the water rushing down the center of the street, lapping up over the curb, flowing around the bases of faked hitching posts like a frothing stream around rocks. In the first block there was one abandoned car snugged into the curb on the left side of the street; farther up the street, two cars squatted, crooked, against the left curb, up there across from the library, by the YMCA, as though the rushing water had beached them. There was nobody on the street. It was as though there had been a nuclear attack, everyone dead and gone, the only thing living now the pale lights.

I snugged myself into the protection of the arch over the front door of the courthouse, where I fumbled for my camera, which had become snagged in my left armpit. Because the mountain behind me protected Broadway from the wind, the storm wasn't as violent here, more of a constant downpour. A metal bucket, a pail, came down the middle of Broadway, rolling back and forth as the force of the water caught it on the side or on the bottom or full-on at its heart, turning it here and there. It made a faint *thump-thump* sound, the water that surrounded it muffling its potential *clang-clang*.

I didn't have a light meter for the camera, but I'd been used to estimating the aperture needed when I used it in college and then bracketing it on either side with extra shots to fill in being off by a stop or two. I aimed up Broadway, using the standard 50-millimeter lens in order to get in the full picture. Shot off three, then moved into the middle of the street, keeping my back to the wind to protect the camera. Rain slapped at the back of my hood as though someone was aiming a garden hose at it.

I planted my feet against the force of the onrushing water, watched a basketball go slithering by on my right, and shot off three more frames, bracketing with one extra shot on either side of the setting.

I moved up the street, fighting the water as it tried to carry me to the waiting river, finding a spot in front of the American Hotel, from where I fired off five shots, holding the camera steady while the shutter flipped up and stayed open a fifteenth of a second. Then three more at a quarter of a second.

Now, more out of curiosity than anything, I plodded farther up the street, occasionally stopping to fire away. I worked my way up by walking on the sidewalk on the right side of the street, stopping between Dugan's Store and the Dimmick Memorial Library, watching the water flow by, mesmerized by it, like watching the newsreel of a man's life go by. Just who was Dimmick, anyway? I'd spent every Saturday morning as a kid in the library, and I realized I had absolutely, positively no idea who Mr. Dimmick, the guy who'd made it possible, had been.

I must have lulled myself into a daze, helped along by watching the illuminated water flow by. Occasionally some object—a broom, a plastic flower-watering can, the branch of a tree—sailed along, all of it headed to the river and from there downstream to the same places wooden barges filled with hard coal used to go.

When the voice emerged out of the dark—"It's a lot worse up Broadway, well over the curb."—I started. Next to me a large, black raven-like beast stood where there'd been nobody last time I looked in that direction. Sheathed all in black, its right arm was thrust out in the direction of upper Broadway, as though I didn't know in what direction upper Broadway lay. "More narrow, tighter up there, the water's up to the first step going into peoples' houses."

I suddenly recognized the voice, even though it was being mangled by the rain pouring onto my back and onto his black canvas duster. A black cowboy hat covered his head and wouldn't allow any light from the streetlights to penetrate what was underneath it. But it was plain it was Null-A. "Ya just about scared the shit out of me," I said above the downward drone of the rain.

He laughed, imitating the Shadow. His hands were stuffed into the pockets on the sides of the duster.

"Tell me you have two nickel-plated .45 automatics in those pockets," I said, hoping I was being funny.

Shit. He pulled out two nickel-plated .45 automatics, just as though he was the Shadow. "Shit!" I said.

"Don't want anybody messing around, looting, stuff like that," he said, leaning his back against the metal fence, sliding the two big guns back into his pockets.

"Shouldn't you be guarding your van Vogt collection from potential book snatchers taking advantage of the storm?"

I could make out his teeth as he smiled. "The house is well fortified," he said, then smiled again. "Next you're gonna ask me about my flooded basement—"

I half-nodded. He was right. I was going to ask about that. Bastard was creeping me out. I felt the hairs up my back stand out straight.

"Three pumps," he said, "pumping their little old hearts out putting the storm water back where it belongs." He nodded toward the middle of Broadway. "And this hain't it," he added.

A squall came around the corner of the courthouse and on up Broadway, as though somebody was driving it and it had Michelin steel-belted radials on it. I nodded toward it as it rushed at us, while I hunkered down in my jacket. Null-A merely laughed as the squall crashed into us like a giant fire hose. For a moment it actually stopped the water running down the street, its force acting like a dam—but only for a moment. A metal garbage can, a forty-gallon one it looked like, came galloping down the middle of the street, making ungodly sounds as it did.

"You're not dressed real good for this," Null-A said.

"You sure are," I answered, hunkering down even more inside my jacket.

"Taking pictures for the big write-up in Monday's paper, huh?"

"Yeah. Including the editorial page. Mauch Chunk don't need no damned dam to hold back the flood. Something like that."

"With a big photo of Broadway looking its best," he said.

I nodded. He seemed to realize that I had nodded. "So you're doing everything you can to piss off Buddy Sward," he said.

"Fuck Sward!" I said, nodding toward the rush of water and junk rushing down the middle of Broadway. "This is his fault."

"He won't think so," Null-A said. "And the little prick's about as vengeful as they come. He'll do something to fuck you up for this."

I nodded toward Null-A's duster. "I can hire you and your .45s to protect me."

Null-A shook his head, and even in the bad light I could see the crooked smile. "They way he'll come after you won't be anything that a pair of .45s will stop."

I spit into the storm, even though I didn't particularly have any spit to spit. "Fuck him and the rock he crawled out from under."

Somehow, out of all the downpour and the wind, Null-A managed to pull a Parodi out of his coat and light it with a wooden match. "Want one?" he asked.

"I don't think I'd be able to light it in this wind," I said. "I'm not as talented at those things like you are."

He took the lit Parodi out from between his teeth and handed it to me. "Here, pard, take mine. I've got another. And don't worry, I didn't lip it very much."

I took it and stuck it between my teeth. I expected to taste some sort of odd flavor, like maybe brimstone or something. But it just tasted like Parodi tobacco from Scranton, Pennsylvania, and when I sucked on it, official Parodi smoke came out.

Null-A lit up another one without any trouble, and we both leaned back against the library's metal fence and vainly tried to make smoke rings in the windstorm.

"Ya did a good job," he finally said.

I turned toward his dark figure, seeing only the red tip of the cigar and his teeth shining under the black hat. "What job?" I was sure he wasn't talking about making smoke rings.

"Finding Elizabeth—"

I laughed. "Shit. It was just dumb luck. Not like I formulated some reason to look for her in the mine. She was just there. And me two weeks too late to do any good."

Now *he* laughed. "You weren't even here two weeks ago. And I'm sure you did some good. At least her mother's got a body to bury, instead of going to her grave wondering, worrying where her little girl is. I'm sure she appreciates that."

I shook my head, took a long drag, held it in my mouth, and spit it out. "I dunno. Maybe I shouldn't have come back to Mauch Chunk. The whole thing, since leaving college, it's like stepping through some sort of a parallel world gate or something. Like I half the time don't even know if I'm here."

"I feel a sci-fi novel coming on," Null-A said.

"Yah, well, I feel like I'm going nuts or something."

"You just gotta slow down a little. Ever since you began work-ing on the paper—What was that, Monday morning? Now it's Saturday evening—you've been hitting on all eight cylinders. You hain't giving yourself no downtime. You need to catch your breath, take tomorrow off, sleep in, read a good book . . . or better still, a bad book. You used to like Spillane. Read some fuckin' Spillane. Smoke a joint. Unlax, man. Catch your breath." Null-A blew out a mouthful of smoke and, honest to god, for two seconds it held fast as a ring the size of a softball, before the wind shredded it.

I considered trying to match him but realized just as quickly that I was no match for ole Null-A. No time, no way.

We continued to lean against the fence, watching the water run down the middle of Broadway, occasionally taking something along with it. We said nothing, watching and listening to the wind-whipped rain. I felt at once exhilarated and depressed, grateful for the jacket's hood protecting the back of my neck from getting wet and chilled.

When the Parodi had burned itself down halfway, Null-A, out of nowhere, shrugged and touched the tip of his cowboy hat, said simply, "I gotta go see how things are holding up at home," and turned and walked up Broadway, appearing as he approached a streetlight and disappearing into the shadows between them.

"Now there goes one weird son of a bitch," I muttered under my breath.

I became aware of the weight of the camera strap around my neck and the bulk of the camera under my jacket. I was, I supposed, finished with my photograph-the-flood assignment. I was sure I had some good shots, and Joe Boyle would be happy, and Buddy Sward not.

I decided to go home by way of Race Street, so I started walking up Broadway, crossing the River Broadway halfway up the block, the current strong against my legs, the current now deep enough some of the water threatened to come up over my boots.

Just as I turned into Race Street, a scantily clad blonde chick began flouncing toward me. More by her movements than by being able to see well through the rain, I was certain it was Alice.

As she got closer, it was plain that it was Alice—dressed in Bermuda shorts (red) and a halter top (white) and bare feet, and that was it.

"Hey, handsome!" she sang as she reached me and pecked me on the lips. "Are you always on the job?"

"Aren't you cold?" I asked, very much aware of her erect nipples through the white halter top. She reached around me and pinched my ass.

"Never too cold, never too warm. Just right," she said, smiling up at me.

"What're you doing out here?"

"Waiting for you."

"Yeah, right," I said.

"Yeah, right," she said. She took my right hand and began leading me down Race Street. "Come in and get warm. I have some cheap red wine opened. Perfect for a lousy night like this. Maybe if we're lucky the power'll go off."

I wasn't sure I was in the mood for fun. I could still feel the stench of Elizabeth Delaney in my nose. Alice immediately picked up on my hesitation. "Your not coming in isn't going to bring her back to life," she said, gently dragging me toward her row house.

Both because she was right and because I didn't want to hurt her feelings—and because certain parts of my anatomy very much wanted to pay a visit with Alice—I let her lead me to her door and then through it.

Candles burned at a half-dozen places, and the two cats were sprawled together beside the sofa. The front room was nice and warm, the building heat augmented by an electric heater across from the sofa. Its red-orange glow looked awfully inviting.

"Take your stuff off," Alice said, while helping me do just that. She helped me out of the hooded jacket, I wrestled the camera strap over my head, and she helped me struggle out of the boots.

She was thoroughly drenched but warm to the touch.

"Help me get out of these wet things," she said, pressing against me, her arms around my waist, while I fumbled at the knot at her back that held the halter top together. She shrugged out of it and in one easy motion unbuttoned her shorts and let them drop. I could feel her nipples through my shirt, which she began to slip over my head. She turned left and right, running her erect nipples along my abdomen, humming to herself. Her hair was parted in the middle and both sides were like a blonde jungle. Her hair smelled like wet flowers.

I kissed the top of her head while she unbuckled my belt, then unzipped my fly and tugged my pants down to my ankles. My dick pressed against her belly. She grabbed it and began rubbing the tip of it back and forth across her belly while at the same time continuing to run her breasts across my belly. I felt rather than heard a moan escape my lips. The cats continued to sprawl next to the sofa, completely ignoring us.

Alice ran her lips across my chest, flicking her tongue here and there. Then slid down to her knees, kissing and sucking my dick. I began to get lightheaded, most of the blood in my upper body now on vacation in my boner. I tried to shift my concentration away from what was happening to me to somewhere else in an attempt to short-circuit another premature ejaculation. I looked at the cats, closed my eyes, and listened to the rain pounding on the street outside, anything to hold off the inevitable.

She got up and led me to the sofa, where she lay back and opened herself. I lowered myself onto her in slow motion as she guided me into her. We stayed perfectly still for a good minute, feeling a kaleidoscope of sensations, trying to draw it out. I knew that as soon as one of us moved, it would speed up toward the end, and it was too early for that.

I suddenly had a flashback to the thing in the mine tunnel that had been Elizabeth Delaney. I involuntarily gasped and pulled out, the blood rushing back into my brain, exaggerating the image. I stood up and immediately began to go soft.

Even in the dim light, I could see the confusion on Alice's face, the sudden wrinkles on her forehead. "What—?" she said.

I went down on my knees in front of the sofa and began to sob.

"You *are* a challenge, aren't you?" she whispered, taking my hand and kissing it.

14
Oral History

My feet felt like lead as I stumbled up the steps between the courthouse and the Asa Packer Mansion. The wind had died down but the rain kept falling like crazy. There were lights on in Weiksner's Bar, but I wasn't in the mood to socialize. If the water kept rising, the folks inside Weiksner's would be fighting over bar stools to keep them high and dry.

Alice and I had held each other for ten minutes or so after my premature dejaculation, and it was tempting to stay there with her, but the time wasn't right. The whole damned thing, at that moment, wasn't right.

She seemed to understand.

She may have understood more than I did.

I was deflated, depressed. I was tired and I wanted to go to bed.

The light in the front common room under which Mr. Jim Thorpe devoured *Moby Dick*, one bite at a time, was lit.

Indeed, when I opened the door and dragged my dripping self inside, Mr. Thorpe and Moby Dick were still together, but the book was resting in Mr. Thorpe's lap while Mr. Thorpe took a nap.

I tiptoed into my room after taking the jacket off and hanging it just inside the door to drip-dry. I changed into a gray sweatshirt and proceeded to tiptoe to the refrigerator to get a beer. I pulled out a Miller High Life and sat down, as quietly as I could, at the table, where the manuscript of the dead Elizabeth Delaney sidebar still rested. I thought about tearing it up but instead pushed it away. I'd give it one more pass tomorrow.

I sucked down a long pull of beer and set the bottle down on the table. It made no sound, so it could not be what caused Mr. Thorpe to rouse with a "Wha—?"

"Sorry," I whispered.

"What? For what?" Mr. Thorpe asked.

"For waking you."

"I don't think I was under very far." He checked his book to make sure he'd left his bookmark inserted, then closed it and set it on the little reading table next to him. He ran his big hand over his grizzled face.

"You want a beer?" I asked.

"Yeah. Yeah. A Bud, please."

I got up and got it for him, popping off the cap into the garbage can next to the sink. He took it, knocked it back, smacked his lips, and looked at me with an increasingly serious look. "Could you do me a favor?" he asked.

"If I can," I said.

"Tell me about your family." I involuntarily raised my eyebrows in surprise. "No. I mean it," he said. "I keep hearing weird and wild stories about your family, and I'd love to hear what you have to say about it. 'Specially since you seem pretty normal."

"It might be a good way to put you back to sleep," I said.

"Then we can pick it up where we left off before I began snoring," he said.

"I dunno," I said, perpetually reluctant to pick and probe through the disorganized history of my family, although it's a family probably no more dysfunctional than anyone else's but more dramatic than some because of its place in the history of Mauch Chunk. It always felt like picking at a scab, especially since most of the characters were still alive . . . sort of. That was sort of referring to my grandmother and my mother and perhaps my grandmother's wayward brother, whom we called Uncle Herby. I took another sip of beer, a long slow one. "How far back you want me to go?"

Mr. Thorpe pointed the tip of his beer bottle toward the front window, where the rain continued to drop as though we were on the tiled floor of a gigantic shower. "Are you planning on going back out tonight?"

"Hell, no," I said, mellowed by the low lighting and the warm atmosphere in Ye Ole Carriage House.

"Start back as far as what you know, you know for sure."

"That'd be the mid-1800s," I said.

"Ready, set, go!" Mr. Thorpe supplied.

"You may already know that at one time, around the mid-1800s, Mauch Chunk, per capita, was probably the wealthiest place in the whole country . . . maybe the world.

"There were two groups of rich people here, the Packers and the Leisenrings. Their wealth came in the way of investments in iron, coal, and the railroads. Packer's big-money investment was the Lehigh Valley Railroad, which transported coal to Easton, Allentown, Bethlehem, Philadelphia, even as far as New York. It just so happened that the wealthiest independent coal operators were Garret B. Linderman and Charles O. Skeer, who happened to be sons-in-law of Packer. Packer's brother-in-law was in charge of the Montrose Railroad.

"On the Leisenring side, John Leisenring Jr. had a coal company and two iron companies in Virginia and Tennessee. He was also a director of the Lehigh Coal & Navigation Company and the Central Railroad of New Jersey, whose station is just down the hill there by the river. Leisenring's son, Edward, was ultimately president of LC&N. Fisher Hazard was also a director of LC&N and owned some manufacturing concerns in Wilkes-Barre; he was a buddy of the senior Leisenring.

"There was a heated rivalry between the two groups. As they battled to become larger and larger, they started banks, took over gas and water and electric companies. The Packer side was Episcopalians and Democrats, while the Leisenring group was mostly Presbyterians and Republicans.

"As an example of the wealth, according to the Federal Manuscript Census of 1870—I did a term paper on this in my junior year in high school; my grandmother was furious—in Easton there was a total wealth of $8.3 million among people worth $50,000 or more;

in Allentown it was $7.1 million, in Bethlehem it was $2.5 million, and in little Mauch Chunk it was $13.7 million. Keep in mind that the relative populations of the four towns in that year were: Easton 14,154, Allentown 13,884, Bethlehem was 8,068, and Mauch Chunk was 5,426.

"Everybody—both sides of the rivalry—built their mansions on this side of town, including some of those who moved into the stone row that's now rundown Race Street. At that time it was known as Millionaires' Row.

"My great-grandfather, one of the Packer gang, was a little eccentric and decided to build his place at the top of Fisher's Hill on the east side of town, called back in those days the Kettle. It was kind of a planned community with streets laid out on a grid; they couldn't do that over here because of all the hills, which is what became the problem—a big problem."

I got each of us another beer. "Geography, which was what originally put this place on the map, is what eventually killed it. The same hills that protected us from the worst of today's storm made it impossible for Mauch Chunk to grow. So almost everyone up and moved to South Bethlehem, where they already had some investments, which then grew to include iron and steel.

"My great-grandfather, who'd made his fortune in building barges to transport the coal downriver and who forged railroad spikes at a shop on Packerton, also owned a brewery—The Indian Head Brewery on the east side—and a bank, The First State Bank of East Mauch Chunk, stayed behind. And for a while was the big cheese in town . . . by default.

"My great-grandparents had two kids: my grandmother, who grew up at the mansion on top of Fisher's Hill, and Herbert, whom we all called Uncle Herby, who as soon as he could get away, went to sea and seldom came back. He'd send me a birthday card and five dollars every year. I saved the stamps. They were from anywhere and everywhere around the world.

"Grandmother married a plumber and for a while was disowned by her parents, but just before they died, they resolved their differences. From what I heard as a kid, the estate was divided in two, but Uncle Herby never bothered to claim his, although occasionally he came through town like a small hurricane to visit family and friends. He was full of stories and full of life, and my grandmother couldn't stand him.

"She had my mother, an only child, and they didn't get along very well, either. My grandfather, Mortimer, the plumber, died of heart failure at an early age, probably from being worn down by my grandmother, who took the occasion of his death as a signal to wear black and black only. She never forgave my mother when she married my dad, who was a miner, and of course set well below her station in life. Grandmother, in one of her greatest expenditures ever, bought them a big ole house on Pleasant Hill, because right after they got married, they were living with her, and she couldn't stand being under the same roof with my mother. They were too much alike.

"My parents had four kids. Donald came first; he's in the Air Force in Alaska. I'm here, boy reporter. Rudy's in jail for using and selling drugs. And Ellie still lives at home, taking care of my always-ailing iron-maiden mother, and probably will be until my mother dies, or until my mother wears down poor Ellie to a nub.

"Our father died in a mine collapse when I was ten. Like Granny, our mother took to wearing only black and after that never came out of the house."

"That *is* weird," Mr. Thorpe said.

"What weirds out everybody in town is that my grandmother is a force of nature, seldom goes outside, could supposedly buy and sell the whole town, but is so cheap she'd steal a walnut from a squirrel if she could catch it. She never pays retail for anything, and nobody much appreciates it."

Mr. Thorpe took another long swig of beer. "And from the ease with which you tell the story . . . the history, besides using the material for a high school term paper, you tell it on a regular basis."

I nodded, took a medium-sized swig. "At least twice a year. Somebody hears where I grew up and they wanna know about my granny. I get to throw my mother in as a coda."

"A what?"

"You know, like an epilogue."

Mr. Thorpe nodded. "And Ellie stands to inherit the same fate."

"Not if she doesn't get herself outside to find a commoner to marry so she can disappoint our mother."

Mr. Thorpe nodded again. He looked as though he had something else to say but was reluctant.

"What?" I said.

"You might not like to hear this, but one local biddy described your grandmother and your mother as Morticia from *The Addams Family*, with a permanent migraine."

I nearly snorted the beer that was in my mouth. "The biddy should be a writer."

"I've never seen or met either of them," Mr. Thorpe said.

I was about to tell him that he hadn't missed much when the phone rang. I picked it up and there was some static, probably from the storm, and then an operator came on. "Collect call from a Mrs. Martinelli. Will you accept the charges?"

"Of course," I said. I was expecting to hear my old running buddyite from Hazleton. Instead, it was her mother.

"Tomorrow morning you will receive a visitor," she said without preamble. "His name is Teddy. You have already met him. At my home. He will stay with you for the next week or for however long it takes."

"But—"

"Sssssh," she hissed. "In tomorrow's newspapers you will read about a van that burned to its axles on Interstate 81 near Hazleton. It contained twelve hundred pounds of marijuana. The van was stolen in Baltimore; the driver is missing. Before the driver disappeared, he claimed that the marijuana was meant as half upfront payment for you to disappear . . ."

"Disappear? Why?" Mr. Thorpe perked up, listening intently.

"If you disappear, well, that's nothing to me other than that you were a distant ally in wanting to stop the drugs. But it would devastate my nasty daughter, the one, you know, who smokes too much. I can't have that."

"But who—?"

"The drugs were bound for Wilkes-Barre, for a small-time rodent I know up there, you don't need to know his name. He knows yours. And where you live. And you might want to advise the Indian living there to find a boardinghouse until this is over."

I winked at Mr. Thorpe. "Tell you later," I mouthed to him.

"Now you listen! They won't come in this storm, but even though their first installment didn't arrive, that won't stop them. They want very badly to make points with these Baltimore people, so they *will* be coming."

"But suppose Teddy and Mr. Thorpe and I take a road trip, throw them off?"

"What my daughter sees in you, I don't know," she said, and hung up.

Mr. Thorpe was all eager to hear what I'd just heard.

"We're going to get a roommate—one less interesting than a professional rassler, and if we had any sense we'd go visit your family in Oklahoma until this drug shit blows over," I said.

Mr. Thorpe looked suitably puzzled.

"Those three punks who came by Friday night to mess with us?" He nodded. "They weren't the first team. They were the frosh. The sophomore team is coming down from Wilkes-Barre to get rid of me."

Without a word, Mr. Thorpe got up, walked into his bedroom, caused a bunch of shuffling and banging noises, and came out with a 12-gauge shotgun that would have taken the head off a lead statue. He lowered himself back into his chair and draped the shotgun across his lap. "Sophomore slump coming up," he said and smiled.

"Well, here's how it is. This guy named Teddy is coming down from Hazleton to protect me, and I'm sure he'd be happy to protect you, too. Apparently all of this trouble emanates from Baltimore—"

"It what—?" Mr. Thorpe asked.

"Originates from Baltimore."

"Tough city, tough thugs," he said.

"You know people down there?"

"Been there often enough. Not as tough as guys in Ohio, at least when it comes to football, but tough enough." He made an elaborate shrug. "Why do they want you? Because you found the girl?"

I shrugged back. "I dunno. I think they think I know more than I do."

"Or you're moving in a direction they don't like. Like an ignorant schmuck that accidently wanders too close to the den where the bear cubs are so mamma eliminates you even though you don't have a clue you're anywhere close to bear cubs."

"Ah—okay," I said, following his reasoning.

"Maybe we should turn off the lights and lay in wait for the bastards," Mr. Thorpe said, moving his hand toward the reading light above him.

I waved him off. "They apparently won't be here tonight. They must be afraid of getting wet—"

"—or they're afraid of the dark," he added.

"Whichever. Maybe we should go to bed early so we're ready and rested for whatever tomorrow brings."

"Naw," he said. "I'm not tired yet." He made a motion with his empty Bud bottle. I went to get us refills, even though my Miller was only about half-finished. "And you know this person who is coming by tomorrow to save our sorry asses, this Teddy guy, so I don't accidentally shoot him—"

"Oh, yeah!" I said, suddenly afraid Mr. Thorpe would kill Teddy and Mrs. Martinelli would join everyone else who was apparently after, as Mr. Thorpe so nicely put it, our sorry asses. "You're sure you're all right with staying here?"

"Up until you rolled in, Mauch Chunk was pretty damned boring," he said. "I was actually getting ready to leave to find wilder places."

"You're a very sick man," I said.

"Thank you," he said.

15
Teddy & the Pirates

As promised, Teddy arrived. At 9:31 a.m. Sunday. Carrying an overnight bag that looked too heavy for its size. And wearing a suit and tie like he'd just come from church . . . which he may have. He drove a battered gray Ford Falcon and parked it next to my Rambler Classic. Obviously the beginning of a classic car exhibit. We had coffee and a variety of Mauch Chunk Baking Company pastries that I had sitting around. It was still raining but with none of the violence of the day before. It seemed almost bored, but it still kept on coming.

Looking out the front window we could see a little clip of Broadway and Susquehanna between the war memorial and the courthouse, and the intersection was under three feet of water eager to make its way across the railroad tracks to the river, damn whatever was in its way. A yellow dump truck with a flashing yellow light on top was parked on the far side of the intersection, and three guys in rain gear were using a crowbar to work on a drain on the side of the street. Just beyond them, where Race Street dumped into Susquehanna, a Mauch Chunk Police cruiser straddled the street, its bubble-gum light on top spinning, the cop turning back traffic.

I introduced Teddy to Mr. Thorpe. Mr. Thorpe extended his hand, but Teddy was having none of it. I indicated an empty chair at the table and he sat down, stiff. He accepted a cup of black coffee and two apple turnovers. He was precise in his movements and his eyes were nervous, as though he hadn't spent much time around a scar-faced guy and his Indian companion. When he was finished eating, he patted his crumbless mouth with the paper napkin and then refolded it into its original format and placed it beside the plate. He sipped his coffee and when finished didn't want a second cup.

Most of his speech came in one- or two-word sentences. "Black." "Thanks." "Just fine."

I glanced at Mr. Thorpe, who rolled his eyes into the back of his head. "You play rummy?" Mr. Thorpe asked him.

"On occasion," Teddy replied. "Stay away from the windows."

Somehow the *Morning Call* paperboy had made it through the deluge. I retrieved the paper from the mailbox, where he'd been repeatedly told to not put it as it was a federal offense, but he put it there anyway, to keep it off the ground and in this case dry. The story on the burned marijuana-carry van was on page 3 of the first section. Under a smudgy photo of a white Chevy van fully ablaze was the headline:

BUNDLES OF POT
GO UP IN SMOKE

There wasn't much more information than Mrs. Martinelli had given me over the phone: twelve hundred pounds of marijuana. How they knew it was twelve hundred pounds if it was all burned up, I could not figure out. On its way north on I-81 just south of Hazleton, under investigation, van stolen in Baltimore, driver unaccounted for. Good thing it hadn't been torched near a population center or, with the rain holding the air close to the ground, a whole swath of Hazleton would have gotten high.

I suddenly hit my forehead with the palm of my right hand. "Shit!" I said. "What the fuck's wrong with me?"

I whipped the paper around as though it was a sailboat main that was going to whip the boom around to the side of my head. I turned back to the front page. Nothing. Pages 2-3. Nothing. Pages 4-5. Nothing. I found it on page 6, all six inches of it under a one-column head that read:

BODY OF UNIDENTIFIED
WOMAN FOUND IN MINE

Unidentified. Dead approximately two weeks. Discovered Saturday morning. Cause of death undetermined. Identity pending further investigation. Under investigation? What kind of a story was this? Cause of death should be under investigation. One-sentence quote from our buddy Inspector James Farrell of the Pennsylvania State Police: "We have no indication of foul play at this time."

A missing girl. A broken neck. Decomposing inside a uranium mine for two weeks. No leads.

Was there anything in her clothes that might provide leads? Some form of identification? Some idea where the clothes came from? Any missing young women anyone knows about? Any footprints in the vicinity? Would a candle inside a Mason jar be a clue?

The outburst had been enough to get Mr. Thorpe out of his reading chair. I handed him the newspaper, folded back on itself so the little item was prominent. He read it through and handed it back. "Search for the big white lie," he said. "I think I'll go back to *Moby Dick*." Which he did.

Teddy waved his hand at Mr. Thorpe, as though to direct him away from the window. "If they try to sneak up on me, I'll know right away. I am an Indian, you know." He opened the book and commenced to ignore us.

I had the urge to call Joe Boyle both to complain about what shoddy journalism it was—not that we could or should do anything about it—and to gloat over the fact that we'd have a much more graphic and detailed version in the Monday-afternoon edition. I had the urge to call someone, someone who'd understand my frustration. But who? Grace Delaney? Null-A? Mrs. Apfelbaum? My brother Rudy? Alice?

I pushed my chair back and got up, feeling the need to move, to do something. "Are we stuck here all day?" I asked Teddy.

"It's still raining," he said.

"Yeah, I can see that."

"You mind if I take some coffee?"

I waved him toward the pot. "I can make fresh if you want."

"Black's fine." He got up, walked stiffly to the pot, refilled his cup, walked back, and sat down, the cup in front of him like a chalice in front of a monsignor at Low Mass.

I banged my right fist into my left palm.

"We gotta get out of this place," I said.

"The Animals," Teddy said.

"What?"

"The Animals. We gotta get out of this place."

"Jeez! I'm trapped with Dick Clark and Captain Ahab."

I marched back and forth across the living room while Mr. Thorpe and Teddy ignored me . . . pretty much. As my wandering took me past a window, Teddy would look up from the crumpled Sunday paper and wave me away, but I ignored him. "I should go down and see how much worse the flood damage has gotten," I said half-aloud.

"No, you shouldn't," Teddy said, now engrossed in a crossword puzzle.

At that moment Mr. Thorpe lowered his book and raised his finger. "Someone just drove by, real slow," he said.

Teddy moved so fast I didn't even know he was moving until he was pushing me away from the front window and toward the wall in which my bedroom door lived.

Mr. Thorpe was up in a flash, his 12-gauge in hand. He'd had it leaning against the wall near his reading chair.

Now I heard it, too: squeaky car brakes that weren't very loud but that were loud enough to just faintly be heard above the drone of the rain. If you listened real close you could hear a car idling. Then two car doors creaked open.

"They need a new car," I whispered to Teddy, who put his hand against my lips. He held a long-barrel .38 revolver next to his right leg. Mr. Thorpe was pressed against the wall between the front door and one of the two front windows.

It was incredible what you could hear if you concentrated, even over the persistent rain. The car still idled out on Packer Hill, and I could hear the *plop-plop-plop* of hard shoes splashing against the gravel driveway. They passed Teddy's car. I could tell by the direction of the footsteps, and now they were nearly in front of the door.

The instant the footsteps stopped, Teddy nodded to Mr. Thorpe, Mr. Thorpe threw open the door, and Teddy ran through it, Mr.

Thorpe on his heels. I followed, just in time to see a flash as Teddy shot at a short, squat man who held aloft a Molotov cocktail, already lit. The flaming bottle fell to the wet ground and cracked and the gasoline spread and the fire fed greedily on it.

The short guy moved pretty fast for a short guy, but he now ran with a limp. The regular-sized guy behind him shot at us using a meaty .45 automatic as he turned to run. It made a lot of noise.

The boom from Mr. Thorpe's shotgun was louder, and at close range just about deafened me. The regular-sized guy juked just in time so that only about 10 percent of Mr. Thorpe's buckshot hit him, most of it in the left buttocks. He did a lurch on one step but on the next was moving like a sprinter.

Teddy held his revolver in both hands and tried to line up a good shot on the short guy, but by the time he was ready to shoot, the short guy was halfway into the car—a dark Plymouth four-door sedan—and the regular-sized guy wasn't far behind him.

We ran out to the street, and Teddy set himself up to take a shot at the retreating car but then canceled because Steve's Diner sat just beyond the car. Mr. Thorpe, the third and last of us onto the street, didn't have any such hesitations. The shotgun boomed again and the Plymouth's right rear brake light exploded.

In another second the car was around the little hillside at the bottom of the street and squealing tires on its way down to Route 209 in a dramatic retreat.

"They weren't very good," Teddy said as we walked briskly back to the house, shedding rain water. "A little better and we would have had problems. I didn't see the gasoline bomb coming."

"What da'ya mean?" I asked.

"I didn't figure they'd use a Molotov cocktail. I figured straight guns, up front after they snuck up on us."

In all the excitement we hadn't realized we'd gotten wet—soaked, in fact. Inside the house, we dripped onto the carpet. I got some towels and we dried off.

"Now I really do gotta get out of this place," Teddy said, pulling himself together and heading for the door. "I don't wanna be here when the cops come."

Mr. Thorpe grabbed his arm before he could open the door. "There won't be cops," he said. "Who's gonna call the cops?"

"Not us," I added. "And with the flooding, god knows where the cops are—"

"But somebody would've heard the shots," Teddy said, straining against Mr. Thorpe's meaty grip.

"So what?" I said. "What are they gonna associate them with? A car backfiring? Lightning? Everybody's so into the flooding that nobody's gonna care. Sit down." I tried to help Mr. Thorpe lead Teddy to a chair.

"In a minute, I'll go clean up the glass in the driveway, and it'll be as though nothing happened," Mr. Thorpe said. "In fact, if you go driving out of here in a car that nobody recognizes, it might be even more obvious."

"Obvious," Teddy muttered. He patted the towel against the sleeve of the arm Mr. Thorpe still held onto. "Yeah, yeah," he finally said. "Yeah." Mr. Thorpe turned him loose and he walked over and sat back down on the chair in front of his cold cup of coffee, patting himself here and there with the towel, as though he wasn't quite sure where he was, as though he'd just come out of a deep sleep.

Mr. Thorpe nodded at me to indicate that he thought everything was all right. "While I'm still wet, I'll pick up the glass," he said, going back into the rain. A few minutes later he returned with his big paw filled with an assortment of glass bits. "A Sauternes bottle stuffed with a rag like they use to clean their hands at a garage," he said.

"That narrows it down," I said. "Somebody in Wilkes-Barre who works at a garage and has bad taste in wine."

Teddy laughed. "That doesn't narrow it down very much."

Mr. Thorpe started. "Was that a joke?"

Teddy shrugged. "That's about as good as it gets—especially after being shot at."

"Better than nothing," Mr. Thorpe said as he reloaded his shotgun and placed it back against the wall near his chair, then dropped into it. He didn't pick up his book. "You don't think they'll come back," he said, talking to Teddy.

"Not today they won't."

"Then let's relax," Mr. Thorpe said, leaning back in his chair and closing his eyes.

At that moment I felt myself begin to come apart. The first jolt was an electric-like spurt up both of my forearms, as though I'd grabbed hold of a live wire. Then an overwhelming feeling of exhaustion, as though my muscles had gone flaccid. I grabbed the back of one of the chairs at the table, managed to swing it around awkwardly, and lowered myself into it

Teddy noticed and laughed. "Just a natural reaction," he said, "to almost getting yourself dead."

"A good feeling but not a good feeling—at the same time," Mr. Thorpe said from his comfortable chair.

"But you guys—" I began. "Nothing affects you—"

Mr. Thorpe laughed. "Why do you think I sat down?" He held up his left arm, the one closest to me, to show me that it was vibrating. Not shaking, vibrating. "Been in a million situations in my life where there's been some danger, from fistfights at a bar to running over a pair of linemen, and after it's over, it's always the same thing. I zing."

"You what?" Teddy asked.

"Zing. Zing!" Mr. Thorpe said. He made his vibrating left arm pretend it was an airplane cutting through the atmosphere. "Zing."

"How about you?" I asked Teddy.

"Varies," he said.

"On what?"

"On how intense. On how unexpected. On the outcome. Lots of things," he said.

"How about now?" I asked. I could see Mr. Thorpe paying rapt attention to the answer.

"A bit. A little bit. But it would have been more pronounced if they'd lobbed the bottle and it'd hit us or the house."

"But the sensations wouldn't have come until afterwards," I said.

He nodded.

"You'd be in a world of shit if it came while you were in the middle of the mess," Mr. Thorpe said. "Your adrenalin pumps to make sure you react, and after it's over you pay the price." He held up his left arm again and began making it shake as though it might fall off.

I picked up an empty coffee cup to throw at him, but didn't. "*You* may think you're funny, old man," I said, "but I don't hear anybody laughing."

He laughed again. "Bring 'em on," he said. "I'm ready for 'em."

I noticed Teddy drumming his fingers quietly on the top of the table. I watched him. He had closed his eyes, as though concentrating. When he opened them he had apparently made up his mind about something. "We can't wait for circumstances to come to us," he said. "We need to take control of this." He formed a steeple with his hands, resting his chin on his thumbs. "Let's go back over everything, from the start, and see what we can do to get off center of this whole plot."

I told him what I knew. Mr. Thorpe fell asleep as the rain continued to come down; he snored, or more precisely snorted.

16
Napmare

The dilemma we faced was simple: we'd come up with our plan but there was no way to launch it until nightfall, so in the meantime we faced hours of just sitting around. Which we did.

I worked over the sidebar on finding the body of Elizabeth Delaney, but I was getting the feeling that the more I fiddled with it, the worse I was making it.

Teddy spent hours sitting at the other end of the table just staring into space. At least that's what it looked like. I fantasized that Teddy had spent time in prison, most of it in solitary confinement, and had learned certain arcane coping mechanisms. He seemed to inhabit a world apart from ours, but I suspected that if a car happened to slow itself coming down Packer Hill, he'd be at the door in a flash, his pistol pulled and ready to do damage.

Mr. Thorpe, well . . . He lounged in his easy chair, going into and out of what seemed like catnaps, reading a page or two of his book, then dozing off, his shotgun never far from his hand. He read, he dozed and snorted in his slumber, he roused, he read, and the rain kept falling, and there was really no place to go without getting really wet and miserable.

It was easy to see, through the sheets of rain, that the intersection at Broadway and Susquehanna was very much a small lake and that Route 209 coming through town was blocked off. Occasionally we'd see a borough truck with its yellow caution light spinning, stopped just off the intersection, and guys in yellow rain suits mucking around with something caught in a sewer drain; then they'd leave, and an hour later they'd be back.

The lights in town stayed on, and the one light we were using, hanging over Mr. Thorpe's chair, was a meager 40-watt deal that threw a golden glow.

After taking one more pass of the manuscript for the sidebar, I got up, made a piss donation to the toilet, and crawled into bed, prepared to try to waste some of the early afternoon by sleeping it away. The hot water in the iron radiators occasionally came on and made a gurgling sound that complemented the steady sound of rain hitting the roof and splattering in the gravel driveway. The longer I lay there listening to it, the more hypnotic it became.

I could barely hear Mr. Thorpe's occasional nap-snorting coming across the big front room and making its way into my bedroom and Teddy's quiet staring and meditating or whatever it was raised silence to a new level of din, and the pattering of rain and the gurgle of the water in the radiator combined with the waves of warmth coming off the hot metal of the radiator lowered me slowly into a stupor.

It was all warm and relaxing and peaceful (in spite of the earlier firebomb incident) and calming, especially knowing that Mr. Thorpe and Teddy were on semiconscious guard in the big room, and that was that and I was gone . . .

It was a garden, an idealized garden, maybe a garden in England where they went out of their way to idealize Nature by making it perfect in a way it never was in real life. There was a perfect dirt path meandering through a perfect green-grass landscape dotted at perfectly spaced intervals by perfect medium-sized trees.

But as soon as I consciously questioned why "perfect" trees had to be medium-sized, most of them changed and became redwoods and Japanese maples while some stayed medium-sized as they were when medium-sized was considered perfect.

There were no animals, and then there were: deer and rabbits and singing birds. And then I wondered why "perfect" was so pastoral and then other animals appeared: a prowling mountain lion, a bison and its calf, three wolves playing tag, not looking for anything to attack and eat.

It was one of those nap dreams where you're not completely asleep and you have enough of your consciousness still engaged that you can take part in the dream, make it take different directions, the kind where if you stir or wake just a little bit, the dream vanishes like cheap fog.

Off in the distance, a girl was walking toward me, but she didn't seem to be getting any closer. I squinted to see if it was someone I knew, and it was and then it wasn't. She was young and then she wasn't, she was wearing one outfit and then another, but none of them seemingly appropriate to the ideal landscape through which she walked.

I tried to will her to come closer so I could see who it was, but that didn't work. She seemed to be beckoning to me, but not with any hand gestures, more with the tilt of her head and the purse of her lips—lips I was not close enough to see, so I don't know how I knew they were pursed.

The wolves, still playing with each other, saw her and ran toward her and I opened my mouth to warn her but my mouth didn't work but it was okay because the wolves ran by behind her as though she wasn't even there. They seemed suddenly intent on leaving the scene; they vanished off the right side of the perfect landscape.

Then the girl/woman came a bit closer, and it was a dark-haired girl I'd lusted after in college. Then it wasn't—it was a woman, in her early thirties, who looked like she came off the cover of a 1950s paperback novel, all beautifully coiffed hair and red lips and a martini glass in one hand and a cigarette in the other, with that alluring nasty look that doesn't know the word "subtle," the kind of woman Mike Hammer might be banging on a regular basis, then tossing aside.

She wore an angora sweater and a bra that made her tits look like the tips of nuclear warheads. The martini glass and cigarette vanished, and she crossed her arms in front of her and began to peel the sweater up over her head. For some reason I didn't understand, I was worried that she might muss up her perfect hair, but somehow she didn't.

Her bra was straight out of the '50s, not sexy like a bikini bra of the '60s but somehow even sexier, like pure sex. She ran her hands along the outside of her breasts, stroking them, then put her palms under them and hefted them, and I felt myself become hard, and then she did purse her lips—and she was close enough now that I could see her purse her deep-red cupid's-bow lips—and she made a motion with her head that asked, "Do you want me?"

And for some stupid reason I could not fathom, I shook my head "No." Was I out of my mind?

Then I realized I wasn't reacting naturally but rather the way I supposed I was supposed to act if my mother were standing behind me. But "No" was all a lie, a setup to rigid good behavior, but I didn't know why saying "Yes" would be bad behavior other than the fact that I wasn't married to her and, in fact, didn't even know her. The fact that she looked ten years older than me didn't even occur to me. She was "hot" in the way my father's generation defined "hot."

For reasons I didn't understand, other than that this was a dream, the woman was very patient. She just stood there, hefting her bra-confined breasts as though they were two cantaloupes at the produce section of a grocery store.

But that in no way made it all less sexy.

She was still very hot—and more patient than any other female I'd ever run into.

She continued to smile, and as soon as I imagined that I was about to change my "No" to "Yes," she began to change in very subtle ways.

The color of her hair began to shift, as though time had sped up and the sun and shadows were making her hair change shades. It went from dark to light to blonde, and then all the way back, but when it became black she had a different hairdo, one that was more modern, more casual.

And she began to lose years, becoming gradually younger, her body changing, too, from voluptuous to more athletic, and then her bra and the rest of her clothing began to fade and she was nude, the patch of pubic hair exactly the same color as the hair on her head, and now she hefted her breasts, breasts that were a bit smaller than they had been when she was Mike Hammer's moll.

She took two steps toward me and smiled and one of her front teeth was chipped and of course she was Elizabeth Delaney, and as she came closer, she took her hands from her breasts and reached out to take my hands, to put my hands on her breasts, and as I did, she began to expand and the pearl color of her skin began to darken and she parted her purple balloon lips and came close to kiss me—

I shouted "No!" and came awake, sitting straight up in my bed, as Teddy crouched in the door, his long-barrel pistol aimed toward me.

17

Pigsty

A t this moment, at this very moment, 8:42 p.m., Sunday, June 9, 1968, I felt as stupid as I'd ever felt in my entire life.

The rain had slowed by half, but it still fell. The darkness that had been here all day intensified as the actual night began to come on.

And here were Teddy and I bushwhacking up from Ruddles Run (aka the Shit Creek) toward the back of the Lawyer Delaney property where we were certain he was, against the desires of the borough council and his neighbors, raising pigs. Certain because the runoff from his backyard was streaming right past us on the way to join the Shit Creek from the pigsty he'd thrown up behind his house.

His property backed onto the bank that dropped off into the valley between South Street and the bottom of Bear Mountain. The days-long rain had turned the back of his property, where we were sure he was slopping his pigs, into a mud bath, and the overflow was flowing right past us as we struggled up the muddy, slippery bank, and the effluent stank to high heaven, but because of the rain holding it closer to the earth, it didn't have a chance to rise to high heaven. The stink just sort of hovered over the piggy-piss creeklet like a purple mist.

Incredibly, Teddy was still dressed in his suit, although he did wear a trench coat over it and had a felt hat atop his head. He looked like a G-man from 1936. But worse, he was still wearing his fashion-statement wingtip shoes, which provided exactly zero traction as we pulled ourselves up the bank by grabbing shrubs and tree limbs.

We stayed over to the side of the pig streamlet, working mightily to not slip into it.

I wore jeans, a sweatshirt, an Espy State varsity wrestling jacket, and my cross-country training flats, which had a little tread but which tread was doing pretty much no good because the little grooves were filled with mud.

Mr. Thorpe wisely stayed back at the house, sitting in his comfortable chair, his shotgun across his lap and the lights out. I pitied any moron who happened to be out selling magazine subscriptions. We had worked out a series of signals that we could employ when we came back—if we came back—that would short-circuit his blowing our dumb heads off.

Teddy had driven us across the bridge, then down to the Lehigh Valley Railroad station, and then up through the little valley between the back of South Street and the Pleasant Hill subdivision on the lower side of Bear Mountain. He'd parked the car in the middle of the one-lane dirt road, confident that no other morons would be out on a night like this.

I knew a safe place to cross The Shit Creek, which right now was about the highest I'd ever seen it, which should theoretically mean that the parts per million of actual shit had been diluted by the massive rainfall only to be countered, to an extent, by the pig shit slurping down from Lawyer Delaney's farmette.

We'd sat in the car before heading up the hill on our fool's errand, me screwing up my enthusiasm for Teddy's madcap plan and Teddy trying to explain, again, why it was a damned good idea. His theory was that we had to make something happen *on our terms*—my emphasis. "On our terms" meant we had to be the active participants, take the whole undefined mess *to them*, and we'd both agreed, after I'd run down a list of people who I thought might be involved in the whole Elizabeth Delaney and drugs thing, that Lawyer Delaney, Elizabeth's loving father, would be a good place to start. Both because he struck me as guilty of something, he struck Joe Boyle as guilty of a lot of things, and he was acting very much like a loose cannon—which meant that just about anything could happen once we stirred him up beyond the level he was already stirred up.

We decided—actually Teddy decided—that we would not confront him head-on by going up to his front door and ringing the bell and asking if we could come in out of the rain. Instead, Teddy said, we should reconnoiter his place, check it out, which is why we were at the moment climbing up a stream of pig shit. If, for instance, we knew he was raising pigs without the blessing of the borough council, we would have a lever, even though I assumed everyone who knew him already suspected he'd jumped the gun on the piggy approval.

If smell is one of the strongest of the five senses, we had all the proof we needed, and we could go home and get warm and dry, right? Not a chance. Teddy wanted to see more, and he wanted to see it up close.

As I pulled myself up another muddy step by grabbing from one shrub to another, it occurred to me that as Mrs. Martinelli's bodyguard, Teddy didn't get to think on his own very much, so perhaps freed from her strong influence, he was letting loose with a talent for detecting that he really didn't possess.

But as our heads came above the edge of the back of the Delaney property and we came face to face with a bristling, grunting, very-male pig that was pawing the mud on the other side of the stiff wooden fence, it occurred to me that Teddy might be onto something.

Confronted with the male pig—what are they called? boars?—Teddy began humming to the pig, and no shit, the pig calmed down and began moving its big ugly head back and forth, its nose twitching like it was rocking to a rhythm that only he and Teddy could appreciate.

While Teddy hummed his serenade, I looked past the boar and saw . . . two more boars. So Lawyer Delaney was stocking up on male pigs—pigs with tusks on both sides of their mouths, pigs whose backs bristled like a porcupine's, pigs that didn't look very domestic to me.

There was a light on in the back of the house up beyond the pigsty and a light on above the deck on the back of the house that overlooked Pig Central.

"We need to get moving," Teddy hissed to me between choruses of whatever love song he was humming to Mr. Tusk. "I grew up on a farm, and I can guarantee you this hain't no nice piggy, and his fascination with my song of love hain't gonna last much longer."

The boar gave a snort and ran his very active piggy nose across the mud in front of us, his front legs pawing the muck, his beady little eyes seeming to glow red in the night.

"Nice piggy," I whispered as Teddy moved left along the fence toward the house. The boar didn't follow us—at least not with his body. Its eyes did follow us, and its front legs were getting more active moving the muck up against its dragging belly.

I took a glance up toward the back of the house and could see two figures moving around in the kitchen. Then, for no obvious reason, I thought about what an olfactory bummer it would be to get invited to a barbecue on Old Man Delaney's back deck—unless it was a barbecue where the last of the three boars was being lovingly rotated on a spit.

I tapped Teddy's shoulder and pointed at the back of the house. He nodded.

We moved along the side of the fence until we were at the steps leading up to the redwood deck, a good dozen feet above us. The backyard slanted toward the Shit Creek, which meant that shit and piss from the pigs had no obstacles in their way to the creek and from there to poison the fish in the Lehigh River.

The boar that had first welcomed us to the sty seemed obsessed with hanging around at the very edge of the yard, where we'd left him. The two other beasts were restive but seemed to be thoroughly enjoying the mud and rain. Both of them bore evidence that they'd been taking the mud cure most of the afternoon.

The rain from the roof came together, dropped into a rain gutter along the side of the house, dropped into a downspout at the corner of the house, and flowed along the side of the pigsty. Even though the rain had slowed, there was a steady flow of rainwater running past us.

Teddy signaled that he was going to start up the wooden steps to the deck when the screen door flew open with a *bang*, the pigs reacted with a collective snort and rushed toward the deck, and Lawyer Delaney stood, in his Sears white underwear, on the deck, protected from the rain by the roof overhang, but wet headed as though he'd just come out of the shower.

I couldn't help issuing a little gasp. Standing in the doorway, wielding a big old black military-issue .45 automatic, stood Mrs. Delaney, the screen door bumped up against her right arm, trying to close itself on the door's spring. She slid along the screen door, and as she moved past it, the spring sprang and the door slammed shut and the pigs let out another snort, as though the banging screen door was the dinner bell.

Lawyer Delaney backed up a step, still three steps from the edge of the deck.

"Honey, honey, honey," he kept repeating, holding his hands in front of him as though he was pushing against a stalled car.

Mrs. Delaney said nothing. The big gun waved back and forth, either by design or because it was big and heavy and Mrs. Delaney wasn't strong enough to control it. From where we crouched, at the bottom of the steps, we couldn't see if the hammer was back and ready to fire.

My immediate thought was that we didn't want to do anything that would spook Mrs. Delaney into pulling the trigger. Maybe Teddy had experience in such matters. He let out a low but growing "Pssssst" sound, and Mrs. Delaney turned toward us. Mr. Delaney stood frozen but turned his head in our direction.

We received two reactions, polar opposites:

"He killed my baby!" Mrs. Delaney cried as she turned toward us, unfortunately the gun also turning toward us.

"Shoot her!" Lawyer Delaney demanded. "She's gonna kill me." Although I hadn't noticed him doing it, Teddy had pulled out his .38 before we reached the steps.

We both raised our hands so as not to freak out Mrs. Delaney. "He killed my baby!" Mrs. Delaney repeated. "The bastard killed Elizabeth!"

"No, no, no," Lawyer Delaney repeated. "It was an accident, all an accident." He moved his hands down a little and then back up, as though trying to send cool air in Mrs. Delaney's direction. The three boars stood together directly below Lawyer Delaney, looking up patiently, hoping something yummy would fall in their direction.

Teddy and I slowly climbed the steps, continuing to hold our hands up. "I'm going to put my gun back in my holster," Teddy said to Mrs. Delaney.

She shook her head, bewildered, as though coming out of an afternoon nap.

Her lips moved. I was sure she was going to repeat, "He killed my baby!" but she didn't. Her lips moved but nothing came out.

"Grab her! Grab her!" Lawyer Delaney commanded, then pleaded. His wet hair looked like a dead squirrel had been taped to his head. His legs were trembling.

"Let's just be calm, ma'am," Teddy said softly. Hearing his voice, his love pig snorted from below.

The steam seemed to be leaking out of Mrs. Delaney now that she had something to distract her. "He killed Elizabeth," she whispered, the big automatic waving back and forth across Lawyer Delaney's chest.

"It was an accident!" Lawyer Delaney whined. "I told you, it was an accident. I didn't do a thing to her. Nothing. It was the drugs. She took drugs and dove. That simple. I didn't want you to know." He turned his head back toward us as though we were witnesses who could confirm his claim. "It was an accident," he said to us, his voice now thinner and weaker. "She fell. Or jumped. From right here. It was the drugs. She was freaking out—"

As much as I hated to admit that Inspector Farrell might be right and I might be wrong, I actually believed Lawyer Delaney. Something about his piteousness couldn't be faked, even by a fake. Snot was running from his nose onto his top lip, but he was afraid to lower his hands to wipe it away.

"Mrs. Delaney," I said slowly and softly as I took a small step toward her, "can I have your gun? Your husband's not going anywhere. We'll make sure of that."

And she actually handed it to me. But, being the amateur gunslinger she was, she handed it to me business-end first. I sidestepped the barrel and eased it out of her quivering hands. The hammer was back and the gun was very much ready to fire.

The instant I had the gun, Lawyer Delaney's attitude changed and he ran at his wife. "You bitch!" he yelled and ran directly into Teddy's fist, which knocked him onto his back, where he slid on the rain-slicked deck toward the edge.

Teddy, consistently quicker than he had any right to be, grabbed Delaney's ankle as the rest of him went over. He now hung, literally, by one leg, the rest of him dangling over the three little piggies, all three of which were now very vocal and excited to see their lord and master offering his very own self to sate their enormous appetites, trying to climb the wall to reach him, and almost making it.

I eased the hammer down on the automatic and set it on the top step as I ran across the slick deck to help Teddy, who actually seemed to have things well under control.

Mrs. Delaney stood just outside her kitchen door, her hands thrown across her mouth, almost a caricature of a 1950s housewife putting forth the classic sign of distress.

Lawyer Delaney was screaming at such a high pitch it would have made ten-year-old choirboys jealous. His wet, matted hair hung down nearly far enough for one of the boars to reach it.

I began to pull on his leg, but Teddy leaned in close. "Take your time," he said under the screeching of Lawyer Delaney, the snorting of the agitated beasts, and the constant pounding of the rain on the roof of the deck.

If someone could see us at this moment, it would look exactly as though Teddy and I were feeding the lawyer to the hogs, an inch at a time.

"How long do you think would be good for getting the best results?" I asked, getting a two-handed grip on Delaney's left leg.

"Twenty, thirty seconds should do it," he whispered.

I could hear Mrs. Delaney going into short, rapid breaths. Maybe she was now torn between feeding the bastard to his illegal pig aliens in revenge for the death of her daughter or spooling out the homemade 8-millimeter film of the good times they'd had together over all of the years: hog food, good memories, hog food, good memories.

I sensed rather than saw her taking short steps to walk up behind us. Out of the corner of my left eye, I could see her in a speeded-up fidget, her hands and forearms shaking in front of her as though caught in an intense cold snap. She seemed torn between the two extremes: hog food, good times.

"Ohhhhhhh—" she wailed, turned and walked, stiff legged, back to the kitchen door.

Teddy had apparently seen all of this, too, but he made no indication that he had. He began to count down from ten, planting himself more solidly, preparing himself to hoist up the evening meal. I did the same.

"Three. Two. One," Teddy said and we literally lifted the bastard straight up into the air, both of us standing at the same time, Lawyer Delaney between us, upside down, not unlike a white-tailed buck hung upside down in the garage to allow it to cool before we began butchering it. "Jeez," I blurted. "He shit himself."

Teddy laughed.

We took two steps backward and lowered him, headfirst, onto the deck. "You bastards!" he hissed. "You bastards! You did that on purpose. I'll have your asses for this--!"

"Maybe we should put him back," I said loud enough for Mrs. Delaney to hear. "I don't think he's done yet."

Since both of us still had his ankles, Teddy obliged by taking a step forward toward the edge of the deck. "Nooooooo—!" Delaney cried.

"Mrs. Delaney? We'll leave it up to you," I said.

She paused . . . a long pause. Her indecision couldn't have been reassuring to Mr. Delaney.

"He's getting heavy, ma'am," Teddy said. "Appreciate an answer."

Indeed, the bastard *was* getting heavy. I was getting so callous to the whole damned affair that I don't think I'd have had a lot of qualms about dropping him over the side.

Mrs. Delaney fluttered her arms in front of her again. "Come inside, so we can talk," she said, retreating before us into the kitchen.

"I'll put on some tea," she said, I assumed for something to say, something to do, rather than taking the offer seriously.

Teddy looked at me over Delaney's feet, and we lowered him onto his back. His boxer shorts were stained brown, and when we lowered him, he sat on his own shit but didn't seem to notice.

I nodded my head at the gun sitting on the step and Teddy bent down, picked it up, and put it in his coat pocket.

"Help me up," Lawyer Delaney said, rolling around, trying to roll himself far enough forward that he would be able to land on his feet. It wasn't working.

"Get up yourself," I said, then called to Mrs. Delaney through the screen door: "Can you get a towel we can wrap him in?"

She scurried off to find one as Mr. Delaney rolled himself over on his hands and knees and pushed himself up off the deck.

He stood in front of us bedraggled and a mess. A sample of his shit slid out of his shorts and plopped onto the deck. He gave us his best "You-pricks!-I'll-get-you-for-this!" look.

Mrs. Delaney opened the screen door and handed out a huge beach towel. I passed it to Lawyer Delaney. "Wrap yourself up in this."

"No, I wanna get dressed," he snarled.

"No way," Teddy said. "You can get yourself dressed when we say you can. Wrap yourself up and get inside."

He did what he was told, wrapping the towel around himself so that he looked like a defeated Roman senator and shuffled into the warm, humid kitchen, where Mrs. Delaney did have a teapot heating over a blue flame.

Teddy pushed Lawyer Delaney down onto one of the four kitch-en-table chairs. We took seats on either side of him. Mrs. Delaney fussed with cups and teabags and hot water. "Did you want some tea, darl—?" she started to say, then caught herself and by her man-ner, withdrew the offer. "I'm sure you young men will have some tea on a foul night like this." The pot whistled, she poured steaming water into three cups, set one in front of each of us, and took the empty chair.

I bobbed my teabag up and down, urging it to steep faster. I looked around. There was a nice, dark-wood dining-room table in the next room; it had six chairs, the one at the far end a captain's chair, a throne, no doubt, for the master of the house. It was obvious, with four kids and two adults, the Delaneys didn't eat dinner in the kitchen like a lot of the rest of us.

"Well," Teddy began, running a spoon around inside his teacup, "we might as well get this meeting started."

"This is all bullshit," Lawyer Delaney muttered, but without the force it needed to impress.

"We either do this here and now or we return everything to what it was when we arrived," Teddy said. He pulled the big black heavy automatic from his coat pocket and set it on the table next to his tea. It made an authoritative *thump*.

"I'm not sayin' nothin'," Mr. Delaney said.

"But you already did," I reminded him. "Remember? 'It was an accident.' That *is* what you said, isn't it? She swallowed a drug and she fell. Or dived. And I assume the fall killed her."

He looked at me the same way he had years ago when he didn't want me to play with his kids—condescending bastard.

His attitude didn't seem to bother Teddy. Maybe he was used to dealing with horrid people in stressful situations.

Teddy removed the spoon from his tea, made sure the teabag was on the opposite side of the cup, and took a sip. He made an appreciative sound. "Here's what you're gonna tell us—" he began.

"I'm not tellin' you nothin'," Lawyer Delaney said, going so far as to attempt to get up and leave the table. From opposite sides, Teddy and I set him back down.

"We want to know how Elizabeth died. We want to know what kind of drug she used. We want to know your involvement with the flow of drugs through Mauch Chunk. And we want to know with whom you're working," Teddy said.

"With whom." I was impressed.

"And just what the fuck do you think you'll do if I don't cooperate?" he said.

Teddy slid the pistol toward Mrs. Delaney. "Don't kill him with the first shot," he told her as calmly as you'd tell someone how to slice apples for a pie. "There're lots of bullets in the gun. And you've got all the time in the world. Shoot him first in an arm or a leg. Then wait until the reality of that sets in. Then if you're not satisfied with the results, shoot another arm or leg. By the second shot, he'll know you're serious—that you're not just using empty words to threaten him."

Mrs. Delaney looked longingly at the pistol and even made a move to touch it, but she didn't. Instead she looked at Mr. Delaney. "Tell them what they want to know . . . what *we* want to know, or I'll do what he says."

"You wouldn't do that," Lawyer Delaney said. "Really, you wouldn't. Maybe before you would have, when you were angry, but not now that you're calm." He smiled his used-car salesman smile that made *me* want to shoot him. I found it difficult to figure out how a guy wrapped in a beach towel who'd just recently shit his pants could have the gall to act condescending to a flea but concluded that he'd practiced it so damned long that it was second nature to him.

Mrs. Delaney must have been having the same thought I was. She gave him a look that would have stripped paint off a battleship.

"Tell us," she hissed. Her hand went to the gun, lovingly turned the business end toward her husband, and three times petted the thing like it was a pet puppy.

Lawyer Delaney had apparently lived with his wife long enough to know she definitely was not kidding. A quick series of looks crossed his face: denial, recognition, fear, resignation. He glanced down one more time at the dark, round barrel opening of the pistol that from his angle looked about as big as a city sewer drain and then back up at his wife. And he decompensated.

He began to well up and actual, real tears dripped down his face. The snot that had been coming out of his nose was suddenly reinforced by a bubble that grew and burst. He unconsciously ran his forearm across his nose and then ran it across his towel, leaving a snail track.

He sniffled and sobbed and finally tried to speak.

"We . . . we needed money," he said. "Business was bad. I knew Liz was using pot, I'd tried to talk her out of it, but it was no use and, you know, we were always close and I never could stop her from doing anything she wanted to do." He shrugged as though we all knew that.

"She was Daddy's little darling," Mrs. Delaney supplied. "He spoiled her." She said it was though that was *not* a good thing.

Lawyer Delaney nodded. "We were very close," he added. "But—"

"But we get that," Teddy said.

"We talked about money. It came to a head when I didn't have any more to give her when she wanted it." He shrugged again. "A few days later she came to me and said there was a way out—if I'd work with some people she knew who were moving drugs . . . to sell at the colleges. At first I said no." He paused as though that was our cue to congratulate him. The bastard actually got a smug expression on his face as though in moving the narrative along, he'd again connected with his bloated vision of himself.

Teddy slapped him across the face as fast as a rattlesnake would strike. "Wipe that smug look off your face," Teddy whispered.

Lawyer Delaney's hand had gone to his face. Now it slid down his cheek and fell back onto the table. Mrs. Delaney had started at the sound of the blow, and I had to admit that I had, too.

"Next time you squeeze that smug face of yours into an expression I don't like, I'll have reporter boy over there dislocate one of your shoulders." I raised my eyebrows. "You *do* know how to do that, don't you?"

Indeed I did. "Yep," I said. "Ya learn that in wrestling."

"Now," Teddy said. "You were saying."

Lawyer Delaney was too scared now to not start. "Ah. I eventually said yes and we made a deal—"

"And what was your part of that deal?" Teddy asked.

"I'd be available as a lawyer—"

"But you're not trained in criminal law," Teddy said.

Lawyer Delaney seemed surprised that Teddy knew that. I know I was. Apparently even contract thugs know how to do research.

"Ah, I knew some judges, some judges that could be persuaded to be lenient when necessary. And I knew some locals who'd be willing to work as couriers."

I was going to say something about him not wanting his kids to play with such riffraff, but I held my tongue.

"And you began to make money," Teddy said, trying to prime the pump.

Lawyer Delaney nodded his head in agreement. "But they kept wanting me to do more . . . for not more money."

Teddy sniffed as though he'd caught a carrion smell. Well, there was the aroma of Delaney's soiled shorts, but that wasn't it. "Just how naïve are we supposed to think you were?" He raised his hand again as though to give him another face slap.

Delaney cringed. "But it helped, yeah, it did." He looked across the table at his wife as though to have her haul out the Delaney household ledger to prove that the cash-flow problem had been staunched. She just looked at him like he had a booger slipping out of his nose.

"But it only put you and Elizabeth closer to the action—and to the drugs," Teddy supplied.

Delaney nodded. "I wanted her to stop, to get out of it, I really did," he said. "But Elizabeth's always been headstrong, and she liked what the drugs did for her, then she wanted to go beyond pot, to try other stuff. I tried to head her off—" He looked across the table again, as though soliciting Mrs. Delaney's confirmation that he'd many times been selected father of the year. She just looked straight at him and gave the gun another pat.

"But she was hooked. They had her hooked, and if they had her hooked, they had me under their thumb," he blubbered, as though to go on he needed our sympathy—which was in very short supply. Better he should have appealed to the three ugly-tusked rutting boars below his deck than appeal to the three of us.

"Get to her death," Teddy said.

He glanced in the direction of the back door, beyond which the rain continued to fall into his pigsty. "Right out there!" he nearly shouted. "Right there." He put his head in his hands and this time it was difficult to tell if it was honest emotion or more playacting.

"What happened?" Teddy asked.

"Lizzy got hold of some of that LSD stuff . . . they gave it to her, and she wanted to try it." He again looked across at his wife. "It was when you were visiting your sister Margie, up in Tamaqua." As though that made it all right. "She insisted that I try it, but I wasn't going to do something crazy like that. That stuff can make you crazy, nuts! That's what it did to her. Right in front of me. She popped a piece of paper into her mouth and told me to stand by to see how things went. She sucked on the paper and nothing happened. But then later, while we were arguing about getting out of all this, it did. Stuff happened. She began getting happy, singing, spinning around. Then she got sad and sat down on the deck and cried. I held her and tried to make it all right, but I couldn't help, she just kept crying. Then she suddenly stopped and got up and just stood there looking down toward the Shit Creek muttering about wasn't it beautiful?

"And all of a sudden she yelled, 'Wheeeee!' and dove off the deck and fell . . . and fell and her neck snapped. I heard it snap." He looked at each of us in turn, wanting something . . . our sympathy for the fact that he was present when it happened?

"I . . . I jumped down and went to her, but she was already dead and her head was...was bent at a terrible angle and she was dead. Just like that. One second alive and thinking things were beautiful and the next second crumpled on the ground, her neck broken." He started to cry, but worse, Mrs. Delaney started to cry, great sobs that shook her shoulders.

I bounced up and grabbed a box of Kleenex that was on the kitchen counter. She grabbed a handful and dabbed at her eyes and blew her nose. "How could you—?" she muttered, looking through bleary eyes at Lawyer Delaney as though she had laser eyes that could burn right through him.

With both of them bawling, we weren't going to get anywhere any time soon.

"Why didn't you call an ambulance?" Teddy asked.

"She was dead!" he said. "What good would an ambulance have done? And besides, there were drugs here. I couldn't have anybody come by."

"But how could you be sure she was dead?" I said.

He actually laughed through his sobbing—in a way that said I was stupid.

"She was dead," he said. "She was very dead. Nobody could not be dead with their neck snapped like that."

Mrs. Delaney sobs increased in volume.

"Okay," Teddy said. "So no ambulance. No cops. What did you do next?"

"Ah . . . I made a call and we moved her as soon as it got dark. We took her to the mine. She liked it there. Sometimes when she ran away she'd go there and live there for a few days. She liked it there—"

"You never told me that!" Mrs. Delaney said, her face full of fury and her lips drawn back over her teeth.

Lawyer Delaney hung his head. "There was no need for you to know—"

"I'm her mother, you bastard!" she screamed as she threw her handful of crumpled-up Kleenex at him. The wet ball of tissues hit his right cheek and fell to the tabletop.

Teddy interrupted. "And what were the candle and the Mason jar about?"

"Lizzy loved candles, but I couldn't just set one there because the draft was too strong and would have blown it out."

"So your daughter's dead. On the ground," Teddy said. "You're in a panic. But you think the whole thing through far enough to take a candle and a Mason canning jar so you can put the candle in it so it doesn't get blown out. Is that right?"

Delaney shook his head in the affirmative.

"So you had time to think up the candle in the Mason jar devotional thing," Teddy said.

"We had a couple of hours before it got dark. I had time to think things through . . . to plan things as best I could."

"And who's the friend who came to help when you called?" Teddy asked.

Lawyer Delaney's face went pale.

He shook his head.

"Who?" Teddy asked again.

"Who was it?" Mrs. Delaney demanded to know, her forehead wrinkled like an elephant's rump. She twisted her hands until they went pale.

Again Delaney shook his head. "I can't," he said.

"You can," Teddy said. "And you will."

Delaney just sat there shaking his head in the negative.

"Mrs. Delaney, may I have some more tea, please?" Teddy said. "Good and hot. It's excellent."

Mrs. Delaney got up to fire up the teapot, and now I shook my head in disbelief. What the hell was Teddy doing asking for tea in the middle of the critical part of our questioning Lawyer Delaney? He was breaking the rhythm.

Well, I found out what he was up to in a few minutes.

While Lawyer Delaney sat still, seemingly hidden behind an impenetrable barrier of self-righteousness and self-defense and self-pity, Mrs. Delaney brought the teapot to the table and poured boiling water into Terry's teacup. Teddy thanked Mrs. Delaney, picked up the hot teacup and poured it into Lawyer Delaney's lap. Mrs. Delaney and I started, but not nearly as much as Lawyer Delaney did.

He screamed and leapt up from his chair, only to have Teddy pull him back down. "You bastard! You prick!" Delaney shouted, while he patted his towel-covered private parts. "I'll kill you, you bastard!"

Teddy nodded at me to help hold Delaney down in his chair. "May I borrow your teapot, Mrs. Delaney?" he asked, as soft and gently as if he were attending an afternoon high tea.

Mrs. Delaney passed it to him.

Mr. Delaney's eyes widened.

Teddy held the hot teapot over Delaney's groin while I held him down.

Delaney screamed again, even before the boiling water came out of the spout.

Teddy let a few drops fall and then stopped.

Delaney just sat there, shaking his head, ready to take more of the boiling water.

"Maybe we should just feed him to his own hogs," I said, "like an inch at a time."

If it was possible, Delaney's face grew an even paler shade of pale.

"Why'd you buy the hogs?" Teddy asked, the hot teapot sitting on a coaster next to him.

Lawyer Delaney seemed flummoxed by the question, like it was too easy after the previous questions about his partner in the drug trades.

He cleared his throat. "I was told to do it," he said, looking furtively at Teddy as though he expected another hot-water therapy session.

"By whom?" Teddy said.

Delaney again shook his head.

I expected Teddy to reach for the teapot but he didn't.

"We're through with him," Teddy said to Mrs. Delaney. "We're gonna take him across town and turn him over to the sheriff for good keeping."

"You can't do that!" Delaney cried.

Teddy smiled. "Watch us."

Lawyer Delaney looked across the table at Mrs. Delaney, and some glances went back and forth, ancient communications.

I caught a look of concern on Teddy's face. I realized what it was. He had just realized that there was absolutely no way he could take Delaney over town and turn him over to the sheriff. Teddy didn't want anybody to know he even existed, much less march into the sheriff's office pushing Delaney ahead of him and demanding Sheriff Neast take the guy into custody until the justice system decided what to charge a man with who watches his daughter dive into a broken neck and then deposits her, in a ritualistic fashion, in a tomb like some Egyptian queen.

I suddenly had a bright idea.

"You know you're dead one way or the other," I said to Delaney. "As soon as your partner finds out we had this little gab session, he's gonna want to do away with your sorry butt."

Teddy looked relieved that I'd changed the tack. Delaney looked as though Teddy had just poured more boiling water onto his nether regions.

Mrs. Delaney looked concerned, even though the potential death would involve someone who at the moment she despised.

"Ha—" Delaney said, "he'll never find out about this."

"Well," Teddy said, "that admission narrows the field down by 50 percent as far as the sex of the partner goes."

"Tell them," Mrs. Delaney hissed.

"Nobody knows you're here," Delaney said, meaning Teddy and me.

"They will when Teddy drives the car around to the front of the house and we march you out in a brown-stained beach towel. We'll make sure we make a lot of noise."

Delaney looked deflated, but I still wasn't sure he was going to break.

He shook his head, depressed but determined. "I can't," he said simply, and I believed him.

"But we're still gonna turn you over to the sheriff," I said. "We have to, after what you did. The system'll have to figure out what to do with you."

Delaney's head came up. You could almost see the light bulb go on over his head. "And I'm gonna tell them just what the two of you . . . the three of you did. That you tortured me!" He again looked smug and unbearable.

"We'll deny everything," Teddy said.

"And who the hell are you, anyway?" Delaney demanded of Teddy.

A look passed over Teddy's fact that I didn't like. Like Delaney had scored a very big point. But almost immediately he recovered. "A member of a task force commissioned to put a stop to the increase in drug traffic in these parts."

Oh, my god, I thought to myself, *why use a phrase like "in these parts?"* It sounded downright Western movie. But Delaney didn't seem to notice. Teddy had scored a point. It was obvious that Delaney had no idea whether there was a task force involved. He didn't need to know it was a task force made up of a suspected Mafia madam and her thugs.

"Besides which," I said, "as a responsible reporter, as soon as we turn you over to Sheriff Neast, it becomes my duty to write it up for Monday's paper. And the *Morning Call* will do the same when it does its daily calls to review the police blotters.

That simple statement seemed to put Lawyer Delaney into a funk. He wouldn't want all of this made public—to either his neighbors or his silent partner. His head dropped and he deflated like a cheap birthday balloon.

"Task force—" he muttered to himself, as though reviewing the case against him.

I pushed the big .45 across the table to Mrs. Delaney. "Keep an eye on him while my colleague and I confer," I said, inclining my head toward the dining room as I got up from my chair. Teddy followed.

"We can't stay here all night going back and forth on this with a guy who's obviously up to his ass in wrongdoing," I said.

Teddy laughed. "Wrongdoing? Ya think?"

I forged ahead. "We gotta turn him over to the sheriff, then somehow stop those nuts from Wilkes-Barre, then track down his partner—"

"—and who they're all working for," Teddy added.

My face went blank.

"You don't think Delaney's partner in crime is Mr. Big in all this, do you?"

I had to admit to myself that I had been allowing myself to think in those terms. Dumb. "Yeah," I said. "Even if we find out who his partner is, it doesn't stop the bigger machine."

Teddy nodded. "I'll go back down the way we came, get the car, and bring it around front. We can't get up Broadway, but we *can* go up to the Heights and come down to the jail from the back way." I could hear Mr. and Mrs. Delaney whispering to each other in the next room. Mrs. Delaney wasn't whispering sweet nothings. I seemed to remember that I'd lowered the hammer on the gun—wouldn't want to have any accidents.

"Okay," I said, "let's do that. At least we'll have Delaney out of our hair and secured."

Teddy nodded and walked back toward the kitchen, went out the backdoor, down the back-porch steps, and into the soggy night. The boars noted his passing with appropriate grunts and snarls.

I sat down next to Mrs. Delaney and slid the gun back in my direction. Mr. Delaney hadn't perked up any. "Last chance to tell us," I said.

He didn't answer. Just let his head hang. But I didn't feel sorry for the bastard. In fact, if Teddy were still here, it would feel real good for us to lower him, headfirst, back into the pigsty. Maybe drop him, accidentally, of course.

"Was he actually close to Elizabeth?" I asked Mrs. Delaney.

She nodded, slowly. "They were always close." She said it as though she was disappointed.

"But you were close, too, right?" I said.

She shook her head. "I loved my daughter," she said. "I loved my daughter very much. I love all my kids."

18

The Agnes & Buster Show

The simplicity of our plan is probably what allowed it to work relatively seamlessly. Teddy knocked on the front door. Mrs. Delaney went to open it, which she did tentatively as though she thought it might be the Fuller Brush Man. She led Teddy back to the kitchen, and he nudged Lawyer Delaney onto his feet, the big beach towel still wrapped around him.

"Shouldn't he change?" Mrs. Delaney asked.

I felt like asking back: "Do you really think he'd ever change?" but didn't. "They'll issue him a set of jail duds when we turn him in," I said.

She stood there twisting her hands into each other as though washing tar off her hands, suddenly seeming very small and soon to be alone. "Will you be all right?" Teddy asked her.

She shrugged her shoulders and then shook her head in the affirmative. "I'll be fine," she said, nodding her head as she followed us to the front door. "What else could possibly go wrong?"

Teddy walked back to Mrs. Delaney and handed her the bulky automatic. "Keep this here, just in case." He pressed it into her hands. "But remember not to pull the hammer back unless you're really gonna shot somebody." He patted her hands and walked back.

The rain was still coming down but almost as though it had become bored in the wake of the mess it had made, or maybe it was just tired. There was no wind, and lights were on in the houses up and down the street, an indication that the power was still on in this part of town.

Teddy handed me the keys, pushed Mr. Delaney into the back seat, and then crawled in with him. "You drive," he said. "You know better than I do where you're going."

His car was a simple three-on-the-column, and the clutch felt as though it had an industrial-grade spring in it. I adjusted the driver's seat to accommodate my smaller-than-Teddy frame, adjusted the mirrors, and we pulled away. Mrs. Delaney still stood on the front porch, cradling the gun like a pet poodle, outlined by the light coming from the inside of the house. I trusted that her three other kids were on the way home to offer help.

I drove over to Center Street, turned left, and headed for the bridge. There were tree branches on the street here and there and a lot of debris, but the road was passable, although we had it pretty much to ourselves. I drove up the Liberties, across the Heights, and down the bus road in the wrong direction. The bus road was built and maintained by the local bus company so its buses would not have to attempt to negotiate the tight switchbacks necessary to reach the Heights by way of the Liberties. It connected with Broadway above the jail after providing a single-lane benign ascent stretched out over a mile instead of the mountain climbing back and forth up narrow winding switchbacks a goat could think twice about taking.

When we came out on Broadway, it was still a minor river, the rushing water up to the middle of the hubcaps.

But by now most of the debris that the flood was taking down Broadway had already been deposited in the river and swept away. The streetlights were still on, still imparting an amber glow to the scene. I pulled into the parking lot next to the jail, opened Delaney's door, and pulled him out like a cork from a bottle. He didn't resist. Teddy stayed with the car.

I had to knock three times on the big, thick door, and when it was finally opened, it was Mrs. Neast who appeared. "Jeez," I said, "it's harder to get into jail than to get out."

She laughed. "The sheriff is out and about helping with this mess," she said nodding toward the wacky world of rain all around us. "I'm sorry," she said. "Do come in."

I pushed Delaney ahead of me, and Mrs. Neast closed the big door behind us. She leaned close to my ear. "What's wrong with Mr. Delaney?" she asked.

"Let's get him into a dry cell and into some dry clothes and I'll tell you."

She led us to the cellblock. I noted that Rudy's cell door was open, but he wasn't inside. "He's nestled in the library," Mrs. Neast said. "He'll be back soon."

She swung open a cell door that stood ajar, led Mr. Delaney inside, and guided him to a seat on the cot. He sat down and slumped. Mrs. Neast wrinkled her nose. "Phew," was all she said. "You stay here with him. I'll get him some clothes." She turned to Delaney. "You just sit there, Mr. Delaney. I'll be right back."

And she was, with a pair of gray coveralls. She had a pair of gray wool socks and a pair of gray cotton undershorts as well as a gray T-shirt on the top of the pile. "Can you help him?" she asked me.

She moved off, going back to the living quarters, and I helped Delaney as best I could, which wasn't much because he was still as limp as a piece of rope. I eventually got him undressed and re-dressed in the clean clothes, folded everything else into his huge beach towel, and took it with me. I locked his cell on the way out and carried the key to Mrs. Neast's kitchen, where she was having a cup of thin coffee.

"What a terrible day this has been," she said, indicating that she'd be happy to make me a cup of coffee if I wanted it. "It's in-stant but it's pretty good," she said as she poured another dose of condensed milk into her cup. "Mrs. Delaney called, just before you arrived, but I'm afraid she wasn't all that coherent. Something about Mr. Delaney killing Elizabeth and then burying her in a mine."

I explained the whole sequence of events to Mrs. Neast and she let me go on, nodding at appropriate places. She apparently hadn't heard all the news from the uranium mine. She wrinkled up her nose at my brief description of Elizabeth's final resting place, but other than that she listened to it like the veteran of life's dark side that she was.

"So once the storm wreckage is cleared up, the DA will have to decide what to charge him with, and there'll have to be a hearing and an investigation, I'm sure," I said. "But most of what he told us"—I omitted the methods we'd used to extract the information—"seems to jibe with the evidence." She nodded her understanding. "He also had an accomplice, whose identity he refuses to divulge."

"We'll keep him comfortable," she said, shaking her head sadly. "Elizabeth was a wild one," she added.

I bid my farewell but before I left returned to the cellblock to say Hello/Goodbye to Rudy. He still wasn't back so I sat on his bunk. As before, he had a copy of the *Panther Valley Pugilist* lying open. I ignored it, figuring that I'd be hearing more from the *Pugilist* than I really wanted to within the next twenty-four hours.

Eventually Rudy returned, a copy of *One Flew Over the Cuckoo's Nest* under his arm. He came toward me but froze in his steps when he saw Lawyer Delaney two cells away. "What—?" was all he said.

I nodded in Lawyer Delaney's direction. "You seem surprised to have a roommate," I said; it was plain that Delaney's presence had been like a blow to the nose for my kid brother.

He lowered himself to the cot, sitting straighter than was usual for him. "The plot continues to thicken," I said. Rudy seemed not to hear me. Then I sort of got it: Rudy knew Lawyer Delaney better than he'd let on.

"What's he doing here?" Rudy eventually got out.

"He was involved in Elizabeth's disappearance," I said. "Latest chapter in an evolving story."

Rudy looked at me blankly.

"He and his partner put Elizabeth's body in the mine," I said.

"Who's his partner?" Rudy asked, his nervousness at the answer palpable.

"Don't know yet, but we're getting closer to an answer all the time," I said.

"Who's 'we'?"

"Those seeking truth and justice . . . of which there are many," I said.

Rudy continued to take furtive glances at the seemingly anesthetized Mr. Delaney, who sat staring at the floor of his cell.

"No, really. Really," Rudy said.

"Really," I said. "The DA, the State Police, Sheriff Neast, Joe Boyle . . . me." I decided to keep the presence of a hit man from the Hazleton Mafia off the list, at least for the time being, although I was tempted to toss Teddy's identity in there in hopes Rudy would get the hint that not everyone looking into Elizabeth's death and the connection to the drug trade was an upstanding citizen looking for justice and not revenge.

"So it's over," Rudy said, half-heartedly.

"Hardly. He needs to give up his partner, and then the partner needs to give up who he's shilling drugs for, and up and up and up until it's all out in the open."

Rudy actually laughed. "You're nuts," he said, smiling at me as though I was a young moron. "You are *one* naïve kid."

"Oh?"

"You really think people involved in this are going to talk? They'd rather guzzle Drano." He put on one of those superior smiles that he sometimes relied upon to get him well under the skin of other people, and I wanted to bash it off his face just for the satisfaction of seeing it vanish.

"You give them way too much credit for having a backbone," I said. "Once the undoing gets rolling, they'll be crawling over each other like cockroaches wanting to be the first to make a deal to save their own sorry asses."

Rudy's superior smirk vanished. I must have known what I was talking about.

"You're nuts," he mumbled. I knew from years of living with the kid what that meant. It meant he'd be closing down the shop for the rest of the day so he could sulk.

I wanted to get up and slap him a good one on the back of the head, but instead I got up, said, "Maybe I'll see you tomorrow," and walked out. The gallows in the middle of the courtyard looked glum, two small spotlights shining on it as though it was center stage at Disneyland while rain continued to fall on it. The

Hollywood types would be lucky to get that final shot done in a week to ten days. The rain seemed parked atop us, as miserable and moody as everyone I ran into.

I waved goodbye to Mrs. Neast as I let myself out the big front door, happy to be away.

Teddy had the motor running in his battered Falcon. I directed him back up Broadway, back on the bus road, across the Heights, and down Packer Hill. We rolled to a stop beside the carriage house and behind my Rambler with a squeal of brakes and a sigh from Teddy. He turned off the headlights but let the motor idle.

"What's wrong?" I asked.

"Something's wrong," he said.

"What? What's wrong?"

At that moment a figure appeared at the driver's-side window, a shotgun barrel the size of a drainpipe pressed up against the window. A second later it retracted. Mr. Thorpe pressed his face against the window and motioned for us to get out and come into the house.

He walked through the rain as though it wasn't really raining, the big shotgun now drooping over his left elbow.

Teddy turned off the motor; we got out into the rain, and followed Mr. Thorpe inside. He set the gun vertical against the wall next to the door. He dripped onto the carpet. "They came back," he said. "Maybe not the same ones but the same kind."

"Are you all right?" I asked, afraid that I'd sucked poor old gnarly Mr. Thorpe into an increasingly bad situation.

He shrugged.

"Car went by, down the hill. This late at night, with nowhere to go? With all this rain? So I took the gun and went outside and hid in the shrubs, and they came back, this time *up* the hill, with the lights off, so when they pulled partway into the drive, I started shooting before they had the car door all the way open. They put it into reverse, gunned it, and got out of here. They'll have a helluva time explaining all the bodywork to their insurance company. And they'll need to replace a rear window." He laughed. "Better 'en hunting rabbits."

He pulled off his jacket, gave it a quick shake to get rid of some of the rain water, then hung it up on the rack next to the front door. "Shooting makes me thirsty," he said, heading toward the fridge, where he extracted a beer. He held it up to us, but both of us declined.

"I need to get to bed," I said. "Early morning tomorrow and it's already the middle of the night."

Teddy yawned. "Me, too. Need to get some rest . . . in case tomorrow is as exciting as today." He hung up his jacket, took off his suit coat and draped it across the back of the sofa, unfurled the blanket that was on the sofa, put a pistol under one of the cushions he was going to use as a pillow, dropped onto the sofa, and pulled the blanket over himself. Within seconds his breathing quieted.

The alarm went off at 4:30. The rain continued to fall. I got myself ready to go to work. Teddy groaned and looked up at me as I pulled on a jacket and my boots. I anticipated that Broadway would still be underwater.

"You get some sleep," I told Teddy. "I'll see you at lunch and we can plan our next move from there. Nobody's going to come barging into the newspaper office looking for trouble besides irate subscribers."

He mumbled in agreement and rolled over. There was no sound from Mr. Thorpe's bedroom.

I went by Steve's and got the usual two apple turnovers and a good strong cup of coffee to go.

Broadway was a mess. There were two borough trucks pulling up crap from the center of the still-underwater street. That crap included chunks of asphalt. Even though the predawn light was still pretty pathetic, it was easy to see where the eddies had shifted what was left of the Hollywood dirt street toward the intersections, where the flowing water had created very artistic formations—long, winding striations, waves of mud. I plodded through the mud and muck and backed-up water, waved at Hurley Higdon, one of the borough crew guys who'd been on the high school wrestling team with me.

The pavement in front of the Lehigh Coal & Navigation Build-ing was barely underwater, maybe an inch or so. Naturally, once I turned up Race Street, I was well above the level of the flood.

The newspaper office was a figurative beehive of activity.

The lights were glaring and the typewriters were hammering. Joe Boyle looked as though he'd been there all night, his sport jack-et hung on the back of his chair and his sleeves rolled up to his elbows. He battered the Underwood with his index fingers until it sounded like a machine gun.

Mrs. Apfelbaum had notes spread out across her desk and a roll of paper running through her typewriter, already a yard into it, the paper drooping behind the typewriter and piling up on the floor.

I found Skip Harrison and gave him the roll of film I'd shot Saturday night, then talked to Abe Schnabel, the chief layout guy, about reformatting the editorial page to accommodate the Broad-way flood photo and the quote from Buster Sward. He laughed out loud at the concept. "You really like pissing people off, don't you?"

"Freedom of the press," I said.

The morning moved along rapidly. We had a two-page spread dedicated exclusively to photos of the flood. At the bottom we add-ed a box inviting people to send in their own personal photos for a special two-page spread on Tuesday summing up the flood and its aftermath.

I could not have been more pleased with the photos of the streetlight-illuminated flood coming down Broadway. We picked what we thought was the most dramatic and laid it across six of eight columns of the editorial page. Joe had knocked out an edito-rial outlining for the hundredth time the benefits of the proposed watershed project and several letters on that same theme had al-ready been dropped off and went onto the page. Except for the quote at the top of the page, nobody mentioned Buster Sward's name.

By noon the floor began to vibrate as it did six days a week as the presses began to build up speed. Like every day I'd been there, Abe Schnabel came up the steps from the pressroom and laid a still-damp copy of the paper out in front of each of us. The sound of typewriters chattering away died down and stopped as we spread out copies of the new issue on the desks in front of us.

The seventy-two-point headline across the top of the paper said it all:

FLOOD!!!

I ignored it and went to the editorial page. No editorial cartoon needed. The photo and Buster Sward's quote summed it all up.

Bundled copies of the issue were being loaded on delivery trucks, but neighbors were coming by with seven cents and buying up copies through the front door, as though they had to read it in the paper to make what was apparent in front of their own eyes real.

Abe wrestled a bundle of papers up the narrow steps and set them on the receptionist's desk just inside the door, cutting the twine that bound them as he did so. "Just put a coffee tin next to the pile and we'll get rich," he said.

It hadn't even reached 1:00 p.m. when the front door was thrown back with a bang and Agnes McCartney barged in. Mrs. McCartney, head of the Carbon County Tourist Promotion Agency, was a force of nature. Big, blustery, she stood in the doorway with the newspaper folded so that the top of the editorial page was displayed. She pointed to it, her mouth opened, but nothing came out.

"Cat got your tongue, Agnes?" Joe asked.

She seemed to sputter for a few seconds. She was making s sounds. I thought she was going to say "Shit!" But her mouth made a garbled somersault and "Wonderful!" is what came out. "Wonderful!" she said again and again.

Her years'-long crusade to get a dam built out beyond Mauch Chunk had obviously just received a shot in the arm.

She stalked over to Joe's desk. "Brilliant," she said, then lowered her voice, but not enough that Mrs. Apfelbaum and I didn't hear her ask: "Has Buster responded yet?"

"Take a little while for the copies to reach Summit Hill," Joe said. "You know. The roads aren't in very good condition today."

Agnes McCartney was literally vibrating. I wouldn't have been surprised to see her break into a jig. She looked around the office and flashed the top of the editorial page, as though the rest of the staff were unaware of it. "Let me know when you hear from him," she said to Joe, then turned and was gone, a big old black hole left in the spot she'd just been occupying.

"Jeez," I said. "You think we have a satisfied subscriber?"

Joe laughed. "When she finds out you're the instigator behind that, she'll be all over you for the next year."

"Is that good?" I asked.

"Well, yes and no," Mrs. Apfelbaum said. "She'll want you to do more, be an advocate, keep beating the drum."

I shook my head. *Politics*, I thought. *God, I hate politics.*

The invitation for walking-around citizens to drop off photos of the flood's effects in their neighborhood was having an effect, but so far no photos. People had to send their rolls of film out to be developed. But they came by anyway, to assure us that they would be bringing flood photos by. Real soon. As soon as they got them back. And they were good ones. Real good. Dramatic.

At close to 2:00 I received a call from Teddy, just checking in. He had some news from Mrs. Martinelli about our friends in Wilkes-Barre, but he didn't want to discuss it over the phone. We'd talk when I got home.

Joe and Nate Dermott and I talked about what kind of coverage we'd give the aftermath of the flood in tomorrow's paper, how many pages we planned to set aside. The rain outside decreased to a drizzle, but the aftereffects would be with us for weeks.

Joe and Nate decided it would be my job to contact the Hollywood people to see what they planned to do about the tons of their dirt that the flood had washed into the river. Were they going to lay down another layer and continue shooting the movie? I got on the phone and began finding that out.

I got as far as talking to one of the production managers who was staying in the Switzerland Hotel over on Broadway and learned that they probably would not lay down more dirt but would likely do close-up shots of the principals interacting "downtown," since much of the preliminary long shots had been done the week before. Mauch Chunk was standing in as "the big city" to which Richard Harris takes Samantha Eggar on a Sunday excursion, where he is to meet briefly with the Welsh coal company cop who is running him as a spy among the Mollies.

I was just signing off after taking the phone number of one of the assistant directors when Mrs. Apfelbaum fielded a call. She held up her right index finger for silence and everything stopped. She covered the mouthpiece and mouthed the words "It's Buster."

"Well you don't have to use language like that, Mr. Sward," Gertrude said in her best offended-lady voice. "I know you're upset. Yes. Of course." She held the phone away from her ear for a moment, and we could hear the electric screech of Buster Sward on the other end, although we couldn't make out what he was saying. We could tell he was talking fast and talking loud. "Now, now," Gertrude hissed into the phone. "Sometimes in life one's words come back to haunt one. Yes, yes. Well, as a newspaper publisher yourself"—Mrs. Apfelbaum covered her mouth to stifle a laugh— "you understand the editorial process. Yes, yes. And the paper's responsibility to its readers." She nodded and smiled. "We'd be more than agreeable to publish a response to the flood picture and your quote. But you don't deny that the quote is accurate. Well, yes, I have that issue of your newspaper right here in my top drawer, with your very words, in eighteen-point type." She again moved the phone away from her ear.

Joe looked at me as though to say, "Just look at the mess you got us into." Then he smiled. He cupped his hands around his mouth and mouthed the words "just kidding." He rubbed his hands together.

"'Bout time that bastard got some of his own medicine," Nate Dermott hissed.

"Yes, yes," Mrs. Apfelbaum said. "You get your letter to us by eleven tomorrow morning and we'll carry it in that afternoon's paper." She wrinkled up her nose and shook her head. "Well, we *do* retain a lawyer, and I'm sure he'd be delighted to hear from your lawyer. Yes." She held the phone away from her head and looked at it as though she was trying to tame a cobra. I thought for a moment that she was going to stick her tongue out at the phone before cradling it, but she had too much class to lower herself that much. Class wouldn't have stopped me.

"Hot, huh?" Joe asked.

"Hot, indeed," Mrs. Apfelbaum said. "He's going to speak to his lawyer. Other than giving his lawyer billable hours, I don't know what the point is." She dropped the phone into the cradle with a *clack*. "He's supposed to be a newspaperman. He should know that as long as you can prove something is true, any suit he brings would be laughed out of court."

"Especially when all we did was repeat his own words," Joe said. He looked buoyant enough to float away.

The phone rang again. Sheriff Neast wanted to talk to me. It didn't take long. Things in the county were still in chaos because of the storm, but he had had time to speak with Lawyer Delaney, who concurred with my brief report of what had happened to Elizabeth. The sheriff had put in a call to the district attorney but had not yet received word back as to how they should proceed, but for the time being Lawyer Delaney was content to stay in a cell at the jail. "You ought to begin charging rent," I said just before he signed off.

If things kept going like they were, it was going to take a crowbar to get my brother out of jail. He was starting to like it way too much.

I decided to call it a day. I'd see Teddy a little later, but in the meantime I felt the urge to go see my kid sister, Ellie.

I picked up the phone again, dialed my mother's number, let it ring once, and hung up. Waited thirty seconds and did it again. Thirty more seconds and repeat it. That was the signal between Ellie and me that I'd be dropping by. When I didn't feel in the mood to see our mother, Ellie and I would meet at the boulder set into the side of Bear Mountain about fifty yards above the family's moldering mansion.

I could call the assistant director of *The Molly Maguires* this evening to get a quote from him about how they were going to proceed with the filming.

I hiked back up to the carriage house, and Teddy saw me coming for my car and came out to meet me.

"I'm leaving," he said.

My surprise must have shown.

"Things in Wilkes-Barre have . . . a . . . stabilized," he said.

"Stabilized," I said. "What the hell does that mean?"

"Means you won't be needing to look over your shoulder for a special delivery."

"So Mrs. Martinelli and this dirtbag came to some sort of compromise concerning my continued existence," I said.

"Something like that," Teddy said. He still wore his suit, and it still wasn't wrinkled. Must be made of some sort of science-fiction material brought in from the future. He moved to open his car door.

I stepped forward, extending my hand. "No handshake?" I said.

He seemed caught by surprise. "Oh, yeah, sure," he said, grasping my hand and giving it a strong squeeze. As he let my hand go, he had a bit more to say. "If our paths should ever cross again, especially in the presence of any of the Martinellis, don't talk to me or make any sign that you know me other than as a statue."

"What?"

"My job description with the Martinelli family does not include fraternization with either a client or an enemy."

"What?" I repeated as he lowered himself into the driver's seat and fired up the trusty old Falcon. He didn't wave or look at me as he backed the car out onto Packer Hill. He was gone in an instant.

And an instant later I was gone, too, on my way to Pleasant Hill, aka Nigger Hill. Ever since anyone can remember, Pleasant Hill has been called Nigger Hill, not because there are or were any Negro people living there, because there never were, but because the hill was primarily inhabited by coal miners and their families: coal miners who didn't own cars and who midafternoon walked from the mines, across the bridge, down past the railroad station, and up the little set of wooden steps to their gray houses on the hill. When they came home they still wore their work clothes and the coal dust that had stuck to them down in the mines. They looked like black zombies—tired black zombies.

Since so few of them owned cars, the borough had built a footbridge between Nigger Hill and the rest of East Mauch Chunk that came out on Third Street, to make it easier for them to get into town. We all called it the Swinging Bridge because if you were in the middle of it you could get it swinging pretty damned good. If you had a car, you went to Fifth Street and drove the winding road that went down past the Silk Mill and then up to the northern edge of Nigger Hill.

Since I was driving a car, that's the way I went to get over to visit Ellie. I drove across the street above the one where our mother's house squatted and parked by the fire hydrant near the pullout next to the beginning of the trail that went straight up the mountain. The boulder where we always met sat like an unfinished sculpture beside the road.

It was the same trail the four of us kids had used to escape home on the day they waked our father. Unfortunately, the following day they tracked us down at our hideout cave and hauled us back home.

I turned the car off and waited for Ellie. As always when I was waiting for something or someone, I wished I'd brought along something to read. When our father used to take us grocery shopping, I used to stand in the cereal aisle and read the backs and sides of the boxes—even if they weren't detailing a prize that waited inside in the bottom of the box.

In a few minutes Ellie came moping up the street, wearing her traditional formless gray dress that made her look like a Catholic nun-in-waiting. (In fact, I'd often urged her to give up being a slave to our mother in favor of becoming a nun. She would make a terrific nun, but she'd have none of it.)

I rolled down the window and called to her: "Hey, kid! Ya wanna sit in the car or take a walk?"

She came to the passenger's door and let herself in. She hung her head, her mousy hair dripping over her face. I patted her lightly on the back. She wasn't much for hugging and embracing. She didn't pull away, but neither did she react as though she craved someone's touch. She lived pretty much by herself in the attic, descending when it was time to make meals for our mother. She didn't go out to play and didn't go to school, although she did know how to read. The truant officer had come after our mother at one point to try to force her to send Ellie to school, and my mother had driven him off with protestations that Ellie was needed at home more than she needed school.

Ellie kind of peeked from under her flow of hair, reached slowly into the big pocket in the front left of her dress, and pulled out a piece of paper. On it she'd printed the word *naïve* in lowercase letters.

This was a ritual we frequently went through. She liked to read but didn't like to use a dictionary. I had bought her a nice *New Collegiate Dictionary* three Christmases ago, but she refused to open it. I came to the conclusion that this was her method of opening a conversation, so I went along with it.

Naïve.

I stopped myself from blurting out, "Well, hell, Ellie, you're the personification of naïve."

"It's the opposite of sophisticated and clever in thought and deed. Sort of like me," I said.

She punched me lightly in the right arm. "Not," she said.

"Is so," I said.

She half-smiled behind her lank hair. "I'm naïve," she said.

"Probably everybody in our family is naïve, except for grandmother."

"I don't mind being naïve," she said.

"But you don't want to be naïve forever, do you?"

She shook her head.

"They found Elizabeth Delaney, and she was dead," Ellie said, playing with her fingers, doing one of those things she often did by changing the topic of discussion in an instant. "You helped her."

"Sort of."

"You see Rudy?"

"Yeah. A couple of times."

"Is he coming home soon?"

"Not for a couple of weeks."

"Mother never asks about him—or about you."

"I'm sure she has other things to think about," I rationalized. Mother never had anything to think about but herself. "Is she actually communicating these days?"

"You mean talking," she said, still playing with her fingers. "She talks once in a while. Sometimes."

"What are you reading that has the word *naïve* in it?"

"I'll tell you when I'm done reading it. Just in case I don't finish it."

We were both quiet for a lot of long moments. The awful rain had petered out to a lowing mist. It was a bit chilly but not cold. Ellie didn't seem to notice the mist or the dampness and there was no indication that she was cold—no shivering or goose bumps.

"Did the roof leak?" I asked, remembering that the house had not had a bit of maintenance done since our father died. How many years was that? Nearly twelve.

"Sure," Ellie said. "I never moved the buckets from the last storm." She looked straight ahead, almost like we were driving along and she was looking for a landmark. "I like your house," she said.

For a second I didn't know what she was talking about. "You like my house?"

"Yeah, the little house next to the spooky mansion."

"When did you see my house?"

"Couple a times." She tucked in her head. "I go out sometimes at night."

This was news to me. "Does Mother know?"

Ellie shook her head emphatically. "She wouldn't like that. You know she doesn't like to be alone." She turned and looked directly at me, troubled. "You won't tell her, will you?"

I patted her on the back. "No way."

"It's nicer at night," she said. "No trouble. And I know most of the dogs, so they don't bark. The only people out are drunken people trying to get home. They don't see me."

"And how far do your midnight travels take you?"

She seemed to be thinking about that, running over a map in her head. She stopped playing with her fingers. "The Immaculate Conception Church on Broadway and up to Memorial Park and the high school the other way."

That constituted about 70 percent of the two towns. "Does anybody ever see you?"

"I can tell if somebody's coming, so I hide."

"Bet you see some interesting stuff."

"Sometimes."

"Maybe we should give you a column in the newspaper: Midnight Ramblings."

She laughed. "You couldn't . . . shouldn't write about some of the stuff."

That piqued my curiosity.

"Why not?"

"Nobody would care." She went back to playing with her fingers, her fingernails chewed down, seeming to concentrate on the little ball of snakes the two intertwined sets of fingers resembled.

"Be a television broadcaster. Give me some of the news you've picked up at night."

She shook her head in the negative.

"Give me some news about the house where I live."

"You already know all about it, you and the Indian man who live there." She tapped the index and middle fingers of her right hand against the palm of her left hand. "Are you two friends?"

"Sure. I guess so," I said. "We're roommates and we get along just fine."

"Good," she said. "He's a famous man that got thrown out of the Olympics."

"Well, he didn't exactly get thrown out. They took back his medals after they found out he'd earned some money playing summer ball."

"What's wrong with playing summer ball?"

"It was against the rules."

"Would they have taken them away if he worked for the summer at the Steel?"

Good question. "Probably not, because that wouldn't have been playing sports."

"But he wasn't getting paid to play the sports he played at the Olympics."

"Good point," I admitted. "You ought to be a lawyer."

"Like Mr. Delaney, the dead girl's dad."

I took half a breath. "No, not like Mr. Delaney. Mr. Delaney's not a very nice man."

"I already know that. And it's not because he's a pig farmer. It's because he hain't nice to Mrs. Delaney."

"How do you know about the pigs?"

"Because I go by and play with them sometimes."

My eyebrows went up all by themselves. "You go by and play with them?"

"Sure." She looked at me, all seriousness. "They like to act mean, but they're friendly . . . if you bring them something."

"What do you bring them?"

"People throw stuff down the Dump, like table scraps. I get a bunch of it together in a bucket and they like it."

"You don't get too close to them, do you?"

"Just enough to scratch them between the eyes. That's what they like the most."

"You should stay away from them. They can be dangerous."

"Not if you're nice to them." She turned back to gaze out the windshield and was quiet for a time. "Are you gonna marry her?" she finally asked.

"Marry whom?" I had absolutely no idea who she was talking about.

"That Alice lady over on Race Street."

I didn't know what to say. "How da'ya know about Alice?"

"You go see her sometimes."

I did the quick math in my head. I'd been to Alice's twice since I graduated from college. "You ought to go to work for the CIA."

"What's that?"

"Central Intelligence Agency."

She hummed "Hmmmmmmm" for a few seconds. "Maybe I already do." She turned to look at me and turned on a huge smile. "I know a lot of intelligence."

"That's what I'm finding out."

"I still have all of your *Detective Comics* and *Batman Comics*," she said. "I'm a creature of the night, just like Batman."

Jeez. That was a little disconcerting. And here I thought she spent all of her time in the attic of the falling-apart old Victorian mansion on Nigger Hill.

"Do you spend any time at home?"

"I'm home all day . . . taking care of Mother."

"And all night roaming the countryside spying on people."

"I'm not spying," she whined. "I'm just keeping my eyes open and my mouth shut."

"How about if you unshut your mouth for a little bit and tell me what's going on around town."

She shook her head in the negative but not as firmly as before. "I shouldn't do that. Then it's gossip."

"Not if it's true."

"Oh, it's true," she said very seriously.

"Just give me ten things you found out."

She looked down at her hands. "I'll make you a deal."

"Okay. And what would that be?"

"You come by and see mother once a week and I'll tell you ten things."

Seeing mother was an ordeal I didn't much fancy. It was like visiting with a mummy. (Sorry.) She sat there looking at me while I tried to make small talk. She seldom if ever opened her mouth, just sat there in her black widow's clothes, getting thinner each trip, saying nothing, looking at me critically as though I'd put her through hell. The closest she got to conversation was the occasional sigh. "How good are these ten things?"

She shrugged her shoulders. "Mostly good stuff. Not all of it great." She smiled a crooked smile. "This hain't the Big Apple, baby."

"Okay. I'll try to come by once a week, probably on Sunday afternoon, when I'm not working."

She held her hand out to shake on the deal. Then she began ticking things off on her fingers. "Mr. Weaver, up on South Street, drinks four gallons of cheap red wine a week." I raised my eyebrows, trying to indicate that I didn't think that was a really good piece of information, at least one not unique. "Harry Fedderer goes on dates with other men." I kind of knew that, but I guess the little spy girl now confirmed it. "Mrs. Spatz's cat had six kittens and none of them look like any of the others." I wrinkled my nose at her.

"Cats do that, when they're in heat," I said.

"Do what?"

"Never mind. What's next?"

"Mr. Kelley up on Center Avenue by the school has two girl-friends."

"So what?"

"He's married to Mrs. Kelley."

"And she's not one of the girlfriends—"

"Of course not, silly."

"You're making the Mauch Chunks sound like Peyton Place," said.

"I know what that is."

"I'll bet you do."

"Your friend from high school, the one you traded science-fiction books with, is out a lot of nights, and he meets people down by the old canal locks, and he always dresses like he's in a movie."

"Null-A," I supplied.

"Yeah, him. I call him the Chameleon."

"And who are these people he meets?"

"I don't know any of them. They're not from here. They meet down in the locks, and they give each other money and packages, and they drive down the road with their lights out." She pulled a spiral notebook from her pocket that was the size of a three-by-five card and about fifty pages thick. "But I get their license plate numbers anyway."

I felt my eyebrows rise again. Not at the fact that Null-A might be involved in something suspicious. I'd have been more surprised if I found out he wasn't. But rather that my kid sister was skating on some very dangerous ice. "And what are you gonna do with the license plate numbers?"

She stuffed the notebook back into her pocket. "I'm gonna keep them."

"Why?"

"Just in case."

"Just in case of what?"

"Just in case I need them someday."

"What would you need them for?"

For a moment she acted as though she wasn't going to answer. "In case I need to blackmail your friend."

I didn't know whether to laugh or have a heart attack. Little Ellie was on the road to becoming a major-league crook, a crook who could get hurt or killed if she got caught sticking her nose in Null-A's business—whatever that was. Whatever it was, of course, seemed pretty plain. He was probably the middleman offloading drugs on their way to Bucknell and Penn State for consumption by the local heads. Null-A had always been a talented boy, always a step or two ahead of the rest of us, whether it came to making baseball and comic book trades or being the first to spot trends— spot them and exploit them. I wondered how close he and Lawyer Delaney might be.

I made a mental note to go back to the county lockup at some point and float the name of Null-A to Delaney as his mysterious partner.

"What else do you have in your notebook?" I asked.

"What kind of wine Mr. Weaver drinks. Mostly Gallo. The names of Mr. Kelley's girlfriends. When you saw that Alice lady."

"It was only two times," I said, much too defensively.

She again pulled out her notebook and consulted it, rifling through the pages. "That's correct," she said, very formally. "Do you want to know the dates and times?"

I shook my head. I was feeling slightly creeped out.

"What else?" The little glance I'd managed to take of her notebook as she rifled through it had registered that there was writing on virtually every page.

"How about the names of the Delaney pigs?" she said.

"The what?"

"What I named the three big pigs—"

"Which is what? Huey, Dewey, and Louie?"

She laughed. "No, silly. Curly, Larry, and Moe."

Now I laughed, then didn't. "How much do you want for the license plate numbers of the people who 'traded' with Null-A?"

"I could use a new car," she said, poking her left elbow into my right ribcage.

If I could get the license plate numbers, I was sure I could get Ronnie to run them for me—for us.

"What will you do with them?" she asked.

"I'll find out who the people are who belong to them."

She thought about that for a moment. Somewhere behind us thunder boomed, as though announcing that yet another storm was lined up out in the Poconos waiting to come marching in to add to the general misery in downtown Mauch Chunk.

"I'll give you a copy of the list if you'll give me a copy of the names and addresses that go with them." She dramatically folded her arms across her little chest as though to indicate that that was all there was to it. No negotiating.

She certainly wouldn't be able to get into any trouble having that sort of information, at least not the way Ronnie and I would be able to.

"Okay," I said, holding out my right hand to shake on the deal.

She shook, her little hand warm and damp.

She pulled the notebook out, opened it, paged to the back where there were still a few blank pages and pulled two of them out, then turned to the pages containing the license numbers, pulled a gnawed pencil from her cornucopia pocket, and began copying them onto the blank sheets.

While she did that, I gazed ahead, kind of blanking out what was in front of me. Just what would Ronnie and I do with the names and addresses? There was no proof that these people were doing anything illegal, other than trespassing on what I assumed remained railroad property. Jeez. Meeting at the old deserted, crumbling stone locks. It sounded right out of the Hardy Boys.

Probably more pressing was the simple question of what I was going to do with Ellie. She was now a teen, she was a shut-in, and for years she'd been the primary custodian of our mother, not an enviable task. (Although with the revelation of her nocturnal adventures, I guess "shut-in" wasn't an appropriate description.) Donald and I had on more than one occasion raised the possibility of bringing in help. I'd even gone so far as to go to grandmother to ask if she'd help financially, and she'd reluctantly agreed to do that, even though she'd seemed appalled at what that kind of care ran a month. "A king's ransom," she'd muttered, but in the end she had acquiesced. We didn't bother to consult with Rudy. For obvious reasons.

But Ellie had squelched our plan.

"I can take care of Mother," she'd said, over and over.

And in frustration, the last time we'd discussed it, just before Donald headed back to Anchorage to resume his Air Force duties, I'd posed the simple question: "And who'll take care of you?"

Ellie had acted like I'd slapped her—hard—across the face. Like I'd undermined all the years she'd managed to take care of—I had to admit it—all of us. She'd spent years making us all breakfast and dinner, and she'd kept the big hollow house relatively clean, while still finding time to spend most of her time cloistered in the attic, amidst the unopened wooden boxes that held, like a series of vaults, our mother's previous life.

We *had*, year after year, taken her for granted. I rationalized it by figuring she'd wanted to be taken for granted, wanted to be left alone in her boring routine, comfortable in the fact that she had a purpose in life, that she was maybe a little slow and loved routine, loved the reassurance of her aerie, her hideout behind dirty windows, among big wooden boxes, like a mouse in the basement of a museum or a bat in a belfry.

This secret nocturnal life, though, this had thrown me. This was not expected, and walked a tightrope between creepy and liberating. More creepy when it came to my two visits to Alice. What hadn't the little shit seen? How many notebooks did she have?

"How many of these notebooks do you have?"

She looked up from her copying. "None of your business."

"Lots, huh?"

She looked at me through the eyes of our grandmother, ancient and critical. As though to ask "Just how dumb are you, anyway?"

I felt a chill go through me, as though I suddenly realized that I didn't know my kid sister at all, that I'd never known her, that as nice as I'd tried to be to her, I'd always done it out of compassion, out of feeling sorry for her.

Now she was feeling sorry for me. I was the one who was slow; I was the one who was dumb. And come to think of it, if my life weren't intruded upon by outside influences, I'd be a pretty pre-dictable routine happening over and over and over, week after week. Wake up, shower, got to Steve's Diner, get a cup of coffee and two apple turnovers, go to the office, check the AP wire service . . . And I'd only been doing that a week and already I was into a rut that would probably cement me until retirement, like a bug with a pin through it at a museum. And then what? Get up, get showered, go by Steve's Diner and get a cup of coffee and two apple turnovers . . .

Ellie poked me in the ribs and pushed the two pieces of paper into my hand.

Her poke interrupted my slow-to-get-it brain's realization that professional wrestlers, Molotov cocktails, bullets from would-be assassins, and a monumental flood had fortuitously interrupted the routine I'd been cementing. Without those few distractions, my last week—my first full week on the job—would have been a dreadful bore.

I took a quick glance at the license plate numbers. Most were Pennsylvania plates, a half-dozen were Jersey, and two were New York. I made a quick estimate and figured there were close to fifty numbers. I made a little whistle.

"Do you ever stay home at nights?" I asked.

"If I'm reading a good book, I do," she said.

"You need me to get you a bag of good books to keep you at home?"

She screwed up her face. "Sometimes I get rammy and I need to get out."

"To get the stink blown off you," I added, something our father used to say if he thought we were spending too much time indoors, especially if it was a pleasant day outside. I guess that's what you say if you spend your days stuck in a dark, dank, dirty old coal mine.

Ellie opened the passenger door and walked slowly downhill back to the haunted house in which she lived—in which we'd all lived.

I decided to go see Ronnie . . . if he was home.

19
Nothing—Much—Happens. Sorta.

I went by way of the Heights, coming down Packer Hill to park at the carriage house, figuring to put on my boots and walk down to see if Ronnie was at home in his red caboose. The way the water had rushed across the tracks to the river, I figured a fair amount of track would be either washed out or moved a few inches or feet, making it imperative that it be repaired quickly.

When I walked through the front door, Mr. Thorpe, unable to do any gardening in the continuing downpour, was still reading *Moby Dick*, and he informed me that Inspector Farrell of the Pennsylvania State Police had come by and appropriated a pair of my shoes. He'd made a kind of receipt on the back of his business card; he promised that I'd have them back within a week. Shit. They were my best pair of training flats, not that I'd be getting in a lot of roadwork over the next few postflood days.

I pulled on my boots, pulled up the hood on my hooded jacket, and headed out the door. I walked down to Ronnie's caboose and knocked on the door, pretty certain he was in because there was gray smoke coming out of the chimney, indicating he had a fire going in the wood stove. I knocked again, and behind the steady sound of the rain falling on the caboose roof, I heard movement.

The door opened and Ronnie stood there in a pair of red long johns. He looked like something out of the California Gold Rush, just emerging from the mines. All he needed to complete the look were a beard and hair a mite longer than what the staties were allowed to grow. "What 'ya want?" he growled. He blinked, looked past the hooded jacket, and waved me inside. "Horrible night last night. Just got in a couple of hours ago. This flood pissed me off." He dropped onto his sofa, where a blanket was crumpled over it, and the indent from his head in the pillow. The blanket and pillow didn't match. Big surprise.

He yawned and made a sign I should get on with an explanation of what the hell I was doing interrupting his precious sleep. I reached into my jeans pocket and pulled out the two little note sheets. "Whazz'dat?"

"License place numbers," I said. As soon as the words came out of my mouth I had the realization that ole Ronnie was not gonna jump at the chance to help me out.

"And lemme guess: you want me to rise from my luxurious deep sleep to run these—Jesus! How many of them are there?" He reached across and grabbed the pieces of paper. "Fuck," he muttered, "some of these aren't even Pennsy plates!" He rolled his eyes, then rolled his head as though it was on a universal joint. Then he did something that made the bones in his shoulders and neck crack without even touching them. He used to do that before a wrestling match in high school. I cringed.

He sat the two pieces of paper on the seat of a chair and again pivoted his head, again making that snapping sound. I cringed again. "Can you please stop that?" I pleaded. "You know it makes me sick."

He smiled his cockeyed smile, the one reserved for his cynical side. "Why the hell do ya think I'm doin' it? Maybe you'll get disgusted enough that you'll leave so I can get back to sleep."

I shrugged and turned back to the door. He fell back onto the sofa and pulled the blanket back over himself. "Take a few days," he said as he waved me toward the door. "Now get lost."

I did as I was told.

Back home I called Joe Boyle at home and asked if there was anything else we needed to do about reporting on the storm. He assured me there was not, that what we had was what we needed. People had been rushing their pictures through the developing process, he said, and we'd be up to our eyebrows in flood photos.

"Some of the folks even got creative," he said, "Mrs. Skoolmacker posed three of her cats in an inverted garbage-can lid and set them sailing down the street and then took pictures. I'm sure she'll be devastated if we don't run them on the front page."

I signed off and offered to get Mr. Thorpe a beer while I put three beef potpies into the oven. "Gonna stop by tomorrow morning," he said, pointing his finger toward the ceiling.

"How da'ya know that?"

"Indians know lots of stuff whites don't know they know." He took a long drag of his beer. "It also said so on WLSH radio."

He lowered his head and looked at me from under his bushy eyebrows, working hard to be at his most menacing. "Means I have to get back to work tomorrow planting summer flowers." He raised his beer toward me, I raised mine toward him, and that was the high point of the evening—other than filling my gut with store-bought twenty-five-cent beef potpies.

I went to my room, tried to read the current issue of *Car and Driver*, and fell asleep over Jean Shepherd's column.

When the alarm went off at 4:00 a.m., I could hear by the silence that Mr. Thorpe and WLSH were right. The rain had stopped. I looked out the window and saw stars.

Took a shower. Picked up my coffee and two apple turnovers at Steve's. Made my way around the rubble on Broadway. Sat down at my desk with a pile of AP stories in my left hand and an apple turnover in my right and Joe Boyle off to my left pecking at his keyboard and Mrs. Apfelbaum on her telephone across the desk from me talking to somebody about the Lehighton Women's Club fashion show being rescheduled due to the flooding.

This morning's copy of the *Morning Call* lay between Mrs. Apfelbaum and me. Somebody had already ravaged it. It lay there in pieces, a few inches of some story cut out by one of our editors so they could follow up on it and expand it. And there, on the lower half of page 7, was an item that caught my eye:

WILKES-BARRE KINGPIN GUNNED DOWN IN BAKERY
Simon "The Stone" Ravich Executed while eating a Danish

What was left of my turnover stopped in midair on its way to my mouth. I dragged the ragged newspaper section across the desk so I could more easily read it. I commanded my right hand to resume its job of transporting what was left of my second apple turnover to my waiting mouth.

Like many such stories culled from out of the area, the news item was only three graphs long. How much would someone sitting at a kitchen table in Allentown or having lunch out of a metal pail at the Bethlehem Steel care about some hood in Wilkes-Barre getting iced?

I stopped chewing when I realized that the news item indicated that this Ravich guy had been eating his Danish in one of Mrs. Martinelli's bakery/restaurants. And I stopped chewing for quite a while, to the point that Mrs. Apfelbaum noticed and waved her hand at me to get my attention. "Daydreams are for the daytime, and it's barely light," she said.

"Mmmmmmmmm," I responded.

She shook her head and went back to dialing her phone. Maybe the Weissport Flower Club wanted to postpone its flower-arranging class until next week.

I was two-stage stunned.

My first reaction was that Mrs. Martinelli had followed through and had the hood in Wilkes-Barre who'd taken the contract on me and whomsoever else was on the drug kingpin's hit list taken out, which was why I had been assured by Teddy before he left that I was now safe to move around under my own direction. Although she was crusty in an old-world sort of way, I couldn't imagine that Mrs. Martinelli would literally have somebody snuffed, as though it was the 1930s all over again. But then a little flickering candle in the back of my head attempted to illuminate me out of my naiveté. Why couldn't/shouldn't she? The increasing drug trade was cutting into her business, and this "The Stone" Ravich was willing to take out anybody who stood in its way, which included me. And Mrs. Martinelli didn't want her only daughter's best friend from college killed over her business. Hence, Teddy. But then I felt some of my ego slip a bit and realized that if I was on the hit list, and I was an outsider, a nobody, there were probably a lot of people on the list who were close to Mrs. Martinelli. Maybe Mrs. Martinelli herself. So I shouldn't inflate my ego so much when the murder of "The Stone" was probably more self-preservation on her part.

And then the second stage kicked in, just like a two-stage rocket. How could she be so damned stupid, so boneheaded, as to have the guy killed in one of *her* bakeries? Man, talk about dumb. But then the second stage seemed to find an extra fuel source, and I changed my mind: how fucking brilliant! Have the bastard killed in one of her bakeries and nobody would *ever* suspect she was involved because nobody would believe she could be so damned dumb. Brilliant!

And then there was the dead guy. Probably a nasty bastard who was very happy to take on a contract to kill a bunch of people who stood in the way of his drugmeisters. The guy probably deserved to die long ago. But now he *was* dead. Even though I'd seen a thousand guys get killed in Western movies, some of them more graphically when *The Man With No Name* hit the screen, I wasn't used to being around people who'd been murdered. People didn't kill each other in Mauch Chunk—at least not since the days of The Molly Maguires.

And then a third stage fired up. What in the hell was Simon "The Stone" Ravich doing in one of Mrs. Martinelli's bakeries in the first place? True, Mrs. Martinelli lived in Hazleton and worked out of the bakery office there and likely didn't get to the Wilkes-Barre bakery more than a few times a year, or as needed, and they weren't likely to run into each other, but if she was on his hit list, why was he patronizing one of her stores?

All of this was becoming just too damned complicated, and now, with the second apple turnover safely in my belly, I was on the verge of admitting that all the last week's stuff was so damned complicated because likely I was making it so. It was probably all very simple, like most things in life—until we step in and try to analyze them or read too much into them or stick our big long noses in them and stir things up that had started out simple.

Maybe Mr. "The Stone" Ravich was in Mrs. Martinelli's Wilkes-Barre store because he liked the baked goods. Maybe it was his habit to eat a Danish or two every day, or every Monday, or every other day. Maybe he even took Mafia meetings in Mrs. Martinelli's Wilkes-Barre bakery, sitting at the same table every week, with his gang sitting around the table munching on shoofly pie, knocking back thin coffee.

Hell, I'd been here a little over a week and I'd already developed the two apple turnover at Steve's Diner habit like someone else develops a tic.

Mrs. Apfelbaum was snapping her fingers not too far from my right ear while Joe Boyle had stopped typing and was looking at me like I'd just dropped in from Saturn. "Earth calling," he said. "Are you okay?"

"Yeah, yeah. I was just thinking, that's all."

"It must have been some thought," Mrs. Apfelbaum said. "You looked like you were in a trance."

I shook my head. "I guess I was."

Mercifully the phone rang and Joe picked it up. "Yeah, yeah," he said. "You're up early." He put his hand over the phone and mouthed to Mrs. Apfelbaum and me: "Sward's lawyer."

Mrs. Apfelbaum tsk-tsked and began shuffling papers around on her desktop.

"You're absolutely correct," Joe was saying. "Not a chance in the world. I don't care if he's a county commissioner. If he doesn't have the good sense to think something through before he says it or writes it down, that's not my problem." Joe was quiet for a full minute, nodding his head "Not a chance in hell." Mrs. Apfelbaum's head came up when she heard brother Joe say "hell." "You tell him he should grow up and stand behind what he says and writes, or else find a different line of work." Another pause. "So what if it was the new kid's idea. It was a damned good idea." Mrs. Apfelbaum shook her head after glaring at Joe when he said "damned." (She would later confide that although she knew all the words, every newspaperwoman did, she'd been on a campaign since she and Joe were kids to improve his conversational English by outlawing all nasty words. "Never gonna happen," she concluded.)

Joe finished his conversation with Sward's lawyer. "He knows he's got no case," Joe said, winking at me.

Mrs. Apfelbaum waved her finger at brother Joe. "Language," she said. "Your language." She tsk-tsked again.

I picked up the phone. "I'm gonna call the Wilkes-Barre police," I told Joe, "follow up on the Mafia assassination up there. Maybe there's an angle: The Return of the Mafia."

Joe laughed. "You *have* been away for too long."

"What da'ya mean?"

"The Mafia never left. Ya virtually have to tiptoe over the bodies if you get out of your car to take a piss"—he looked toward his older sister across the desk, egging her on—"along the Northeast Extension of the Turnpike. It's a damned dumping grounds for Mafia kills."

Mrs. Apfelbaum shook her head and threw up her hands in surrender.

Joe looked at me ten seconds longer than was necessary. "Yeah, sure, go ahead. It'd be nice to have something else besides news of flooded basements and leaky roofs." He smiled and went back to his pecking.

I pulled a notebook over and dialed "0" to get an information operator to get the Wilkes-Barre Police Department number. She offered to put me through, but since there was an extra fee for that, I opted to do it myself. Besides, I was working on putting together my own little phone directory of important numbers I might need in the future.

The desk sergeant who answered was Sgt. Luther Studnik. He had a voice only one shade on the human side of a bullfrog. I pictured a guy who'd been promoted to desk duty because he could no longer get into and out of a patrol car. Maybe he was sitting on a lily pad instead of a swivel-desk seat.

I identified myself and he made a sound like a belch. "Whad'da'ya want?"

I told him.

"Somebody down there in Mauch Chunk know this guy? That why you wanna put it in the paper?"

"No. Just seems like news, but news needing more detail."

"Ya kin find all the dead hoods ya want along the Turnpike," he croaked.

"That's what our editor says."

I heard the shuffling of some papers. "Boyle? Ya mean Boyle?"

"Yeah, Boyle," I said. Joe looked up from his pecking. I mouthed the name "Studnik," and he nodded.

He reached for the phone and took it. "Hey, Luther, help the boy out, will ya?" Joe smiled and made an "okay" sign with his thumb and index finger. "Yeah, yeah, yeah. Any day of the week. You couldn't hit the eight ball with a bowling ball. Here, I'm gonna give ya back to the kid." He passed the phone back.

"What da'ya wanna know? And understand that I'm only cooperating here because I feel sorry for anybody gotta work with that pool shark."

"How'd he die, Ravich?"

"Lead poisoning," Studnik said. Jeez, I thought, I'm caught in the middle of a 1930s B-movie. I decided to play along.

"One application or two?"

"Three. Two to the chest, one to the head. Bang, bang, bang. And don't ask. Nobody saw nothin'."

"How many Danish?"

Studnik laughed. "Hey, kid! You're my kind-a news guy. Details. The ones that get solved always come down to a moron as a perpetrator or some wiseass gets tripped up on details."

Studnik shuffled more papers. "Let's see here," he muttered. "The vic's habit was to consume three cherry Danish each weekday morning along with two cups of coffee, two teaspoons of sugar, no milk. That from the counterman who served him every day."

"So he was a creature of habit—"

"Who hain't?" Studnik asked.

He had me there. "Any information on the caliber of gun or a getaway car?"

"ME expects to have ballistics in a few hours. Nobody saw no getaway car 'cause nobody saw no crime happen. Mr. Ravich just happened to slump down at his table while eating a cherry Danish. Just like he had a heart attack from eating too many gooey baked goods."

He shuffled more papers. I figured to let him go on if he wanted to go on. "You wanna know what he was wearing?"

"Sure," I said, poised with my pen over my pad.

"Brown two-piece suit, brown tie, white shirt, which proves he was a hood, 'cause in the middle of summer up here nobody but a banker or a hood wears a suit." He paused for a second. "Also brown socks and brown shoes . . . and Fruit of the Loom boxer shorts with teddy bears on them." Studnik laughed. "I hain't makin' that up. Who could?"

"Maybe his grandkids bought them for him for his birthday."

"Maybe he shoulda got a vasectomy."

"Anything else?" I asked.

"You hain't gonna use the boxer shorts in your article, are you?" It sounded like I could get him in some Dutch if I did.

"Not relevant," I said. "Although the wearing of a suit probably is."

"Like I said, a banker or a hood."

"Was he armed?"

"No firearms found on deceased's body."

"So he was shot inside the bakery?"

"No," Studnik said.

"He wasn't?"

"No. He was shot in the chest and the head. I told you that."

"I mean the scene of the crime—"

"Yeah, sitting at a table in the front coffee shop, little restaurant section of the bakery, got to finish two of the three cherry Danish."

"Did the responding officer confiscate the third Danish as evidence?"

"Of course not. It would have never made it back to the station house alive."

"So he left it there."

"For the detectives and the lab guys to scoop up before they went over the scene and then mopped up the blood—"

"They didn't make the counterman do that?"

"They always do it themselves. The mayor likes a neat, clean city, at least as far as we can make it that way."

"Well you've been very helpful, sergeant."

"Tell Boyle to give you a raise. But call the ambulance boys first, 'cause they'll have to get his heart started again—if he has one."

Joe was busy pecking out a story so I didn't interrupt him to tell him what Sergeant Studnik said about a raise. Mrs. Apfelbaum was again on the phone, talking very quietly to someone who I gathered was a personal friend.

I sat for a minute or two, the sound of other keyboards clicking from the next room, the occasional vehicle going by outside on Race Street. Elizabeth had apparently been an accident—a very unfortunate, and very preventable, accident. The attempts to get me off the scent of the emerging drug trade were not accidents. And the fatally interrupted breakfast of Mr. Simon "The Stone" Ravich was no accident. It was still inconceivable to me that Mrs. Martinelli, for all of her orneriness, would have a guy killed in the middle of enjoying one of her baked goods. I tried to laugh to myself. That'd be awfully bad advertising: a cherry Danish can kill you.

I tried to laugh to myself because no matter how many used-up, bullet-ridden bodies were dumped along the Northeast Extension of the Pennsylvania Turnpike, I didn't know any of them. Technically, I didn't know Mr. Ravich, either, but I felt we had a history. He'd tried to fulfill a contract to kill me.

I couldn't imagine that whoever in Baltimore was behind this was going to let this ride. There were bound to be recriminations. And although little Mauch Chunk was not necessarily in the middle of it, it could get caught in the crossfire.

I had the urge to pay another visit to Mrs. Martinelli but held back. Also held back from calling her to see if I could read anything behind whatever story she would feed me.

Instead, I banged out an expanded story about the Ravich killing and passed it to the copy editor. "I'll be back," I said to nobody in particular and walked out the door and up Race Street, toward Broadway. The morning was about as opposite what the weekend had been as you could get and still stay on the same planet: co-balt-blue sky, temps headed toward the mid-70s, a slight breeze. Weighted down by the drug mess and the death of a guy who had wanted me dead, I began to feel buoyant, unable to escape the healing powers of good weather. I wondered for a moment what kind of weather Donald was enjoying—or suffering—in Anchorage.

There were still massive reminders of the flooding. Asphalt chunks sat here and there, water still ran in ribbons down the street, only a handful of cars had been reparked on Broadway. And pedestrian traffic was light. Here and there an old lady was out front with a broom, sweeping debris off the sidewalk and into the street, where, I suppose, borough crews would eventually come by and shovel it up.

When I'd gone far enough, I stopped and stood in front of Null-A's house. Even before ringing the bell, I could see and feel that it was abandoned. It just had that forlorn look, like its innards had been scraped out and it was just sitting there waiting for the next assault against its existence.

I went up to the door and rang the bell. I heard it go off inside, but it had one of those echoing dismal sounds.

I tried again, with the same hollow results.

I tried to peer in the window to the right of the front door but could see nothing. It was as though I was looking into a coal mine. I flipped up the lid on the mailbox that hung on the wall beside the door. There was a circular for Bright's Department Store in Lehighton and an electric bill. I put them back into the box, and just as I turned around to walk through the alleyway beside the house, an elderly man from across the street scurried over, using his cane to ward off an oncoming car.

The old man looked vaguely familiar, but then in a town as small as Mauch Chunk, everyone looked vaguely familiar, simply because you'd been exposed to them at some point along the way.

"He's gone," he said. "Left Sunday, near midnight. The storm was still going pretty good. Had two big vans. Loaded up and he led them in a pickup truck out Broadway."

"He didn't say anything to anyone about leaving?" I asked.

"Out of the blue," the old man said. He snapped his fingers. "Just like that. Lived here for as long as I can remember then, poof, gone—like a thief in the night." He rubbed his chin. "I probably shouldn't say that, 'cause I don't know, but ever since the old man died, things've been strange over there, that side of the street."

"Strange how?"

"Maybe I've already said too much." He rubbed his chin again. You could actually hear the noise of his fingers rubbing over the stubble. "Lots of comings and goings. Nothing loud or bothersome, nothing like that. In fact, just the opposite. Furtive. Yeah, that's exactly the word. Furtive."

I suddenly remembered the face. Furtive. Mr. Ganger, the English teacher in the junior high school. I'd never had him and he was near retirement when I passed through junior high, but it sure enough was him.

"Furtive," I said. "That's a good word, Mr. Ganger."

He raised his eyebrows. "Do I know you?" He took a longer look. I turned my head so he could see the scar on the left side of my face. "Of course, of course," he said. "I had your older brother in ninth grade. David."

"Donald," I supplied.

"Yes, of course," he said. "I should get over to the east side once in a while. Lost touch with most of the people I worked with, the kids in my classes. Had a heart attack, you know. Not a big one, but big enough to keep me close to home."

I hated to interrupt. "Anything else you can tell me about what strange things went on here?" I nodded my head back in the direction of Null-A's empty house.

"Just like I said. Too quiet for a young fella his age. Too quiet and too much sneaking around. Sometimes cars with Jersey plates, sometimes New York. I copied them down. Have them somewhere inside," he said, indicating his house across the street.

I was about to ask myself if anybody in this town minded their own business, and then canceled that thought. Hell, it was *my job* to mind everyone else's business.

NOTHING—MUCH—HAPPENS. SORTA

I suddenly had the urge to see Alice. I pulled a three-by-five card from my pocket and wrote on it my name and phone number and asked Mr. Ganger to call if he remembered anything else.

He shambled back across the street while at the same time examining what I'd written on the card as though it was hieroglyphics.

I abandoned the idea of walking into Null-A's little backyard since if he was gone, he was gone. Instead, I hurried back down Broadway, and at the corner where Doc Dougherty's massive home loomed, I turned down Race Street.

On the way up the street, I'd been so focused on finding Null-A that I'd completely ignored Alice's row home. Now, as I reached it, it gave off the same vacant vibes as Null-A's had. And to confirm its emptiness, a For Sale sign peered out of the window to the right of the door. I looked through the window and the place was empty, stark bare. Even our love sofa was gone.

This was so plain that even I got it:

Things were getting too hot for Null-A so he split. Alice was in cahoots with Null-A so she split, too. Wherever they were, they were probably together. I wondered if they'd gone to Baltimore.

Null-A had taken subtle pains to nudge me off of the drug-trade thing. Alice had diverted my attention and had been a willing listener to what I was doing on virtually every front on which I was doing something.

I wondered if the Jersey and New York plate numbers Mr. Ganger had copied down were the same ones Ellie gave me. I turned around and walked back up Broadway, rang Mr. Ganger's bell, asked him if I could copy down the numbers. "No need to," he said, handing me the yellow tablet paper with the numbers scratched on it, "'cause I assume they won't be coming back to visit an empty house. But if they do, I'll make sure to start a new list." Mr. Ganger offered me coffee, tea, beer, or soda, but I told him I was in a hurry, which he could plainly see, so I got out of there faster than was polite.

I went back to the office where Joe was pecking out stories built from the scribbled notes in his reporter's notebook and Mrs. Apfelbaum was still on the phone. I made a quick pass through the lay-

251

out department, where the day's pages were coming together. Cy Apfelbaum was, as usual, fussing about the grocery store ads, making sure no sale prices fell off the overly complex ad layouts. The grocery store ads were like intricate puzzles, especially the way Cy drew them up in his chicken-scratch style. Johan Hoffman, honcho of the layout department, was not above getting into terrible—and loud—arguments with Cy over what his scribbling actually meant and the finished product of whoever in layout was unfortunate enough that day to be assigned the A&P ad. Today it was doubly bad because it was a double-truck spread across two full newspaper pages. The two of them were revving up for a classic duel.

I ricocheted off the edge of layout and went through the knot of press guys who were wrestling with a huge roll of newsprint that they intended to, miraculously, lower downstairs into the press room. When they saw me they sang out, in chorus, their usual refrain: "The press runs at noon!" It was their warning that whether or not the editorial and layout departments had their work done on time, when noon came, the button to start the press rolling would be pushed.

It was a singsong warning that would dog me during my entire tenure at the *Times-News* and in fact would, years later, echo through various nightmares. "The press runs at noon!"

As I came back into the front office, Mrs. Apfelbaum reached out to hand me a note while she continued to talk to someone on the phone, wringing from them some material for her daily column on the back page, Strictly Personal.

The note was a phone message from Ronnie. He'd been able to bag a few of the license plate numbers. Come by at 6:30.

At that moment my telephone rang. Were you ever psychic enough to know by a telephone's ring—the same ring it produced for every call that came through—that there was trouble on the other end of the line?

I'd barely gotten "Hello—" out when a shrill female scream issued from the earpiece.

"Come now! Please! You've got to come! I think I killed him!"

"Who is this—?" I tried to edge in sideways.

"I think I killed him!"

"Who—?"

"Get here—! Quick!"

"Where—?"

"Delaney!"

"Mrs. Delaney?"

"Yes! Come now—!"

She hung up.

I grabbed Joe's car keys from his desk. "I'll bring it back!" I yelled as I bolted out the door. Parked in the No Parking spot on Susquehanna Street like it always was, Joe's car started right up. I dropped it into gear and did a U-turn that strained the anemic motor but managed to raise a puff of gray smoke from the rear tires.

I took a right at the light, ignoring the fact that it was red. Mid-morning traffic was light, and I was across the bridge and up River Street and up Center and over to South without killing anybody.

I slid to a stop in front of the Delaney house. The screen door was closed but the front door was open. I let the screen door bang behind me and rushed down the hall to the kitchen. Mrs. Delaney was out back on the deck, the big black .45 automatic in her hand.

There was a racket coming up out of the pigsty, snarls and what sounded like belching. Mrs. Delaney stood like a statue, looking down into the domain of the boars, where the three of them were rapidly tearing apart what looked like a mannequin but wasn't.

I put my arm around Mrs. Delaney, took the gun from her, and led her into the kitchen. There was nothing anybody could do for the poor bastard who'd fallen—or been blown—into the pigsty. He had been wearing a suit, blue, and a white shirt. He'd been white, about six feet and maybe 170 pounds. It was hard to tell much more because of the mud and the press of boar bodies.

"He said he was a police detective, looking for Mr. Delaney," she got out, her shoulders shaking as though the temperature was minus-fifteen.

I rushed outside and down the side stairs and like an assassin put two bullets into the foreheads of all three boars. The racket of the rapid fire killed off the horrible sound of the boars' smacking and chewing and snorting. They sprawled together with what was left of their brunch like so many sleeping monsters.

I looked at the gun, black and business-like. A few years after high school graduation a classmate, Mike Lennon, had one of these. We'd walked it to Glen Onoco and placed a Budweiser beer can eight feet away and each took twenty-five shots at the can. We each managed to hit the can once. My aim with a .45 automatic had apparently improved on its own.

Mrs. Delaney was apparently drawn back onto the deck by the thunder of the six shots. She looked over the side with a hand over her mouth. "Call the cops!" I called up to her. "Call them now!"

She very slowly backed into the kitchen, still looking down at the mess in the pigsty. I jogged up the steps and went inside with her, where I ran into the business ends of three .38 Police Specials, one of them wielded by Pennsylvania State Police Inspector Farrell.

"Drop it," he said.

I gently sat it on the counter near the backdoor and put my hands up over my head.

"Get it," Farrell said to one of the other guys. He came forward slowly as though I had a dozen sticks of dynamite strapped to me and slid the .45 away from me.

Mrs. Delaney stood stone still, her hand still over her mouth.

"But he came to help," she managed to whisper. "I called him."

Farrell made a head motion to the other guy to check out back. He pushed his way past me as Farrell continued to train his gun on me.

"Shit," the guy said from out on the deck. "Shit."

"What—?" Farrell called to him.

"He's dead . . . more than dead. They started eat—" I heard a gulp, then the familiar sound of a guy barfing, then barfing again. Two weeks out of college, I knew the sound only too well but more usually associated with too much booze.

It was obvious Farrell wanted to get out there to see what was going on, but at the same time he didn't want to let me out of his sight. I decided to outtough them.

I inclined my head toward the deck. "We can all go out," I suggested. "Except for Mrs. Delaney. She's been through enough."

"Cole," Farrell said to his partner. "Stay here with Mrs. Delaney."

I couldn't believe it. Farrell was going to do what I suggested. He grabbed my arm and turned me around, herding me out the back door by jamming his revolver in my lower back.

The guy who'd already seen the scene of slaughter below was down on his hands and knees, spitting out the last of his second spew of vomit. I could smell it even over the stink of the pigsty.

"Fuck," Farrell said when he saw the mess below. He turned to me with a rage I could smell over the pigs and the vomit. "You bastard!" he said, raising his gun to slap me across the face with it.

"What?" I said. "I didn't kill him, ya moron." Then, just for fun: "You make a move with that gun and I'll break your forearm in half." Well, it was theoretically possible, if I could get the right hold on his wrist and upper arm.

He looked momentarily confused, as though someone he trusted told him that water wasn't really wet.

Mrs. Delaney had apparently seen or heard what was going on. She opened the screen door and stepped out, making sure to stay near the door and away from the edge. "I shot the bastard," she said.

"How'd you get here so damned fast?" I asked Farrell at almost the same moment Mrs. Delaney spoke. I let my question die so as not to interrupt Mrs. Delaney:

"He came to the door . . . the front door . . . and said he was a policeman . . . held up a badge, but I wouldn't let him in . . . said he had to see Mr. Delaney." She stopped for a moment, seemingly unsure if she should be speaking at all. Cole, the guy who was supposed to be keeping an eye on her, nodded to her to continue. "I . . . I told him to wait there, I'd call the police to see if he was okay . . . but I really wanted to get to the kitchen to get the gun . . . the gun that was there . . . in the drawer." She paused for a moment and took another breath. "But he began crashing against the door . . . so I grabbed the gun and came out here and hid against the wall . . . here"—she pointed to a position just to the right of the door—"and he broke in and came rushing out here . . . with a gun in his hand . . . and when he got out here and turned to see where I was . . . ah

. . . I shot him, twice." She turned to me. "Like you told me, I pulled the hammer back first and held on with both hands . . . and he went backwards and fell off . . . and the pigs came . . ." She put her hand over her mouth and turned away. "He wanted my husband. He came here to kill him. I know it, I know it." She began to cry and, of course, four big grown men didn't have the first idea of what to do to calm her.

I stepped forward and the movement caused Farrell to raise his gun. "Oh, grow up!" I spit at him and went to Mrs. Delaney and hugged her. "Ya did good," I whispered to her.

"I don't know," she muttered. "I don't know about any of this."

"Of course you don't," I whispered to her. "Detective Farrell's men will call Grace, and she'll come and get you, and you can go and stay with her until this is all over."

Detective Farrell made like he was going to take control of the situation and not let his men call Grace, but Cole was already in the kitchen with the wall phone in his hand asking Mrs. Delaney what Grace's number was. Mrs. Delaney told him, and I walked her back into the kitchen and sat her down on one of the chairs.

I went back to join Farrell and the barfer, who I learned was Inspector James. "How *did* you get here so damned fast?" I asked again.

"We were already here," James aid. "Down the street. Watching"—he pointed his .38, which dangled slack in his hand, at the body of the guy sleeping with the pigs—"Faraski, keeping him under surveillance." Farrell became agitated, making a cutthroat sign to James, urging him to shut up. James seemed to outrank Farrell, though. "We didn't expect anything like this—"

"How could you?" I said. "It's crazy."

"You don't know what the hell you're talking about," Farrell said.

"You're absolutely right," I admitted. "Why don't you educate me?"

Farrell seemed disinclined to do so. His face went through several distortions as though somebody invisible was mashing his balls. He couldn't make himself speak.

Inspector James, after again wiping his sleeve across his mouth, stepped in. "We've been keeping an eye on Delaney—"

"You know he's in the county jail," I interjected.

Both of them looked first stunned, then incredulous.

"He is," Mrs. Delaney confirmed. "To keep him safe, it looks like."

"Your sister's on the way," Cole said, coming back out onto the deck. "I also called the tech boys to come do their thing with this"—he inclined his head toward the remains of Faraski—"but we can wait on contacting the medical team 'cause it's gonna take forever for tech to finish up this mess." He looked back and forth at Farrell and James. "What? What'd I miss?"

"Delaney's apparently sitting safely in the county lockup over on Broadway," James said.

"How?" Cole asked.

James shrugged.

"They came and got him," Mrs. Delaney said, indicating me. I hoped she wasn't going to say more, implicating Teddy, an implication that I had no way of explaining away.

"Why weren't we told of this?" Farrell wanted to know.

"I assumed that after the flood mess Sheriff Neast would be in touch with everyone who needs to know," I said.

Farrell looked likely to blow a gasket.

"If Delaney'd been here, the way it looks, he'd probably be dead," I offered.

"How'd we miss this?" Cole muttered to himself.

"Can we go inside?" I asked Mrs. Delaney.

"Oh. Oh, I'm so sorry," she said, leading us back into the kitchen. "I can make tea," she said.

There was a unanimous shaking of heads. She sat down at the kitchen table where she and Teddy and I had spent so many happy minutes with Mr. Delaney. Cole pulled out a chair and sat down. Farrell sank into a chair, not sure whether to whip up another round of indignation or be quiet for a while until he gathered more information. James indicated that I should take the fourth chair. He leaned against the backdoor jam.

"Let's review," I said. I looked around for consensus, certain I wouldn't be getting any from Farrell. The others nodded. Mrs. Delaney folded her hands in front of her and sat back as though waiting for a show to begin.

"Let's start with Elizabeth Delaney," I said. Mrs. Delaney's hands tightened. "We learned that Mr. Delaney and a player to be named later arranged Elizabeth's body in the uranium mine after Elizabeth broke her neck"—I reached over to put my hands over Mrs. Delaney's hands; she smiled weakly—"when, under the influence of a hallucinogen, she dove off the back deck." Mrs. Delaney nodded.

Farrell looked as though someone had kicked him in the balls.

"That's right," I said. "Case closed."

"It'll be closed when I say it is," Farrell shot back.

"But that's right," Mrs. Delaney said, pushing strands of loose hair back behind her ears. "It was an accident." She looked at me. "It was, wasn't it?"

I patted her hand. "Yes it was."

"But what about my husband?" Mrs. Delaney asked. "Why were you surveil—why were you watching him?"

Inspector James answered after giving Farrell the hot-tamale eyeball when he started to interrupt. "We suspected he was involved with the drug trade," James said.

"Oh, he was," Mrs. Delaney said. "He told us that. Right here." She indicated the very kitchen table at which they were sitting.

"He was hired to do some lawyering for some suspected drug people," I said. "What's that called, their 'mouthpiece'?"

Cole nearly laughed.

"You watch a lot of gangster movies?" James asked.

"About average," I said.

"I wanna know just how you're so involved in this shit?" Farrell said to me. He looked at Mrs. Delaney as though to ask her permission to ask me. "How do you manage to be involved in this at every turn?" he asked me, giving me his most belligerent stare.

"It's a small town," I said. I hoped he was talking about only the instances I wanted him to talk about. I didn't have any idea if

I'd been under surveillance along with Delaney. I had no idea if he knew how active the carriage house had been to roving criminals over the past several days.

Farrell had begun sweating inside his coat. He began to tick off those instances where I'd been "involved." "You're in on the discovery of Elizabeth Delaney's body in the uranium mine. You're apparently here hassling Delaney and then escorting him to jail." I was glad he didn't mention Teddy, my accomplice. "And now you're here when a guy wanting to probably kill Delaney gets himself killed—"

"—and half-eaten," James aid, apparently recovered from his bout of nausea.

"Like I said," I said, "it's a small town and I work for the newspaper and it's my job to be where things are happening and to report on what I see."

Mrs. Delaney now patted *my* hand. "He went looking for my Elizabeth and he found her. Something nobody else had been able to do."

"He found her by accident," Farrell insisted.

"'Accident' involves being in the right place at the right time," I said, wanting suddenly to get out of there and take a long shower.

"But you were watching Mr. Delaney because you suspected him of wrongdoing," Mrs. Delaney said, looking at Farrell. "What had he done besides agreeing to be a lawyer for some people if they got in trouble?"

James and Cole looked at each other, passing something back and forth. "Wha—we're not at liberty to talk about that at this time," he said.

"About time you hotshots try keeping your mouths shut," Farrell blurted out.

"But somebody should explain to us who this Faraski is . . . was," I said.

"Need-to-know basis," James said.

"Okay," I said. "I need to know."

James kind of smiled. "No," he said.

"That's the official answer of the Pennsylvania State Police?"

"Yes," James said.

Now *I* smiled. "That kind of a stance isn't going to go over very well when I put this story together. Let's see if I have it: Mysterious hit man whom state police investigators will not identify, even though they know full well who he is, comes to East Mauch Chunk to assassinate Lawyer Delaney, who has potential affiliations with the drug trade that is currently escalating throughout Carbon County and Lehigh Valley, so damn it, stay in your houses, lock your doors, load your guns, because you're on your own."

Mrs. Delaney's right hand went over her mouth. "Oh, goodness," she said. "That doesn't sound like what the State Police are supposed to do."

I was beginning to like Mrs. Delaney more and more. Apparently the longer she stayed away from the old man, the more backbone she grew.

"So it's no-go," I said. "You're not going to tell us anything about Faraski."

"That's right," Farrell said, sticking his head forward over the table like a terrier that's about to nab a rat. His confidence was growing like a blocked-up drain.

I got up, pushed my chair back, and walked through the house to the front door. "Where the hell da'ya think you're going?" Farrell called after me. "You'll leave here when I say you can leave—"

But by that time I was out the front door and walking down the street, checking license plates until I found the one I was looking for. Just as I began smiling to myself like a self-satisfied twit, a car pulled up, a VW bug, and Grace Delaney popped out.

She grabbed my arm as we headed back to the Delaney house, where Farrell was standing on the front porch, looking like he wanted to take a shot at me. I patted Grace's hand. She was wearing a lovely Victorian gown that was ivory on top and burgundy for the billowing skirt. "How *do* you manage to drive a little stick shift while wearing such a huge and lovely outfit?" I asked.

"Is my sister-in-law all right?" she asked, squeezing my arm.

I wondered for a moment how to answer that. "She seems to be in fine fettle for something who's just killed a guy," I said.

She stopped in her tracks and put the back of her right hand over her mouth exactly as though we were in the movies. "Oh, my dear," she said. "She killed somebody?"

"Guy named Faraski who came to kill your brother," I explained. "Shot him dead, thank goodness."

"You can't tell that information to a civilian!" Farrell shouted, coming down the steps, bristling like a porcupine.

Grace and I walked right past him. "I'm going to ask you to not go out onto the deck out back," I whispered to Grace. She looked confused. I showed her to one of the kitchen chairs, opposite her sister-in-law.

"Baltimore," I said to Cole and James before Farrell could make his way back to the kitchen. "Faraski's from Baltimore."

Cole and James looked at each other. "Where'd you get that?" James asked.

"I'm a trained journalist," I said.

Grace sat cooing to her sister-in-law, who looked to me to be quite engaged in what was going on around her and didn't need to be cooed at.

"You're not going to put that in your article," Cole said, his face pinched.

"Why not?" I asked.

"Because it could blow a lot of stuff we're doing right now," Cole said.

"All we're doing is sitting around the kitchen table of a woman who just shot an assassin who was here intent on killing her hus-band because some drug dealers in Baltimore are afraid that he's so stressed out that he might spill the beans," I said, enjoying the distressed looks on Cole and James and the purple fury building in Farrell, who caught the last 8 percent of what I'd just said as he returned to the kitchen.

"You'll do nothing of the sort," Farrell blustered. "I'll put your ass in jail . . . in the farthest cell from sunlight."

James held up his hand. "Calm down, please."

"Yeah, you're making matters worse," Cole said.

Grace Delaney looked from face to face, not sure what was go-ing on, holding her sister-in-law's hands across the table.

"Can you ask him to leave?" I asked, meaning Farrell.

Cole and James looked at each other, and it was easy to see from their expressions that they had the authority to do just that.

"We could—but we won't," James said.

"What da'ya want from us?" Cole asked.

"First of all to allow Grace here to take her sister-in-law to her house so she can have some peace and quiet, so she can lie down in a dark quiet room and take a nap if she so wishes."

"That's so kind of you," Mrs. Delaney said, "but maybe I need to stay here."

"As soon as the technical squad arrives, this place is going to become a zoo," I said. "Is that okay with you guys? You'll know where to find her if you need her."

"Oh, we'll definitely need her at some point—to answer more questions," James aid. "But that's a good idea—to let her get out of here before the tech boys and then the ME show up."

Cole made gestures to have the ladies rise and aimed them at the front door. "See the ladies to the car," James said to Farrell, who didn't move at first. "And then wait out on the front porch to direct the tech boys around the side of the house, not through it."

"But I'm—" Farrell began, only to be met with a cold stare from James.

"And when you *do* come back, I want my shoes to be with you," I said to Farrell.

Cole and James looked like they were out to sea.

"He came to my house when I wasn't home and stole my running shoes to compare them with footprints in the mine where Elizabeth was found, when I wasn't even wearing those shoes that day and he already knows I was there and left footprints. Hasn't he ever read *The Hardy Boys' Detective Handbook*?"

"It was to eliminate them from the other footprints," Farrell said, halfway between doing as he was told to see the ladies out and resisting following Cole's orders.

"You have his shoes?" James said.

For a moment it looked as though Farrell was going to put up some resistance, but when Cole additionally turned to him, it was pretty much over. "Yeah," he said. "Yeah, I got his damned shoes. In the trunk."

"Bring 'em in when you come back," James said.

Farrell sulked out, too late to walk to the VW with the ladies. The screen door slammed.

"How long have you two known each other?" James asked. "This looks like it goes back a long way. You steal his girl?"

"Known him since last Saturday," I said.

"Love at first sight," Cole said.

"He's sometimes hard to love," James added, then made his hands into a steeple. Cole and I sat there at the table. "How do we resolve this?" he asked.

"Nothing to resolve," I said. "I have a batch of facts and a story to write with some missing pieces, but they get written around until I find 'em. You guys could give me some good quotes, make the State Police look good, like you're on top of this but must hold back some information until it's appropriate to release it. Or," I added, "I could ask Farrell for some choice quotes." I smiled a fake smile.

James smiled a fake smile back.

"Beyond what you've got, we can't give you any more," Cole said. "We don't have all of it ourselves at this point."

James nodded.

"So tell me about Baltimore."

"Nope," James said.

"Can't," Cole said.

I shrugged. "I'm gonna have to infer a connection with Maryland," I said. "Dead guy's got a Maryland license plate, which I've already memorized, and a Baltimore Orioles bumper sticker. I'd be compelled to infer that that's where the drugs are originating. On their way to a college town near you." I winked. "Parents of college kids aren't going to like that. Not especially since their kids are the first in the family to go to college. Lotta pride involved." I made my hands into a steeple.

But didn't get to pursue the point further because at that moment Farrell stepped back inside to inform us that the tech van was pulling into the street. "Show them around," James called to him.

Before he went back outside he tossed my training flats into the dining room. They bounced across the floor, landing in the archway between the dining room and kitchen.

Cole grunted. "He really *does* like you."

James stood up. "We're through here. We know where you live in case we need to get back in touch with you—"

"—which we will," Cole added.

"I wouldn't send Farrell if I were you," I said.

"Not much chance of that," James said. On his way to the front door he reached down and tossed my shoes to me. "Real light. Gotta get me a pair of those."

"See ya around," Cole said as he walked out the back door.

* * *

I sat in Joe Boyle's car, parked in its usual No Parking spot along Susquehanna Street, just downhill from the *Times-News* office. The motor was turned off. Afternoon traffic went back and forth. I stared straight ahead at the Mansion House Hill, the main—and only—road out of town to Packerton and Lehighton, climbing out of the river valley and hugging the shoulder of the mountain atop which the Flagstaff Park sat. I stared straight ahead, feeling like an empty gas tank: run dry, hollow, echo filled, drained, pretty much useless.

I'd been on the job about ten days and had already seen two dead bodies: Elizabeth Delaney's bloated thing of a body and a partially eaten thug/killer named Faraski who drove all the way up here from Baltimore to kill a guy in broad daylight to make sure he didn't fold up and squeal to the authorities about a drug ring. I'd been sucker-punched in the side of the head by a longhaired biker, been marked for death or destruction by first some guys from Slatington and then from Wilkes-Barre, was living with Jim Thorpe, arguably the greatest all-around athlete of the 20th century, and getting laid by Tinker Bell-like Alice, only to have her spirited away by a guy who lives his life through the books and stories of a second-rate science-fiction writer.

I'd often heard the phrase "sick and tired." At that moment I think I knew, profoundly, what the term really meant. I felt sick to my stomach and sick at heart and I felt like I'd just put in not an all-nighter but an all-weeker. My head wanted to slump down against the metal steering wheel and maybe sleep for a month, or until they came to tow away the car.

I knew what I needed to do: get into the office and start putting together the story on the death of Faraski, whose first name I didn't even know. I'd need to make calls to the telephone people in Baltimore to see if they had a listing for a Faraski. I could call the Baltimore cops and hope they would cooperate in getting me the full name and address of the Faraski who owned the car parked down the street from the Delaney house. Which might or might not help me, because if Faraski was any kind of a pro—a pro who let an innocent woman put two bullets square into his chest—he wouldn't have driven his own car here. It was probably stolen, maybe from the parking lot at the stadium where the Orioles played ball, hence the bumper sticker.

I wasn't going to get any help from the State Police investigators and certainly wasn't going to get any from the East Mauch Chunk Police Department, because it didn't want to have anything to do with a murder, thank you very much, when it didn't even have to do any work to let it slide nicely over to the staties.

This was not going to be easy. I had the idea to drive back over to the east side and, before they had it towed away, check Faraski's car a lot closer to see if he'd used a key to start it or if he'd hot-wired it. But I felt that I didn't have the energy to both do that and then start writing the damned article.

If Alice was still at home, it would behoove me to pay a visit for an hour or so, to get back on track—a track that apparently no longer included her.

With a heave I pulled myself from the car and walked up to the *Times-News* offices. "You look like shit," Joe said when I walked in.

"Tsk-tsk," Gertrude said.

At least some things stayed the same, thank god.

I whispered the tale of Faraski and Mrs. Delaney to Joe and Gertrude, not wanting to cause a panic in the rest of the office. Joe listened intently, shaking his head. Gertrude inserted the occasional "Oooooh" and "Ah" and nodded at the appropriate points.

When I was finished, Joe said that he'd try to use the contacts he had at the State Police to wring what information he could from Farrell's and Cole's and James's superiors.

"You call Aggie," he said to Gertrude. "See if Frank can shake anything loose for us about Baltimore."

"Why're you calling Aggie McCartney?" I asked.

Gertrude laughed. "Her husband, Frank, was Commissioner of the State Police from '59 to '63. Some of the guys who worked under him are still there." I guess I had a lot to learn when it came to who was who in Carbon County, even though I'd grown up here. Gertrude dialed and got Agnes McCartney on the phone, but I could tell by the way the conversation was going that it would be a long shot. Mrs. McCartney didn't seem to want to get Frank involved in this.

"Murder's a dirty business," Joe said, cradling his phone. "Especially around here, since it never seems to happen here." He scratched his head. "Not much murder since the Molly Maguires, now they come to town to make a film about the murdering Molly Maguires, and we get murders. It's like a bad movie." He scratched his chin, then tugged at his ear. Then stared at the ceiling. Then held up his right index finger which, for all the pecking at his keyboard it did, should have had the strength to lift a car and the callous to go along with it. He began dialing again. "I'll let the coroner's office know that I'd appreciate a call back when he returns with the remains."

I picked up the phone and asked the operator to connect me with the Baltimore Police Department. She did. I was transferred to a Detective Hollingsworth who had the dedicated voice of a heavy smoker. He confirmed that diagnosis by proceeding to cough a hacking cough that couldn't be anything else. I explained to him what I was looking for. He explained I should explain to him what had happened. I did. He called someone else over to his desk so they could hear at least his half of the conversation. They were very interested to hear the name Faraski. They even cooperated by providing a first name: Vince. And a nickname: Liver Lips. "Has some disease," Hollingsworth explained, "that makes his lips the color of raw liver."

I felt like talking tough and saying something like, "Well, he hain't got them lips no more," but that would have been sophomoric. I still don't know why I just didn't do that since I am sophomoric and all.

"So you say he was eaten by pigs," Hollingsworth said, also telling whomsoever was standing next to him.

"He was shot in the chest by a local housewife whose husband he apparently came to kill, and he fell off the deck and got nibbled on by three boars," I explained.

"Where'd you say this happened?" Hollingsworth asked, after being encouraged to do so by whomsoever was with him.

"Mauch Chunk, Pennsylvania," I said.

"Jeez," he said. "Tough place." A pause. "You know Joe Boyle?"

"He's right here," I said.

"Put that son of a bitch on," Hollingsworth said.

I covered the phone and said to Joe, "A Hollingsworth from the Baltimore Police Department wants to talk to you."

"Hollingsworth?" Joe said. "He retired two years ago."

I uncovered the phone. "You retired two years ago," I said.

He snorted—sort of like a pig. "I did," he said, "but I didn't like it so I came back."

I relayed that to Joe, but I could hear Hollingsworth ranting even though the phone was a good foot away from my ear. "Put that son of a bitch on the fuckin' phone!"

Mrs. Apfelbaum's hearing was not especially good but still good enough to hear Hollingsworth. She covered her ears and shook her head.

I passed the phone to Joe. "Harry, Harry, Harry," Joe sang. "Which is it? Too bored to stay away or just too dumb?"

Hollingsworth was loud enough—maybe he had a hearing problem—that even with the phone up to Joe's ear, I could follow the conversation.

"Yeah, both of those," Hollingsworth said, chuckling. At least I assumed it was chuckling. His chuckling was followed by a hacking cough.

"Still smoking those awful Pall Malls?" Joe said.

More hacking. "Yeah," Hollingsworth said.

"People still think you're wearing a gray shirt when it's actually white but it's covered with cigarette ash?"

"Since Mary died I send 'em all out to be cleaned and they come back just as gray as they were when they went in." More coughing.

"So my boy here told you about this Faraski guy," Joe said.

"Yeah, Vince Faraski. Mean mother." More coughing. "Did he really get plugged by a housewife waving around a .45 automatic?"

"That's what I'm told," Joe confirmed. I shook my head in agreement.

"And then got eaten by pigs?"

I mouthed the phrase "wild boars."

"By wild boars," Joe said.

"Partially eaten," I mouthed.

"Wasn't totally eaten. My boy here plugged the wild boars before they could finish lunch . . . ya know, so there'd be evidence of who it was . . . instead of waiting until he came out the other end."

Gertrude held her head in her hands and shook her head. "Men," she whispered.

"Ya know old Vince has a younger brother, Zeke, who's just as nutso as Vince is . . . was. Good chance he'll want to purify the family name by coming after this Mauch Chunk housewife," Hollingsworth said.

"East Mauch Chunk," Joe corrected. "The Mauch Chunk proper housewives are even meaner."

"Well, the Faraski family is not a family to mess with."

"Nor is Mrs. Delaney," Joe said.

"Touche."

"So can you do something to slow down this Zeke character?"

"Could bring him in under the guise of needing him to identify what's left of his brother, but that might make him even more pissed off . . ."

"So what's the specialty of the people Vince Faraski was working for?" Joe asked.

"You name it, they play it."

"How about drugs?"

"At one time I'd've said no, but over the last two years they're seeing a lot of profit there." He coughed again. "They're like the hub on a wheel—drug business radiating out in all directions."

"Including up here, apparently."

"Apparently. They seem to have a penchant for college campuses," Hollingsworth said.

"They have a what?" Joe asked, winking.

"A penchant. A penchant. Look it up if ya don't know it."

"Is that like word of the day or something?" Joe asked.

"How the fuck should I know?"

Joe held his hand over the phone. "Good cop but dumb as a brick. Steals one new word a week and runs it into the ground." He took his hand away. "So Harry, is there anything else we should know about this?"

"Not if you're just writing a story. Be different if you was trying to put a stop to these guys. Like we are. I'd love to get the okay from the commissioner to put together a team and just go in there and do away with them all."

"But you really wouldn't do that," Joe said.

"A guy can fantasize."

"Well look, let me know if you're ever in this area. We'll go have a beer . . . or ten."

"Now why the hell would I ever be in your area?"

"If you're learning a new word every week, you must be working to give yourself a little class. Get a little more class and you'll wanna get out of Baltimore and come up here where we all have more class than we can use."

"Nothing up there but used-up coal ash."

"Now it's people saying stuff like that that gives us an undeserved reputation," Joe said. "Hey. I'll be in touch if we get anything else on this Faraski stuff."

Joe handed the phone back to me and I hung it up. "How'd you meet him?"

"Doing a series on the workings of the Bethlehem Steel Company. They have a plant in Baltimore, and there was some sabotage going on, and Hollingsworth was on the case. Real character."

"I guess," I said.

"So I guess we'd best let the staties know about Faraski's kid brother, just in case he heads this way."

"Yeah," I said. "I can't imagine Mrs. Delaney being good enough to plug two of 'em."

"How long you think it'll take you to knock out the piece on Faraski?"

"Ninety minutes. Then I gotta go see Ronnie Von Renner," I said, rapping on the typewriter keys.

```
A suspected hit man for a Baltimore crime syn-
dicate died violently yesterday afternoon . . .
```

* * *

I sat on the top of the lawn at the Packer mansions, just across the gravel drive from the carriage house. I'd already polished off one Miller High Life, and had dropped it onto the edge of the lawn, and had opened the next one with a church key. The weather was ideal: around seventy-five degrees, 70 percent humidity, and a breeze from the west of about five miles per hour. Because the mansions were around the hillside from the western breeze, nothing on the property moved except Mr. Thorpe, who was inserting some kind of red, white, and blue flowers into the beds next to the Asa Packer Mansion, hoping they would last until the Fourth of July holiday. He worked with slow determination, gentle with the flowers for the bulk of him. He'd waved when I walked out with the two beers. Just too early to skip down to visit with Ronnie; he was still out there apprehending speeders, although with the aftermath of the storm still clinging to many of the roads, he was probably coming up short on his ticket goals for this month.

There wasn't much traffic downtown. One borough truck, yellowish/orange, had rumbled by with a load of storm debris, headed for the dump. The flag that flew above the Flagstaff Park flapped lazily in a breeze that didn't reach down here.

When I arrived home, I'd called Grace Delaney to learn that Mrs. Delaney had been extremely animated for about a half hour, and then it was like someone had let the air out of her, and she deflated into a nap on the sofa. I offered to go find a replacement gun for Mrs. Delaney to keep around just in case Zeke Faraski got it into his head to take out the middle-aged housewife who'd iced his mean-as-a-junkyard-dog brother. Fuckin' wimp!

But Grace didn't want to have anything to do with a gun in her place. I'd try again later, when Mrs. Delaney was awake, and I suspected that the answer I'd get would be a little different from Grace's. If one of the Delaney women could take out a professional hood, just think what two of them could do to Zeke Faraski.

I was finished with the second beer and leaning back on my elbows when I saw the State Police cruiser come down Susquehanna Street and take a right through the town's only traffic light.

It was near dinnertime and Ronnie was now home. Maybe I'd be able to talk him into chowing down at Weiksner's over a pitcher. I patted my left front jeans pocket to make sure the list of license plate numbers Mr. Ganger had given me was safe. But I'd had enough time contemplating the world from the ground level of the Packer lawns that I had no idea what we'd be able to do with the two lists even if there was some crossover. What were we supposed to do? Charge them with entering Pennsylvania illegally? We couldn't prove that they'd done anything illegal. Ellie saw them at the old canal locks; Mr. Ganger saw them parked in front of Null-A's house on Broadway. Big fuckin' whoop! Maybe we could get the canal-lock parkers for trespassing on railroad property, but the cars on Broadway hadn't even been illegally parked.

I dropped the empties and the church key inside the carriage house and made my way down Parker Hill and across the street and the tracks, able to sneak up on Ronnie just as he was walking in his caboose door and sidle in right behind him and scared the shit out of him. I made sure to put my opened hand over the butt of his service revolver so he couldn't go for it.

He turned quickly, but I had anticipated that, and I managed to lay a half nelson on him, but he squirmed halfway out of it, so I whirled him around against his attempted escape and followed through with my weight so that both of us crashed onto the sofa. He instinctively twisted his torso and tried to plant his feet to corkscrew his way out of what was left of my hold, but I was on top of him, and very much illegally wrapped an arm around his neck. "Loser, loser, loser," I whispered into his ear.

He relaxed and hissed, "Fuck you, moron!"

I rolled off him and sat on the floor in front of the sofa.

He sat up and flicked his uniform so it was uncreased. "Been in the sauce already, huh?" he said.

I cupped my palm over my mouth and nose and blew. "Miller High Life, 1968, western side of the wheat field."

"You keep doing stupid shit like that and one of these times you're gonna get yourself killed."

"Fuck," I said. "It's still broad daylight. You don't think I'd try that after dark against a highly trained combat machine like yourself, do you?"

He began unbuttoning his uniform shirt and loosened his belt, letting his holster and cuffs drop to the sofa. "Get out two beers," he said, nodding toward the kitchen, "while I change." He disappeared into the bedroom while I pulled out two Coors. Illegal Coors.

"You got a new delivery from Louie the Leech," I said, referring to Louie Luginski, a long-haul trucker who graduated a year before us. "How do you manage to dispose of the empties so nobody traces them back to you?"

"Lotta mine shafts around here," he said. "Someday one of them mine shafts is gonna be your home for eternity, you don't wise up." He emerged from the bedroom wearing an East Mauch Chunk High School wrestling T-shirt, a pair of red gym shorts, and white socks. He grabbed one of the Coors and knocked it out in three mighty gulps. "More," he said, marching around the living-room space like a drum major. I got him more. "Riding in that damned cruiser all day puts kinks on top of kinks. Maybe we oughta go a few rounds just so I can get those fuckin' kinks smoothed out." He took the second Coors and drained half of it.

He sat down at the kitchen table, pulled out a drawer, and handed me a typewritten sheet of paper with the names, addresses, and phone numbers of—count 'em—eleven people on the license plate list I'd gotten from Ellie; there were even three out-of-state names.

"You check these against criminal mischief lists?"

He shook his head. Nodded outside. "With this storm, I haven't had time to take a good shit." He banged down the second empty Coors can on the kitchen counter, compacting it. "More," he rumbled like a pro wrestling ring announcer.

I got him another one and pulled the sheet of paper out of my pocket that Mr. Ganger had given me. I placed them side by side. "What's this?" Ronnie asked.

"Corroboration," I said.

I scanned the two lists. Seven matches. Ronnie reached over and pulled them in front of him. "Hmmmmm," he said. "Where'd you get the new list?"

I explained Mr. Ganger's retirement hobby.

"You know this doesn't mean shit," Ronnie said, then drained his beer can. "Nothing we can lay on these people."

"You could begin to keep an eye on them," I suggested.

"You could begin to keep an eye on them," Ronnie sang. "With what? With who?"

"Whom?"

"With whom? You gonna hire detectives to follow each of these people around twenty-four hours a day? To prove what? That they drop by to buy some pot? Hell, you can go to any street corner in Philly and get all the pot you want."

Of course he was right. I'd come to the same conclusion.

"Did you know Null-A's gone? Cleared out. Took everything he owns and scrammed."

Ronnie raised an eyebrow then got up and pulled two more Coors from the fridge. "Not surprised."

"Looks like Alice went with him."

He reraised his eyebrow. "Too bad."

"But you're not surprised."

"Not surprised."

He did the ole Adam's apple hully gully while he downed more beer.

"So what's our next move?" I asked, taking my own more modest swig.

Ronnie shrugged.

"I assume you heard about Mrs. Delaney shooting a hit man," I said, wondering why I'd put the stupid license plate list before something really important, earth-shattering even.

Now Ronnie really raised his eyebrows—both of them. "I heard over the radio there'd been a shooting on the east side. Mrs. Delaney?"

"He was a pro from Baltimore named Faraski, come to take care of Lawyer Delaney, we assume," I said.

"Who's 'we'?"

"Farrell, Cole, and James."

"Holy shit!"

"Yeah, all three of them were there."

"And you were there."

"I seem to turn up at a lot of bad scenes lately." I explained about Mrs. Delaney's call.

"So was the Terrible Trio staking out Delaney's house or were they tracking this Faraski dude?" Ronnie asked.

He saw immediately that I was stumped. I shrugged my shoulders.

"Didn't you even ask?"

"No, but I guess I should have."

"Makes all the difference," Ronnie said, ignoring his beer.

"I wonder if they told Lawyer Delaney about all this?" I asked.

"Wouldn't count on it."

"But somebody should," I said.

"So why don't you go up to the jail and visit him and break the news that somebody higher up in the drug organization he works for thinks so highly of him that they sent a professional hit man to kill his sorry ass? Oh, and yeah, your wife just happened to be in the way and there was no way the hit man was going to leave her alive when he left, 'cause those sorts don't like to leave witnesses loitering around a crime scene. Go ahead, go tell him." Ronnie knocked back another long swig.

I'd been around Ronnie enough years to know where this was headed. He was building up a head of steam that was probably going to wipe out his stash of illegal Coors Banquet Beer.

"Somebody *should* let Delaney know," I agreed, "but I don't know that it's our place to do it. You're not on the case, and I've got enough people pissed off at me as it is." I took a sip of beer. Then something occurred to me. If ole Ronnie was going to go off on a bender, and I was going to get caught up in his wake, I'd better make a phone call. "Pass me the phone."

I rooted around in my pocket until I found the slip of paper with the Hollywood assistant producer's name and number on it. I dialed the number, and he answered on the second ring. I asked him a few questions about the shooting schedule, jotted the facts down on the same slip of paper, and stuffed it back into my pocket. Research for little item on *Molly Maguire* shooting schedule done and filed away. "Get me another beer," I said, sucking the remaining drops out of my current one.

Ronnie obliged and got another one for himself. He'd been tossing them in the wastebasket so I couldn't add them up to see how far down the road he already was.

"Let's get some grub over at Weiksner's," I suggested. I wanted to get some food in his stomach to absorb some of the beer he'd poured down his gut.

Incredibly, he agreed. "I could eat a pig," he said.

Ah, Jeez—

20
Mail Call

The night went downhill fast. We went to Weiksner's, gobbled up the lobster special, and continued to knock back the beers. Around midnight we decided that we wanted to shoot some darts. Bad idea. The darts went so errant that most of the bar patrons hid out in the now-closed dining room until John threatened to call the cops to take us to jail.

We staggered back to the caboose, had one more beer each, and Ronnie dropped into bed, very much unconscious before his head hit the pillow. I trudged uphill toward the carriage house, where Mr. Thorpe had kindly left on a light so I wouldn't get lost.

I dropped into bed and was afraid it would begin to spin, but it didn't—but not by much—and I dropped off.

The next thing I knew, Mr. Thorpe was roughing me up, bringing me out of a nightmare where a bear was roughing me up while being directed to do so by half of a grapefruit that lay cut-side down on a flat rock, talking as though through a mouthful of saliva.

"Phone call," Mr. Thorpe tried to tell me. "From your brother. Says it's important. Sounds important."

"Brother," I muttered. "Which brother?"

"The one in jail. He's calling from jail."

Mr. Thorpe helped me sit up in bed and helped me get my legs onto the floor. I staggered toward the phone, which Mr. Thorpe picked up from the table and handed to me.

"Rudy?" I whispered into the receiver, afraid to talk too loudly for fear of deafening myself.

"You gotta come quick. Now!"

"What?"

"It's Delaney. He's dead."

"Huh?"

"He hanged himself. He wanted to get out of his cell, and I got the key for him, and he walked around talking to himself and went down to the gallows and went up the stairs and put the rope around his neck and jumped."

"Wha—?"

"Sheriff Neast just called Doc Dougherty, but it's too late for that. He's dead."

"Ah. I'll be right there," I muttered, hanging up the phone after my first try to do so missed the cradle.

Delaney. Dead. Jesus.

Fortunately, I'd gone to bed with most of my clothes still on. I pulled on a pair of desert boots and ran out the door, fired up the Rambler while giving it absolutely no time to pump some oil up to the top of the engine, and shot downhill. Twice on my way up Broadway, I lurched through enormous potholes left from the flood, and when I pulled into the little parking lot next to the jail, I barely slowed before jumping out of the car.

The big front doors were unlocked, and I could hear another car approaching at high speed out on Broadway. Probably Doc Dougherty.

I ran to the yard, and Sheriff Neast and Rudy were on the gallows, which was illuminated by the two ground-level spotlights the movie company had installed to illuminate it at night.

There was absolutely no argument that Lawyer Delaney was dead. He'd apparently sprung the trapdoor, then put the noose around his neck, and dropped through the opening. The wrench when he'd run out of rope snapped his neck, and it hung crookedly. *Just like Elizabeth's*, I thought to myself. His body drooped, his arms hung at his sides.

Sheriff Neast motioned me up the steps. He was in the process of reaching out over the trapdoor's opening to get hold of the rope to pull Delaney's body to him. I reached out and helped him do that. Rudy stood off to the side, doing nothing.

278

Although he wasn't particularly heavy, Lawyer Delaney's body was dead weight and difficult to get hold of. We maneuvered him closer to us, and I loosened the noose around his neck while Sheriff Neast supported the body. He shit himself again, and for the last time ever, and I avoided touching him anywhere near his ass. I would have nightmares about loosening the noose for years to come, coming in contact with Delaney's newly dead skin. But I didn't think of that at the time. I just worked some slack into the noose, slipped it over his head, and rushed to help the sheriff lower the body to the gallows' platform.

We had just lowered him when Doc Dougherty, huffing and puffing, came up the stairs.

He pushed us aside and bent over the body. "My god," he said. Shook his head. "Nothing we can do for him." Shook his head some more, made to open his black bag, and realized he had done that out of habit and that there was nothing in it that would help Lawyer Delaney at this point.

"This is going to kill Mrs. Delaney," Sheriff Neast muttered.

For no reason I could think of, I reached up and patted the sheriff on the back. He looked at me in the stark light of the floodlights and shook his head. I could feel Rudy, who was behind me, inching away from us.

"Not your fault," I said, half-turning. "You didn't know he was going to do this. Right?"

"I thought he just wanted to walk off some energy," Rudy said. "Cells get confining." He coughed. "I should have cleared it with the sheriff."

"Yes, you should have," Sheriff Neast said, his voice flat, his head bent.

"Nothing we can do for him," Doc Dougherty repeated.

Nothing.

And everything.

I felt like the spinning bed from overimbibing that I'd avoided several hours ago had followed me and was taking over.

Sheriff Neast steadied me before I managed to plunge off the gallows. "You okay?" he asked.

I shook my head. "Not used to so much happening in such a short time," I said.

He let out a hollow laugh. "Neither are we." He directed me toward the steps and walked down them next to me. Doc Dougherty remained bent over Delaney's body, as though fascinated by a body that was inanimate. "I'll call the coroner," Sheriff Neast called up to Doc. Doc waved his arm but remained kneeling on one knee next to the body.

Rudy, in true Rudy fashion, had managed to skulk his way down the steps without anyone noticing, beating us to the bottom. He stood there as though waiting to get a good whooping—which on some levels he deserved.

I still felt a bit unstable and put my arm out to nudge Rudy back toward his cell, but he pulled away and walked back in that direction himself. "Pull it 'til it locks," Sheriff Neast called to him, his hand still on my upper arm, making sure I didn't stumble.

"Next will come pestilence and then fire," the sheriff said. "Somebody sure has it in for Mauch Chunk."

I stopped and turned toward hm. "Does this kind of thing ever get to you?"

"What kind of thing?" he asked, looking down at me from a good four inches advantage.

"You know. Death and disaster."

He smiled a weak smile that was made spectral by the stark floodlighting. "Been doing this for years and never had so much bad happen so close together, so no, I'm not used to . . . coping with this. I don't know that anybody around here is."

"I'm starting to feel guilty about all of this," I floated.

Mr. Neast's wry smile faded. "Guilty of what?"

I put my hands out in front of me, palms up. "All this. All this horrible stuff started happening when I came back. I'm back here, working a job, for maybe ten days, and it's ten days of horror. Deaths, murders, hogs eating people, the flood, suicide—RFK getting killed." I felt as though I'd just run a fast mile, started gasping.

The sheriff again reached out to steady me.

"You can't possibly think you had anything to do with all this . . . this stuff happening," he said. "And RFK? Really?"

"If I hadn't found Elizabeth—"

"Delaney already knew all about that."

"And Mrs. Delaney . . ."

"Was lucky you let her keep her gun."

"And this," I said, making a motion toward Delaney's body on top of the gallows, where Doc Dougherty had finally stood up, continuing to regard the body as though by doing so, he could resurrect Delaney.

"You should go back to bed for a while," he said, waving his hand in front of my face, as though warding off the toxic exhaust of too much beer breath.

"Ronnie and I—" I began and then let it drop.

"Just don't leave town, all right?"

I looked blank, as though shocked.

"That was an attempt at being humorous," Sheriff Neast said, slapping me on the back. "At a time when nothing seems funny."

"I need to stay up, get to the office, get on top of this. I'll call you later, for some comment," I said, feeling stupid saying something so obvious.

"Of course you will," he said. "My initial comment is 'Tragic,' but on reflection, it might go beyond that."

I paused, turned back to him. "I'll go lightly on how Delaney got out of his cell. Like not really incarcerated, but being housed, something like that—"

"You do what you need to do," the sheriff said, turning toward his office, to make yet another call to the usually underemployed coroner. But just as he left me he left me with this: "The DA hadn't yet brought charges, so Delaney was not technically under arrest so didn't have to remain in his cell."

I was confused. Wasn't that what I'd implied?

The Rambler fired right up and I headed right on home. I realized that I didn't have a key to the office, it was too early for Steve's to be open, and at home I could either take the sheriff's advice and get a little sleep before I *had* to wake up, or scratch some notes on a pad of paper so I had a jump on getting into the office to try to write this up.

There was no sound from Mr. Thorpe's bedroom. I groped my way back to my own bed, not wanting to turn on the light. I tried to reassemble the covers and crawled under them, folding my arms over my chest as though wearing an invisible straitjacket.

I closed my eyes and saw Mr. Delaney swinging at the end of the rope, so I snapped my eyes open and stared at the dark ceiling, where it was a lot safer to dwell.

It wasn't that long ago that I was still in college, the safe bubble of college, where none of the journalism courses taught you about professionally reacting to dead bodies and where every example was from the *New York Times*, which was as far from the *Mauch Chunk Times-News* as Earth was from Pluto. On a per capita basis, Mauch Chunk was coming up as a much more dangerous place than New York City.

I played around with various leads for the Delaney story and finally decided to lead with Lawyer Delaney himself. "Well-known local attorney Lawrence Delaney, apparently despondent over the accidental death of his daughter, took his own life last night by hanging himself from the movie-set gallows in the courtyard of the Carbon County Jail." Wait. Did I need to write "allegedly" took his own life, when in fact, a witness—my own brother—saw him do it? Yeah, I guess I did. ". . . allegedly took his own life . . ." I wrapped my hands around my head and exerted as much pressure as I could, allegedly trying to implode my own aching head.

That felt strangely relaxing, so I did it some more. I absently wondered just how much pressure I'd have to exert to actually implode my head. I did it some more and realized that I was doing it in order to postpone dealing with yet one more death. And that litany of death didn't include "The Stone" Ravich, late of the Greater Wilkes-Barre Area.

Then I wondered about Mrs. Delaney.

Would the news actually kill her? Or would she be relieved? She and Mr. Delaney didn't exactly seem to have the most harmonious marriage. And where were the kids? Two boys and one girl who were supposed to come home for the funeral of their sister now could save on airfare and double up on funerals. I flashed back to

Lawyer Delaney's warning to me to steer clear of his kids, that I wasn't sufficiently upper crust to associate with them, even though my eccentric grandmother could afford to buy up half or perhaps all of the town. I felt a little red ember of anger. I do tend to hold a grudge until it gets rusty. And thanks to the good nuns, now I got to feel, in the middle of the night, guilty for thinking badly of the dead. Was I allowed to think badly of a dead Mafia chief in Wilkes-Barre and a partially eaten assassin from Baltimore? Hell, why not feel guilty about everything? That would force me to feel guilty about drinking way too many beers last night, but it was hard to feel guilty about that, since as best I could recall, Ronnie and I had fun while we wasted away the evening.

But now, in the middle of yet another terrible night, I felt obliged to feel guilty about having a good time.

It was almost time to get up to go to work to write up another death. But all I wanted to do was torture my head while I pulled the covers up over that poor head . . . and maybe stuck my thumb in my mouth.

I marched the people of Mauch Chunk with whom I'd recently had contact across a stage, trying to find the one I felt most sorry for, and I kept coming back to Mrs. Delaney. But she kept coming across as a paradox: at once a victim but, the more victimized she was, the more steel spined she became, until she ended up like Annie Fucking Oakley, putting two .45 slugs into a guy who'd purposefully killed how many people? How badly would she take the news of her husband's death, his suicide, which made it worse still, nothing to live for, rub her nose in it, you're not worth living for, nor are my kids, because it's all about me, so there, take that, I'm thumbing my nose at all of you as I dive out of this life. Me and Elizabeth, we'll be together now, away from all of you, away from the disrespect, the money problems, and the damned pigs. But definitely away from my dear wife, who held a gun on me, who turned on me when I most needed her support.

I suspected Mrs. Delaney would survive, but she'd probably always from now on go to sleep with a big handgun nearby.

I wondered who would call her with the news. And would they call a priest first to be on hand when they delivered the news?

Maybe Sheriff Neast. Maybe Doc Dougherty. Maybe the coroner. Who the hell was the coroner? I should know that. Would they do it before she had her first cup of coffee for the day? I sure hoped not. Or should I do it? Could I drag myself to do it? No, I couldn't. It felt as though I was still drunk, still asking questions a drunk would tend to ask. And then I must have fallen back asleep because I awoke to the alarm going off, the Pavlov's dogs' signal to once more go through my now deeply established routine: crawl out of bed, shit, shower, go by Steve's Diner, get a cup of black coffee to go and two apple turnovers to wash down the coffee, walk to Race Street, open the door, walk inside, set the turnovers and coffee on my desk, hang my jacket over the back of my chair, mutter "Hello" to whomsoever looked up, and get to work separating AP wire stories and then start typing on my own story of the day.

"Jeez, kid," Joe Boyle said, "you look like you never went to bed last night. Did you and Ranger Ronnie go back to Weiksner's to play more darts? Did you manage to impale anyone?"

Mrs. Apfelbaum waved an impatient finger at Joe. "Can't you see he's not feeling well?"

"To be honest," I admitted, "I don't feel well."

"Summer cold," Mrs. Apfelbaum said, trying to be helpful.

"No," I said, "leprosy of the soul."

"Well, don't you worry. Time heals—" Mrs. Apfelbaum began. "What?" she said.

I looked back and forth between them. "You mean you haven't heard?"

They looked at each other as though discombobulated by the possibility that they, recorders of all that occurred in Mauch Chunk, had missed something.

They both turned to me and didn't have to say a word. It was now my duty to tell whatever it was I'd learned that had skulked past their wary eyes.

I took in a breath of stale air, hoping to get a start on the answer. "In the middle of the night, Mr. Delaney hanged himself on the movie-set gallows at the jail." Neither of them moved a facial muscle. "He's dead. Broken neck."

They turned toward each other.

"Where in hell did you hear that?" Joe asked.

I almost hated to admit that I'd seen the body; it was only further confirmation that wherever I was, the dead bodies piled up. "I saw it. Rudy called me and I went up there. He's dead."

At the outer edge of our little trio bent over our desks, other people stopped to edge toward us. They had not heard what I'd said. They were newspaper people, and they sensed something terrible was up, like dogs following the scent toward a recent roadkill.

"What's up?" Nate Dermott asked. Being managing editor, he had the authority and seniority to interrupt us on behalf of everyone else in the room.

"He says Delaney took his own life last night, up at the jail," Joe said, exactly no inflection in his voice.

"No," Nate said. "Why?"

"That greatest of all human gifts bestowed upon we human beings by God: guilt," Joe said.

I nodded my head. "Sounds feasible," I added, unnecessarily.

"You mean guilt about what happened to his daughter?" Nate asked.

"Well, sure," Joe said. "His favorite kid, dead in front of his eyes, and he couldn't manage to do anything to stop it."

"A tooth for a tooth, a broken neck for a broken neck," Mrs. Apfelbaum said, shaking her head. She turned to me. "But you'd need somebody to say that so you could quote them," she said.

"Right," I said. "But couldn't I quote you? You just said it, right?"

"It would be better coming out of a padre's mouth," Joe said. He looked at his watch. "Father Begley should be just about to say Mass. I could give him a call to see if he'd say anything like that."

"I suspect that by now Sheriff Neast has Father Begley kneeling over Mr. Delaney seeing if he can get his eternal soul an escort to a better place," I said.

"Not if he committed suicide," Mrs. Apfelbaum said. "Well," she added, shaking her head to underscore the conclusion, "we all know where he'd go." She made the sign of the cross.

"Nate, can you handle the AP copy while the kid here gets started on yet another story of death?" Joe said.

"Sure, sure," Nate said. "I'll get right on it." He walked off to wrestle with the teletype, which had recently been converted to a Friden punched-tape system and which, once gathered, had to be run through a reader machine to see what they said. They didn't always say what they said very intelligently, which is why the low guy on the totem pole got to take on that chore every morning.

"You think I should call the jail and talk to my brother to get more of his story?" I said.

"How much more will he give you now than he gave you when you were there?"

"Hmmmmm," I said. "Come to think of it, he's had a couple of hours to inflate it. Maybe I'd be best to stick with what I have. Not much more that the sheriff can add, either. We were both there."

"Call Doc Dougherty and get the official cause of death from him instead of waiting for the coroner's report. That'll take longer than we have time for."

I looked up Doc Dougherty's number and called. He answered. And he was short winded. "Cause of death was a broken neck," he said. "Wasn't that obvious?"

"I can't say that," I told him. "Needs to be official. Now you've said it, it's official, all well and good, in your professional opinion."

"Well it sure as hell wasn't caused by strep throat, was it?"

I was getting the impression Doc Dougherty, for all of his years making house calls, was put out about being awakened from his sleep to attend to someone for whom he could do nothing.

"You've been a big help," I said. I refrained from advising him to take two aspirin and go back to bed.

The rest of the morning was spent massaging the story. At several points along the way, I thought of calling Mrs. Delaney to either give her the bad news or offer my condolences. And around 8:30 I nearly did that. Instead, I called Grace Delaney, figuring that Mrs. Delaney was still staying with her sister-in-law.

Grace answered on the second ring. I asked if she had heard the bad news. She had, she said, from Sheriff Neast, who'd called an hour ago. Mrs. Delaney was still staying with her and she'd taken the news well at first, then not so well, and now well again.

"She's lying down right now," Grace said. "Do you need to talk to her for your story?"

"No, no," I said, "that's okay. How are you holding up?" I thought of her rather delicate features.

"I'm fine . . . for now," she said simply.

I offered condolences to both of them. Grace thanked me for the call. "It'll take some time to sink in," she said. "It's been a stressful month so far."

Boy, talk about understatement.

At one point midmorning, a few hundred words into the second draft of the story, I took a break and walked up Broadway to the five-and-dime store and bought a pair of sympathy cards that I filled out and sent off to Grace's house.

Once the second draft of the story was finished, Joe and Mrs. Apfelbaum went over it, made a few changes, and Joe told me to take the rest of the day off since I'd been to bed so late and up so early. Mrs. Apfelbaum told me to take a nap, that I'd feel much better for it.

I left before the presses in the basement came near to starting their earth-shaking rumble. I was at the front door of the carriage house a few minutes before 10:00. Mr. Thorpe was back putting in flowers down at the Asa Packer Mansion. I waved at him and he saw me and he immediately pushed himself to his feet and began trudging up the lawn, waving a hand to have me wait for him.

He wasn't exactly out of breath, but he was breathing hard by the time he reached me. Some of the breathlessness was apparently from excitement. "Did you hear them? Did you hear them?" he gushed, his usually pallid face florid.

He could tell from the vacant expression on my face that I didn't know what he was talking about.

"Them. There," he said, pointing to the intimidating Harry Packer Mansion. "Last night. They were back. They were moving around—"

"Who was moving around?"

"Them. The ghosts." He kept looking back and forth from me to the massive mansion. "They were wandering around, making noise. Last night."

"That was probably me coming home, around 2:00, after Ronnie and me got asked to leave Weiksner's," I said, sure that's what it was.

"No, no, no," he said, going to his arms to emphasize what he was saying. "This was around midnight. I was reading, it was quiet, and then it wasn't. I went outside and I could hear them moving around. They were so scary even the crickets shut up."

I was about to say, "Ah, come on, Mr. Thorpe, get it together," but something in his face advised me not to do that.

"They were walking around, like they had bricks tied to their feet, and they were moaning and groaning and whimpering," he said.

"But how could you have heard them through those stone walls?" I asked, seriously considering Mr. Thorpe had seriously gotten into some serious magic mushrooms.

He looked puzzled for a moment. "I don't know. That's a good question. But all I know is that I heard 'em."

"Were there any lights inside, any other indication there was something going on? Did you tell anyone about this earlier today?"

"No and no. No lights. If I told anybody again, they'd want to lock me up." He looked around as though searching for men in white coats sneaking up on him. "But it's true. I'm old but my hearing's still okay."

I patted him on the shoulder. "You probably did hear something, but it was probably due to the wind brushing trees against the side of the building."

"No wind. No scraping tree branches. Not crazy."

I didn't know what to say. So I simply said, "Next time it happens, wake me up, and we'll check it out."

For a solution so lame, it apparently was enough for Mr. Thorpe to not be called a nut. "I'm gonna do that," he said before turning away and heading back to his flower-planting duties. He waved. "There's mail on the table for you," he called back.

Indeed, there was mail. Two circulars for department store sales, a copy of *Newsweek*, a copy of the *Saturday Evening Post*, and three envelopes, piled neatly one atop the other, each of them totally different from their fellows.

I felt a jolt in the gut when I looked at the return address of the envelope on top. It was a light-brown envelope, and the return address was from the Selective Service office on Broadway, about a quarter mile or less from where I stood. I tore open the envelope, and it was what I expected. It welcomed me to Uncle Sam's service; I had two weeks to get my affairs in order, at which time I would be transported by bus to the induction center in Wilkes-Barre, where I'd be tested to see if I was proper fodder for chasing after small men in pajamas in a country on the other side of the world.

I wasn't eager to give two years of my life and possibly the one life I owned toward a war that I thought was ill-advised. Of course, I could have enlisted for four years in a branch that probably wouldn't see action in Vietnam, like the Air Force or the Coast Guard.

The letter slingshot my mind back to sophomore year in college where a freshman down the hall, Dave Gundel, had taken on Vietnam as some kind of hobby. He could recite rice-production figures, give current population of a number of towns and cities, and knew several words and phrases and even some complete sentences in the language. I'd always wondered if it was a ploy, reverse psychology, a guy so eager to go to Vietnam to help out that the Army would be obliged to turn him down because under the current circumstances, he'd be thought to be rather unstable.

Was he smart enough to outsmart the Army? Considering the oxymoron "military intelligence," who knew?

I wondered what happened to Gundel. But wait. Why was I trying to figure out what happened to him? He was a year behind me, so he was now a senior at Espy State. Heavy-footed ghosts in the Harry Packer Mansion, draft notices. I was becoming unmoored.

I picked up the phone from its cradle and called the *Times-News* office and asked to speak to Joe. I felt it was my obligation to let him know immediately that he would probably have to start interviewing to fill my job when I left for the Army in two weeks.

He listened without comment. When I was finished he heaved a sigh. "This is the work of that son-of-a-bitch Sward. This is his way of getting back to you for the flood photo and the quote. He's a vindictive little troll." Another pause. I could almost hear Joe's gears meshing all the way through the phone wire. "Your brother's in the Air Force. In Alaska." I confirmed that. "Your father's dead but served in World War II." I didn't feel a need to confirm that, since it was common knowledge. "And your grandmother's gonna be pissed as a coiled rattler," he added.

I hadn't thought about my grandmother or about what kind of a reaction she'd have. I did know that as far as whatever passed as a favorite among her grandsons, that would be me. How deep that regard went, however, was difficult to tell with Granny. But she would take it as a personal affront that someone, *anyone*, would attempt to strong-arm someone under her authority. Buster Sward obviously hadn't thought this one all the way through. He'd reacted in anger and haste, a decidedly unwise strategy. Whether Grandmother could move against the forces of the United States of America or not, I did not know, but she would certainly move against one Buster Sward.

All that went through my mind as Joe again sighed through the phone wire. "That little weasel hasn't got the brains of a fruit fly," Joe said. "And his fellow county commissioners aren't going to appreciate the attention I'm going to be sure this move receives." I was struck by how formally Joe was speaking. Maybe Gertrude was leaning over him, editing his words, culling out all the "bastards" and "pricks" and "assholes."

"So what do you want me to do in the meantime?" I asked. "It's not like I have a whole lot of stuff to get packed away for my departure, and what little I do have can go into grandmother's dungeon. I should let Miss Grace know that I'll be vacating, though."

"No. Don't do that. Not yet," Joe said. "This whole thing'll blow over like a February scarecrow."

A what?

"Just keep working on the Delaney story, updating it for tomorrow. Just keep working as though that letter never happened. Now go take that nap." He hung up.

Take a nap? Under these circumstances? Yeah, right.

I pushed the phone away to the end of the table where it usually rested and hefted the fattest of the three letters. This one looked like it had traveled around the world, twice. It was postmarked more than a smallpox victim is pockmarked. There were tremendously elaborate artistic postage stamps in the top right corner, things with parrots and palm trees and brilliant sunsets. And best of all, the return-address area contained no return address—just my great-uncle Herbert's name, in his precise script, with a drawing of a skull and crossbones under it. Wow.

Uncle Herbert, as I'd told Mr. Thorpe how many days ago, was a wonderfully strange character: big-boned, big-bearded, big-haired, with precise small handwriting that could have belonged to a monk and a soft squeaky voice like a small boy's. It wasn't easy tearing through all of the tape he'd used to reinforce the envelope. But when I'd finally breached it, I tilted it to let whatever was inside drop out. What came out with a dull clunk was a gold coin, about the size of a quarter, not much the worse for wear for having been minted in 1876. There was a guy's head in profile on the front and the name Alfonso XII. The back looked like some sort of coat of arms.

I turned the coin over in my hand, back and forth. It felt solid, heavy, substantial. I resisted the urge to bite it to see if it was soft enough to be gold the way I'd seen pirates do in cheesy movies. Instead I twirled it on the tabletop. It twirled with some enthusiasm, and when it finally stopped twirling it flopped with a satisfying *blonk*. I let it rest there and began fishing around inside the envelope to find a note. Sure enough, there was one, but I had to work at unwedging it.

It was written in Uncle Herby's beautiful penmanship on a thick, rich yellow paper with purposely frayed edges, as though it was . . . well . . . a prop in one of those cheesy pirate movies.

"Brother Skar," it began. Uncle Herby always referred to me as "Brother Skar," as though we were mates.

Brother Skar:

Little something enclosed to pique your interest and to prove the old boy hain't always off base. There's plenty more of these where

*this one came from. Whole chests, as in pirate chests, but these
wonders haven't felt the salt of the sea for near a century. I'll be
rollin' in around the end of the month. See if you can get me old
room free of cobwebs and dust between now and then and let Sis
know that I'm on my way so she can creep out of town so as to
avoid me should she feel the inclination.*

*In the meantime, don't spend this all at one time. And keep the yap
zipped. Other than you and Sis, nobody needs to know anything
about where I am or what I'm doing—or not doing. Soon.*

It was signed with a larger-than-usual signature, again with
skull and crossbones affixed under the signature.

It suddenly felt like I was in the middle of a Hardy Boys novel.
Then I realized that I'd probably be gone into the military, somewhere on some godforsaken base, halfway through basic training
when Uncle Herby came skulking into town under the cover of
darkness. Yeah, "skulking" was the word. Don't let anybody know.
Most of the people who knew Uncle Herby were either dead or on
their way to their graves. It wasn't like the next generation had ever
even heard of him, he was so regularly gone abroad somewhere.

I stood the coin up on its edge and hit it with my index finger.
Once again it began its spin and this time was more fascinating
than the last time. I watched it as though for the moment it was the
only solid thing in the universe.

Something about its color was fascinating, something about its
being gold. Something about how, over the centuries, gold had
driven people mad. "There's plenty more of these where this one
came from."

I could almost feel where the gold crackpots were coming from.
I'd seen *Goldfinger* numerous times, from its Christmas 1964 release
to just a few months ago when a bunch of us, anticipating graduation and being expelled into the real world—a world where you
could get your sorry ass shot up in some faraway rice paddy—we'd
loaded the car with near-graduation guys, four cases of Yuengling
lager, a dozen big bags of Wise potato chips, some Ben Franklin
cigars, and drove to the drive-in in Berwick, where we reabsorbed
Goldfinger. "No, Mr. Bond, I want you to die." We'd returned less

than sober but more than willing to see the best damned James Bond film again if the opportunity offered itself.

Some of the Auric Goldfinger passion for the shiny golden metal flowed out of the Spanish coin. "Whole chests . . ." Uncle Herby was the richest male in the Mauch Chunks but he'd gone off to find more wealth. What people who lived here didn't realize was that, for him, it wasn't wealth that mattered, it was the game played in finding and hoarding it. Local folks still harbored the absurd notion that grandmother's house sported a foundation of gold bars and that there was money and jewelry salted throughout the old drafty dump. Like any wealthy person with any brains, she kept her money in banks, in her case banks scattered all over the world.

I wondered if, from the muddy fields of Fort Leonard Wood in the middle of Missouri, I'd get word from Joe Boyle that my ancient uncle had rolled into town in a gold-plated Rolls-Royce, accompanied by manservant Odd Job, stirring up the napping ill feelings against him. Forget that before he left on the last adventure he'd given East Mauch Chunk yet another park, this one five acres and complete with an Olympic-sized swimming pool that very few people bothered to use and those who did complained because the town was responsible for the pool's upkeep.

The clock on the top of the courthouse rang out three o'clock and brought me back to the real world, as did a mournful wail from a freight train chugging along across the river on the Lehigh Valley Railroad tracks.

I let the gold coin's slow revolutions wear themselves out, and this time when the coin flattened itself on the tabletop, I let it.

The third letter was a regulation-sized business envelope type letter. Again, there was no return address, only a capital *A* with a horizontal line across the top: the mark of Null-A. The postmark was typed on a standard typewriter in Courier font. The stamp was the plain-Jane current first-class six-cent variety.

I looked at the damned thing for a long, long time, like looking at a snake charmer charming a cobra. It startled me that what brought me out of the envelope-induced trance was the bell on the top of the courthouse chiming 3:15!

I turned the letter on its edge and gave it a rap against the tabletop, forcing the letter inside against the edge of the envelope,
the way a smoker snaps his pack of cigs to compact the tobacco
against the filter. I tore the end of the envelope and shook out the
letter. With typical Null-A precision, it was folded neatly in thirds.
I opened it carefully, as though it might contain a sample of something terrible. A neatly rolled joint fell onto the table.

Dear Skar:

By now you may have noticed that I left town in a
bit of a hurry. Preservation is always a priority,
as I'm sure you can understand. I didn't have time
or space to take everything. Go through what I left
and help yourself to what you want. The backdoor key
is in the bottom of the mailbox.

I'm not exactly sure how to put this. I owe you an
apology for getting your sorry butt in trouble with
some real bastards who don't tend to see shades of
gray in anything in this whole world. I tried to
warn you off, but in typical Skar fashion, that had
little effect. You're a stubborn little shit. Some
of what happened was merely the result of momentum
picking up. I never meant to let you get into danger. The whole drug-movement thing was just business, that's all. Just one more business scheme to
perfect before somebody less able comes along and
gets it done half as well.

I know it's a waste of time to try to warn you off,
but were I you I'd switch to researching subjects
other than the drug trade. First of all because, as
you've seen, it can get ugly. And secondly, as you
will see, it's got a momentum of its own that's going to be impossible to slow down, much less stop.
(If you get the chance to go to 'Nam as some people
up there would like, you'll find that it's pretty
universal over there, so what's the use of resisting?)

I'll do what I can to keep the bastards from doing
you in if you can help me out by cutting it out. Let
some other dildo get his ass killed.

Don't bother looking for me. I'll be particularly
hard to find. And what would you do if you managed to
find me? You can't prove anything. I didn't so much
as leave town owing the paperboy money.

Take care, man. Alice says Hello and says she misses
you. She actually getting nostalgic — — already!— —
for the whole damned miserable little burg. Hain't
that the shits? I suspect that at some point she'll
actually break down and move back. Keep a space
open.

Bye and bad riddance and all that.

Your bosom buddy,
Null-A.

I put the letter down and picked up the joint, turned it over and around, ran it under my nose. I thought about flushing it down the toilet but then thought better of it. It wasn't much in the way of evidence of Null-A's nefarious activities. It probably had his spit on it, but spit was spit. What was that going to prove? What was one joint going to prove? I wouldn't be surprised if Ronnie had some stashed away in his caboose.

Maybe Null-A was right: fighting the drug traffic was an increasingly losing battle. Why not just give in and let it run its course? But then I thought of Rudy and slid the joint into my shirt pocket, handling it as though it was a baby asp.

I looked outside. The afternoon was brilliant. The sun was still high. Life was moving inexorably along. The flowers Mr. Thorpe had been planting along the front of the Asa Packer Mansion were as brilliant as the day. One oversized too-white cloud hung over the Flagstaff, looking like Andrew Wyeth had painted it just for us. I felt like shit. So I went outside, hoping that by allowing myself to absorb the day, it might be a bit healing.

With Null-A's joint in my shirt pocket, I walked across the gravel road between the carriage house and the slanted lawn, picked out a bit of lawn toward the very top, and dropped onto it. The grass was cool and moist but not wet. The sound of the traffic from the corner of Susquehanna and Broadway filtered up but in a muted way, as though a see-through mosquito net had been thrown over the mansion grounds.

I closed my eyes and tried to let the day's crap melt into and fertilize the lawn. When it didn't happen right away, I tried harder. Then I realized that for it to happen, I couldn't force it, I had to let it happen on its own. So I did.

I thought about constructing two mental lists—one for the crap that had happened so far today and the other for the good stuff. But considering what kind of a day it had been so far, that would be launching the positive stuff on a terribly dangerous journey.

Let's see: simplified, Mr. Delaney hanged himself out of guilt for what he let happen to Elizabeth. Sheriff Neast was likely to get in some trouble for allowing inmates to run freely, Rudy among them, Rudy in trouble for letting Mr. Delaney out of his cell; but everyone in town knew the kind of prison Sheriff Neast ran, and until now, nobody had ever had a complaint. So maybe that fear was overblown. Hell, Mr. Delaney could just as well have hanged himself in his cell.

I wondered briefly what effect Delaney's suicide would have on Rudy. Would it shake up his crappy attitude toward life and the world in general? There's always hope.

Then the mail.

You're getting drafted. Uncle Sam wants you. Joe says don't worry about it, you won't be drafted. Worse yet for the local office of the Selective Service when Granny learns of this. She'll ruin Buster Sward if, indeed, he's behind it.

Uncle Herby is coming to town after lo these many years, with treasure chests filled with long-lost (and now found) Spanish gold coins, thereby making himself even richer than he has always been, and stirring up the locals to the point that they might actually assault the Castle like a bunch of berserker villagers, waving shovels and torches, not too unlike that Hardy Boys Mickey Mouse Serial where Applegate's property is put under siege by the greedy neighbors, as though they have some right to his gold.

Null-A and Alice are gone, now living somewhere near Washington, DC, and Null-A, who was seldom wrong about anything for the two decades or so I'd known him, predicted that the drug trade was inevitable, get used to it, might as well get in on the ground floor and make a profit from it. Marijuana, I'd agree with him, was generally pretty harmless if it wasn't overdone and profitable for the local pizza parlors when the munchies struck, but too often it led to more serious crap, like I'd too often seen on weekend excursions to Manhattan. Maybe Null-A was right about the inevitability, but that didn't make it right.

I felt rather than saw or heard someone sit down on the grass to my right.

The blades of grass being compressed must have been protesting louder than usual.

"A beautiful day," Mr. Thorpe said. "Mind if I take my break here?"

I shook my head, indicating that I didn't mind. In case he wasn't looking when I shook my head (I still had my eyes closed), I confirmed that it was just fine with me. Mr. Thorpe hummed a little tune that was basic enough it might have come from his days as a child in Oklahoma. "You seem troubled," he said.

"You think?" I said without thinking, putting an edge on it. "Sorry," I added.

"No need to be sorry. When we're troubled we're often troubled on many fronts at once." He hummed a few more notes. "Yeah, sure," he said. "He don't mind. Join us."

I felt someone lowering himself to the grass on my left. "A beautiful day," he said. With an accent like that it had to be Dickie Harris. "We're between shots. It's nice to come up here and relax."

"I often see you do that," Mr. Thorpe said. There was a long quiet when the only sound was the muffled traffic from below, a few birds cavorting through the trees, and our own breathing.

"This young man is troubled," Mr. Thorpe said, as though I was a lump of protoplasm unburdened by ears and a brain.

"Ya know, they're really good these days with plastic surgery. Half the people in Hollywood look different than they did when they arrived. You should look into it. It'd help you get laid more often."

"I been laid," I said, way too quickly, too defensively.

"He looks just fine from over here," Mr. Thorpe said.

"Yeah, but you're on the good side," Dick said. "It don't look so good over here." Dickie lightly touched the scar down the left side of my face. "They could cut a lot of that scar tissue away and make it thinner," he said. He paused. "I'd be glad to put a thousand toward it," he said. "Really."

He slapped me—hard—on the back as though he'd known me all my life. I felt grateful and angry at the same time, like he'd invaded my individuality—and my dread.

"It still looks just fine over here," Mr. Thorpe said.

"You wanna change seats?" Dickie said.

Mr. Thorpe laughed.

"Only if you give *me* a thousand bucks," he said.

For some reason this whole thing was getting ridiculous, and I started laughing. That seemed to send the whole discussion up in a quickly dissipated vapor. "I like myself the way I am," I said.

"Sure you do," Dickie said.

"Sure you do," Mr. Thorpe said.

Mr. Thorpe's seeming betrayal seemed the worst of the two.

"When they bring my sorry ass back from 'Nam you can spend your thousand dollars on sewing up my sorry ass," I said.

Dickie slapped me on the back again. This time it felt soothing, like he understood.

"Do you think if we nudge him just enough he'll tell us what's troubling him?" Dickie said.

"What little I know of him, he's not much of a talker, more of a doer," Mr. Thorpe said.

"And you?" Dickie asked.

"Often," Mr. Thorpe said. "Sometimes." He laughed. "Over the years I've been both . . . and neither."

"You keep it to yourself," Dickie said.

"When I am not trusting of a person," Mr. Thorpe said.

"Do you feel he does not trust us?" Dickie said.

"I do not know whether he knows either of us well enough to have formed an opinion, although he and I have had some manly adventures since he came to be my roommate." Mr. Thorpe laughed again. "I wish I was twenty years younger. I might like it more. At my age I worry about my heart giving out among all the running and shooting and plotting. I wish I was younger."

"He may be tired from having such a rich life now that he is out from the protective bubble of college," Dickie said.

"This old town hasn't seen this much excitement since—"

I'd had enough. "Hey! I'm right here." I sat all the way up, eyes wide open. Mr. Thorpe sat next to me smiling, his cottage cheese complexion sagging but his smile huge. He wore work overalls and a straw hat that should have been retired months ago.

On my left, Mr. Richard Harris was still sporting his fake mustache, a go-to-town Irish cap, and a suit that looked all too hot for such a nice day. He turned up one collar. "It's why I come up here between shots," he said. "Damned hot with these duds on midafternoon." He pulled a cigarette from his jacket pocket and lit it with a wooden kitchen match he fired by flicking it against his thumbnail. He drew in a lungful as though it was perfume, paused, then blew the smoke out through his nose.

"You ever smoke, kid?" he asked.

"Tried it once and didn't like it. Smoke a cigar or a pipe every once in a while."

"Very relaxing," Dick said. He looked down at me. "So what's the trouble, kid?"

I didn't really want to answer him. I hadn't had enough time to go through each of the topics bothering me, to digest them carefully. So in typically stupid, impatient fashion, I blurted out: "I'm getting drafted, my great uncle is a pirate and is coming home with chests of Spanish gold coins, and one of my former friends admitted to being the local drug lord."

Over my head, Mr. Richard Harris looked at Mr. James Thorpe and laughed. "I'm sorry I asked," he said.

"So you have something, some things, to be troubled about," Mr. Thorpe said.

Both of them laughed.

"Every time I turn around, things get worse, there are more and more loose ends hanging, and none of them seem to get tied up."

"Well, hell, son, that's how real life works—and doesn't," Mr. Harris said, yawning. "The only time you get to tie up all the loose ends is when you die, and they usually aren't all that tied up then, either. You just leave them for someone else to tie up."

"Life is messy," Mr. Thorpe said, "then we die and it isn't. That's what you were saying, isn't it, Dickie?"

"Exactly," Harris said.

"You need to lighten up on yourself," Mr. Thorpe pronounced.

Dickie took another drag of his cigarette, a very slow, meditative drag. "So let's see," he said. "You can run away to the South Seas with your great-uncle to avoid the draft, and while there you can open an island branch of your friend's drug business so you can support yourself."

Mr. Thorpe grunted. "I think they already have enough drugs on South Sea islands."

"That's the Caribbean," Mr. Harris said. He looked down at me again. "You're in a world of hurt, son."

"No shit," I said. "That's what I been trying to tell you."

"So what to do?" Harris said.

I closed my eyes again. "When you come up with something good, let me know."

"You could go to Canada," Mr. Harris said.

"You could hide out in the haunted mansion," Mr. Thorpe said, nodding his head in the direction of the Harry Packer Mansion. "Nobody would ever think of looking in there. I could bring you those frozen potpies you always eat."

"What's the downside to your great-uncle returning to town flush with chests of Spanish gold coins? You could buy your way out of the army."

"Or you could vanish into the slums of a big city and sell drugs with your buddy," Mr. Thorpe said.

I sat up and extracted the joint from my shirt pocket. "Ole Null-A already sent me a sample."

"Is it real?" Mr. Thorpe asked.

"I doubt Null-A would bother sending me a fake," I said.

"Here," Mr. Harris said, snubbing out the butt of his cigarette and taking the joint. He put the end in his mouth and lit it up, took a drag. "Yeah, it's real," he said, passing the joint to me. "Here, you take a drag. If you become a drug addict, the army isn't gonna want you."

What the hell, I thought, and took a drag, held the smoke in my lungs, and passed the joint to Mr. Thorpe. He took it and pulled in a drag. "The unfortunate story of my life," he said after he'd blown it out. "My weakness has always been to never find a bad habit I didn't like."

"Can't have the satisfaction of breaking a bad habit if you don't have one to break," Mr. Harris said.

I closed my eyes and concentrated on the sounds around us. A car horn blew on Susquehanna Street, two birds got into an argument, a light breeze rubbed some leaves together. My past experience with weed was that it tended to make me sleepy. Maybe I should take a nap. Maybe when I woke all of my problems would be in the past. Yeah, sure.

"So what is the lad to do?" Dickie Harris asked the world in general. He posed the question around trapping a lungful of smoke, then slowly exhaled.

"Since I'll probably end up getting killed in Vietnam and won't be able to share it with anybody, you could tell me what 'MacArthur Park' is really all about," I said sleepily.

"But if you *didn't* get killed in Vietnam, when you came back I'd have to kill you myself so the secret would remain inviolate," Harris said.

"Did you really say 'inviolate'?" I asked.

"I guess I did," Harris said.

Mr. Thorpe took another hit. I guess that since I lay there with my eyes closed they assumed I'd had enough because they didn't offer me any more.

"We've already offered several good ideas," Mr. Thorpe said without a trace of humor. Did he really think that the solution to my problems was to haunt the Harry Packer Mansion?

Oh, yeah, wait.

We *are* smoking weed. That does tend to alter one's perception, doesn't it?

"Who's that?" Dickie asked.

I opened my eyes. Coming up the top of the steps down at the bottom of the lawn was none other than Joe Boyle, his sports coat open, his Polaroid camera hanging around his neck, his eyes behind his horn-rimmed glasses, looking about. He spotted us and waved, marched toward us.

"Put it out," I said, not sure which of my two bosom buddies I was talking to. "Joe Boyle's coming."

"Put what out?" Dickie said.

"The pot," I said.

"It's gone," Dickie said.

"It is," Mr. Thorpe confirmed.

Joe strode toward us, his legs moving slowly, almost ponderously. Joe wasn't in the best of shape.

When he got to within five yards of us, he motioned us to sit closer together so he could take a picture. As he swung his Polaroid up to focus in on us, Dickie whispered, "See no evil, hear no evil—"

"Which one's which?" I asked.

"In sequence," he said.

He covered his eyes, I covered my ears, and Mr. Thorpe covered his mouth. Joe snapped the shot, yanked the picture out of the camera and waved it around, stood there for a full minute looking at the Polaroid, peeled off the chemical layer, and again waved the photo in the air to dry. "Three monkeys," he said, before showing us the picture.

He would later apply the preservative goop and once *that* dried, he'd post it on the editorial office bulletin board where it would stay for more than a decade.

I wouldn't get killed in Vietnam, as is obvious by the fact that I wrote this story. In fact, I wouldn't get drafted, but that's a whole 'nother story. Uncle Herby would come back to town claiming he'd found a vast treasure of gold coins. He'd arrive, in fact, wearing an eye patch he didn't need, his head covered with a bandana like a real pirate, and with his usual bluster. He wouldn't have a parrot on his shoulder or a peg leg, but he would manage to get himself kidnapped and nearly killed by a trio of numbskulls. Null-A would occasionally resurface in one form or another, but I'd never again see Alice, who vanished into the bowels of Washington, DC, although she would send me a gift several years hence.

And Mr. Thorpe would leave Mauch Chunk at Thanksgiving and move to Southern California, where a year later he would die of a heart attack.

They killed Bobby Kennedy that summer. That's what the summer of 1968 was noted for.

Author's Notes

Mauch Chunk and East Mauch Chunk really did exist, on either side of the Lehigh River in Carbon County, Pennsylvania. Jim Thorpe died in 1953 in Southern California and his widow persuaded the towns to join together and take Thorpe's name. In 1954 they joined to become Jim Thorpe, Pennsylvania, even though Jim Thorpe had never set foot in either town.

In 2008 I wrote my childhood memoirs under the title *Jim Thorpe Never Slept Here* (University of Scranton Press).

Many of the characters in this novel really existed in Jim Thorpe.

Richard Harris and Sean Connery came to town in 1968 to film *The Molly Maguires*, the story of Irish coal miners who revolted against the repressive mining companies in the 1870s. A group of them were hanged in the yard of the Carbon County Jail on Broadway after going on trial at the Carbon County Courthouse.

Weiksner's Bar was located exactly where it is placed in this novel; today it is called Molly Maguires Pub and Steakhouse.

Cy and Gertrude Apfelbaum were very much involved with the *Times-News*. Joe Boyle was the editor of the *Times-News*, which in 1967 was sold to Pencor, a Palmerton, Pennsylvania, holding company [which also owned Blue Ridge Cable, the world's second-oldest television cable company]; Pencor moved the paper to a converted movie theater in Lehighton. Joe left the newspaper in June 1968 to take a job as PR manager of Split Rock Lodge in nearby Lake Harmony. He would later return to the newspaper. Cy Apfelbaum served as the advertising director of the newspaper. The *Times-News* building on Race Street is today a bed-and-breakfast. Joe Boyle, who died a bizarre death in 1992 when a parade float he was standing on crashed, was the most ardent promoter the town of Jim Thorpe ever had.

Sheriff Neast also existed. He presided benignly over the county prison and was well-liked and perpetually reelected to the office of county sheriff. Think of Gary Cooper.

Agnes McCartney was head of the Carbon County Tourist Agency and very active in attempting—against much local resistance—to turn Mauch Chunk into a tourist destination, which it certainly is today. Even though she has been dead lo these many years, some "Chunkers" still despise her for bringing the borough Mauch Chunk back from the dead.

The half-dozen wrestlers employed in this story were also real and frequently staged their terrible duels at venues in Hamburg and Allentown. Professor Tanaka appeared in the 1981 film *An Eye for an Eye*; he also appeared in Chuck Norris's *Missing in Action 2* in 1995. He died in 2000. Chief Jay Strongbow was my favorite pro rassler. He was born in Oklahoma, the same state that gave us Jim Thorpe. His most famous moves were the (now politically incorrect) Tomahawk Chop, the Sleeper Hold, and the Indian Deathlock. He died in 2012 while this novel was being written. I admit to whiling away many an evening watching the Chief and other pro rasslers go at it; I wrote a column for the *Times-News* on the pro wrestlers; it is available at *www.richardbenyo.com*: go to Shorter Stuff and scroll down to *Times-News* and click on "When Professional People Meet."

When we were kids we were convinced the deserted Harry Packer Mansion was haunted. Apparently so did the folks at Walt Disney, for when they built Disney World in Orlando, they used the Harry Packer Mansion as the inspiration for the Haunted Mansion. Today it is a very upscale bed-and-breakfast that specializes in hosting murder-mystery gatherings on weekends. Check it out on *www.murdermansion.com*.

The rest of the characters are all fictional and do not resemble real people who lived and worked and died in Carbon County. Mostly.

Today Jim Thorpe, Pennsylvania is a thriving tourist mecca, much as Agnes McCartney envisioned it. In 2012 Yahoo.com voted it the Most Fantastic Town for Fall (beating out Sedona, Arizona for the honor). National Geographic Adventure voted Jim Thorpe, Pennsylvania, one of the Best Places to Live + Play: Mountain Towns.

It thrived as a tourist destination at the turn of the 20th century and does so again at the turn of the 21st century, but it sure took its knocks in the years between.